# The Winning Score

Book 4 in The Playmakers Series®

BY G.K. BRADY

Trefoil Publishing

This book is a work of fiction. Names, characters, places, and incidents are the product of the author's imagination or are used fictitiously. Any resemblance to actual events, locales, or persons, living or dead, is coincidental.



ISBN 978-1-7354558-4-6

Cover design by Getcovers
Edited by Jenny Quinlan, Historical Editorial
Proofread by Word Servings

# Contents

# *Dedication*

To my late father-in-law, Russ, whom we lost too soon to COVID-19. Thank you for your courage and kindness, for your unwavering support, and for raising your amazing sons. Or, as someone so succinctly put it, for being a damn fine man. Though you never read a romance book in your life, you were the living, breathing embodiment of everything we love in our heroes.

# Chapter 1

## SLAPSHOT

Quinn Hadley's primary goal when he strolled into the Denver ChopHouse was to get a good buzz going. He needed to let loose. Hell, he'd needed to every day since his home life had been knocked on its ass a month ago. At twenty-five, up to his eyeballs in money and downtime distractions, he'd never expected to be living with a mother who'd always found him lacking. Second best. If he'd had another sibling, third best. Technically, though, she'd moved in with *him*, but the end result was the same: an epic crimp in his free-wheeling bachelor lifestyle. One he'd enjoyed immensely and now missed the hell out of.

Radar tuned for his Colorado Blizzard teammates, he caught sight of a hand waving from a dark corner amid a cluster of noisy guys. "Hadley!" Quinn squinted against the gloom, trying to make out which of his buddies had hollered his name as he threaded his way toward them. They'd commandeered a large booth and a few smaller ones, though the boys were mostly standing as they talked, drank, and cut up.

"You assholes started the party without me," he joked, trying to zen himself into casual mode and lighten his mood.

The guys greeted him boisterously—even Hunter McMurphy, who hooked an arm around his neck. "That's what you get for being fashionably late, dickhead."

"Couldn't be helped." Quinn brushed it off, belying the unyielding knot in his stomach—a knot of endless complications more twisted than an unwound roll of hockey tape, brought on by his latest frustrating argument with his mother. But hey, he was going to leave all that behind tonight, wasn't he?

*Time to get my Quinn on.*

Hunter tapped the side of Quinn's head before releasing him. "Don't worry. We left you some."

"Booze or women?"

Hunter guffawed. "Booze, of course. Get your own women." He shot a glance over his shoulder.

Quinn followed his gaze, landing on a few babes snuggled up in a booth with Wyatt, the team's temperamental goalie. "Looks like Wyatt's taking more than his fair share, as usual."

"Don't worry your pretty little head, Hads. There's plenty more where those two came from."

Hunter jerked his head toward the front door, where a fresh gaggle of hotties blocked the entrance. They zeroed in on the team and wiggled their fingers in girlie waves. Hunter pounded Quinn's shoulder. "What'd I tell you, Hads? Stick with me, and you'll never be without."

Quinn chuffed in response. He'd never completely shaken off his dislike for Hunter, though he'd tried his damnedest. Great hockey player, but the cocky son of a bitch just rubbed him the wrong way. Maybe because Hunter was always gunning for whatever Quinn had. They seemed to be locked in a competition Quinn hadn't signed up for, whether it was on the ice, in the locker room, or in social settings—not unlike the competition his older brother, Ronan, constantly goaded him into. One asshole at a time was more than enough, thank you very much.

Quinn joined a small cluster of teammates where a waitress was trying to nudge her way in, balancing a tray loaded with longnecks, pints, and cocktails. As the guys swarmed her, she did her best to hand them their drinks. Someone grabbed her ass, and she snapped her head up and glowered at Quinn. "Jerk," she muttered.

He threw up his hands in surrender and mustered one of his trademark lady-killer smiles—the one that showed off his dimples. "Wasn't me, sweetheart." Making a show of dipping his eyes to her cute tush, he added, "But I wish it had been."

"Ha!" she shot back. "Funny man."

"Just wanted to get you to smile, sweetheart—although I totally meant the part about your very fine, uh, asset." She glared, and he shrugged. "Obviously, my attempt at humor is an epic fail."

"Obviously," she said dryly.

He kept the fake smile plastered on his face and let his mouth gallop away from him. "What have you got against someone trying to coax a smile from you? I'll bet it's pretty."

She narrowed her eyes at him. "Charmers are smarmers. You're all alike."

Brushing off her barb, he slid a hundred-dollar bill from his pocket and placed it on her tray. "I can see you're busy, but when you have a minute, I'd love a rum and Coke." He'd found that coating everything with honey—no matter how thick—usually got him what he wanted, so he used charm liberally on a regular basis, even if at times he turned his own stomach.

He grabbed one of the pints. "And in the meantime, may I?" Without waiting for an answer, he took a sip of the beer that wasn't his and sent her a wink. "Not all alike, sweetheart."

Though she gave him the expected eye-roll, one side of her mouth curved up and a telltale blush colored her cheeks. This always baffled him. Was it the money, the bullshit, or the fact he was a pro athlete? Lovers, past and present, said it was the hair, while others fawned over the bod. He wasn't sure. He was *never* sure. And sadly, none had ever mentioned his articulation prowess or juggling acumen, two skills he himself was immensely proud of.

Still, there was a tiny triumph in the waitress's softened expression, and he'd take what he could get. Not that getting a woman to smile—and then some—was a challenge anymore, not since he'd been playing at an elite level. And since he'd signed the big contract? Like shooting fish in a barrel. These days, he just opened his mouth and let the words fly without a second thought. He was an automaton, like a parking lot entry machine that expelled identical ticket after identical ticket. *Here's your ticket. Place it on your dash and have a nice day.* And it got him the same response every damn time. No matter how ridiculous his spiel sounded, some sweet thing was always willing—sometimes without him having to reel out a line.

While he had a healthy ego, he wasn't stupid enough to believe they wanted *him*. They wanted to screw him to say they'd screwed a hockey player. He got that. And that was okay by him because he was only after guilt-free sex. An even bargain where no one got hurt. And over the years, he'd taken advantage plenty and had enjoyed the hell out of himself. Lately, though, the luster had come off—or was it in need of a good buffing to bring it back? Whether he was in a funk caused by his mother or just downright bored, he didn't know. And right now he didn't give a flying fuck.

"Hey, Hads."

Quinn glanced toward the voice, pleasantly surprised to see his favorite teammate, Gage Nelson. One of his favorite people, actually. Nelson rarely joined them socially, especially now that he was with his girlfriend, Lily, and had taken on the role of dad to Lily's little girl. The guy had better things to do than hang out with this bunch of dumbasses, as he often reminded them. But Nelson wasn't alone, and the woman with him wasn't Lily.

Quinn hid his surprise and held up his pilfered beer in greeting. "What inspired you to slum with the boys today, Nelsy?"

"Lily took Daisy to the dentist a few blocks over, so I thought we'd grab some brewskis with the boys and hang for a bit while we kill time." He tilted his head toward the woman. "I think you've met my sister, Sarah, before?"

Quinn's inner light bulb blinked on. "Oh, hey! The engineer from Seattle, right?" He'd met her a year ago at a team dinner, and they'd started talking as soon as they discovered they had engineering in common. But a warning glance from Nelson that night had made Quinn back the hell away—not that he'd considered tapping Nelson's sister. Not only was she so *not* his type, but he would never pull that bullshit on a teammate. Sisters, significant others, mothers, aunts, grandmothers, and women who belonged to someone else were strictly off-limits.

Even so, his inner rate-o-meter went to work, quickly taking in Sarah Nelson. Short, hot pink hair framed a heart-shaped face. Medium height—about a half foot shorter than he—with a lean, athletic build in jeans and a body-hugging long-sleeved T-shirt that read, "My Eyes Are Up Here" with an arrow pointing north. His eyes immediately jumped back to hers—she didn't seem to have noticed they'd wandered to her chest, thank God—

and caught on a tiny twinkle on her nostril. Other than the nose jewelry, she was without any other adornment, including makeup. The fresh-scrubbed look suited her. Wide, intense eyes now studied him over the rim of her pint glass, though he couldn't make out their color in the dimness.

She lowered her glass and gave him a half-smile. "Good memory."

"How did you know she's an engineer?" Nelson asked.

"Because I'm one too, and that's what got us talking. Right, Little Sis?" He turned on a high-wattage smile. Though Sarah's face was blank, his imagination had him seeing a hint of disgust flit through her eyes, which threw him for an instant.

Nelson's eyebrows hugged his hairline. "You're an engineer? No way."

Quinn laughed. "Way. I got my degree from DU before I went pro."

"DU? As in University of Denver?"

"One and the same. I grew up not too far from here."

"Huh. You think you know a guy …"

"Yeah. I get that a lot," Quinn said. Sarah's eyes had been bouncing between the two of them, and he felt a twinge of guilt, even though they hadn't purposely left her out of the conversation. "It's nice to see you again, Sarah. We fellow engineers gotta stick together. So what brings you to Denver?"

She tipped back her half-full glass and emptied it in one swallow. "I moved here."

"Like, two hours ago," Nelson added.

Quinn was picking up on something so thick and ripe a swipe of a knife could slice it open, though he had no clue what it was. Nelson hadn't mentioned his sister moving to Denver, not that he'd been obliged to, but still … "When we talked last year, I thought Seattle was your dream job."

"Things change." Sarah held up her empty glass and waved it at the waitress.

*Okaaaaaay.*

"Quinn Hadley?"

Quinn swiveled his head toward the feminine voice. A sexy blond wearing bright red lipstick and a tight dress—God, Quinn loved blonds in tight dresses—gave him a dirty smile and pointed toward one of the booths. Did he know her? No, but he could change that. She blew him a kiss, and he blew one back without thinking. *Automaton.* In the process of turning back to Nelson, he caught the sister's eye-roll.

"I've always suspected puck bunnies are internally prewired with a GPS device in their panties," she said. "Must be how they find you guys so easily."

Nelson busted out with a laugh, but Quinn wasn't amused. Heat rose up the back of his neck, though he couldn't say exactly why. The uncomfortable feeling reminded him of being a kid caught red-handed by his mom.

His irritation must have been obvious because Sarah Sunshine finally gave him a pittance of a smile. "Sorry. I didn't mean to offend you."

"Not possible, sweetheart," he blurted.

She flinched, then folded her arms over her chest and in an icy tone said, "I prefer 'Sarah' over 'sweetheart' or 'little sis.' And for the record, it would be 'big sis' to you."

*Ouch! Okay, Big Sis. You just go right ahead and put me in my place.*

Nelson seemed to wince. He cleared his throat. "Uh, Sarah, maybe we should step outside and see if Lily's waiting?"

"It's fucking freezing out there, Little Bro," said Miss Sunshine. "I'm sure Lily will let you know when she's here."

Quinn couldn't recall seeing this prickly side the last time he'd talked to Sarah. She'd been downright pleasant, smiling and laughing easily, and they'd had a great time talking. Unsure what the hell her problem was, he decided to pull the plug on the conversation and save his charm for a more appreciative audience—like the friendly blond.

The waitress brought him his drink, and he downed it in nearly one gulp. Soon he and his teammates were surrounded by giggling women who smelled like the perfume counter at a department store, which, along with an excellent two-to-one ratio, gave Quinn an adjusted attitude. And it improved even more when he spotted the hot blond patting the seat next to her in one of the booths.

He took his time ambling toward her, keeping it cool and casual. The waitress brought him another drink as he claimed the seat beside the blond, and he instructed her to keep them coming.

Hunter caught her as she walked by, which was when Quinn noticed he had cornered Sarah Sunshine, whose take-no-prisoners gaze was trained dead-center on Hunter's forehead. *Ha! She's going to hand him his balls.* The thought brought Quinn a dose of perverse pleasure.

"I'm Dory," the blond beside him said, yanking him back to the present. She was giving him a heated once-over. "I love your long hair."

He let her rake her red talons through it. It seemed to do more for her than it did for him. "I'm Quinn, by the way. Do you watch hockey?"

Her expression grew overly animated. "I know who you are, and of course I watch hockey! I love it!"

"Yeah? What's your favorite part?"

She rolled her bottom lip between her teeth, and her eyes took a trip around the room as though she were searching for the right answer. "The part I like most is in the last seconds of the fourth quarter, when the goalie leaves the net."

He stifled a guffaw. *Fourth quarter?* Yeah, this chick might *watch* the game, but her hockey IQ matched her age. While it wasn't a mark against her for what his libido had in mind, the fact she hadn't even bothered to pick up the basics bugged him. If you're gonna hang with the boys, at least have a clue about the game they play.

Christ, he was still annoyed. Apparently, he hadn't had enough alcohol yet. He waved the waitress over.

She walked over with an arched eyebrow. "Spill the last one?"

"Nope. But I'd love it if you'd speed them up. And make them doubles." He slipped her another Benjamin, and her smile told him she would.

Around him, players and girls were engaging in figurative foreplay. Dory's leg grazed his, and he draped his arm around her shoulders. Still chasing that elusive feel-good vibe, he shifted all his attention to the blond.

"Dory." He dragged out her name as if test-driving it.

"Like the fish in *Finding Nemo*," she explained.

"Uh, you're named after a fish?"

"More like the fish was named after me," she tee-heed.

"Oh, right. Because it's so"—*don't say ditzy*—"so cheerful. Like you."

This earned him a series of eyelash bats. Soon she was shimmying against him, and she dropped her hand on his thigh, draining some of his brainpower. Playing in his own backyard was a danger he tried to avoid, but he liked his odds tonight. This girl seemed to have lots in common with his "regulars," the women he routinely hooked up with: enjoyed sex as much as he did, weren't clingy, and didn't care if he slept around. Love 'em, leave 'em, return occasionally to love 'em again, but never let things get serious. That shit was okay for guys like Nelson and his other favorite teammate, T.J. Shanstrom. Those dudes were totally committed and happy about it. Good for them, but it wasn't for him.

As Dory glued herself to him and he pretended to listen to her chatter, an annoying inner voice sounded off: *Where's the challenge?*

"Hads!"

Quinn looked up, and Nelson gave him a wave from across the booth. "We're heading out. Catch ya later."

When Nelson turned to leave, Sarah placed her hand on Quinn's shoulder and whispered in his ear, "Looks like someone's getting lucky tonight. Enjoy your lube and tune, Sparky."

*Da fuck? Did she just say what I* think *she said?*

A beat passed before his brain pulled itself together. Unfortunately, the best he could muster was, "Oh, you bet your sweet ass I will."

She gave him a wink and walked away. He didn't have time to give it much thought because his phone vibrated. When he glanced down at the screen, panic bloomed in his chest. He mumbled an apology in Dory's direction and lurched out of the booth.

"Mom? What's wrong?"

# Chapter 2

## WELCOME TO MY WORLD

Sarah slouched in the backseat beside Daisy and stared through the window at lights streaking against an ultramarine backdrop. Winter in Colorado. Harsh. Was she really doing this? What choice did she have?

Lily sat behind the wheel, Gage next to her in the passenger seat as she drove them home from the bar. He threw Sarah the occasional concerned look over his shoulder.

"I'm okay," she reassured him. Her brother was ultra-protective, and she didn't want to worry him. After all, *she* was the big sister, though she sure didn't feel like one now.

"Can't fool me, Sar-bear."

"I'm just tired, Bro. I drove over mountain passes in lousy weather to get here. I'll be fine by morning."

"Yeah, about that."

"About what?"

"The sleeping arrangements. You okay sleeping in Daisy's room while she's on the couch?"

Oh shit. Sarah had been in such a panic to flee Seattle that she hadn't considered how disruptive her presence in Gage's and Lily's lives might be. She'd just blindly run to her safe haven, which was her brother. Of course, she hadn't realized at the time that he'd just sold his big-ass house and was squeezed in with Lily and her daughter in a two-bedroom, two-bath box.

She straightened in her seat and glanced over at Daisy. "No way. I'm not kicking you out of your room, Crazy Daisy. I'll take the couch tonight and find an Airbnb tomorrow."

"But I want to sleep on the couch, Aunt Sarah!" Daisy protested from her booster seat. The grin on her cute six-year-old face telegraphed she wasn't really upset.

Lily glanced at Sarah in the rearview mirror. "We want you staying with us, Sarah. And Daisy's been looking forward to her big adventure on the couch."

Gage turned in his seat, his eyes on Daisy. "We're turning it into a fort when we get home, aren't we, kiddo?"

*Aw, damn! He's so good with her.* Sarah felt a hot tear prick her eye. There'd been too much of that lately, she admonished herself.

Daisy's head nodded vigorously. "Yes! My babies are having a sleepover. And Archer's coming too."

Gage flicked his eyes to Sarah. "Well, I'm not sure the fort will be big enough for all your babies *and* a dog. Besides, I think Archer will want to be with Aunt Sarah tonight, especially since he's in a strange place."

Archer, Sarah's lovable lab, had been a big hit with Daisy from the moment Sarah had arrived hours ago. But then, he was a hit with everyone who met him. A service-dog school dropout, he was a well-behaved pup who'd captured her heart when she'd gotten him a year ago. And if she hadn't had Archer in her life, she would've shattered into irretrievable pieces. Eager to please, loyal, dependable. Trustworthy. Too bad those traits were absent in men—besides her brother.

"Lily," she pleaded, "I never intended to displace anyone. It just didn't occur to me that Gage would've sold his house, and now I'm kicking myself for not asking before I came plowing into your lives."

"Don't argue, Sarah," Lily said. "You're staying in Daisy's room. Period." Lily's fake sternness warmed Sarah.

An unexpected laugh bubbled up, and it felt good. "Okay. I know when I'm beaten." She patted Lily's shoulder. "Thank you."

Gage dangled his hand over the back of his seat. "We're moving into the new place in a few weeks, and it has a guesthouse in back. It's yours if you want it." His usual calm demeanor was in full sway, and Sarah glommed onto it like a life preserver in a boiling ocean. Where he was all chillax, she was constantly abuzz. They were opposite sides of the same coin. He'd gotten more of their grandmother's personality, while she'd wound up with their mother's—and the realization terrified her. Not only was their mother the poster child for "overbearing," but she was certifiably *nuts.*

"Any chance I can see the new house?"

"Absolutely," Lily said. "You remember Paige Miller from last summer's Stanley Cup party?"

Sarah chuckled. "You mean the one where you and my brother were scouring each other's throats in front of dozens of people?"

Gage shot her a lowered-brow warning and slid his eyes toward Daisy.

"What? She saw you guys kissing." She elbowed Daisy. "Didn't you, Daze?"

Daisy squirmed and crinkled her nose. "Everyone saw them kissing. And they still kiss. *All the time.*"

Gage's mouth quirked. In the rearview mirror, Lily's face had turned crimson. She cleared her throat. "Anyway, Paige is meeting us there tomorrow. Why don't you come with and check it out?"

"I'm in."

For the rest of that evening, Sarah sat back and observed the little family in their comfortable cadence. Gage's "girls" had brought so much richness to his life, and Lily was his perfect match. Sarah had never seen him happier. If it hadn't been her brother's life she watched from her front-row seat, the ache inside her might've blossomed into unrelenting envy. Instead, soaking up the loving vibes gave Sarah hope and, by inches, lightened the burden her own devastation had brought. But she didn't want to think about that anymore. Sleep—oblivion—was what she craved, and when she finally climbed into Daisy's neon-pink bed, she did something she'd never done before: she urged Archer out of his bed and into hers, then curled herself around him.

The smell of bacon greeted her when she stepped into the kitchen the next morning to let Archer into the backyard. She'd slept like the dead and found herself trying to catch up to the buzz of a fully awake household.

She slurped the eye-popping coffee Lily deposited in front of her. "Ooh, I'm liking my soon-to-be sister-in-law more and more. Where's Crazy Daisy?"

"I took her to school," Gage replied, "and you've got about a half hour to get ready to see the new house. You and I are riding together, and Lily will drive on her own because she needs to measure stuff. Then I have to drop something off for a teammate. Why don't you bring Archer? Our cat hasn't come out from under the bed since you got here—this'll give her a little reprieve."

"Oh shit. I'd totally forgotten about Hobbes."

Gage raised his eyes to hers. "Language?"

"Fuck. That's right. Except Daisy's not here, so I can say shit out loud, right?"

Lily burst out with a laugh. "Sarah, you can damn well say shit anytime she's not in fucking earshot."

Sarah held up her cup in a toast. "Lily, you and I are going to get along fucking splendidly."

Gage rolled his eyes.

An hour later, they stood in a circular driveway facing what could have passed as a golf course clubhouse. Petite, auburn-haired Paige waited at the front door and waved.

When they reached her, she hugged everyone, ending with Sarah. "So I hear you're moving to our beautiful state."

"Moved."

Paige pushed open one half of a double front door and motioned them inside. "Is this for a job?"

Though Paige asked innocently, the question jabbed Sarah in an uncomfortable place—like poking at an open sore. "No. Just wanted a change of scene. I'll start job hunting tomorrow."

What Sarah didn't tell Paige was that the job she'd up and left was one she would have a hard time replacing. Not only had it been a promotion, but it had been a prestigious one that promised an express elevator ride to the top. When she'd discovered, however, that she hadn't gotten the job entirely on her own merits, the luster had rubbed off quickly and, along with the rest of her sham life in Seattle, had gone into the crapper.

She lingered with Paige in the foyer while Gage and Lily wandered off.

"What do you do?" Paige asked.

Sarah let her eyes travel around the interior. Though architects drove her nuts, she appreciated their artistry, especially loving the lines of living spaces like this one. "I'm a structural engineer."

Paige's green eyes lit. "Ooh. So can you look at an old house and configure weight distributions for moving a load-bearing wall? That sort of thing?"

Sarah shrugged. "Totally. Those are usually pretty straightforward."

They ambled toward a monstrous great room. "Would you be interested in consulting on some remodels I'm contemplating?"

From around the corner came Lily's disembodied voice. "Paige hires all of us."

Sarah's confusion must have shown because Paige gave a little shrug and said, "I only hire the best, so I hired Lily and Natalie."

Sarah followed Paige into a to-die-for kitchen where Lily stood behind a stone counter, grinning. "We're becoming an all girls' club. We should call ourselves something like Paige's Petunias."

"Oh God no!" Paige laughed. "That's too close to 'Pansies.' We need a more kick-butt moniker. Maybe Paige's Powerhouse Playmakers. P-Cubed." She swiveled her head from side to side. "Is Gage where I think he is?"

Lily flicked her hand. "Yep. Checking out the basement. Again."

"Good. Let's plan a girls' night out so we can pick an official club name."

Gage entered from a doorway that led downstairs. "What are you three plotting?"

"Paige's Plotters!" Lily and Paige sang together.

Sarah never hung with women—too whiny, too catty—but she felt a tug to be part of this career girls' club. "I may not be part of the club—"

"Yet," Paige interrupted, a mischievous twinkle in her eyes.

"Oh boy," Gage muttered. "Look out, Denver."

A half hour later, Gage and Sarah had left Lily and Paige behind and pulled up to the teammate's house. Correction, mansion. Castle. The teammate turned out to be Quinn, the babe-magnet engineer from the bar. So what if he had smarts? He still was a jock hockey player. Emphasis on *player,* judging by the hair and the take-no-prisoners dimples he flashed repeatedly at members of the opposite sex. He was one of those guys who *knew* how he affected women, and he was skilled at working it—practice makes perfect and all that.

Like Wolf. *Prick.*

"Hey, Bro, I'm just gonna stay out here so Archer can do his business and have a sniff-around." She leashed her dog and led him out of the backseat.

"You sure you don't want to see this house? I hear it's got a swimming pool and a racquetball court and a home theater almost as big as a real theater."

*Nothing worse than an entitled player.* "No, thanks. I'm good."

"Suit yourself," Gage called back. "If you change your mind—"

"I won't."

The gonging doorbell startled Quinn. It always did, even though he'd been in this ridiculous house over a month now. He threw open the door to Nelson's grinning face. "Hey. C'mon in." Over Nelson's shoulder, he spotted a woman walking a dog along the grass median. When she turned, he caught the flash of electric-pink hair. "Your sister's welcome to come in too."

Nelson glanced over his shoulder. "She's gonna hang with her dog."

*Fine by me.* Quinn wasn't in the mood for Sarah Nelson's acerbic tongue today anyway, especially not with the hangover mercilessly pounding his skull.

"Quinn," came his mother's shrill voice from somewhere. Hell, the house was so big it was hard to tell which wing she might be in. Not so far away, judging by the telltale thumping of her approaching wheelchair. She rounded the corner into the foyer. Her eyes landed on Gage, and she smiled. "Who's this?"

Quinn made the introductions. "He's just here to drop off some new gear from one of the companies that sponsors him."

"Oh." Her eyes darted out the front door, and her face lit up. "Who's the girl with the dog?"

"That's my sister, Sarah," Gage answered.

Mom practically flattened Gage on her way to the front door. "I love dogs! Yoo-hoo! Hey, doll! Come in! Bring your dog."

Quinn suppressed his eye-roll. It would've only added to the thudding in his head anyway. Instead, he offered Nelson an apologetic shrug. Nelson answered with a no-big-deal shrug of his own.

Judging by the way Sarah Nelson's head swiveled on her shoulders, she was surprised his mother was cajoling—no, roping her in. And who the hell wouldn't be? Sarah didn't know his mother, nor did she know that once Elizabeth Hadley set her mind on something, you'd better get out of her way. And even though he didn't particularly like Miss Sunshine, he inwardly wished her luck.

"Yes, you," his mother called to Sarah. "I'd like to meet your dog."

And just like that, Sarah Nelson and her big, yellow, panting dog crowded into the foyer with them. Well, not that the foyer was small enough to become *crowded* with a mere five souls, but everyone was clustered together. The dog seemed to zero in on his mom, thrusting its head into her lap. She patted it and crooned, "There's a good boy. Oh, aren't you a beauty!"

The dog responded with an enthusiastic tail wag.

Sarah smiled at his mom—a genuine, eye-brightening smile. *Green eyes?* "His name's Archer." Her voice held a huge dose of pride.

"Like the cartoon character?" Quinn and his mother both said at the same time. Though his mother didn't seem to notice, his chin probably hit his chest. How did his mom know about *Archer*?

Sarah bobbed her head, her pink strands fluttering around her face. "Yes, *that* Archer." That's when Quinn noticed only the very front strands were pink. The rest of her short do was dark brown, a rich color that caught the light and reflected it in reds.

He managed to cough out, "You've watched *Archer*, Mom?"

"I own every season on DVD," she murmured, though all of her attention was riveted on *this* Archer.

Suddenly, the dog backed up and out of her grasp and sat on its haunches, doing a canine version of standing at attention. It seemed to sniff the air, then glanced over its shoulder at Sarah and let out a whine.

Sarah's dark brows knotted in a frown. "What's up, Arch?"

Another little cry and he fidgeted like he wanted to jump up and take off. Sarah pointed. "Seek." The dog loped toward the kitchen, and they all fell in line behind, coming to an abrupt stop when it parked its furry butt once more and stared up at the kitchen island. It was making a whiny-pant sound, its head swinging between Sarah and the island.

His mom gasped and pointed. "Oh my God! I forgot to take my pills this morning."

Quinn snatched a little zippered cloth bag where his mother kept all her meds. As soon as he handed it to her, the dog seemed to settle down.

"Good boy, Archer," Sarah sang.

Baffled, Quinn said, "What just happened?"

Sarah's eyes danced with excitement. *Gray?* "I'm not sure, but I think … He was trained to be a diabetes alert dog. They can smell when something's off with their human—like their blood sugar level is too high—and they alert a family member. I've never seen him actually use that skill, though." A little laugh escaped her. "Ironically, he flunked his training, and that's how I ended up with him."

"Well, he gets an A-plus from me," Quinn's mother said, causing his mind to whir. Most of their arguments were over caregivers he hired and she fired. Could he hire a *dog* as a caregiver? How much kibble would it demand in payment?

He filled a glass with water for his mom while she fiddled with the paisley pouch. He held out his hand to help her open it, but she ignored him and fought the zipper. Fine motor skills were eluding her today, but as usual her stubborn streak was sharp. Sarah also extended her hand, and to his surprise his mother relinquished the bag. He bit back the sting, telling himself at least his mother was willing to let *someone* help. As Sarah finessed the zipper, his mom told her which pill container she needed. Sarah plucked it out, uncapped it, and tapped out a pair of pills into Mom's open palm. Just like that. If only he could get the same cooperation.

After downing the pills, his mother looked from Sarah to Nelson and back again. "I'm Liz."

"Oh shit, I'm sorry. I should've introduced you."

Mom darted daggers at him. "Quinn Anthony Hadley! Jar!"

He returned an eye-roll, grabbed his wallet from the kitchen desk, and stuffed a bill into his mother's idea of the perfect cure for swearing: a three-foot-high glass cylinder she lovingly called the "swear jar." So what if the container was already half-full?

"Wow, dude," Nelson chuckled. "Is that all you?"

His mom nodded and gave Nelson a smug smile. "I keep telling him he's going to go broke." Her eyes then riveted on Sarah. "Is your nose pierced?"

Sarah had been wearing a smile since she'd set foot in his house, and now that smile widened. "Yep. It's a recent addition. What do you think?"

"Oh, girl, I love it! Is that a diamond?"

*Oh girl?* Quinn took a step back. Who was this woman in the wheelchair, and what had she done with his mother?

"Yes, it is. It was a recent splurge." Sarah twirled her index finger.

"Celebrate a birthday or something?" Quinn asked.

She turned and looked at him for the first time since she'd walked in, and that brilliant smile slid from her face. "No. Just a whim."

His mother whooped and clapped her hands. "I want one!"

"I'll take you to get one, if you like," Sarah offered. The smile was back in place as she addressed his mom. Her jacket had parted, giving him a look at a different T-shirt from yesterday's. This one said, "I Do What the Voices in My Head Tell Me."

Quinn stared at the scene in front of him. Since his mother had come to live with him—correction: since he'd traded in his awesome condo for this leviathan of a house just to accommodate her—she hadn't been so lively.

Nelson jarred him from his woe-is-me wallowing. "Hey, Hads. Can I check out your home theater? I'm trying to get ideas for what I want to put in our new place."

"Yeah, sure." Though Quinn didn't want to, inviting Nelson's sister was the polite thing to do. "Do you want to come with us, Sarah?"

"No, she's going to stay here and keep me company," his bossy mother tossed out.

He arched his eyebrows in question at Sarah.

"I'll stay here and chat with Liz," she said with warmth directed at his mom.

Relieved, he led Nelson to the theater room. Nelson whistled softly. "Wow, Hads. This place rocks. You must love living here."

"It's okay." Truth was, he missed his condo. A lot. It had spanned the top two floors of a stunning building—an architectural marvel with endless walls of glass. Perks of the building had included a rooftop gathering area complete with a heated infinity pool that drew lots of eye candy.

Clinging to the hope his mother's unexpected presence in his life was a temporary setback, he couldn't bring himself to put his one-of-a-kind bachelor pad on the market. So he'd let the building's rental staff fill it with strangers who enjoyed it while he languished in suburbia.

He realized Nelson was staring at him, and he felt the need to elaborate. "Living here wasn't my first choice, but I needed to rent a one-level quick, which meant slim pickings."

Nelson nodded. "Your mom …"

"She's got Parkinson's. She doesn't usually need the wheelchair, but with the way the disease progresses, it'll become more and more of a necessity. She was living with my brother, but when his third kid arrived, she needed a more relaxed environment." Quinn left out the part that she'd become more dependent on the wheelchair, and that he suspected it was amped-up stress caused by living with *him*. Damn, he didn't want her to backslide, especially on account of him.

"So how does that work when you're gone? Do you have someone come in?"

Quinn smiled at the irony. "I've been trying. She's gone through three caregivers in a month. Last night, she called me at the bar to tell me she'd fired the latest one." Seeing his mom's number pop up had scared the ever-loving shit out of him. But after he took the call, he'd been royally pissed off.

Nelson nodded. "That's gotta suck."

Quinn puffed out a breath. "Yeah, it slowed me down for a hot minute. Somehow, though, I still got hammered enough to need a ride home." He'd pounded down a slew of rum and Cokes before switching to tequila shooters. Bad idea. He hadn't had an abundance of brain cells to spare as it was, and the partying had disabled the few he did have—as he'd proven when he wound up in the backseat of his Ram truck with the blond fish. Dory. They'd steamed up the windows fucking each other stupid. Not his smartest play, but the drunker he'd gotten, the better she'd looked, and lust mixed with frustration had given logic a swift kick to the curb.

In the end? It hadn't been nearly as hot as his dick had led him to believe it would be, but that seemed to be the way with all his hookups lately. In this case, he'd been left with a twanged butt muscle and buyer's remorse.

He glanced over at Nelson, who was inspecting the screen. "So you and Lily. Things good with you being crowded together in that tiny little house? Wedding's still on for August?"

A shit-eating grin spread all over Nelson's face, followed by a look Quinn could only call blissful satisfaction. Wonder what that felt like?

"Wedding's definitely still on," Nelson said, "and we'll be settled in the new place and able to spread out before that. Sarah and Archer will move into the guesthouse."

This brought to the fore a question that had been spinning in Quinn's head. "So what made your sister move all of a sudden?"

"I'm still trying to figure that out. But I plan to drag it out of her today."

"Well, good luck with that, Nelsy." Judging by the glimpse Quinn had had of Sarah Nelson's prickly personality, she wasn't the type to do *anything* she didn't want to. Just like his mom. They could have been peas hanging out in the same pod.

# Chapter 3

## I Wasn't in Line the Day God Handed Out Smarts

"Okay, Sis. Time to spill."

Trying to ignore Gage jabbing at her for answers, Sarah intently stared out the passenger window as they streaked along the freeway toward Denver's sawtoothed skyline. The flat browns and grays brought to mind the homespun clothing worn by characters in a favorite period series she'd watched. Dull. Different from Seattle's cityscape. And yet the sky here, unlike the treeless late-winter terrain it spanned, was so vivid it practically shimmered. *Big Sky Country.* Or was that Montana? Not that it mattered because she'd see it every day going forward. Her stomach clenched with the recognition that this was her new reality.

"What do you mean, Little Bro?" She put as innocent an inflection in her voice as she dared.

"What I *mean*, Big Sis, is what the hell happened in Seattle?"

"Who says anything happened?"

He chuffed. "This is me you're talking to, Sar. If you showing up on my doorstep isn't evidence enough of some epic disturbance in the Force, I don't know what is. Plus, you were pretty cold to my teammate, and that's not like you."

"He's a ladies' man who reminds me of someone I don't like." *Shit! My kick-ass self has devolved into a whiny teenager.*

Gage side-eyed her. "Quinn may have a reputation as a fuckboy, but he's a good guy."

"What *you* perceive as a good guy and what a woman perceives as a fuckboy are parts of the same man that are in two entirely different universes."

His brows puckered. "I have no idea what you just said."

Neither did she, which pissed her off. She was speaking in tongues *she* couldn't understand. *Get a grip.* Somehow she couldn't. "He's full of himself. Just look at his flow."

"You're judging the guy by his *hair*?"

"It's just part of the same deliberate package." She flung her hand out. "Everything he does—the easy lines, the two-day stubble, the ridiculous dimples—is contrived. It's so he can schmooze women into bed."

Gage blew out a breath as he took an exit. He rolled to a stop at a red light and turned toward her. "We're getting sidetracked. Quinn isn't the reason you're here, so let me ask my question a different way. What's *really* eating you? And don't give me any lame excuses or Mom-like dodges."

Her brother was absolutely right. She wasn't *mad* at Quinn. Frankly, she couldn't have cared less what the guy was into. If anything about Quinn made her mad, it was what he represented. He was the poster boy for the type of guy she told herself she'd *never* fall for. Spending time around Gage's hockey buddies had taught her what sort of man to steer clear of, yet somehow she'd let herself be hoodwinked by the humdinger daddy of them all, with a tongue made of solid sterling. Not only had she parked her brain, but she'd unlocked her judiciously guarded vault and thrown it wide-open for him. Then she'd handed him the key and watched him bash her heart in with it.

She'd always thought herself too sharp and independent to give up control to a man. The takeover had been incremental, but why hadn't she seen it before it was too late? Mom and Grandma had raised her to be smarter than that. And for a while, she'd nailed it. A rising star who was always professional, always put together. With double engineering degrees, she was a Spanish-speaking consultant brought into prestigious resort projects in Mexico, earning her more feathers in her already crowded cap. She'd wowed them all—herself too. Where was all that confidence now?

Gage's voice startled her back to the interior of his car. "I'm waiting." He said it in a *Princess Bride* Vizzini voice, and she let out a chuckle.

Before she could formulate her careful answer, they glided to a stop in front of Lily's house. "We're home," said Captain Obvious. "Looks like she's not back yet. And, Sar? We really are happy to have you here."

The way he said it made tears suddenly surge, and she swallowed them down. *Kick-ass women do not cry.* Clearing her throat, she willed the kick-ass girl to come through in her voice, and not the wimp who'd taken up space in her psyche. "It's oddly nice to hear you say 'we,' Bro." He'd always flown solo, like her—until recently. And irony of ironies, until four days ago she'd been part of a "we" he knew nothing about. Funny how quickly your life could transform from idyllic to total shit.

Gage headed up the walkway, and she led Archer out of the Range Rover. "And while I appreciate your hospitality, I still have to find another place so you have some breathing room. I've gotta say I never thought I'd see the day you'd go *back* to living in a cramped house with multiple females."

A goofy grin sprouted on his face. "Some things are totally worth it." He opened the front door and held it for her and Archer. "You're doing an awesome imitation of Mom by avoiding an obviously unpleasant subject, by the way. But you'll need a little more practice to be as evasive as she is." He chuckled, completely oblivious to how deeply the comment cut, and a frightening thought slammed into her like a fully loaded freight train. "I haven't told Mom. You didn't say anything, did you?"

His keys landed with a *clink* in a bowl on a side table. "Absolutely not. Bro code."

She heaved a sigh of relief. Yeah, she'd always been able to count on him to keep her secrets and mistakes to himself—not that she'd let him see many of the latter. Worse, the doozy she was currently fighting to forget outweighed all her other blunders combined.

Gage started rifling the fridge. "Something to drink?"

She shot him a backward glance as she let Archer into the backyard. "Got any bourbon and Coke?"

"That bad?" He hauled down two glasses and a bottle of Blanton's. He poured the tawny liquid into the glasses, doctoring one with ice and Coke before handing it to her. He pointed at the kitchen table. "Sit."

*Moment of truth.* Maybe he'd be satisfied with the incomplete version of the story. Yeah, she'd go with that. He sat, and she plopped her butt into a wooden chair and took a deep breath. "First I need to back all the way up and tell you the *real* reason I moved to Seattle."

"It wasn't for the structural engineering job?"

"Yes. No. That was part of it. It was also for a man. Named Wolf." *Damn it!* She practically flinched from saying it aloud. Not only had she been bricks shy of a full load to uproot herself for him, but the precious job was one he'd arranged for her—*after* grooming her for it, so he'd said. All without her knowledge. She tried to convince herself she could have landed it on her own, but the notion was hard to swallow.

Though his eyebrows climbed his forehead—the only note of surprise in his expression—Gage remained quiet and sipped his bourbon.

"I first met him in the Bay Area. He's an architect who designed one of the buildings our firm was hired to engineer. He told me he was Swedish and that he split his time between Sweden and here."

Ice-blue eyes in an angular face. Fair hair graying at the temples. Sophistication. Intellect. Style. The images had conspired against her, and she'd fallen ass over teakettle.

Marshaling the force of her anger, she tried to herd the pictures into a box and slam the lid, managing to cram everything inside but those haunting glacial eyes.

"I was on the project team, and we worked long hours together. All of us did. He and I started spending more time alone. That is, until the project ended and he returned to Sweden." She paused, and Gage gave her an encouraging nod. "He stayed in touch. Then he announced he was traveling to Seattle to check out an opportunity and asked if I would spend a few days with him there. I thought, 'Why not?' He bought my plane ticket, then wined and dined me. He pulled out all the stops."

She tapped nervous fingers against her glass. "We did the long-distance thing for a while. Sometimes we saw each other in Seattle, other times in Chicago or New York. We went to museums, shows, and we walked the cities and looked at the older buildings. Then we'd talk for hours about the architecture and the engineering behind it. I ate it up. Eventually, he told me he was seriously considering taking the opportunity in Seattle, but only if I'd move there too."

*Little did I know he was dangling his business like a carrot in front of the firm's owner. In return, the owner had to hire me.* The pain in her heart was so sharp she swore she'd been struck by *shuriken*—the proper word for ninja stars, Wolf had instructed her.

Gage sat back. "So you did."

She nodded slowly. "Yes, I did. I mean, the job was fabulous." Her words came out in an odd mixture of defensive and sad.

Wolf had been an expert salesman, and she'd been as overwhelmed as a sapling in a gale-force wind. She'd heard "beautiful" often enough, but Wolf took it way beyond her mere physical appearance: he admired her independence, her intellect, her ability to see the world in 3-D, her accomplishments, her sophistication—which she'd never before thought she had. He was masterful at pushing all the right buttons. She was a woman rising to her full potential, he'd smoothly said, and if she let him mold her, groom her, she'd soar to her pinnacle even sooner. He became her mentor, her lover, her lavisher. Her everything. In turn, she inspired him, made him feel youthful again, fascinated him. Yes, she'd fed his ego too, but at the time she hadn't cared because she'd *wanted* to.

"I stayed at his place in the beginning, intending to get my own apartment. His house had a beautiful yard and a view of Puget Sound, and I just … never left. It made sense to stay there, especially after I got Archer.

"Then Wolf started traveling for long stretches. He said he was having problems with his business in Sweden. I missed him, but I wasn't worried. I had my amazing job, and he reassured me that once he got everything straightened out, he'd be around more."

She took a slug of her drink.

"But something happened," Gage murmured.

Sarah nodded. "Yep." She kept her eyes averted from his. "I found out the reason he was gone so much wasn't because he was in Sweden. It was because he had someone else. Might've been more than one, for all I know, but I didn't stick around to find out."

"Aw, shit, Sar."

When she raised her eyes to Gage's, she only saw concern, and it broke free the tears she'd been holding back. He placed his hand on the table between them, palm up, and she rested her hand in his.

"Guy's a total douche," Gage said softly. "You know this, right? He didn't deserve you."

"He sure as shit didn't. But I fell for him, damn it. I'm usually smarter than that."

He squeezed her hand. "We can't always control who we fall for."

She laugh-sobbed. "God, you sound just like Grandma!"

Releasing her, he grinned. "Right? I've been practicing."

Sarah rolled her watery eyes. "Does Lily appreciate what a rare breed you are?"

"All the time."

"Thought so. She's a smart cookie." *Unlike yours truly.* "So how come there aren't more of you—unrelated to me, that is?"

He stood, passed her a box of tissues, and let Archer inside. "There are lots of us. You just have to look a little harder. We don't all flash signs that say, 'Your perfect man standing right here!' In fact, steer clear of *those* guys."

"I think 'perfect' and 'man' together equal an oxymoron." She plucked a few tissues and dabbed at her eyes. Archer laid his head in her lap and wagged as if to say, "How 'bout me? I'm perfect." She stroked his soft fur, inwardly agreeing.

Gage chuckled. "All I'm saying is don't judge a book by its cover. You never know what's written in those chapters until you crack the spine."

"Omigod, listen to my little brother! You're like Dear Abby and Yoda rolled into one." She let out a snort.

"I thought *you* were Yoda." He cocked a brow.

"I think I lost my title. Damn, you're four years younger. How'd you get to be so much smarter? I'll need to earn my place back and lord it over you again." Some of the tension drained from her shoulders, and she rotated her neck.

"Ha! It's taken me a long time to get here, and I'm not giving up my Yoda throne that easily," he joked.

"What's a Yoda throne?" Lily stood in the kitchen doorway, surprising them both.

"Didn't hear you come in, Goldilocks." Gage rose, strode to her, and swept her up in his arms, laying an embarrassingly long kiss on her. Sarah debated excusing herself.

A breathless Lily pulled away. "Well, hello to you too, Professor."

Sarah stood. "I'll leave now."

"No, Sarah, sit." Lily flapped a hand. "That's all the kissing we're going to do in front of you."

Gage smirked. "For now."

"Between the cutesy nicknames and PDAs, you two make me want to puke!" Sarah barked.

Gage and Lily turned wide eyes toward her.

She grinned. "I meant puke in a *good* way."

Gage's phone rang, and he stepped into the living room and answered.

Lily's eyes took in their drinks. "Are you guys celebrating something?"

Sarah tugged her fingers through her hair. "No, more like burying something."

Lily's expression morphed into what Sarah could only describe as motherly. She reached for Sarah and pulled her into a hug. "I don't know what happened, and it doesn't matter. I just want you to know we're glad you came *here*."

That simple act made Sarah's chest squeeze and wedged fresh tears in her throat. *Stop it!*

Lily patted her back, then held her apart. "You gonna be okay?"

Sarah nodded as the waterworks spilled over. "Eventually."

"Well, in the meantime, you're coming to the game with Daisy and me tomorrow night. We may not be able to take your mind off all your troubles, but it'll be a distraction."

"I don't think I'd be very good comp—"

Gage poked his head into the kitchen. "That was T.J. Wyatt's birthday is tomorrow, so we're having a surprise dinner after the game."

"That sounds fun." Lily bobbed her curly head. "Doesn't it, Sarah?"

Sarah opened her mouth, but nothing came out. Gage barreled into the quiet. "No staying at home alone, Sar. I already bought you a ticket, and I told T.J. to count you in for dinner."

"But, Gage—"

"It's better to sulk among friends than to sulk at home alone. Another pearl of Yoda wisdom for you."

Sarah relented with an exaggerated eye-roll. "Oh, well, since you put it *that* way, Yoda … How can a girl say no? It sounds like a blast." *Not.*

Gage shot her a fake glare right before he and Lily said in unison, "It'll be good for you."

What was *good* for her was to crawl under a rock and never come out. Unfortunately, that option wasn't available. Sarah sighed and finished her drink. Maybe all the yelling in the arena would drown out her mother's inner voice telling her what a moron she was for putting on rose-colored glasses and letting a man blindside her. She hadn't told Gage everything—she wasn't ready to. She might never be. Admitting her epic mistake would also mean admitting that their mother was right.

# Chapter 4

## Oh Hell No

That evening, Sarah hovered uselessly while Lily manned the stove, Daisy set the table, and Gage shredded cheese. What could Sarah do to help? God, she hated being an intruder in this little family's sweet routine, contributing nothing while sucking up the scant spare space in their crammed house.

Her phone rang, and when she checked the screen, she suppressed a groan and thumbed the call off. She'd been dodging her mom for days, sending texts saying she was busy with work and would call later. If she didn't call soon, she ran the risk of Nola Nelson flying to Seattle and organizing search teams.

With a sigh, Sarah plopped into a kitchen chair and started folding paper napkins into fancy shapes.

Daisy executed some rapid-fire sneezing, and Gage craned his head over his shoulder. "You okay, kiddo?"

Nodding her head, she rubbed her eyes. They were bright red.

Gage turned back to his shredding. "So has anyone been following this virus in the news?"

"COVID-19," Sarah chirped, feeling suddenly helpful. "I heard about it on the radio as I drove cross-country. Started somewhere in China. Wuhan, I think."

"Yeah, well, it's popping up in South Korea, Italy, and Iran, to name a few, and it just showed up in the US." Gage flicked his gaze to Sarah. "In Washington state."

Her eyes widened. "What? How did I miss that?"

Gage gave her a grim nod. "I don't know much about it, but there's talk the World Health Organization might declare a pandemic."

Lily stopped what she was doing and faced him. "Which means what, exactly?"

He shrugged. "I'm not really sure."

Lily's blue eyes popped with something akin to panic.

"There are only a few reported cases in Colorado, sweetheart," Gage soothed. "Mostly they're on the west coast, so we're okay."

When Sarah climbed into Daisy's Pepto-Bismol room that night, she surfed the Internet and read what she could about the virus. Honestly, what was the fuss about? It was the flu. During flu season. People got sick. Some died. Gage, Lily, and Daisy were healthy, and so was she. They'd be fine.

"I can't believe you fucking beat me!" Quinn set the video controller down on Wyatt's coffee table.

Hunter sat beside him on the couch, his voice laced with smug condescension. "Admit it. I'm that much better."

"No, you're not. But I guess even a blind squirrel finds an acorn once in a while," Quinn groused.

He rose and took his empty beer bottle into the kitchen, where Wyatt was finishing off a plate of tortilla chips covered in orange goo that looked like plasticized neon.

"Dude, how can you eat that shit?" Quinn pointed his finger down his throat, faking a gag.

"Until I find me a Playboy centerfold who cooks like Betty Crocker, this is it."

Quinn couldn't stop himself. "Oh, you mean like McMurphy's ex? What was her name? The one who caught him boinking her best friend?"

"Fuck you!" Hunter snapped.

Wyatt shook his head. "Jesus Christ, you're a jackass, Hads." Then he offered up an orange-toothed grin. "My perfect centerfold Betty is gonna take a while to find. Meanwhile, I'll have hella fun auditioning candidates for the part."

"Speaking of which," Hunter stood and joined them, "you're clubbing with Wyatt and me tonight, right?"

"Nope. My head's still pounding from last night, and practice about killed me today. I wanna be ready for tomorrow night's game."

"Oh, come on, you big pussy." Hunter shoved his arm, and Quinn bit back the urge to flatten him.

Wyatt licked his thumb and chuckled. "Hunts needs you there, Hads. Only you can wheel the ladies and spin one his way. Otherwise, he's got no one to nail."

Hunter glared darts at Wyatt. "Fuck off, motherfucker."

Restlessness spiked inside Quinn, and he was suddenly anxious to be out of this stupid conversation and away from these asshats. Why was he here anyway? Oh right. To get away from his mom for a few hours. They were the only two losers who didn't have anything better to do, which left him with the unsettling thought he was a loser too.

Wyatt's chuckle turned into a full-on laughfest. "Your epic comeback says it all, Hunts." Wyatt flicked his eyes Quinn's way and jerked his thumb toward Hunter. "Know what this asshole was doing last night while you were balls deep in that blond?"

"Who said I was balls deep in *anyone* last night?"

"Her girlfriend saw you guys putting on quite a show in the backseat of your truck." Wyatt wasn't laughing anymore, but he still wore a stupid-ass grin.

*Goddamn.* Quinn pushed down his alarm. Not only had he been stupid enough to screw this girl in his truck, but he hadn't checked his surroundings once they'd gotten going. He dragged a hand across his neck. "As much as hanging out with you two dipshits is the highlight of my day, I'm out."

"Wait. Don't you want to hear how Hunts was begging—and I mean *begging*—for a piece of ass? Fuck, it was embarrassing." Wyatt giggled like a girl while Hunter cussed him up and down. Shit was getting old.

"I don't give a fuck about what Hunts—or you—do off the ice." Except Quinn somehow always wound up in the middle of whatever *they* were doing. Why was that? He picked up his jacket and headed for the door.

"We're starting at the Red Room at ten," Wyatt called.

Quinn waved a noncommittal hand behind him. *Maybe if I'm ready to stick needles in my eyes because my mother is bugging the shit out of me …*

By the time he strolled into his house, he'd zenned himself into a state of calm—only to be yanked out of it when he reached the kitchen. His mother lay on her side on the floor. Several feet away, out of her reach, sat her upright wheelchair.

*Fuck!*

He dropped beside her, and her eyes fluttered open. *Thank God!* Patting her face, he scanned her. "Mom? Are you okay? What happened?"

"Oh, Quinn. There you are." She said it matter-of-factly—as if she *weren't* in a prone position on the floor—before grasping on to him and hauling herself up onto one elbow. "Help me sit up."

"Hold up, Mom. I don't want to move you until I know you didn't break anything." He slid his arm along her back.

"I didn't break anything," she sighed. "That darn chair and I had a disagreement, that's all, and then I couldn't get my legs to work in sync."

*Christ!* "How long have you been like this?"

She craned her head and peered up at him. "No idea. Forty-five minutes? A few hours?"

"Jesus, Mom!" He pulled her upper body into his arms and cradled it. Guilt swamped him. *I should have been here instead of wasting time with the two yokels. This wouldn't have hap—*

"Swear jar!"

"For fuck's sake—"

"Quinn! That's ten bucks!"

Yeah, she was okay. He dropped his forehead to her shoulder and began laughing. And couldn't stop. Whether it was relief, the absurdity of the situation, or a combination of the entire FUBAR day, he had no idea. Soon her shoulders were shuddering along with his, and she let out a few whoops.

"Isn't this great, son? We're finally getting some quality one-on-one time."

He brushed tears from his eyes with the back of his hand. "Yeah, on the fucking floor!" She opened her mouth to say something, but he cut her off. "I know. Ten bucks. Twenty. I don't give a shit."

She shook her head, but he caught the chuckle in her voice. "I taught you better."

"Yeah, you did, Mom, but guess what? I unlearned most of it." Judging by his dumbass behavior of late, a truer statement had never been spoken. "C'mon, sassy. Let's get you up."

"'Sassy.' I like it."

After he'd gotten her situated in her wheelchair, he handed her a glass of water and guzzled one of his own, keeping a wary eye on her. "Mom, we've gotta get someone in here for you. Any of the ladies that were here before know the setup and—"

She shook her head so hard he thought it might fly off her neck. "No, no, no! I will *not* tolerate any of those Nazi cows. I'll get back on my own two feet, and I won't *need* a Nurse Ratched. I'm fully capable of taking care of myself."

"Your stubborn streak's the reason you fell down today. You could've broken your neck!"

She flapped her hand. "Not really. Besides, a Nazi cow babysitter would've been completely useless. A waste of couch space while she sucked down popcorn and watched soap operas. Did you know not one of them knew how to play Parcheesi? For heaven's sake! Who can't play a simple child's game?"

He pushed a cleansing breath through his lungs. "Parcheesi skills are not a job requirement."

"Well, being smart is," she scoffed. "What about your friend's sister, Sarah?"

*What the actual fuck?* Feeling as though he'd been doused with a bucket of ice shavings, he coughed. "You can't be serious."

"I am serious. We're simpatico. She's spunky. Way better than any of those stodgy biddies you've hired. I want her as my caregiver." She bobbed her head as if signaling the end of the discussion.

"No. No way."

"Why the hell not?"

Fighting the quirking at the corner of his mouth, he pointed his finger at her. "Swear jar."

"I'm allowed one a day."

"Since when? You can't just arbitrarily change the rules to suit yourself." He bit back his amusement. "Look, Mom, there are a million reasons why Sarah can't be your caregiver. Let's start with the most obvious ones." He held up his index finger. "First, she hates my guts."

A little gleam came into his mother's eyes. "Why don't you just use your charm on her?"

Oh no. He was not about to let this train leave the station. "Sarah Nelson is deathly allergic to charm." He held up a second finger. "Second, she's a structural engineer, which means she's not qualified to be a caregiver."

"Why not? Her smarts qualify her for *any* job. Besides, you can pay her far better than whatever she could earn as an engineer."

"While that may be—and thanks for spending my money for me, by the way—they're two different jobs from two completely unrelated industries." He blazed ahead. "Third, she has a dog, and I'm not having a dog here. The lease probably doesn't allow it anyway."

His mother clapped as though she hadn't heard a damn thing he'd said. "Yes, *and* Archer was being trained as a service dog. Did you see what he did? Of course you did. You were standing right there. I love dogs. Archer would be perf—"

"Did I mention Sarah hates my guts?" Quinn flicked out another finger. "That leads me to four: You don't need that kind of tension around you. Fifth, *I* don't like *her*."

"Really? What's wrong with you?" Now his mother held up *her* fingers and began counting off. "First of all, I like her. Second, she's cute as a button. Third, she's sharp as a tack. Fourth, she makes me laugh. Fifth, I like her dog. Sixth, she'll take me to get my nose pierced. At least talk to her, Quinn. For me."

His mind was wobbling like an unbalanced top. How was he going to derail his mom from this beyond-insane track? He pondered relenting for a nanosecond before giving the idea the heave-ho. Sarah Sunshine in his house? Twenty-four-seven? Hell no.

Even if that meant it was all on him to take care of his mom?

*Fuck me.*

The only retort he could muster was, "Pretty sure there's an age limit for getting your nose pierced." As he opened his wallet and emptied bills into the swear jar, he huffed. "Discussion closed."

He was pretty damn sure his mother mumbled, "We'll just see about that."

# Chapter 5

## Because My Mom Made Me

The next night, as the team celebrated its win over the Rangers, Sarah realized they might *not* be safe from COVID-19. They were back at the same restaurant they'd visited a few nights ago, in a private dining room tucked out of the way. She was seated between Gage and Natalie at a noisy table filled with Blizzard players and their WAGs—wives and girlfriends—or would that be WADs? Wives and dates? She suppressed a chuckle just as Wyatt, the birthday boy, held up his phone.

"Basketball's just been suspended for the season."

The boisterous group went quiet, voices stilled in mid-speak.

Quinn, who sat across from her, piped up. "*What?* Why?"

"They think it's unsafe for big groups to congregate. Like, this stuff is super contagious. The NBA suggested playing without fans, but the players balked. So no basketball," Wyatt answered with a shrug.

Six seats away, Hunter leaned over the table. "Any word on what's happening with the NHL?"

"Not yet," Wyatt shot back. "The league's announcing their decision tomorrow."

Quinn rocked backward in his seat. "Jesus, aren't they blowing this whole thing out of proportion? A few cases in the US and suddenly we're shutting down the NBA?" He shook his head and grumbled. "If they're gonna throw everyone into panic mode, the least they can do is leave them their sports for a distraction."

Last night, Sarah would have agreed. But tonight? The NBA wouldn't just shut down because they were scared of an everyday flu bug. Unease flared up her spine. This had to be a lot more serious than she'd initially thought.

Hunter called to Quinn, "Hey, idiot." Quinn darted him daggers, but Hunter barreled on. "Do you have any idea how many people have died from it already? The stuff's lethal. And just because it hasn't taken hold here doesn't mean it won't."

Gage held up his beer. "Then I propose a toast. If this is our last game for a while, it was a great note to end on."

"Hear, hear!" someone shouted.

Ringing of bottles and glasses filled the space with cheerful sound. Feeling out of place, Sarah raised her beer halfheartedly. Across from her, Quinn folded his arms across his chest. He reminded her of a sulking six-year-old, and it almost pulled a smile from her. *Kinda puts a stop to the puck bunny parade, doesn't it?*

The table soon returned to its former decibel level, and conversations around her were drowned out in the din. Natalie hopped up to visit with some of the WAGs, or WADs, leaving the seat beside Sarah vacant. Gage's back was to her, his head bent to Lily's.

Sarah pulled her phone from her jeans, intent on fading into the background while she checked job apps, but she never got the chance. A big body pulled out Natalie's chair and sat, taking up so much space his shoulder brushed hers with heat and hardness.

"Hey," Quinn said. How had he snuck up on her?

She looked around. "You talking to me?"

"None other. I wanted to ask you something."

She sat back and braced herself. Just what she was bracing for, she wasn't sure. "Fire away."

"Have you considered being a caregiver while you're job hunting?"

To say this question came as a surprise was the understatement of the year. Her brows knitted together. "Uh, no. Why would I do that?"

He shrugged. "Oh, I don't know. Maybe because I have a job opening that pays really well?"

"Giving care to a certain body part?"

His dimples made an appearance despite the fact he hadn't turned on his brightest smile, and he trained liquid brown eyes on hers as if he was trying to read something. She disguised her body squirm by crossing her legs.

When he spoke, his voice rolled out in a sexy, whiskey purr. "Tempting as that sounds"—he waggled his eyebrows—"I'm actually thinking of my mother."

"You want me to take care of your mother's body part?"

He chuckled. "In a manner of speaking, and not just one part. *All* her parts."

Sarah's confusion must have shown all over her face. When she didn't chuckle back, he rushed on, the liquor-and-sex tone gone from his deep voice. "She hasn't stopped talking about meeting you and your dog." In a quavering falsetto, he added, "'When are you going to have that nice dog and her grumpy owner back over?'"

"Your mother said I was grumpy?" Sarah cringed a little inside, recalling Gage's words about her coldness that day.

"Not exactly. That was my contribution." He flashed her a smile that showed off his pearly whites, and her mind made a quick detour to whether they were all his. "She loves your dog, and apparently—though I have no idea why—she loves you too."

Her cringe factor evaporated. "Um, thanks?"

"Right? I'm baffled too. Anyway, I was thinking since I can't seem to hire a professional she likes—mostly she denies she needs help, but that's another story—why not hire a non-professional she *does* like? And bonus, the dog is tuned in to her. It'd be like having two caregivers for the price of one." His grin broke free, deepening the dimples. The thought of licking them sprang into her head, and she blinked rapidly, trying to bat away the ridiculous, intrusive image.

No way was she going to work for this playboy. She'd probably have to be on her guard twenty-four-seven to deflect his roaming hands and lips, and it had nothing to do with her being attractive. No, it was the mere fact she had X chromosomes that acted like a magnet to his steel dick. *Whoa! Do not think about his dick and steel at the same time. Do not think about his dick. Period!*

To distract herself, she blurted out the first thing that popped into her head. "So what would I have to do?"

"Be there during the day to help her do the little stuff. Her fine motor skills come and go, and sometimes she needs help buttoning something, or she can't brush her hair, for instance. The more stress you can take off of her, the better she does. When I'm on the road, you'd need to spend the night. This is still new to her and me, so we're working it out as we go."

"How did you end up with her living with you anyway?"

He tugged a hand through his hair, and her eyes followed the motion. Jeez, he had thick hair. With lustrous streaks that reminded her of gold satin ribbon. She'd kill for hair like that. Why was it wasted on a dude? And did he go to a salon and have his hair highlighted? Yeah, she could totally see him being *that* guy. Nonetheless, she couldn't avoid thinking of her fingers plowing through his thick strands. *Stop!*

His baritone pulled her back to the here and now. Thank God he wasn't a mind reader because she didn't need him getting the wrong idea. "She's been living with my brother, Ronan. He and his wife recently had their third kid, and the house got a little rowdy for Mom, so voila." He flipped his hands outward as if presenting something. "Quinn's turn."

When she didn't respond right away, he helpfully added, "Voila is French for 'ta-dah'!"

She gave him her best eye-roll. "Any other siblings? What about your dad?"

"Ronan and I are it. As for my dad, let's just say Europe's his home base and leave it there." The tone of his voice told her way more than his words had. Something shifted in his eyes, like he'd eased open a window, catching her off guard.

"What does he do?"

"He coaches hockey. In Poland."

Surprise overtook her features before she could reel it in. "Is he Polish?"

The window Quinn had cracked open snapped shut. "Long story."

"So you're your mother's keeper, and you're not happy about it."

An exhale whooshed out of him. "It's not that I'm *un*happy. It's just … it was unexpected. She's never been that fond … Ronan's the golden child, and it never occurred to me she'd want to move out. But that doesn't matter. I just wish I could've planned … Yeah, if we're being honest here, I guess I'm not thrilled. But I'm trying to adjust."

Sarah snickered. "Having your mom around must make it tough to entertain the ladies."

His mouth parted, and he regarded her for a moment, as if thoughts whirred through his mind that he debated spilling. Instead, he shrugged again—a little too casually. "However you wanna look at it. I did have this really cool place with incredible views, and I miss it. But no way would it have worked for her. So I rented the ludicrous house you saw yesterday."

Huh. The thought of him doing something selfless for his mom might've nudged her opinion of him slightly to the positive side. "The house is ludicrous? I thought it was *Architectural Digest*-worthy."

"It's too big and pretentious. It reminds me of that person who tries too hard."

She bit back the "Like you?" on the tip of her tongue. Instead, she went with, "But your mom has her wing and you have yours. Lots of privacy. Not to mention a sweet hot tub, a park for a backyard, and a gorgeous pool." Jeez, now she was gushing like she was really impressed by his house. It occurred to her he might think she was equally impressed with *him*. Which she most certainly was not.

The appraising look was back on his face, though there was a smug quality to it now, lending it a "gotcha" vibe. *Troll.* "You saw the hot tub, and you liked it," he said with a hint of … of triumph?

Her answer was a snarky huff.

He shifted his posture and his expression. "Okay. So we've established you like the house. That's good … No, great! Means you'll like working there."

She held up her hands. "Whoa, whoa, whoa. Not so fast, Sparky."

He snorted, sounding like a moderately annoyed bull. "Why do you call me that? And what the hell did you mean the other night with your 'lube and tune' comment?"

She leaned back—way back—to stare down her nose at him, praying she wouldn't tip over. He was bigger than she'd first thought, and the best she could do was try to level a smirk at him. "It looked to me like you were about to get lucky, so I was just being friendly and wishing you a good time." She wiggled her eyebrows. "You did get lucky, didn't you?"

He narrowed his eyes. "None of your damn business."

"Well, it will be if you expect me to stay overnight on occasion. *No es bueno.* After all, I might be bumping into puck bunnies every morning. Not that I give a rat's ass, but if it happens often, I'll need hazard pay." Wait. Was she actually considering his offer? *Nuh-uh. No way.*

"Well, good—that you don't give a rat's ass—because it'll still be none of your business," he tossed back. His eyebrow dipped. "How does your brother put up with you?"

She batted her eyelashes. "Aw, did I hit a nerve? Sorry. You just seem to bring it out in me."

To her surprise, his glare morphed into another one of his big-ass smiles. "Yeah, well, you bring out the worst in me too. But to show you what a great guy I am, I'm still willing to hire you. For a ridiculous amount of money." He signaled the waitress.

Sarah twirled her nearly empty drink. She hadn't noticed she was getting low, but apparently he had. Which made total sense. Any good Casanova was tuned into what it took to get into a girl's panties, and it was usually damn quicker with liquor. Not that she'd ever assume he was aiming for *her* panties. It was just that he had this built-in pickup autopilot thing going on. Whatever it was, she didn't want him thinking he could keep sitting with her just because he ordered her a drink.

"I don't think me working for you is a good idea, Sparky."

His smile didn't waver. "And why's that, Sunshine?"

She burst out with a laugh. "*Sunshine?* Are you kidding me? Where'd you come up with that one?"

"Must've been your sunny personality that inspired me." He downed the rest of his cocktail.

The waitress materialized beside them, her hip jutting into Quinn's face. He seemed not to notice. *Probably used to it.* "A bourbon and Coke for the lady, and a rum and Coke for me, please." He slid a twenty into her apron pocket so discreetly that Sarah wouldn't have noticed if the waitress hadn't given him a hip bump along with a sultry "Thanks." *Like stuffing a stripper's G-string. Probably used to that too.*

He raised his empty glass to Sarah. "So what do you say, toots? You could have your own wing. Hell, your dog could have his own wing."

Her prickle-meter shot upward, and she felt as though every flea that had ever lived aboard Archer had suddenly taken up residence on *her.* Why, she wasn't exactly sure. Quinn just affected her that way, apparently. She shook her head. "Thanks, but no thanks. I'm not the caregiver type."

"Meaning?"

"I'm not caring or giving, nor do I have a bottomless well of patience." *Not true, though I'm turning over a newer, meaner leaf. Starting now.*

"Tell me something I don't already know," he shot back. "The caring crap doesn't matter. As for a bottomless well of patience, you'll definitely need that to deal with my mother. I know I do."

So he agreed she wasn't the caregiver type? For some unfathomable reason, this *really* irritated her, and she let mouth run wild. "I wasn't referring to your mother."

A defeated sigh *whooshed* out of him. "Then I take it that's a no."

"That's a no."

He let out a mirthless laugh. "Shit, I'd sure like to know what I did to piss you off."

"You're a man, and you're breathing," she bit out.

His head jerked backward, but he quickly recovered. "So's your brother."

She raised her own empty glass in a toast. "He's the exception."

Quinn rose, all traces of his smile gone. In a frosty timbre, he said, "I'll be sure the waitress brings you that drink. Nice talking to you, Sunshine."

As she watched him walk away—trying not to focus on his broad back spanning his fitted button-down shirt—a twinge of remorse needled her. She'd been a bitch. Maybe, just maybe, he hadn't earned the full force of her fuck-all-men salvo. But in her own defense, guys like him wielded their confidence without thought. With practiced ease. Like pulling breath into their lungs. And they invariably broke women's hearts. Women like her mother … like *her*.

While she chatted with Lily and Natalie, she glimpsed him lavishing his brilliant smile on two blonds at the bar. One of them was practically sprawled over him, and they were scarfing up whatever BS he was feeding them, giggling every time he opened his mouth. As if they weren't thinking of his big fat bank account. As if it was only because what he had to say was so damn witty.

Normally, she didn't let annoyances distract her, but for some baffling reason her gaze was continually pulled toward the cozy trio. *Call me sociologically curious.* The sprawling one looked like the woman who'd been with him a few nights ago. *Girlfriend? Doubtful.* He probably had a "type," and they all looked like these two. Barbie dolls with laughably out-of-proportion busts. How did they not tip over? Her engineer's mind would puzzle that one out later.

Sarah glanced down at her own chest. Not busty, but not flat either. Today she wore a T-shirt that said, "Warning! I Do Dumb Things." *Yeah. Like wasting way too much brain power on lady-killers and the ladies they kill.*

Before Wolf had ripped her heart out with his pointy fangs, she'd never worried much about her looks. That's not to say she didn't take pride in her appearance because she did. She was toned and lean because she was disciplined about her fitness. Though her office environment was casual, she dressed impeccably—not to turn heads, though she'd done plenty of that, but because she enjoyed presenting a professional appearance. And it had paid off. Despite her junior rank, she'd been tapped for some plum projects. Her boss had said her image, the way she carried herself, caused people to take her seriously, and by extension, their firm. That same confidence had been what drew Wolf to her, he'd once confessed.

Ironic that the very part of her he'd found attractive was the first one he'd tried to manipulate. More ironic, she'd let him do it. Hadn't she always striven for independence? Worn her sass like a badge of honor? But she'd twisted herself into a pretzel to please him, to be all things to him. Why she hadn't registered the maneuverings in their relationship she hadn't a clue, but now she found herself constantly second-guessing her appeal.

Blind love made people do stupid things.

She stood and blazed a path to the ladies' room. No sooner had she locked herself in a stall but Sparky's giggly groupies stumbled in. Cocking her head, Sarah peeked through the door's gap.

One of the blonds fanned herself. "Oh my God, Dory, he is even hotter in person! You lucky bitch!"

The one named Dory pushed her friend's shoulder. "On top of *that*, the man is *packed*. I thought I was gonna choke when I went down on him."

A shock of electricity jolted Sarah's gut. *Oh God, oh God, oh God! No, no, no! TMI! I do not want to hear this.*

"I *love* those dimples. And his hair! And he's so funny!" Not-Dory squealed. "Now I get why you nailed him in the backseat of his truck the other night."

*Gah! And now more information I can't unhear!*

Dory applied scarlet lipstick and puckered at herself in the mirror. "His very *nice* truck. That was fun once, but tonight he's gonna have to take me to his place or a nice hotel if he wants to fuck me. I am *not* a slut."

Sarah suppressed the overpowering urge to explode with a laugh.

Not-Dory's manicured eyebrows bounced. "Maybe he gets off on doing it in cars."

Dory grabbed her double-Ds and gave them a squeeze. "*This* is what he gets off on. And he can have them in his fancy house or a high-end hotel with room service."

They broke into a gigglefest and headed out of the restroom, Not-Dory saying something about a freeway. *Or was that a three-way?*

The jolt that had zapped Sarah's gut took on a roiling sensation that made her wonder if she'd be able to keep her dinner down. She pulled in deep cleansing breaths, willing her stomach's contents to settle down. As she did, her mind wandered for a moment. Were these the kinds of women men really *wanted*? Dainty, top-heavy darlings who spent more time sculpting their assets than their brains?

Well, it appeared to be what *Sparky* wanted, just as it appeared he was about to get himself another lube and tune tonight. Probably more than one. Good on him.

But who gave a flipping fuck? Not her, that was for damn sure.

# Chapter 6

## Never Proposition a Fish

Quinn parked inside the unlit garage at the back of his dark house and threaded his way inside. What time was it? 5 a.m.? Jesus, he was beat. Crawling into his own bed was his prime mission.

Until he walked into his house and found his mother curled up on the couch in the family room.

*Shit! Busted!*

She hadn't been there an hour ago, when he'd sneaked himself and Dory out of his own house. Did Mom know he'd brought a girl home? Nah. Impossible. He'd taken Dory to an unused guest room in a separate wing and had made sure they kept the noise down—though Dory's voice *had* climbed when he'd told her it was time for him to drive her back. Yeah, he'd felt a little douchy about that. Not that he hadn't taken care of her too because he had, and she'd acted as though she'd enjoyed herself.

Nevertheless, girl had to understand the score. He didn't cuddle, and he *never* let them stay over. Hell, he never brought them home! He was still trying to figure out why he'd let himself get talked into it. Once again, he'd turned over common sense to his low-IQ dick. Dory had been clinging to him like a statically charged piece of plastic he couldn't shake free. Between her rubbing her hot body against him and just enough alcohol in his system to hip-check his smarter self out of the equation, turning over control to his libido had taken on an undeniable appeal.

They couldn't go to her place, and she wouldn't do the backseat again, so he'd brought her here because it seemed easier than trying to grab a hotel room at 2 a.m. *Rookie mistake.* Well, he wasn't bringing her here again. Didn't plan on *seeing* her again.

Meanwhile, his mother seemed to be asleep, and his prime mission shifted to getting away without disturbing her. Guilt tugged him toward her still figure. She looked peaceful, and relief spread through him.

As he crept toward the stairs, her sleep-raspy voice nearly launched him out of his socks. "You're late."

*Fuck me!* She'd always had eyes in the back of her head. "I'm too old for curfews … in my own house," he retorted. He pivoted in time to see her pull herself upright, and he softened his tone. "Why are you awake?"

"Couldn't sleep. I thought moving out to the family room would help, but I was wrong."

He took a seat beside her. "Bad night?"

In the dim light, he recognized the mother from his youth. No lines, no gray. The sight tightened steel bands around his chest, and he quickly forgot his fatigue. When he'd been a kid, he'd thought his mother was the most beautiful woman who ever lived. And now? She was still there.

A sigh escaped her. "Yes. No. Just the usual." She zeroed in on him, like she used to do when he lived at home and her sixth sense had tipped her off that he'd been up to no good. Pretty much all the time. "I saw you won the game. Did you have fun celebrating?"

He drooped with an added helping of guilt. "The team went out to dinner, and we ran late. I didn't want to text and wake you up."

Her eyebrows arched, and a little smile played across her face. "What was her name?"

His spine went ramrod straight. Why was it his mother could *still* make all his defenses snap into place? With one look, one word. "Who?"

"The girl you brought back here. The one you just took home."

*Shit!* "Does it matter?"

"Not if it doesn't matter to you, and I'm guessing it doesn't. I take it I won't be meeting this one either."

He ran his hand over the back of his head to mask the squirming inside his body.

"You're fidgeting." A hint of amusement laced her words.

"You're not helping," he fired back. "And what do you mean by you won't be 'meeting this one either'?"

She flipped her hand. "You never introduce me to your girlfriends. Not that I could keep them straight if you *did*. I'd need a color-coded chart."

How would *she* know? It wasn't as if he'd ever paraded them past her. On purpose. Most of Quinn's hooking-up happened on the road, where he kept things casual with about a dozen girlfriends in different cities—a third as many as his teammates gave him credit for, a misconception he'd never bothered to correct.

He found a certain advantage in staying away from the local talent. The out-of-town women knew the score, and if they tried to change the rules, any possible drama remained contained, geographically speaking. They were down to fuck without strings, which suited him perfectly. Denver hookups, on the other hand, *might* be down at first but had the potential to turn needy, hunting him down in his favorite hometown hotspots. Like Dory. That's what he got for playing in his own backyard—with the same person more than once.

He let out a slow exhale and reminded himself he needed to limit sex to the road again. *If* he got back on the road. In his own defense, that very question had played on his mind when he'd decided to take advantage of what Dory offered because who knew when he'd get laid again? As it was, he'd been pretty damn proud of himself for turning down the opportunity to include her girlfriend. A modicum of logic had cut through the murk of lust and made him consider his mom catching him with *two*, though he'd never expected to be caught with the one in the first place.

"Tell me something, Quinnie."

*Quinnie.* No one but his mom had ever called him that—maybe his brother when he was riding his ass—and it had been a long, long time since he'd heard it. It sounded strange but kind of nice. "Mmm?"

"Do you have anything in common with them besides … Well, besides the obvious?"

He burst out with a laugh—the wrong reaction, judging by her disapproving frown. "Mom, you're killing me here! A mother and son should *not* be talking about this sh—stuff."

She side-eyed him. "It's no different than talks I've had with Ronan."

Quinn didn't bother hiding his surprise. "You've talked to Ronan about his, uh, love life?"

She shrugged. "Before he married Jennifer and settled down."

Quinn's throat contracted at the reminder of Ronan and Jen, and he felt as though he were trying to swallow past a piece of barbed wire. "You so sure Ronan has 'settled down,' Mom?" Ronan had been the biggest manwhore Quinn had ever known—which was saying something—and from the way he bragged whenever he talked to Quinn, didn't sound like the guy had changed his ways. *Douche.*

"He'd better not to be running around on Jen. Do you know something I don't?"

Shit, why had he even brought it up? Because he didn't like his brother, and anytime he could make him look bad—especially in front of either of his parents—it was a rare Quinn win. He was extremely fond of those.

"No. He just likes to talk up what a big man he is."

"Have you ever considered that's strictly for *your* benefit?"

"*My* benefit? Why?"

She squared up her body so she faced him. "You two have been competing with each other since you were born. Your brother may be two years older, but he envies you. You snatched the golden ring that was out of his reach."

Without thinking, he blurted, "Is that why he stole the girl I was dating?"

His mother drew in a sharp breath and let it out slowly. "Oh, Quinn, I thought you'd gotten past that. You and Jennifer weren't—"

"Just because she and I weren't serious didn't make it okay for him to make a move on her. I mean, who does that? *Especially* to their own flesh and blood?" Jen was sweet, fun, and cute, and Quinn had been dating her a few months when Ronan met her. Truth be told, Quinn hadn't been ready to take it to the next level with her—might not ever have been, though she was the rare one who had made him at least ponder the possibility. Apparently, *she* had been ready because shortly thereafter she'd broken it off with Quinn. Not long after *that*, she was pregnant and on her way to the altar. With Ronan.

Though Quinn had closed that chapter of his life years ago, the betrayal still stung. Not to mention that the occasional family get-together was awkward as hell.

His mother's voice dragged him back to the present. "If he's bragging about other women—and God help him if it's true because I will beat him black and blue—it's only because he wants to sound as if he's outdoing you."

"Really? I understand competitive streaks, Mom. I absolutely do. But if *that's* the reason Ronan took my girl *and* mouths off about conquests? No, that's totally jacked-up."

"I'm sorry. I didn't realize it was still a sore spot."

"It's not," Quinn sighed. "All I'm saying is even if Ronan's full of it, he shouldn't be talking like that. No matter *how* things ended between her and me, she doesn't deserve that kind of treatment."

His mother's eyebrows flew to her hairline. "Is it possible the pot's calling the kettle black?"

He turned her question over for a beat. Maybe she had a point in a convoluted sort of way. He shrugged. "It's different. I'm not married." *And what's the point of getting married if you're going to keep fucking around?*

"Which leads me back to my original question: Do you ever take the time to talk to these women? Get to know them?"

A dull thudding started behind his eyes. "It's not that I don't want to get to know them. It's just …" *My priorities don't usually include talking.*

"One of these days, Quinnie, you're going to fall hard, and you won't even see it coming. Jennifer was too nice and pliable, and that's why it wouldn't have worked. The girl for you will take you to task, and I just hope I'm around to witness it. She'll be something else!"

He couldn't picture the kind of woman his mom was talking about. What he did know was that when—*if*—the day came when he finally committed to one, she'd be it. Done. No one else. Unlike his dickhead brother. "Chances are she doesn't exist, Mom."

"Chances are," his mother countered, "she *does* exist, but you'll need to have graduated in Adulting before you recognize her."

He chuckled. "I have at least two, four semesters left, right?"

His mother's eyes gleamed with mischief. "Maybe. Whoever she is, you'll probably butt heads at first, like your dad and I did. Then she'll give you a run for your money because she'll be the rare woman you can't impress with just your smile."

*Your dad and I.* Why weren't they together? Sure, she could be a pain in Quinn's ass, but she was a vibrant, attractive woman, so why had his dad left? Quinn could remember listening to his parents' laughter late at night when he'd been tucked in bed. He'd loved hearing the sound because it meant safety and love and warmth.

Had his dad cheated? And why hadn't she moved on? Tempted as Quinn was to ask her, he always stopped himself short. Why stir up her private, painful memories to satisfy his own curiosity?

He laid his hand on her shoulder, unsettled by how bony it was. "Can I get you anything?"

She surprised him when she covered his hand with hers. Affection wasn't something they often shared since he'd become an adult—well, physically grown anyway.

She gave his hand a little squeeze and released it. "No, Quinnie, but thank you."

He slid his hand off of her and was about to head to bed, but she didn't seem ready to let him go. "I saw on the news that the NBA shut down. I was shocked. This thing must be bad." She locked her gaze on him. "Do you think the NHL will do the same?"

"I have no idea. But honestly, I'm not convinced it's as bad as everyone's making it out to be." He waved his hands in the air, and in a singsong voice said, "The sky is falling! The sky is falling!"

"I don't know. I've never seen anything like this in my lifetime." Her lips curved up in a half-smile. "I kind of hope they do suspend your season. Then you can stay home and stop with the Nazi cow babysitters."

He scrubbed his hand over his face and gave her a fake glower. "Mom. Whether I'm home or not, you need someone here full-time."

"No, I don't." Her familiar tone told him there was no point in arguing, and he was too tired anyway.

Puffing out a breath, he reached for his beanbags on the coffee table and started juggling. It always helped settle him when his nerves got too jangly.

Though he wasn't looking at her, he could tell his mother's eyes followed the little stuffed cubes. "You're so good at that." Her voice drifted, as though she were hypnotized, so she surprised him when she slipped in, "The only person I wouldn't fight you on is that cute little Sarah."

He dropped one beanbag, and the rest tumbled without him managing to catch even one. *Shit!* Recalling his laughable proposal, offered out of pure desperation, made him wince—at least Sarah had laughed at it when she'd shut him down.

"Porcupines aren't cute, Mom, and she's definitely a porcupine. She's also a royal pain in the ass and—"

"Ah! Ah!" His mom held up her finger, then pointed toward the kitchen. "That's a buck for the swear jar."

"Since when is 'ass' a swear word?" he chuffed.

She shook her head. "No arguing or it doubles."

"Fine," he groused as he pulled out his wallet. Yeah, something else he was having trouble adjusting to with his mom under the same roof. He wasn't even allowed the satisfaction of cursing out his exasperation in a blue streak. Like when he was a kid, he had to do it under his breath in his bedroom. No doubt she knew about *that* too.

In the kitchen, he slid out a dollar and stuffed it into the mega vase. Sadly, this was only one of many she'd strategically placed around the McMansion. His mind wandered to Sarah and her potty mouth. If she *did* live under the same roof, she'd be stuffing these damn things too. The thought brought a smile to his face.

As irritating as Sarah was, though, he couldn't deny that trading barbs with her was the most stimulated he'd been last night—intellectually speaking. Girl had a mind—and a tongue—as sharp as a skate blade. It had kept him dancing on a boot toe, unlike Dory and her friend. Those two had laughed at everything he'd said, whether it was funny or not. Had they even paid attention to the shit that came out of his mouth? He'd toyed with describing what it was like to watch someone get pegged with a hundred-mile-an-hour puck in the kisser to see if *that* made them giggle too.

His mother's sarcasm returned, jerking him from his thoughts. "Quinn, you should probably get some beauty sleep after your busy-bee night. Don't you have a team meeting later today?"

*Goddamn! Almost forgot.* "Yeah, Mom." He trudged toward the stairs, stealing a glance at her as he went. Though she might appear frail, his mom had a spine of steel. She reminded him of Sarah Nelson. Thank God Sarah *had* turned down his job offer because, Christ! He couldn't imagine living with *both* of them under the same roof. Even in this twenty-thousand-something-square-foot house, there wouldn't be enough room to contain the fireworks.

He chuckled to himself—and immediately stopped. If this virus was as bad as they said and they started shuttering everything, where would he find someone to help take care of his mother?

*Oh shit. Sparky's got a big problem.*

Sarah woke up early the next morning, pulled from sleep by the urge to check her email. Had she received any replies to her rental inquiries?

As she scrolled through her phone, she drooped with disappointment. Getting her own place wasn't going to happen today. Not only was the inventory already low, but landlords were temporarily pulling their places off the market to reduce the risk of coronavirus exposure. There was even talk the government might shut down short-term rentals. *What?*

She tossed her phone to the side, wrapped a thick robe around herself, and beckoned Archer. She padded to the back door and let him out. The only noise was the TV in the living room, and she went to investigate, discovering Gage and Lily watching the news.

"What's up, guys?"

Lily looked over her shoulder, wide-eyed. "More people are testing positive for COVID-19 here in Colorado."

Sarah plopped her butt in an armchair. "Any word yet on what the NHL's going to do?"

Gage shook his head. "No, but we have a team meeting in an hour, so I'll learn more then. Lily's going to the store to stock up."

A chill ran through Sarah's limbs. She was in a twilight zone, suspended between a sci-fi movie and a dystopian reality. "I'll get ready and go with you, Lil."

Lily sent her a relieved smile. "Thank you, Sarah."

If Sarah thought the news was surreal, Costco was like touching down on a different planet. The place was jammed. Had everyone in Denver decided to shop at the same store at the same time? The air was thick with tension, as though everyone was keeping a lid on simmering panic. But what they loaded on their carts was downright puzzling.

"Why are they stocking up on toilet paper?" Lily asked after the umpteenth cart piled high with the stuff rolled past them.

"Big sale?"

They ambled toward the paper goods section. When they arrived, a fight was breaking out between customers over a package of toilet paper.

Lily tugged Sarah's sleeve. "Uh, Sar, I think we're good on TP."

"I feel you, Lil. I'm gonna grab extra bags of dog food, then let's get the hell out of here."

Back home, they put away their purchases and were high-fiving as Gage walked in. His eyes bounced between them. "Somebody win something?"

While Lily filled him in, Sarah took Archer into the backyard while she checked the rental apps again. Nada. Zip. Zero. As she was corralling her disappointment, her phone vibrated with a call, and her blood froze. Why the hell was Wolf calling? Hadn't she told him specifically what he could do with himself? Anger—or the adrenalin shooting through her veins—made her hands shake as she slid his call to the red zone. She slipped the phone into her back pocket, but it went off again. She ignored it. The fourth time, she whipped it out to silence the damn thing, but it was a different incoming number.

"Oh hell," she muttered. "Just what I need." She tapped her screen to accept. "Hi, Mom."

"Sarah!" her mother gasped. "Finally!"

Alarm bells went off in Sarah's head, but she knew better than to get sucked into her mother's frantic, guilt-laced rants before gathering a little intel. "Hey, Mom. What's going on?"

"Where have you been, honey?"

She ran her fingers through her hair. "Well, actually, I've been making my way to Gage and Lily's."

A silent beat went by, then another. Sarah could practically count down to the "What? Why?" that exploded from her mom. Only it didn't come. Instead, she got a mild "Oh."

"Yeah, the company cut us loose to work from home, so I decided I could just as easily work from Colorado. I'm sorry I haven't called. Between work and the drive, I've literally just found a little downtime. You happened to beat me to it." She cringed and instantly reverted to her naughty little-girl self, hating that an unstoppable force pulled her there.

"Well, thank goodness you're with your brother," her mother whooshed. "Family *should* be together at a time like this."

Not the third degree Sarah had prepared for, and now *her* worry bloomed. "Why? Is everything all right? How's Grandma?" Her grandmother, who suffered from dementia, was both a source of ludicrous, laugh-out-loud stories *and* the depths of melancholy. An odd push-pull of emotions came into play every time Sarah thought of their once-vibrant supreme matriarch.

"I just saw your grandmother, and she's fine. The senior home announced they're going on lockdown, so unless it's end-of-life, I can't see her." A little sniffle came from the other end.

A pain jabbed at Sarah's chest. Though she and her mother constantly rammed heads, she hated for her to be unhappy. And, well, there was her grandma too, locked away and alone. "I'm so sorry, Mom. Maybe this is a case where the dementia is actually a blessing. If she doesn't know what's happening, she won't miss us and she won't be scared."

Her mother quickly recovered a cheery note in her voice. "I hope that's the case. At least she's got Oscar there with her. I'm grateful he's in your grandmother's life."

Sarah pulled the phone from her ear and stared at it. *Invasion of the body snatchers. Has to be.* Oscar was Grandma's sweet gentleman friend who lived in the same senior center, and Mom had been dead set against their relationship. So much so, she'd ripped Oscar a few new assholes for the horrible crime of doting on Grandma.

Sarah wiggled her tongue and got it working again. "Sounds like maybe you've had a change of heart?"

Her mother actually trilled. "I'm learning that the right someone to help shoulder your load can be a real blessing, Sarah."

*Okaaaaay.* "You're not trying to say *you've* found, uh, a right someone, are you, Mom?" Flabbergasted, Sarah searched her memory banks for a time when her mother had been on a *date*, let alone caught up in a romance. Not surprisingly, she came up empty.

"Could be," her mother sang like a high soprano, "but right now I need to scoot. I just wanted to check on you. Now that I know you're with Gage, I won't worry."

So pod people *hadn't* snatched her mother's body and taken control, turning out a kinder, gentler version of Nola Nelson. No, but love might have. Sarah nearly laughed out loud at the incongruity. Her mother, the Queen of Anti-Romance, who'd always warned her against giving her heart to a man, sounded like a sixteen-year-old schoolgirl tripping along Cloud Nine.

After the call ended, Sarah—still in a state of bemusement—went back inside with Archer. "Gage, did you—"

Her brother was leaning against the kitchen counter quietly talking to Lily as she scrubbed the kitchen sink. His gaze lifted to Sarah when she walked in, and a look of concern flickered in his blue eyes.

"What's the word, Bro?"

He blew out a breath. "The NHL decided on an indefinite pause"—he air-quoted the last word—"and Lily and I have been talking about what to do."

She kept her tone casual. "What do you mean, what do to?"

"Lots of guys are heading to their homes outside the U.S. to hunker down."

"Where would *you* go if you left town? And what about your new house?"

"I talked to Paige," Lily said. "Our closing is on hold, and she has no idea when we can move in."

Gage added, "So no place to go, and we're not sure what'll happen with Daisy's school. For now, I guess we stay put."

In that moment, reality slammed into Sarah full force and rocked her hard. "We're not in Kansas anymore, are we? This shit's getting real."

Gage's eyes slid to Lily, and Sarah's followed. Lily made an attempt to smile at them, but her wobbly mouth gave her away. The look tugged at something inside Sarah, and she pulled her almost-sister-in-law in for a tight hug, needing it as much for herself as to offer Lily comfort.

# Chapter 7

## Corona's Served with Lime, Right?

*Fuck me.*

Those two words had been on a constant loop in Quinn's head since the league's announcement yesterday that play was paused indefinitely. Suspended. Stopped. Just when playoffs were about to start. Just when the Blizzard was having one of their best seasons and stood on the brink of winning it all.

He stood at his stall in disbelief as he cleaned out his shit. Who knew how long this would last? Would they get paid? How would they stay in game shape? And over what? A few seniors dying of the flu. He shook his head in disgust.

*Utter bullshit.* And it wasn't just the league that was panicking. The whole fucking globe was panicking. He picked up three rolls of tape, tossed them in the air for a few spins, then let them fall into his bag.

"Hey, Hads."

Quinn looked up, meeting Hunter's gaze. The guy had a smirk on his face that Quinn itched to knock off, so he turned back to packing his bag. "'Sup, Hunts?"

"What do you say you and me hire a dozen girls from the Sapphire Club to shelter in place with? Gotta do our part to keep the economy going. Between us, we can keep them in bank for at least a month. Maybe by then this thing'll have blown over. Otherwise, those poor girls are outta work, man."

Quinn raised his head again, noting Hunter's waggling eyebrows above his leer. Yeah, this had absolutely nothing to do with benevolence and everything to do with Hunter's dick. "No, thanks."

Only a few guys knew that Quinn was taking care of his mom, and even if he hadn't been, the thought of being cooped up with Hunter—even with twelve strippers between them—held zero appeal. Strippers were fun to watch every blue moon, but room with twelve of them? For that matter, he couldn't think of twelve women he'd done that he'd *want* to hang with. Over the years, he'd been disappointed with the conversations, and pillow talk was downright awkward. Which was why he didn't engage in it. Fuck and go, that was his motto.

The conversation in his mind was suddenly thrust into a bright glare, as if someone had turned on a searchlight inside his head. Floored by his train of thought, he brought it to a screeching halt. *When did I turn into such a dick? When did I turn into Ronan?*

As he stood, blinking at Hunter like an idiot, another disturbing thought speared him square in the chest like the butt end of a stick. He'd always thought himself better than Hunter—maybe because his charm quotient was higher—but now he wasn't so sure. The cocktail waitress's voice echoed in his head. *Charmers are smarmers.*

"What's gotten into you anyway?" Hunter taunted.

*No fucking clue.* Maybe it was this stupid coronavirus getting to him. He was on edge after getting shot down by every service he'd called to help out with his mom, and now he was facing the very real possibility it would just be him and her, which scared the crap out of him on so many levels—the most terrifying being whether he was capable of doing a good job by her.

He turned away from Hunter without answering him, and the asshat finally got the hint and focused his attention on their team captain. Big mistake. "Yo, Grims! How about you and me—"

"Fuck off, McMurphy," Grims growled. "I don't like hanging with you on a good day. I'm sure as hell not going to hole up with you." Grims was no one to fuck with, especially since he'd been placed indefinitely on the IR and he and his girlfriend had broken up during training camp. Guy was like a wounded bear. Big, mean, and thoroughly pissed off. All. The. Time.

Which was great when they were battling another team on the ice, but in the locker room or during social time? Not so much. Not that Grims participated in social time anymore—not since he'd been busted doping. Quinn and his teammates weren't supposed to know. The violations hadn't gotten back to the league, and management had kept a lid on it, but Grims's girlfriend had blabbed to the Blizzard SOs for some damn reason, which meant *everyone* knew. Despite the guy's troubles, Quinn liked and respected his captain, so he gave him a wide berth.

Quinn had turned back to his packing when Coach LeBrun ambled in. "We're holding a press conference. I want some of your pretty faces in there to help field questions." He looked around and pointed. "Shanstrom, Nelson." He stopped and eyed Grims. Grims took a step forward, obviously anticipating the call to duty as team captain. But then Coach pivoted toward Quinn, gave him a chin lift, and jabbed his thumb over his shoulder. "And Hadley. You guys are up."

*Damn it!*

Quinn gaped at Grims. Anger flared in the captain's eyes before he hooded them and turned back to cleaning out his space. Quinn didn't miss how Grims clenched his fists before he started shoving shit into his bag.

Picking Shanny and Nelsy made sense—they were the alternate captains. But why bone Grims? Coach had looked right at him, then dismissed him deliberately.

Someone slapped Quinn's back, and he wheeled to face Shanny, who grinned at him. "Let's go, lover boy."

Quinn followed Shanny and Nelsy down the hall to the press room, which was filled with eager, annoying sports journalists who'd somehow been anointed the "experts" in a game they'd never played. *Self-serving bastards. And bastardettes.*

Reporters began firing questions at them as soon as they joined their coach on a platform that held a podium loaded with mics. Quinn never caught the first volley. But as they settled into the Q&A and he heard the absurdity in everything they uttered, his irritation climbed. *These people actually get paid to ask these stupid ass questions?* Yeah, he already knew the answer to that one.

One particularly eager beaver fired a particularly aggravating query at Quinn. "What do you make of all of this, Hads?"

*Hads?* This little prick didn't get to call him "Hads." Only his teammates did.

He could practically hear the snapping going off inside him, and he cleared his throat to hold it back. "I don't pretend to understand what's going on here. Obviously, people with pay grades *way* above mine are calling the shots, based on information the rest of us don't have."

The reporter smirked. "I'm sure they don't get paid nearly as well as you do, Hads."

"Whatever. All I'm saying is I'm not in charge, so I'm not the one making the decisions."

"Are you saying you don't agree with their decisions so far?" the reporter goaded.

Quinn drilled the guy with a steely look. "I'm not gonna pretend I could do a better job. That would be ridiculous. Now do I think some people *might* be overreacting? Of course. But we're in uncharted territory here, and who's to say what's too little and what's overkill?"

"Maybe you oughta just stick to hockey there, sport," the little weasel said. The room chuckled. Well, the reporters chuckled. No one connected with the team did.

Quinn wasn't normally a hothead, but God, he hated it when people who didn't know him talked down to him like he was a dumb jock. "You're looking at a bunch of guys"—he waved his hand toward his teammates—"who work their asses off every night, and now they're told they can't play—probably won't get paid. That includes coaches, trainers, equipment staff." He paused a beat as another thought struck him. "And what about the other people who depend on the game for their livelihood? People who work concession stands, who clean up the arena after a game, who maintain the ice, to name just a few. How do they pay their bills?"

"Maybe the president oughta tap you for his task force, Hads. No doubt you could tell him a thing or two."

Quinn tried to rein in his mad. He really did. "Look, I don't know who the hell you are or why you're sitting in this room, but I don't think it's unreasonable to question if the kneejerk reaction of shutting everything down might be worse than the damn virus. All these measures have a cascading effect with far-reaching consequences, and I'm not convinced those consequences have been given enough due consideration." He dragged a hand through his hair.

The buzzing room grew very, very quiet.

"Who says it's a kneejerk reaction?" Weasel Prick challenged. "I mean, c'mon, man. You're no scientist, though you might pass yourself off as an economist."

A wave of nervous laughter swept through the room.

What possessed Quinn, he had no idea—maybe his inner surly teenager—but he reached out and smacked every mic on the podium. Wide eyes fastened on him as he stepped off the platform and, with the advantage of surprise, grabbed the iPad the pencil-neck reporter had been using to record the Q&A. Quinn breathed on it and shoved it back into the tweeze's hands. "I might have it."

People stood frozen, stunned into a stupor, and he repeated the action with a few other reporters. "Now we all have it," he announced. The entire room seemed to shuffle.

Behind him, Coach hissed, "Hadley! Get back up here!"

Ignoring his coach, Quinn pointed at the audience he'd commandeered. "We're one small group in one private room, yet we have the power to do exponential damage merely by breathing on everyone we meet. So how is shutting down sports venues going to protect us exactly? This is all bullshit. Bull. Shit!"

All hell broke loose. Reporters jumped up and players stepped off the platform, looking like two gangs squaring off. Well, one small gang of hulking athletes against a crowd of squawking dickwads. And dickwadettes.

Someone grabbed him and hauled his butt down the hallway. *Shanstrom.*

Shanny shoved him through the doorway into the locker room. "What in the fucking name of fuck is wrong with you?"

Quinn stumbled backward, but T.J. kept coming. "Do you know what you just did in there?"

Normally, Quinn would never contemplate messing with this motherfucker—he liked the guy, and more importantly, his survival instinct was too strong—but adrenalin was still pumping through him, and it apparently fueled his inner Stupid Man.

"No, Shanny," he shot back. "Please enlighten me. What did I just do in there?"

Now Grims appeared, filling up the space next to Shanny, looming larger and more badass than Shanny, if that were possible. "What the fuck's going on?"

Shanny gave Quinn's shoulder another push. "This asshole ran his mouth off about having the virus. Then he touched every goddamn mic and grabbed the reporters' shit and breathed all over it."

Before Quinn could spit out a comeback, the locker room door burst open, and in stalked a fuming Coach LeBrun. Seeing Coach red-faced jarred something inside of Quinn, and his anger evaporated. He took a step back in the face of his coach's fury.

"Hadley," LeBrun said in a scary-low voice, "That was the stupidest thing I've ever witnessed in my entire fucking life." Coach was breathing so damn hard his nostrils were flaring, but somehow he kept his voice chillingly quiet. "Is this a joke to you? People are scared *shitless* over this, and you're acting like a stupid little kid whose ball got taken away at recess. Now get your shit and get the hell out of here." Coach stepped back and parked clenched fists on his hips.

Quinn's gaze took a quick tour around the locker room. His teammates had gathered around, and while some gaped at their normally unflappable coach, a number of them fired Quinn looks that could have sliced him to slivers. In that moment, it struck him how badly he'd screwed up.

# Chapter 8

## CASTAWAY, AKA SOCIAL DISTANCING

A scant few days into shelter-in-place, and Sarah was losing her mind. Scratch that. Her mind had already walked out the door, and she couldn't go after it because the six of them—which included Archer and Hobbes—were in fucking lockdown. In a tiny house that shrank by the second. If Sarah had to listen to her brother and Lily through these thin walls one more time … Shit, she knew *waaaay* more about her brother's sex life than a sister should ever know.

Added to that awkwardness was a buzzing undercurrent of tension. No one was barking at anyone—yet—but Daisy's every sneeze seemed to send the household into a panic about her coming down with the coronavirus. And man, that little girl sneezed a lot! Sarah was trying her damnedest to summon her inner mother—which, apparently, was buried as deep as the Marianas Trench—but the girl's misery was beginning to scrape Sarah's already frayed nerves even further.

She was tip-tapping on her keyboard in the Pepto Bismol-pink bedroom—*her* room for the foreseeable future—engaging in another futile search for a new place when her phone vibrated.

"Just what I need," she grumbled, expecting to see Wolf's number. He continued calling and texting, and though she hadn't responded, each of his attempts jolted her like a dentist's drill without novocaine. She snatched up her phone and was instead delighted to see a local number.

*Finally! A job! A place to live! Paige Miller needs a consultation!*

She slowed her racing heart and answered in her most professional voice. "Sarah Nelson speaking."

"Well, hello, Sarah Sunshine."

*Shit!* "What do you want, Sparky?" Just like that, the words flew out quick and snarky. Not at all what she'd intended. Oh well. His overinflated ego would register the slight about as much as a buffalo would notice a ladybug landing on its hide.

He chuckled, which unsettled her even more. "Ah, see, that's what I love about talking to you. You're so warm and fuzzy. And your repartee is priceless. You'd be an awesome date."

"Haha. Save yourself the trouble of asking because I am *not* going out on a date with you."

"Say it isn't so! My poor heart will never recover."

"I'm sure you'll survive, Romeo," she snorted.

"Look, toots, even if I *could* take you out—which I can't because of social distancing and your brother's threats to kill me slowly—you're the last person I'd call. In fact, if we were stuck on a deserted island together, I think I'd prefer floating in the water as shark bait over rolling around in the sand with you."

*Ouch! Okay, Sparky. Game on.* She put her best I-don't-give-a-fuck attitude into her voice. "Pretty sure the sharks wouldn't want you either."

"Were you an inquisitor in a former life?"

"You get funnier by the second, Hadley. As scintillating as sparring with you is, I'm in the middle of something important—"

"Oh? Sharpening your teeth?"

She made a rolling motion with her hand, even though he couldn't see it. "Can we get around to the real reason for your call sometime today?"

A thunderous throat clear came through the line. "Yeah. About my offer the other night."

"Offer? Um, are you confusing me with the puck bunny who blew you in your truck?"

A gargling noise came from the other end.

"Oh my heavens!" she gasped in an over-the-top voice. "Did you offer *me* the chance and I missed it somehow? Damn! I think I'll fling myself into my niece's baby pool and drown myself now. Good-bye."

"As usual, I have no idea what the fuck you're talking about." His voice grew muffled, as if he were covering his phone, but she thought she heard the words "swear jar," and then he was back. "The caregiver job offer. Remember? It's possible you didn't think I was being sincere when I put it out there," he said dryly, "but I wasn't kidding."

*Huh?* "Meaning?"

"Meaning, with what's going on, I can't hire anyone to come in and take care of Mom. And she likes you. And she also likes your dog. Not to mention, I have a huge-ass house with plenty of room to accommodate the four of us."

He couldn't be serious! Could he?

Her inability to speak gave him room to ramrod his way in. "Consider this. Gage and Lily are already crammed into their Cracker Jack-box house, and who knows how long we'll all be sheltering in place? That'll get real old, real quick."

*It already has.* She opened her mouth to toss something back at him but stopped short, unable to muster a pithy comeback as she recalled the unending space in his big-ass house. Instead, distractions, like the thought of being cooped up in a tiny house without soundproofing for weeks—months!—were messing with her. Not to mention she was ten days into a one-month agreement with an ex-coworker in Seattle who'd been generous enough to let her cram her leftover crap in his storage unit. Those boxes had to go *somewhere.*

But surely she could find another solution besides living with *this* egomaniac, couldn't she? Sarah was no masochist, and subjecting herself to Quinn Hadley twenty-four-seven would be masochism on steroids.

"You have plenty of time on your hands now. Why don't *you* take care of your mom?"

"Well, besides trying to stay in game shape and take care of her in other ways, there's … woman stuff, and that's … She's my mom. But hear me out. By you being here, you won't be couch-surfing at Gage and Lily's and comingling COVID. Here, you've got plenty of room to spread out, and we can totally pull off the social distancing thing."

*I'm not a couch-surfer!* she wanted to protest. "Wait. Let me see if I have this straight. I'm supposed to take care of your mom while staying six feet away from her. We'll all live in our own wings. When we come into common areas, we'll be masked and gloved. Oh! And we'll carry around drums of antibacterial wipes so we can disinfect everything, and each other, as we go."

"Something like that, but we can work out the details later. By the way, I don't have that many *wings*, and after two weeks we can be as cozy as we want because we'll either all have it or we'll have dodged a bullet."

*Cozy*. He didn't have ulterior motives, did he? No. He hadn't given off so much as a glimmer of that vibe. In fact, he'd made it clear he preferred to be shark bait. Which was perfect.

When she didn't answer, he answered for her. "See? You don't have a comeback because it's a brilliant plan."

Living under the same roof with Quinn, no matter if his house *was* the size of several ice rinks, ranked right up there with root canals. On the other hand, she did like his mom, a lot, and … Holy moly, was she really considering this? No way.

"Brilliant?" she guffawed. "A little full of ourselves, aren't we?"

"I can't get anybody else. Would you please help me take care of my mom?" he pleaded. The little-boy voice totally threw her. "I promise I won't look at you or talk to you. And I'll make it worth your while."

Without censure, her mouth galloped away from her. "We'd better be talking cold, hard cash, Sparky. If it's the same kind of 'making it worth my while' you use with your fan club, then you are barking up the wrong tree."

"Whoa, whoa! Talk about being full of our ourselves. That's not what I meant. This is strictly business. I *was* talking about cold, hard cash—lots of it."

She hmphed.

Quinn barreled ahead. "First of all, Sunshine, even though your brother is my best friend, he'd separate me from my balls if I tried anything. I'm rather fond of them, and I have no desire to give them up. Second of all, and no offense, while you're not *bad* looking, you're not my type."

"Well, thank God for that! I would never want to be confused with *your* type." Whatever the hell *that* was. Oh yeah. Blond, busty, and skanky. In other words, not her. "Yeah, still not interested."

He sounded like a deflated balloon on the other end. "Right. Okay. I'll tell Mom I tried. Bye, Sunshine." He hung up.

"Hello? Hey, Sparky?" She stared at her phone. Wait! That was *it*? That was all the fight he was gonna give her? Wuss!

Sarah fell into a restive sleep, punching pink pillows at every turn, though she couldn't say exactly whose face she pictured as she punched. There were any number of candidates: the virus, the people spreading it, the governor of Colorado, the president, Wolf, Quinn Hadley. In her less agitated, more lucid moments, she admitted she couldn't lay the blame on any of them, though she was surely tempted.

It was this merry-go-round of thoughts spinning in her head—along with the pins-and-needles sensation in her legs—that forced her from her bed. *Daisy's bed.* As a kid, Sarah had suffered from something they now called Restless Leg Syndrome, only they didn't have pills for it back then. Grandma would fix her a warm mug of milk and pull her against her pillowy body while she stroked her hair. Before long, Sarah would drift off to sleep. If only the drug manufacturers could turn *that* into a pill, the world would be a much happier place.

Though she no longer had Grandma's comforting body to sink against, there was milk in the fridge she could heat—her go-to cure for her fitfulness even now. As she was stealing down the hall into the kitchen, she heard a grunt from the living room. A manly grunt. Followed by a heavy thump.

She stilled a moment, picking up a gruff "Son of a bitch!" *Definitely* not Daisy.

"Gage?" she hissed into the dark.

"What?" came her brother's growl.

She tiptoed to the couch. "What are you doing out here?"

Her brother's torso sprang upright on the couch. "Daisy's sleeping with Lily." She could practically hear the clench in his jaw.

"Wait. Why isn't Daisy out here? And why aren't you sleeping with Lily?"

He huffed and scrubbed his hand over his beard. "We're pretty sure Daisy's allergic to dogs now that Archer's been here a while, and the congestion's keeping her awake. She's decided sleeping out here is scary—something about the trees through the windows. So I offered to swap."

"How long?"

"Going on a couple of nights now," he sighed.

"But I thought …" Coincidentally, it *had* been a few nights since she'd heard the distinctive coitus noises through the walls. She began pacing the width of the couch. "Gage, I'm sorry. I didn't mean—look, why don't you sleep in Daisy's bed and I'll sleep out here?"

A night-light glowed in the kitchen, reflecting pinpoints in his eyes. "Uh, nice of you to offer, Sar, but it really doesn't get me any closer to sleeping with Lily."

"Oh. Right."

Well, shit. He looked dejected as hell. Or maybe he was exhausted from sleeping on the too-small couch. And it was Sarah's fault. Not only had she insinuated herself and her allergy-inducing dog into their tiny house, but now she was the reason they slept separately. Guilt pinched her.

"I know what you're thinking, Sar, and Lily will not tolerate you sleeping on the couch, so just march your ass back to bed and go to sleep," he grumbled before flopping back down and hitting his head on the armrest. "Fuck!"

Milk forgotten, she turned for the bedroom, feeling like a class-A heel. Then she stopped and pivoted. "Gage?"

"Mmph?"

"Um, so I got this offer from Quinn …"

Gage shot upright again. "What the hell? In the middle of all this, he's putting the moves on you?"

"No, no, that's not it. What I meant was, he wants to hire me to take care of his mom on a live-in basis. I guess he hasn't been able to hold on to caregivers, and now with COVID …"

He seemed to calm down. "Right. It's gotta be near impossible to hire someone."

"Exactly. So …"

"That might not be a bad idea, Sar."

Her brother was actually going along with this wackadoodle idea? "I thought you said you'd kill him if he laid a hand on me."

Even in the gloom, she could see Gage appraising her. "Who says he's going to try anything? Quinn likes them young and dumb anyway, and you're neither."

"Gee, thanks."

"What I meant was, you're what? Five years older than he is? He likes them just old enough so they can drink legally, and like I said, he goes for the stupid ones. You're not stupid, Sar."

"And this guy is your friend why?"

He chuckled. "From a guy's perspective, he's got his good points. *Most* of the time he thinks things through. He'd do anything for his friends. He'd be the first guy I'd call after T.J. if I was in trouble because he'd drop everything."

"So you'd be okay with me living with him and his mom? Temporarily?"

"It's up to you, but yeah, if that's what you want. Then when Lil and I move into the new place, you can move back."

Whoa! The idea sounded so reasonable when her brother sussed it out. Maybe she'd been letting her emotions run roughshod over her and cloud her judgment. "All right, Bro. I'll think about it."

Sleep remained at bay that night, but she finally came to a conclusion that would solve everyone's problems. Well, almost everyone. And five happy people out of six was way better than *none* out of six.

Quinn lay on top of his covers without a stitch on, yet he still couldn't cool off enough to fall back asleep. Slumber was as elusive as a unicorn. His buzzing phone surprised him, but more surprising was the name on his caller ID at 4:12 in the morning. Should he answer Psycho Sunshine's call? Was she drunk or high and looking to entertain herself by chewing him another asshole?

*Yeah, not in the mood for her vitriol.*

He stuffed the phone under his covers to shut it up. Several seconds after the vibration stopped, a text chimed.

*Goddamn, what does this woman want?*

He told himself he was a dumbass for giving in to his curiosity, that it wouldn't help him get to sleep, yet he hauled the phone to his face. A poke at the screen, and the little bubble with her message was crystal clear. And it shocked the hell out of him.

*If the caregiver offer's still open, I'm in.*

Wiping his eyes, he looked again. The message hadn't changed. He fumbled as he tapped out an answer.

Quinn: *You are seriously texting me at four in the morning to tell me you've changed your mind about taking care of my mother?*

Sarah: *Give Sparky a gold star. Yes, that's exactly what I'm telling you.*

Quinn shook his head. *When can you start?* Shit, he hadn't meant for that to come across all eager-beaver. She'd get the wrong idea that he wanted to hire her after all. Except he *did* want to hire her. Well, he didn't *want* to hire her, but he *needed* to hire her. He'd run out of choices. And somewhere along the way, he'd gotten on board with the crazy idea that Sarah as a caregiver could work—maybe because facing his mother's constant gimlet eye as she fumed at him was a less attractive alternative.

"Better to be plastered against a hard place or spread eagle across a rock?" he mused aloud. As he thumbed his response, he half expected to A) never hear from Sarah Sunshine again or B) have her tell him to go fuck himself. His mind hadn't caught up to scenario C yet, which was exactly what she hit him with: *I'll be over at eight.*

Quinn: *As in 4 hrs?*

Sarah: *Exactly. Archer and me. Does that work for you?*

Numbly, he typed two little letters and hit send before he could reconsider. *OK.*

He sat up, flipped on his bedside lamp, and looked around. Maybe he'd been dreaming. He glanced at his phone screen. Nope. *Jesus Christ!* Had he really hired this wildcat?

On his nightstand were three red beanbags, and he snatched them up and started tossing them in the air while thoughts tumbled through his brain. *Which room do I put her in?* The one farthest from his, naturally. *No, next to Mom.*

"Shit!" he grumbled. "I'm stuck inside for God knows how long with two crazy women. I would've been better off holing up with Hunts and his strippers."

The beanies looping through the air were hypnotic, soothing, and other thoughts bubbled to the surface. Like how happy his mom would be when he told her the news. Yeah, the news that a pink-haired, weird T-shirt-wearing spitfire was moving in—in four hours. With her dog. A spitfire whose life's motto was *Fuck All Men!* And not in a good way. No doubt she had *that* slogan emblazoned on a T-shirt.

With an enormous exhale, he caught his beanbags and piled them back on the nightstand, then dragged his hand over his face. What had he just signed up for?

# Chapter 9

## Good Roommates Are Hard to Find

Hours later, fresh from a workout and shower, Quinn was still basking in the glow of his stunning accomplishment. His mother had been delighted when he'd told her about Sarah. That glow, sadly, dimmed when his brother called.

"Ronan the Accuser. 'Sup in the mighty state of Kansas?"

"Oh, you know. Living the life." A child screamed in the background as if to punctuate Ronan's declaration. "So I hear you finally got off your lazy ass and hired someone to take care of Mom. 'Bout damn time."

Though Quinn knew full well Ronan was deliberately pushing all his buttons at once, he couldn't keep his jaw muscles from bunching. Why did merely hearing Ronan's grating voice make Quinn want to throw a fist in his face?

"It's not like I haven't tried, asshole. She's fired everyone I hired."

"Yeah, well, the way I heard it, you didn't exactly make the best choices. So what's this one like?"

"She's a piece of work. They should get along fine."

"Mom says she's got a dog that can help?"

"Yeah, we'll see."

"Mom also said this girl's pretty hot. That why you hired her?" Ronan started laughing—no, cackling.

"Fuck you."

"Besides being unable to find the right people to help her," Ronan poked, "how are you and Mom getting along?"

*Like Raid and roaches. Like Round-Up and weeds.* "Good. She's stubborn as hell, though."

"Ha! Like you're not?"

"That's not what I meant, dickhead. Did she tell you I came home and found her lying on the floor the other day? She'd had a little run-in with her wheelchair and lost the battle. But Jesus Christ, suggest she needs help and you'd think I'd just threatened to take her damn arm off. Did that shit happen when she was living with you?"

"No, but then Jen and I made taking care of Mom priority one."

God, Ronan just couldn't stop himself, could he? Quinn wanted to throw out that, from what Mom had told him, Jen had done most of the heavy lifting—taking care of Mom *and* the three rug rats—while Ronan golfed, partied, acted like Ronan. Instead, Quinn kept his mouth zipped.

"It's been rough for Mom, Q," the sanctimonious son of a bitch added.

"Like I don't know that?" Quinn snapped.

"Well, it's good you finally stepped up to the plate. That's all I can say."

*Not really all you can say, asshole.*

"Oh, hey," Ronan droned on, "I heard from Dad."

This had all of Quinn's attention. He hadn't heard from his dad in what? Two years? Nor had his mom, for all Quinn knew. So why the hell was Dad in touch with Ronan? Right. It was *Ronan*; his shit never stank. "What did he want?"

"To say he's stuck in Poland until this blows over."

"Well, no shit. He's been *stuck in Poland* for the last three years!"

"Don't be such a dick. Contrary to what you tell yourself, you are *not* the Mighty Quinn."

Quinn rubbed stiff fingers over his forehead. "Look, Ro, as awesome as talking to you is, I gotta go. Sarah will be here soon, and I wanna be sure everything's ready for her."

"Oh, Saaarah! Smile for meeee," Ronan sang. "Seriously, Baby Bro, don't screw this up. Mom likes her. Keep your dick zipped unless you're about to fire her ass, then by all means, tap it." Ronan gave him a dirty chuckle. "Not that you need to get up in *that* with all those hotties hanging all over your NHL-playing ass. Good thing that's what you do for a living, otherwise you'd never get *any*."

*Fuck, here we go.* Only this time his mom's words streamed through Quinn's consciousness. *Was* Ronan jealous? "Yeah, too bad not all of us have what it takes to make it to The Show. Later." Quinn hung up before his brother could get in another word. As for Sarah, Quinn would have no problem keeping his dick in his pants where Miss Sunshine was concerned.

Right on cue, the doorbell rang. Quinn pulled in a breath to fortify himself.

"Quinnie, I think she's here," his mom called helpfully from some hallway somewhere in the labyrinth of hallways.

"Got it," he growled.

Plastering on a semblance of a smile, he jogged to the front door and threw it open, his eyes landing on Sarah. The hot-pink hair wasn't quite so hot anymore, having faded to a hue he wasn't sure was on the color spectrum. She seemed to be sizing him up with those big forest-green eyes of hers. Or were they hazel? Beside her, Archer sat on his haunches, his lips drawn back in a smile. *Do dogs have lips?*

"Hey, roomie," Sarah said.

"Hi. Welcome to your new home." Sweeping his hand in a welcoming gesture, he held the door wide. "Temporary new home," he clarified. His eyes darted above her head and landed on a teal Jeep. "That yours?"

She turned to look over her shoulder, and when she did, her dark zip hoodie gaped open, revealing a T-shirt that read, "Zombies Hate Fast Food," and the hint of curvature beneath. She swung her gaze back to his, nearly catching him. "Yep."

"I'll show you where to park it later and give you a garage remote. In the meantime, come in." He made way for her and the dog in the foyer.

Her eyes shot up to the recessed dome that held a monstrous two-tiered chandelier, then took a turn around the space. "I love the lines of this entry. I feel like I just walked into an Italian villa."

He shrugged. "Follow me. Party's back here."

Sarah and Archer trailed behind him as he padded to the family room. Archer's nails—*or are they claws?*—clicked over the polished marble. His mom sat upright, her legs stretched out on the couch, her head bent over something in her lap.

"Hey, Mom?"

Mom lifted her head and whipped off her glasses before breaking into a bright smile. "Hello, hello!" She held her arms wide and beckoned the dog. "How's my handsome man today?" she cooed. Archer rewarded her with a serious tail wag and several swipes of his long pink tongue.

Sarah looked on with a wide grin, one hand loosely holding Archer's lead. "It's lovely to see you again, Liz. I'm looking forward to hanging out with you."

"Me too." All his mom's attention was focused on Archer, and Quinn felt himself sag with relief. If this could work out, he'd find a way to put up with Sarah Sunshine's snark. It might take barricading himself in his room, the gym, or the in-home theater, but he'd figure it out.

"Let me show you your room," he invited. They left Archer behind with his mom, and as they walked he pointed out this and that. "Feel free to go wherever and use whatever."

"What's down that way?" Sarah indicated a hall with the rooms he never used—except the one time.

"Oh. Anywhere but *there*. Those are the forbidden rooms," he joked with an evil *bwahaha*.

"Got it. So the rooms equipped with the dance poles and BDSM gear?"

He gave her a smirk. "Not a bad idea. Think Amazon ships trapezes, poles, and those neon light-up dancing platforms strippers use?"

"You wish," she scoffed. "Come to think of it, they probably do. Did you know that since they've had to shut down for the pandemic, some strip clubs have put in drive-throughs?"

"I have no idea what that would look like, but strip clubs aren't my thing. And wow, aren't you a wealth of information? Were you doing job research?"

She shrugged him off with a cold shoulder. In front of a large door at the end of a wide hallway, he came to a stop. She'd halted beside him, and he had to lean past her to grasp the door handle. She hopped backward as if she didn't want any part of him touching any part of her. Fine by him, though he couldn't avoid the sweet vanilla-flowery scent that wreathed her. Shit, that smelled good. Not what he'd expected from her, though he couldn't say *what* he should have expected. The scent of burnt rubber? Motor oil?

"This is your room," he announced as he threw the door open. She gave a little gasp and covered her mouth with both hands. He couldn't have cared less about impressing her, but he wanted her to be comfortable, and her reaction gave him an unexpected surge of gratification.

"Oh wow!" Her eyes were wide as pucks, and she seemed to hesitate on the threshold.

He tried not to laugh at Miss Badass looking bowled over. Stepping into the room, he urged her in. "I picked this room because it has access to the backyard. I figured it would be easier to let Archer in and out."

She gingerly moved into the space, taking it in with owl eyes.

"If you don't like it," he continued, "there are plenty more rooms to choose from. But this is one of the biggest, it's close to my mom, and it should accommodate all your girlie stuff."

*I can't imagine having enough girlie stuff to fill a tenth of this suite,* Sarah thought to herself as she gaped. She didn't care that Quinn was smirking at her. The room was beautiful! Soaring ceiling, a marble fireplace, a towering bay window with a table and armchairs, and French doors that opened onto a private deck. It was decorated in heavy, dark furniture and rich golds and reds—not exactly her style, but it imbued the room with luxury and comfort. Definitely an upgrade from Daisy's pink room.

Quinn was in the bathroom now, which was on the other side of the fireplace, going on about a steam shower, jetted tub, towel warmers, blah, blah, blah. Sarah's head reeled. When she peeked in, all she could think was that the bathroom resembled a spa and was bigger than the two bathrooms in her childhood home combined.

"No shortage of space, is there? Hope I don't get lost," she said, cutting the "Wow!" from her tone.

A chuckle rumbled in his chest. "I'll leave you a rope so you can find your way back out. Oh. And a little tip? Watch your language around my mom, or you'll be stuffing all those strategically placed money jars."

"Thanks, Sparky. I'll keep it in mind." Now all she wanted was for him to get out so she could explore her new digs alone. As if he'd read her mind, he excused himself and left.

"Wow! A girl could get used to this," she muttered to herself. Why didn't Quinn like this place? Oh, right. It had to be the antithesis to the swinging bachelor penthouse he'd been so fond of. "Bet *that* place has the stripper poles," she giggled to herself.

After fetching Archer, Sarah unpacked. Sadly, it took all of ten minutes, with her filling only one miniscule portion of the room's available storage space. Liz stopped by to check on her and let her know she was going to lie down, and Sarah found herself with some time to burn. She changed into workout togs and jogged to the kitchen—getting lost twice—but it was deserted. Perfect. She'd been hoping to avoid Quinn.

Plugging in her earbuds, she found the way to the walkout basement fitness center he'd shown her—it was bigger than any gym she'd ever joined—and marched past the racquetball court into the weight room, where she pulled up short. Facing away from her, poised in front of a wall of glass that looked out on the swimming pool, Quinn was doing bicep curls with big-ass free weights. He didn't break stride, and she soon figured out why. He too was sporting earbuds and was obviously in a zone.

Despite the voice in her head telling her not to, she ran her eyes over him as he pumped iron in a baggy tank that revealed more than it hid and gym shorts that moved with him, highlighting a well-formed ass. Up and down, he alternated arms, slowly curling first one then the other. Her gaze paused and lingered on his flexing, sweat-sheened biceps. What could it hurt? He might be a twit of epic proportion, but he was a fine specimen of a twit, and she was simply … evaluating his … form. And what a nice form it was too. Different from Wolf's leaner body, yet no less beautiful, in a masculine sort of way.

"See something you want, toots?"

She jerked, instantly admonishing her body for betraying her surprise. *Shit, shit, shit!* Worse than showing her shock, though, was the fact she'd been caught watching him in the first place. Now he'd get the wrong idea, fanning the flames of his out-of-control ego even higher. How had he known she was standing there anyway? He deposited one of the weights on a rack, plucked out an earbud, and turned. His chest was heaving. A cocky smile was plastered all over his face, and out popped those damn dimples. As if he read her mind—again—he pointed to the windows. "Saw your reflection when you came in."

"Then why didn't you say something?" Her inner petulant child shot through her tone, giving her away. On the defensive, she cinched her arms over her chest.

One corner of his mouth hitched up even higher. "Looked like you were enjoying the show. I didn't want to spoil it for you."

"Oh, for Christ's—" She rolled her eyes to the ceiling. Yeah, and *now* she was broadcasting that he'd gotten to her. He knew it too because he laughed. Damn him. Maybe she should leave.

"I'm glad you're going to use the equipment," he said cheerfully. "It's top of the line but hasn't been put through its paces."

"Didn't you get in a workout this morning?" she grumbled.

"Strictly cardio. Thought I'd break it up since I've got the whole damn day."

"I'll come back."

"Don't leave on my account, Sunshine. In fact, I could use a spotter. You willing?"

When she didn't move, he added, "It's either you or my mom."

*Oh hell no.* "You make your mom spot you?"

"Not yet, though desperate times and all."

"All right. Jeez." She pushed herself into the room. "Where do you want me?" *Fuck. Did I just say that?*

He arched an eyebrow at her, and a predatory gleam lit his eyes. Yeah, no way was a guy like him going to miss the softball she'd just pitched. Mercifully, he didn't say anything. She really didn't want to clock her employer on her first day of work. Even if that employer was Quinn "Asshat" Hadley.

He walked over to the bench and started adding weights on either end of the bar while he hummed. In between the *clink-clunk* of the disks slipping into position, she said, "You should get Gage over here to work out with you. They shut down the team facility *and* his favorite gym, and he's got nowhere to go. I'm not sure Lily's gonna let him do chin-ups in the bedroom doorway for hours on end."

Quinn flicked his eyes her way before returning his attention to what he was doing. "I'll give him a call." He swung one long, thick leg over the bench and lay back, wiggling his big body into position. His hands wrapped around the bar. "Ready, toots?"

She shuffled to the head of the bench, not daring to get too close to all that thick hair. His eyes slid from the bar to her. They were a deep, rich chocolate color that matched his dark eyebrows.

"Move a little closer, toots. I don't bite. Unless you ask nicely."

That did it. Snapped her right out of her stupid zone. She gave him a snort and placed her hands below the bar as he lifted and cleared the stand with a grunt. A deep pull of air in, and he pushed it out and extended his arms to their full length. Muscles in his arms, chest, and shoulders were taut under smooth skin. Another whoosh of breath, and he began to lower the bar slowly. Now the show was full on, his muscles rippling and flexing as they strained. Corded veins grew more defined along his powerful forearms. Even his enormous quads were working as he dug his feet into the floor.

Sarah tore her eyes from Quinn's various body parts and helped him guide the bar onto the stand. God, she'd always loved the look of a fit hockey player's physique. Too bad their annoying personalities couldn't be separated from their bodies.

After a few sets, he sat up and gave her a nod. "Thanks. Wanna give it a go?"

She waved her hand. "No, thanks. I'm more of a runner."

His eyes swept her from head to toe. "Yeah, I can see that."

The look was all business, no heat, yet she felt completely undressed in front of him. "I'll just …" She pointed toward one of the treadmills.

"All yours. Thanks for your help." He stood and yanked off his shirt, rubbing it over his slick skin before draping it around his neck. God help her, her eyes dropped to his well-cut abs and drifted to his solid obliques, visible above the waistband of his shorts that had slipped below his flat navel. Was the man commando? She darted her eyes away before he could catch her surveying him and misinterpret her examination for something it wasn't. The mystery of his underwear would be put aside for now. No, for*ever*.

Her focus didn't sharpen on what she was supposed to be doing until he left. Trying not to consider how ridiculous she was, she instead formulated how she could time her gym visits so she wasn't sharing the space with him. Except he needed her help with the bench press. *Wait.* This wasn't *her* dilemma because that would mean she gave a rat's ass about him, which she most certainly did not.

# Chapter 10

## Let's Flamingle

Quinn ordered Chinese delivery for Sarah's first dinner to make it easy on everyone. She jumped right in, making herself comfortable in the kitchen as she found and laid out plates, napkins, silverware. She even found chopsticks and opened a few beers. Like she belonged there. In order to keep his borderline aggravation under control, he reminded himself she was *supposed* to act like she belonged there.

As she buzzed around the table, she kept commenting on how good everything smelled. He got the idea it was more for his mom's benefit than her own because honestly, girl looked like she could stand a few extra pounds. Nelson had mentioned something about her having a hard time in Seattle, and maybe that was the reason she was on the skinny side. *Wonder what happened?* She'd changed from her workout clothes and apparently showered because her hair was still damp. Tonight's T-shirt was turquoise, and bright pink flamingos adorned it. The saying read, "Let's Flamingle." Christ. Maybe she owned a T-shirt shop that had gone belly up?

They sat down to eat, and she surprised them when she popped out of her seat. She reminded him of a jumping bean. "Shit! I forgot the soy sauce."

His mom fixed an amused eye on Sarah Sunshine. "Did Quinn tell you about the swear jar?"

In a cosmic, comical spectacle, Sarah froze and gave Quinn wide eyes. "Told you," he mouthed at her before settling into a smug smile.

She straightened the hem of her T-shirt and faced his mom. "Um, how much do I owe?"

His mom giggled. Actually giggled. Then waved her off. "Nothing this time."

"What?" He let his outrage come through. "How come she gets a pass?"

Pointing a chopstick at him, his mother said, "Quinnie. I give you all sorts of passes all day long. You just don't know it. This is Sarah's first day, so she gets a pass too." She gave Sarah a Cheshire-cat grin and bobbed her head as if to punctuate her edict.

Sarah bit her bottom lip. The corners of her mouth tipped up, and her hazel eyes brightened. Shit, that was kinda cute. *Wait! Poison ivy is not cute, and neither is Sarah Nelson.* He shoveled in a mouthful of food and mumbled PG curses while he chewed.

Dinner conversation was animated, all over the map, and his mother participated fully, to his delight *and* frustration. They barely talked at the table when it was just the two of them, with him forever stretching across awkward silences for *some* commonality, something they were both interested in that would catch a conversation on fire. Fortunately, he'd been on the road a lot, so it hadn't been an everyday issue, but when he'd been home, he'd taken to eating in front of the TV to avoid the discomfort. But tonight—this … wasn't so bad.

As Sarah served her a second helping—*how the hell did she get Mom to eat that much?*—his mother peered at her. "How do I get pink hair?"

Quinn nearly dropped the beer bottle he'd tipped to his lips. Sarah clapped her hands, reminding him of a little kid. More cute behavior that caught him off guard. Thank God he wasn't into cute. Hot, dirty, sexy as fuck. That's what he was into, and Sarah was none of those. Not that he'd ever look at her that way anyway. A picture of a pissed-off brother loomed in his imagination.

"I don't know if you color your hair," Sarah spurted, "but I picked up supplies in case."

His mother's eyes danced. "How fun! What about the pink? I like what you have."

Sarah flipped a hank of her own hair and craned her head to inspect it. "The pink's not holding up as well as I thought. I do have a cool teal we could use on you. Or we can order something off of Amazon."

Quinn watched in stunned fascination as they chitchatted about hair dye and girlie shit. He never even knew his mom colored her hair. Didn't know his mom was into girlie shit. Why hadn't that occurred to him before? He couldn't say taking a trip to Girl Twilight Zone was unpleasant, though. Just weird.

"Are you going to finish your meal?" he asked Sarah when they were finishing up. She'd had maybe half a plate, and her portion hadn't been big to begin with.

Without looking up, she flapped her hand at him. "No, you can have it."

"That's not what I meant. I just thought … Aren't you hungry?" *Aw, crap. Maybe she doesn't like what I ordered.* Except he'd ordered just about everything on the menu. Was she a picky eater? Probably. It would go along with her pain-in-the-ass persona.

She gave him a shrug. "I had plenty. I'll get the dishes."

"Um, no."

He was hyperaware of his mother's bemused gaze bouncing between them.

Sarah stood and began collecting plates. "I got this. I have to get used to your kitchen anyway."

"But I didn't hire you to cook or be a maid."

"Chillax, Sparky. It's what I usually do. No special treatment for you."

"Sparky!" his mother howled. "Oh, that's priceless!"

Sarah grinned at her in response.

Annoyance spiked, but the phone on the counter vibrated, and he rose to check caller ID. A split second later, the phone in his pocket went off, and he pulled it out. Sarah arched an eyebrow at him as he stood there, a phone in each hand, looking from one device to the other. He chugged into a different part of the house before answering the first phone. The second one he ignored.

"Hey, Nelsy. What's up?"

"Just wondering if you and my sister had killed each other yet."

Quinn let out a mirthless laugh. "No, but there's still plenty of time."

"Sarah can be a little … intense, but she's good people."

*Intense.* Yeah, Quinn would go with that. It was more PC than any of *his* descriptions. "So she mentioned you don't have a way to work out. Why don't you come over tomorrow and help yourself to the equipment here? This house came with a full gym that's a fitness nut's wet dream."

"Can't. Team says no mingling. At all. Which is the other reason for my call."

"Yeah?" Quinn plopped on a formal couch in a formal room he'd never used and tossed a formal pillow into the air. He caught it and tossed it again.

"Heard from anyone on the team?"

Another catch and toss. "You're the first since our fun times at the press conference. No one else is talking to me." Yeah, he'd been a dumbass, but cut a guy some slack. "What's going on?"

Nelson blew out a breath on the other end. *Uh-oh.* "So one of the trainers is sick, and they're testing him for COVID-19. On top of that, that dick of a reporter's whining that he's sick too, so the team's paying to test him."

Quinn let the pillow fall to his feet. "You're shitting me."

"Wish I were. It'll take a few days to get the results. I wanted to give you the heads-up so you can lay low. People are still worked up over the press conference."

"You're not, though, are you?" In that moment, Quinn needed to know he and Nelson were okay because neither Shanstrom nor Grimson were talking to him, though he'd tried apologizing by phone, by text. Multiple times. With barely a response, which bothered the shit out of him.

"Nah, we're good. Don't get me wrong. That was a really stupid move on your part, but I know where you were coming from. You're not out to hurt anybody, but a little more impulse control on your part would've gone a long way. Feel me?"

"Yeah, I feel you. But shit, I couldn't have given them the virus." *Could I?* Cold needles of ice spiked along Quinn's shoulders and neck.

"Doesn't matter right now. Everybody's on edge. Like I said, I wanted to let you know so you don't get blindsided."

"Thanks, man. I appreciate you."

"Oh. And another piece of advice? Don't be putting moves on my sister unless you want me beating your ass."

Like Quinn needed the reminder. "Ha! Farthest thing from my mind, dude. Your sister's safe with me." *Can't imagine being that desperate. Besides, that little wildcat would scratch my eyes out just for trying to read her latest ridiculous T-shirt.*

When they hung up, Quinn sat in the dark, turning over Nelson's words. When he'd touched the mics, he'd done it … Why? *Just another jaunt into Quinn World.* Impulsive. And senseless. Wouldn't be the first time. No, he never did anything halfway. But damn, he'd never intended for anyone to get sick. Hell, how could anyone have gotten sick from him when *he* wasn't sick?

His second phone was tucked beside him on the couch, signaling he had a voicemail. Without bothering to listen, he stuffed the phone back in his pocket. The other phone, his *regular* phone, he carried in his hand as he padded back into the kitchen. The soft giggling of women, all high and musical, reached his ears. He rounded the corner and stopped. The kitchen was completely buffed, as if a tornado had scoured and polished every surface, and on the family room couch sat his mom and Sarah Sunshine. His mom was stroking Archer's head, which was planted on her thigh, and Sunshine's head was down, as though she was looking at something in her lap. What was obviously a chick flick played on the TV screen—he knew because a trio of hot girls were laughing at some clueless guy.

His mom's head turned toward him. "Quinnie! Come join us." He squinted to get a closer look. She was smiling, and she looked about ten years younger than she had the other night. Maybe Sarah had colored her hair already? No, he hadn't been gone *that* long. Besides, it looked the same. But her cheeks were rosier, her face less lined.

A little gust of air left his body, unwinding a few coiled muscles. "Uh, I'm good, thanks." Life might be going to shit, but there sat his mom, actually enjoying herself, and for a moment he didn't feel guilty. So hey, a silver lining in a black thundercloud. Miss Sunshine didn't look up, and he found himself wanting to make her acknowledge him.

"Got everything you need?" he directed at both of them. His mom nodded, but Sarah stayed focused on whatever the hell was in her lap. "How about you, Sunshine?"

She didn't raise her head. "I'm good, Sparky."

*Sparky. Great.*

He couldn't help himself. "Whatcha got there?"

"The latest issue of *Civil Engineering.*"

"Can I read it sometime? Sounds interesting."

"Mm-hmm." She still hadn't looked up.

It occurred to him that her magazine was way more interesting than he was. With a puff of his cheeks, he spun and retreated to his room, where he shut the double doors behind him. He scrolled through his regular phone, relieved to find nothing on his outburst in the press conference—yet—and laid it on top of the nightstand. Sliding the second phone out of his pocket, he stared at it a beat before powering it off and stowing it in his nightstand drawer. He threw himself on his bed, locking his hands under his head. Stared at the ceiling as if he could find the answer to what the universe had in store for him written on its surface. Whatever the future held, he was pretty damn sure it involved adulting.

Quinn slept in late the next morning. His bedroom was isolated in a separate part of the house, and usually his mom texted him when she needed his help. He bolted upright and snatched his phone off the nightstand. No messages. He pulled on gym shorts and a T-shirt and jogged down to the kitchen. Everything was quiet except the unaccustomed sound of a tail slapping carpet.

"Hey, Arch. Where's your mom?" *What the hell am I doing talking to a dog?* Archer hopped up and rushed over, greeting Quinn as if he were a long-lost bone that needed a good licking. Quinn hadn't spent time around dogs—any animals—and wasn't sure about pet protocol.

When Archer nudged his hand so it landed on top of his furry head, he gave him a stroke, surprised at the softness. Soon he was rubbing the dog's silky ears. "So where is everyone this morning, buddy?"

Archer swung his head toward the basement stairs.

"Seriously, dog? You psychic or something?" Quinn gave him one last pat, trod down the stairs, and shuffled along the hallway past the racquetball court. He froze in his tracks when he picked up Sarah Sunshine's voice.

"Look at you, Ms. Awesome. You are *owning* this!"

A sort of muffled giggle came next. "I think you're feeding me a line of you-know-what, Sarah."

"No, I'm not. Raise your head for a sec and look at your posture compared to mine in the mirror. See? Your butt's as high as mine."

This had all of Quinn's attention, and he let his curiosity pull him toward the gym. When he peered around the corner, two asses in stretchy black fabric mooned him.

"What's this called again?" one ass said.

"Downward dog," the other ass—a really nice one—answered. He crossed his arms over his chest and leaned against the wall to enjoy the view.

"Hold that pose a little longer, Liz. You're doing great." Lean legs walked toward fingertips braced on the floor, then Sarah's upper body slowly rose, vertebrae by vertebrae. She glanced at him over her shoulder, turned, and in two quick strides stood in front of him. A smirk twitched her lips. "See something you want, Sparky?"

Quinn's tongue wouldn't work. Before he could spit out the clever comeback that hadn't come to him yet, Sarah winked and walked away with a chuckle. *Shit! What if she thinks I want her? Which I absolutely do not.*

Now her arms were on his mom's waist, and she was giving her instructions on how to bring her body upright. "You good?" Sarah asked when Mom was fully standing.

Even from here, he could see the smile that lit his mother's face. "Better than good. I can't believe I didn't do yoga before."

"Didn't your doctor ever say anything about it?"

"Just in a vague 'get more exercise' kind of way."

"Well, I've been doing a little research, and if you're game, I've got some other things I'd like to try with you. But not today. I think we've done plenty. Unless you want to get in the hot tub and soak for a bit?" Sarah's gaze lifted to his.

His mother turned, and her eyes widened. "How long have you been standing there, Quinnster?"

*Quinnster?* Another term of endearment he hadn't heard in a long while. "Long enough, Momster. Looks like Sarah Sunshine's got you working out." *After only twenty-four hours!*

His mother looked between him and Sarah and beamed. "Sarah Sunshine? Sparky? You two have the cutest names for each other." A little twinkle in his mother's eyes had him thinking he needed to set her straight. ASAP. *Not gonna happen, Mom.*

"Okay, clear out." He used a pushing motion with his hands. "There's too much estrogen in here. It's man time."

Sarah looked around dramatically. "Don't see one anywhere."

Annoyed again, though not completely sure why, he barked, "Out!"

"Oh, Sarah. I think he's serious," his mom said in a conspiratorial tone.

Sarah seemed unconcerned and took her time picking up their scattered belongings. "Well, then, let's leave ol' Grumpy Gus alone while we check out the hot tub. Maybe later we can do hair."

As he watched them walk up the stairs, he scratched his stubbly chin. How the hell had his mom gotten so comfortable with Sarah Sunshine so damn fast? With a headshake, he picked up the remote and turned on and muted ESPN. He plugged in his earbuds and went through his stretches. As he climbed onto the rowing machine, he flicked his gaze to the TV. And stopped breathing. On the screen, he recognized himself holding the prick reporter's phone before shoving it back at him. *WTF?* This couldn't be good. He whipped the earbuds out and snatched the remote, jabbing the volume button. Prickface had turned toward the camera, waving his phone. "Did you catch what Quinn Hadley did? Did you get that on tape?" Next, Quinn's team photo flashed across the screen with his name in big letters. It looked like a mug shot.

Even if he'd tried, he couldn't have done a better job fucking up his PR or the team's.

He switched off the TV, shoved his earbuds back in, and attacked the rowing machine at a furious pace. Too bad none of it tamped down the embarrassment and self-recrimination twisting inside him.

# Chapter 11

## Checkout Time is at Eleven

Quinn bolted up the stairs so fast Sarah nearly dropped the mug of steeping tea. "Wow, I can see a contrail coming off of you, Sparky."

He came to an abrupt stop and stared at her like he had no idea who she was. Wet hair was plastered against his head, and sweat was beaded on his face, neck, and chest, as though he'd been drenched in a thunderstorm. "Just finished an intense workout," he panted. His eyes drifted to the cup she held. "What's that?"

"Stress relief tea for your mom. Want some?"

"Stress relief? Why? What's got her stressed out?" His eyes brightened as though a switch had flipped on, then a look of panic overtook his features. "Shit. *You're* stressing her out, and now she's gonna fire your ass, and I'll have to start all over again."

"Hang on just a hot minute. I am *not* stressing her out."

His head turned one way, then another. "Where is she?"

"She's relaxing in the hot tub, and I'm taking the tea out to her. Three bucks for the swear jar."

He did a double take, then pinned his eyes on her. "How so?"

She counted off on her fingers. "Two bucks for 'shit,' and a buck for 'ass.' That's what Liz told me."

"Wait. Did she give you a price sheet or something to torture me with? And 'ass' is not a swear word."

Sarah gave him an exasperated eye-roll. "No, she didn't give me a price sheet, but she did make me put a few bucks in for 'shit' a little while ago. Oh, wipe that ridiculous smirk off your face."

His dark eyebrows quirked. "And she pegged you for 'ass' at the same time?"

"No, just the one word, but she said lesser swear words are a buck." She paused a beat. "Is 'ass' really not a swear word?"

"Nope. Know why? I could say, 'That woman has a very fine ass,' and I wouldn't be swearing, whereas 'shit' is 'shit.' It's a pure swear word."

"That's ridiculous. You could also say, 'You look like shit,' but you wouldn't be swearing."

He pointed at her. "Two bucks."

"No! That was an example."

"Technicality." He shrugged. "And speaking of money, do you use Zelle? I need to deposit your first paycheck."

Sarah couldn't stop her mouth swinging open. "I just got here. You're supposed to pay in arrears, not in advance."

He shook his arms and rolled his neck in a loosening-up motion. "Well, I'm paying in advance. And I have a feeling you're going to need every penny for the swear jar, toots."

A phone rang—it was an old-fashioned kind of ring—and he slid a device from his pocket. *Huh. Which of his two phones is that one, I wonder?*

"Aw, shit!" He shot her a warning glare. "Don't say it." He pressed a button and put the phone to his ear, barking, "*Now* what?"

Sarah took it as her cue to clear out, and she carried the mug outside to Liz, who looked as though she were being blissfully boiled in steaming bubbles. "Here you go."

Liz flashed her a happy smile. "Aw, thanks, doll."

Sarah had grown up wary, thanks to her mother drumming daily messages into her head that most people—*especially* men—were only interested in what they could get from you. As a result, she didn't usually bond with people quickly, and certainly not people of her mom's generation. But this woman? Inwardly, Sarah admitted she'd already developed a big soft spot for her. She was drawn to Liz's smarts and her lively spirit. As Sarah watched her take a careful sip, two things occurred to her. One, why couldn't her mom be more like Liz? And two, how could someone like Liz raise a womanizing, conceited, pretty boy like Quinn?

A pretty boy who wanted to pay Sarah early. Okay, so he wasn't *all* bad. Then again, with what *he* got paid, he could afford to be generous. *Oh shit! Is he getting paid? No play, no pay?* She had no idea.

"I'll come back and help you when it's time to get out, okay?" Sarah leaned down to pat Archer, who lay on the hot tub decking.

"Take your time. I'm in no hurry." Liz made a shooing motion with her hand.

Sarah eyed the phone within Liz's reach. "Just call or text if you need an early rescue from prune skin."

Back inside, Quinn was still on the phone. He was shaking his head, unknowingly flicking his wet strands, and his face was a study in frustration. "Yeah, I get it," he huffed. "Right. I'll make sure I'm ready." A beat passed. "Oh, don't you worry. I'll be wearing the biggest fucking smile you've ever seen." He grumbled a good-bye and hung up.

Sarah decided to hold on to the swear jar snark itching to leap from the tip of her tongue. "Troubles in Sparkyland?"

A distant look haunted his eyes. He dragged a hand over his face, which was when she noticed his dark whiskers. *Nice. No! Not nice.* "I guess there's no point keeping it quiet. You'll find out, if Gage hasn't already mentioned it." He told her about slapping microphones at a press conference.

A laugh like the crack of a whip escaped her. "What are you, five fucking years old?"

His eyebrows knotted together in a fierce glower.

"You gotta admit, even for you that was really dumb."

"What do you mean, 'even for me'? Never mind. Management agrees because now I have to do this PR connect-with-the-fans virtual interview thing in a few days. And apologize to the stupid-as-fu—reporter." His shoulders sagged, and he nodded his head solemnly. She *almost* felt sorry for him. "Hindsight's twenty-twenty," he groused.

*Says the man who seems to live by impulse.*

His head snapped to hers, and his eyes zeroed in on her. "Did you say something?"

"Me? Nope. I was just wondering where your second phone was."

His head did a little jerky shake thing. "My what?"

"Your other phone. The one you had on you last night. What's it for?"

"Jesus Christ, you're nosy."

Yeah, none of her business, but she couldn't resist needling him. "Does 'Jesus Christ' fit in the swear word category?"

"No. And speaking of Mom, why's her wheelchair in the family room and she's outside in the hot tub?"

"Well, she says her legs felt pretty good after the stretching, and she wanted to walk to the hot tub and back. I thought that was a good sign, so I encouraged her."

A look of alarm spread over his features. "You weren't just planning on leaving her out there, were you?"

"Of course not! What do you take me for?"

His lips quirked. "Don't even get me started."

Her mad-o-meter started to climb, and she narrowed her eyes at him. Why did this guy get to her anyway?

He took a step backward. "Whoa! What's with the stink-eye? Seriously, what did I ever do to you?"

She smirked. "It's not about what you did or didn't do. It's about what you *want* to do—well, not to *me*, per se, but to women in general—and what you want to do is completely controlled by that." She pointed at his crotch but kept her gaze fixed on his.

He gave her a cocky grin. "Well, at least you noticed I have one. Envious, toots?"

"You're such a tool."

He crossed his arms over his chest. "The more I'm around you, the harder it is to believe you and Gage are related. For one thing, I think you swear more than your brother does, and that's saying something considering he plays hockey for a living."

"Gage is the polite one."

"Yeah, I totally get that."

Arms still firmly crossed, he seemed to appraise her. His scrutiny made her insides squirm like tadpoles teeming in a pond. Well, that and the modicum of guilt building inside of her for disparaging her brother's teammate.

"So tell me something," he drawled. "Did you acquire your sunny personality in engineering school, or do you come by it naturally?" His smirk deepened, making one dimple appear. She felt an overpowering urge to scrub it off his smug face.

"No, I learned it in common sense school—someplace you obviously didn't attend."

"Oh, ow. Burn, Sunshine." He covered his heart and laughed, then spun and headed toward *his* wing. With a backward glance, he said, "This has been fan-fucking-tastic. Let's do it again real soon. And yeah, I owe the swear jar five bucks for that. Totally worth it."

With that, he jogged down the hall. God, it was only her second day, and she wanted to throttle him even more than she had on day one. This wasn't going to work out. Suddenly, Daisy's bubble gum room was looking a hell of a lot better. Damn it, even Gage and Lily's *couch* held more appeal than Sarah's sumptuous suite if it meant not living under the same roof as Quinn "God's-Gift" Hadley.

Why *not* go back to Gage's? She could take care of Liz during the day and let Quinn handle the nights since he was stuck here anyway. As her mind ran through various scenarios for setting that up, her phone rang. She hadn't loaded in Liz's number yet, but the Colorado area code was a dead giveaway Liz was calling, looking for hot tub rescue. Sarah answered it. "Ready to get out now?"

"Well, well, well, she *does* answer her phone," said a sinfully silky male voice.

Sarah's jaw clamped down like a pair of fully locked vise grips. *Damn it!*

"Sarah? My love?"

*I am not your love!* "What the fuck do you want, Wolf?" she hissed. She was already kicking herself for being so damn stupid. Of *course* he'd figure out a way to get a local number. She shouldn't have expected anything less; he'd proved how adept he was at deceit.

"My sweet, fierce little ball buster. It's one of the things I love best about you, you know." His chuckle slid a greasy chill along her spine. How had she never seen this side of him before? "What I *want*, Sarah, is that dirty mouth of yours. God, I've missed it."

Her cheeks blazed, sending sparks skittering across her scalp. Every hair stood on end. Every nerve ending zipped, then zapped, and not in a good way. "I told you I never wanted to hear from you again," she gritted out. "What part of that did you not understand?"

He tsked. "I understood it all, love, but what *you* didn't understand was the part where *I* said you don't get to walk out on me. I'm coming to

Colorado to bring you home, Sarah." Another slimy laugh. "Oh, you thought I wouldn't know you'd run to your brother's, didn't you?"

"How's *Ingrid*?" she snapped, trying to keep the tremors from her voice while she reined in her shallow breaths. *Calm. Stay calm. You can do this.*

His voice frosted over, turning to ice. "Ingrid has nothing to do with us."

Sarah's hand flew out. "There is no *us*, Wolf, and Ingrid has *everything* to do with it. What world do you live in?"

Without missing a beat, he smoothly said, "Why, Wolf's World, of course."

Movement in her peripheral vision drew her gaze to the hallway entrance. Quinn was lasered in on her, his mouth a hard, straight line, as if he was trying to bite back words. *Damn it! Now I'm flinging all my dirty laundry in front of Sparky, who looks like he's going to fire my ass. Can this get any more fucked up?*

"We're done, Wolf," she bit. "Don't waste your time coming to Colorado, and do not *ever* call me again." She hung up, raked her fingers through her hair, and pushed a huge breath through her lungs. Setting her phone down, steadying her shaking hands on the kitchen counter, she psyched herself up to look Quinn's way.

He hadn't moved. He was frozen, like a hulking statue. She darted him a quick glance. "I need to get your mom out of the hot tub."

"You okay?" His unnaturally soft voice both warmed and threw her at the same time.

Without looking at him, she waved a dismissive hand and pivoted toward the patio doors. "Never better."

On the counter, her phone rang. She came to a sagging stop.

"Sarah?" Quinn called, his voice gentle and filled with concern.

"What?" she rasped.

"I'll get my mom. You take care of your phone—or not—and maybe figure out what, or if, I should know about … whatever's going on with you."

*Nothing! You don't need to know anything!* Quinn brushed past her as he headed toward the doors, and his just-worked-out masculine scent enveloped her, oddly pleasant. As she watched his retreating back, a thought jolted her. Wolf was capable of finding out where Gage lived. The thought of staying put at Quinn's morphed into a necessity. For everyone's sake.

*Da fuck was that?* Quinn's stomach was wound into knots after hearing the wobble in Sarah's voice. She'd sounded so off that he'd come to an abrupt standstill in the hallway. He couldn't help but hear the almost desperate edge in her voice—such a contrast to her usually snotty tone—and it had riveted him in place.

*There is no us, Wolf. What world do you live in? Do not ever call me again.*

As he glanced at his mother relaxing in the hot tub, his mind churned. Who the hell was this Wolf asshole, and why was he harassing Sarah? Then it struck him. The douchebag must've been why she left Seattle. Was she running from him? Did Gage know? Not that it mattered because Sarah was in Quinn's house now. She was a bro's sister, and now she was Quinn's responsibility.

Overwhelming protectiveness surged within him. It was a weird feeling, one he'd only experienced once before, when his dad had left his mom behind to gallivant off to Europe.

"Quinnie!" His mother interrupted his thoughts with a frowny face. "Where's Sarah?"

He nearly laughed out loud. Two times in his life he'd felt a primal urge to safeguard someone, and each time that someone had been a crabby, mouthy woman.

Before he could ponder it further, his mother's scowl returned him to the here and now. "She had to take care of something inside, and I told her I'd come get you. Do you need me to lift you out?"

A triumphant little smile curved his mother's lips. "No. Watch this."

Slowly, she levered herself out of the hot tub while he stood there somewhat stunned, arms tense in case she stumbled and he needed to catch her. But to his utter amazement and delight, she didn't stumble. Instead, she stood on the decking and smiled up at him proudly before breaking into body-shuddering shivers.

"Oh shit!" He snatched up a towel and threw it over her slight shoulders. "Sorry, Mom."

She pointed an accusing finger at him.

"I know." He gave her an eye-roll. "Two bucks." Shit, he was going to go broke.

When they got back inside, Sarah Sunshine seemed to have recovered, acting as though no Wolf had sunk his fangs into her. Though the afternoon passed quietly, Quinn fought the urge to pepper her with questions; her affairs were none of his business. Nonetheless, the unsettling episode bothered him, and he ran through different scenarios to shake the truth from her. All this played in his mind as he watched her maneuver his mom with a finesse he obviously lacked. Maybe it was because they were bonding over girl shit, like the stinky dye Sarah was currently slathering on his mom's hair as they chatted.

"We'll do the tips in teal and the rest in this golden brown. How's that?"

"Oh yes, please," his mom said. "But what about you? Aren't you coloring your hair too?"

"Yep. Well, I'm turning it back to its natural color. I'm over the pink." Sarah hummed, then said, "Liz, have you thought about setting some mobility goals? I know you're dying to spend less time in the wheelchair, and we could build on your good days a bit at a time. What do you think?"

"I love that idea!"

Wow. Only here a few days, and Sarah was light years ahead of anyone else he'd hired. Maybe because she seemed to give a damn. Why hadn't *he* thought of setting up a plan, just like his trainers did with him?

Feeling a little sheepish—and wanting to get away from the god-awful smell—he retreated to his bedroom, relieved he could do so without worrying about his mom. There, he scooped up his beanbags and began juggling—which was when he remembered his *other* phone. He pulled it out and fired it up, listening to a dozen or so voicemails from his out-of-town regulars. The messages were all pretty much the same, hoping he was doing okay and saying how sorry they were that they wouldn't be seeing him soon. *Yeah, me too.*

The last three voicemails were from Dory, which set off his wacko radar. Why the hell had he given her this number? The more important question was, why the hell had he slept with her? His fear factor took a step back from the ledge as he cued them up and listened. Nothing stalkerish. Simply pleasant, brief hello-thinking-of-yous. He blew out a breath he didn't realize he'd been holding, then typed out the same text to each woman—even Dory—who'd called him: *Thanks for thinking of me. Hope you're staying safe and that this doesn't last much longer.*

A knock on his door commandeered his attention, and he stuffed the phone in his pocket.

"Dinner in ten."

*Dinner in ten?* He wrenched his door open, and Sarah Sunshine nearly flew backward. "You made dinner?" he said. Her short do was one color, a rich, dark brown that caught the light and reflected it in reds. The pink hadn't bothered him—he hadn't cared, honestly—but now he found himself wondering why she'd ever want to change it. It was really pretty.

"Well, yeah. I … There's a lot of fresh stuff that I didn't want to see go to waste, so … But don't get your hopes up, Sparky. This is *not* what you're used to. No five-star gourmet fare by any stretch of the imagination. My cooking's more like Betty Crocker's newbie apprentice."

Wyatt's comment about finding Playboy Bunny Betty streaked through Quinn's head. Would she be a brunette? He shoved the thought aside. "Who says that's what I'm used to? Oh, by the way, I have something for you."

She took a step back and cinched her arms over a black T-shirt that read, "May the 4th Be With You." He slid the phone out and handed it to her.

"What the hell's this?"

He arched an eyebrow at her. "That's a buck."

"Your phone's a Buck? Never heard of that brand."

"No, Sunshine. 'Hell' is worth a buck. For the swear jar. That"—he pointed at the phone—"is a spare phone I'm not using right now. If you want to give the number to your family, anyone you want to be able to reach you, feel free. Then you can leave your other phone off in case … Well, if you don't want certain people trying to reach you."

Her eyes fixed on the phone in her hand. "Um … Wait. Is this your hookup phone?"

*Well, shit.* He shifted his weight from side to side. "What, now?"

"You know, like you have your *phone* phone, and then you have your *phone* with a private"—she used air quotes around the last word—"number you only hand out to hookups. Girlfriends. Whatever you call them. That way they can't bombard your regular phone."

He stood there gawking at her like a total idiot.

She waved her hand at him. "Pfft. You forget I've had a front-row seat to hockey players and their shenanigans for *years*. I'm wise to *all* their tricks. And I'm older than you, which makes me just downright wiser all the way around." She shoved the phone back at him. "You might want to close your mouth before a fly moves in."

With that, Miss Sassy Sunshine turned and marched her cute little ass down the hall. Not that he was checking out said ass. She was his buddy's sister after all. And an older, *wiser* woman. Not that the label "older woman" was a deterrent. To the contrary, it sounded sexy as hell for some reason that escaped his comprehension.

"How much older?" he called after her, unable to stop himself.

"Four years older than Gage, so whatever that adds up to."

Whoa. He could've sworn she was the younger of the two when he'd first met her, and when he'd learned she was older, he'd figured by no more than a year, two tops.

She stopped and turned, her side to him. "In case you can't do the math, I'm thirty … and way more woman than you can handle."

Part of him was irritated that she'd read his mind *and* dismissed him like he was a punky teenager, and another part was all kinds of inappropriately heated up. "Hey, don't you want the phone?"

"Um, no. I don't want to be fielding calls from women hot for your bod day and night."

Oh, this made him break out in a wide grin. "And that's how it is. Day and night. Night and day. They can never get enough of the hot bod."

A hand planted itself on her hip. "Oh my God, you are so full of yourself! How do you pass by a mirror without swooning?"

"Toughest thing I do every day, toots. Not gonna lie. It's especially hard when I'm trying to shave. You know, I see myself and pass out with a razor in my hand. Then I get up, see myself again, and fall down again. Super dangerous. And shaving takes. For. Fucking. Ever."

He got the eye-roll he'd been after, along with an extra snort. Tossing the phone on his bed, he followed Sassypants to the kitchen. "I can block everyone on that phone so you won't be bothered—not that there were that many to begin with. Or I can get you a burner phone."

"Five bucks goes to the jar," she called over her shoulder, "and I'll think about the phone. Thanks."

Why this made him happy, he had no idea. *One winning score for the Quinnster.*

# Chapter 12

## The New (Virtual) Normal

Over the week, they settled into a routine that smoothed out like a freshly Zambonied sheet of ice. Quinn's mom—whose blue-tipped hair he'd finally adjusted to—continued to improve while her stress level decreased. Begrudgingly, he admitted to himself that Sarah exercised far more patience than he'd thought her capable of—and far more than he could have mustered himself.

Archer was included in their workout games. The dog not only motivated his mom to go for short walks with Sarah, but he seemed to soothe her at the same time. For some freaking reason, the dog even knew her meds schedule and went off like a whining timer if Mom wasn't getting to it fast enough. Un-effing-believable!

Sarah hadn't had any more uncomfortable phone calls that he knew of—not that she'd confide in him anyway—and that wicked tongue of hers gave him a daily lashing. Oddly, it had become the highlight of his day. He even found himself pushing her to get her rolling. Probably because he was bored out of his ever-loving mind, being cooped up twenty-four-seven with his mother and her mouthy caregiver. A guy could only take so much working out and playing video games. Shit, Quinn couldn't even banter with his teammates, who were either still giving him the cold shoulder or fully focused on their families. As for TV, he avoided it because his mother held a morbid fascination for COVID-19 numbers.

So when he veered into the family room one day and the TV was blaring stats on mask-wearing, he veered right back out and found himself in front of a space he'd dubbed the "solarium." Shaped like an oblong octagon, the room served no purpose but to hold plants and offer pretty views of the grounds. Surrounded by floor-to-ceiling windows and topped with a glassed-in dome mimicking the room's perimeter, it also let in lots of light … which must have been why Sarah had chosen it to construct 3-D puzzles.

She was hunched over a table, chin in her palm, frowning at a partial foundation. Intrigued, Quinn casually drifted in and peered over her shoulder. "Where'd you get the puzzle?"

She didn't look up. "Amazon. Where else?"

"What is it?"

"It's supposed to be the Taj Mahal," she huffed.

He grabbed a chair and slid it perpendicular to hers. "Want some help?"

"You don't have anything better to do?"

His eyes darted between the picture and what she'd assembled. "Not really. I've already worked out twice"—*and I'm in the best damn shape of my life*—"and Mom's got the TV tuned to Covid Network News again. I'm so over it."

"Mmph." Sarah picked up a piece and eyeballed it.

He pointed. "I think that goes—"

Her eyebrow dipped in a spectacular stink-eye. "Really?"

He grinned. "I'm helping!"

"Okay, smartass. Help." She handed him the piece, and to his delight, he snapped it in place after only a few tries.

"Piece of cake," he chortled. "I think we're going to need glue, though."

"I was thinking the same thing, but we don't have any."

They worked quietly for a half hour. Unlike the rest of his existence, hanging with Sarah wasn't dull. Grating, annoying, irritating, yes. She was sharp as razor wire, with wit to match. Girl was ruthless *and* competitive. But like this? Surprisingly, it wasn't so bad.

He stole a glance at her. Something glimmered on her cheek, and he reached out to brush it off. Her head snapped back, and she looked at his finger cross-eyed. He pulled the finger back, but not before he registered the unexpected softness of her skin. "Sorry … just some … You've got … glitter."

"That's my nose stud."

He shook his head.

She peeped at him through long, dark lashes, surprising him when she placed her fingertip on his jaw and smirked. "So do you."

Her light touch shot a bolt through him, and he barked, "I do? Where the hell did it come from?"

She glanced at the bag that held puzzle pieces. "From the Taj, I think."

Heat percolating in his veins, he ran a hand through his hair. "And speaking of the Taj, I think I'll go get us some glue." He shoved himself up from the table. "Need anything?"

Hopeful hazel eyes tracked him. "Flour? And TP? I can't find them anywhere, and I'm worried we'll run out."

"How much TP do we have?"

"Not enough. According to the Internet quiz I took, we have another ten days' worth. I should've waded into the TP wars when Lily and I went to Costco."

He shrugged. "We'll be fine. And if we do run out, I read about some substitutes."

"Such as?"

"Rocks—that's a favorite among backpackers, apparently—and leaves."

Her mouth swung open. "Are you serious?"

"Absolutely. Oh, and my personal all-time favorite: pine cones. Never used them myself, but we have an endless supply in the backyard."

She gave him a horrified look. "Pine cones?"

"That's what the article said. Highly effective, but you only use them going in one direction." He bit back his laughter and patted her shoulder. "Don't worry. I'll find us some TP." How hard could it be?

An hour later, waiting with other TP seekers in a line that snaked through the store, Quinn wasn't laughing. Shoppers jockeyed their carts to get in better position. Had he wound up at a car race? Adding insult to injury, just as he turned the corner into the paper goods aisle, a clerk announced they were sold out for the day.

With his glue and a few meager groceries, he popped into the liquor store next door and loaded up his cart. The place was packed. Evidently, everyone was on the same wavelength.

As he waited his turn to pay, a customer at the front of the line laid a case of Rolling Rock on the counter. "Yeah, drinking the cheap stuff for now. What I was pouring at the arena is better than this, but when you got no money coming in, what else can you do?" he joked.

Quinn peered over the heads in front of him to look the guy over, not that he'd recognize him. The sight brought him full circle to his comment at the press conference. The arena hired a fuck ton of concessionaires. If *this* guy was out of work, how many more were? He looked at the people behind him in line and what they held in their hands, then glanced down at his cart brimming with expensive craft beer, high-end rum, and several cases of wine.

When he reached the cashier, he mumbled a few instructions. The guy's eyes went wide. "Are you serious?"

"As a heart attack."

The clerk glanced at Quinn's American Express, and a knowing smile spread over his face. "Nice" was all he said before ringing him up.

Quinn hustled out of the store before anyone could slow him down. Didn't want or need the attention. Hey, if folks could buy burgers for the people behind them in the MacDonald's drive-through, why not do the same for people in a liquor store line? Though it wasn't a big deal, it buoyed him and got the gears in his head turning. Before he could call any of his teammates, though, Coach beat him to it.

Bracing himself, Quinn picked up the call. "Coach LeBrun, how are you and your family?"

"We're good, Hadley. Thanks for asking." Coach's voice sounded way different from the last time they'd spoken. *Thank fuck*. "So the reporter that's been such a pain in the ass?"

Quinn swallowed hard. "Yeah? Any news on him?"

Coach let out a mirthless chuckle. "You're gonna love this. He tested negative. But even better, they found COVID-19 antibodies in his blood."

"*What?* He's *had* it?"

"Yep. Little bastard claims he didn't know because he had it in late February. Which means he spread it himself to everyone he came in contact with."

"That's unreal!" Quinn said. "So management isn't mad at me anymore?"

"Let's just say they're enjoying having a good laugh right now, but I'd keep my head down if I were you."

"I can do that. But I have this idea I want to talk to you and the team about."

By the time he parked in the garage, he'd relayed his idea to Coach and some of his teammates about pooling their funds to help out the furloughed arena staff. The players' pay structure was still on the fuzzy side, but they'd work it out. And in the meantime, he had something productive to do.

He walked into the house with an extra bounce in his step that made him happy to have Archer greet him with a head bump. Sarah Sunshine's voice drifted from the general direction of the family room in a soft, almost sensual lilt. He stopped dead in his tracks.

"She quivered with anticipation as he laid her pliant body upon rosy satin sheets that matched her taut, throbbing nipples."

*What. The. Fuck?*

Frozen in place, he sharpened his hearing.

"He lowered himself between her pillowy thighs, and his throbbing member grazed her wet entrance, making her gasp and faint dead away."

"Oh, throbbing's in there twice," came his mother's very practical sounding voice.

A shock of electricity raced through him. *What the hell is going on?*

"Well, hey, when it throbs, it throbs," Sarah laughed.

Unsure what to do, Quinn stood like a tree that had just drilled roots into the ground.

"Keep going," his mother urged. "I can't wait to find out if he's going to do the dirty while she's out cold."

They both giggled before Sarah went on. "'Millicent, my love. Wake up, darling.' He was as hard as a hickory log, and the throbbing—"

"That's three throbbings!" his mother exclaimed. "This author needs to learn her way around a thesaurus."

"Okay. Here's the good part. Creamy mounds alert!" Sarah sounded wickedly gleeful.

Quinn burst out of his trance. *Oh hell no!* He coughed. Loudly. "I'm home." His voice sailed out of him a few octaves higher than normal.

He rounded the corner, and two pairs of eyes fastened on him.

"Quinnie!" his mother exclaimed—without a trace of guilt.

"What," he warbled, "what, ah, are you guys doing?"

Mom rubbed her hands together with delight. "Sarah's reading me a smutty romance novel about an eighteenth-century duke who's about to have his way with the chambermaid he's been lusting after." She shrugged. As though this were the most normal pastime in the world for a fifty-something mother of a grown man. Said grown man nearly choked on his spit. Meanwhile, his mom's face brightened. "Come sit down. You can listen in."

His voice cracked. "No, thanks. I'm good."

"C'mon, Sparky. You might learn a thing or two." Sarah's eyes gleamed with pure evil.

He glared at her, ready to throttle the smirk right off her face. Every last one of his good feels from the liquor store had been utterly pulverized.

His mother stood and fluttered her hand against her chest. "Whew! On second thought, maybe I need a nap after *that* literary walk on the wild side. I'm going to my room for a rest now."

Sarah giggled. "We'll pick up later when Grumpy Butt isn't around."

When his mother was out of earshot, Quinn rounded on Sarah. "What the hell was *that*?"

Sarah flipped the cover closed on her e-reader. "Afraid of a little competition?"

"From an eighteenth-century count who's not even real?" he snorted. "I doubt there's anything *he* can teach me."

Sarah rose from her seat and sauntered toward him. "From a woman author writing romance *for* women about stuff *women* like. You could add it to your arsenal and learn to be a better lover."

"Who says I need—never mind," he groused. "I'm not sure I could deal with all the *throbbing*. And you should *not* be reading that shit to my mother." He went for his wallet before Sarah could tell him to pony up the two bucks—three, if she took note of the "hell" he'd thrown out. As he stuffed the bills into the swear jar, he said, "This stack grew. Is this you?"

She bit her bottom lip and shot her eyes to the ceiling, where they lingered for a few beats. Oh shit. There was that cute look again. "Well, I was wrangling the stupid blender to make smoothies, and your mother happened to overhear—"

He let out a whoop, blowing off some of the tension that had built up inside him, though he couldn't say exactly where the tension had come from; he hadn't been tense when he'd first walked in. Whether it was being annoyed Sarah was reading this crap to his mom or whether it was *hearing* the crap in her sultry voice, he couldn't be sure. *Wait! Since when has she had a sultry voice?*

Sarah took the opportunity to size him up, raking her gaze from the sunglasses on top of his head to his feet. "I never took you for a prude."

"What the fuck does *that* mean?" *Shit! Another five bucks. Goddamn!* In pure frustration, he wrestled all the money from his wallet. "There! Now I can swear all I want."

Sarah stood on tiptoe and pretended to inspect the wad he'd thrown in. "Not *all* you want, Sparks."

He dragged a hand through his hair. "That shit you were reading. Is that *really* what women want?"

She patted his chest. "Only if they can't have you, big guy."

He face-palmed. "I give up."

"Hey, Gage was telling me about some virtual interview thing for the team in"—she dashed a look at the microwave clock—"fifteen minutes. Aren't you part of that?"

He'd been so distracted he'd nearly forgotten. "Oh shit!" Before pivoting away, he pointed at the jar. "I'm covered."

Today was his PR virtual appearance, and three of his teammates had been added to the mix. Yep. Nelson, Shanstrom, and McMurphy were now part of the fun and games. Probably to diffuse the ongoing fallout from the press conference.

A grin broke out on his face. *Wish I could've been there when Weasel Prick heard the "good" news.* The guy had sure milked the situation for all he was worth, whining on social media about Quinn and the team. *Scumbag.* Much as Quinn wanted to announce it on today's show, it wasn't his place. But he'd make sure Wyatt found out because the goalie had gotten sick and was still pissed as hell at Quinn.

"Hello, Quinn! Glad you could join us today," a voice bellowed from his computer, jerking him back to what he was *supposed* to be doing.

"Uh, hey. How's it going?" He gave a little wave to the tiny black eye above his computer screen.

The interview went the way Quinn had expected. Softball questions about what he'd been doing to keep in shape and stay busy—same questions his teammates fielded. Sarah Sunshine had sashayed past a few times with piles of clothes, making him wonder what the hell she was up to. When the interview wound down, Quinn tried to catch T.J. for a few minutes—he really needed to clear the air with the guy, but Shanny gave him a curt "Not now."

Quinn had been juggling off and on during the interview and lobbed one in frustration when Shanny cut him off. Unfortunately, it bounced off Sarah's right shoulder as she was breezing by. She stopped and turned. "Trying to tell me something, Sparky?"

"Sorry, it got away from me. But jeez, toots. That's your third or fourth pass. Miss me that much?" he taunted.

She parked her fist on her hip. "In case you didn't know, there's a laundry room down this way. I'm doing the dirty clothes—including yours—and this is the shortest route, so passing by your office is a necessity, not a desire."

"So sue me for not knowing. There are like five laundry rooms in this place. Wait. You're doing *my* laundry?" Why the hell was she doing that? She wasn't the damn maid.

"Uh, because your mom can't and she asked me? No maid service while we're sheltering in place, Sparky."

Oh. Right. Well, didn't he feel like an ungrateful jerk. "Uh, thanks for doing that."

"How'd the interview go?"

"Meh, about what I expected. You know, though, there's one thing that always bugs the shit out of me." Why was he going here?

"What's that?"

"Whenever they find out I've got an engineering degree, they act so damn surprised. Like I'm too stupid to have graduated in basket weaving, let alone earned a BE."

"I get the same thing."

"You do?" Stupid and Sarah didn't go together. *Annoying* and Sarah, yes, but not stupid.

"Oh yeah, but it's a little different. It's more of a shocked look they get when they discover a woman could be a structural engineer."

"No way. Not in this day and age."

"Way. There are lots of holdouts who haven't caught up to the twenty-first century. I feel like I'm being patronized sometimes, like they think what I'm doing is 'cute' when I really should be home taking care of my man."

"Nothing wrong with that." He knew better, he really did, but he couldn't keep from needling her. Nor could he keep from making it worse. "Maybe if you had the *right* kind of man at home—"

"You're really going there?" She shot him a look that told him he was skating on thin ice. "Don't tell me, let me guess. If I had someone as awesome as 'The Mighty Quinn,' he'd become the center of the universe and I would be completely fulfilled?"

He grinned. "Sounds about right."

She stooped, and before he knew what was coming, she hurled the beanbag at his head—and connected—then stomped off.

# Chapter 13

## Caution: Slippery When Wet

*What an ass!*

Sarah huffed and puffed into the kitchen. "Jerk! Why do I even try talking to the man? And why, oh why, do I let him get under my skin?"

"What did you say, Sunshine?" His closeness caught her by surprise, and she wheeled and yelped. When had he come up behind her?

"I need to hang a bell around your neck."

He snorted. "Not gonna happen. Now what did you say?"

Instead of backing away, she pulled herself upright with all the kick-ass she had and waved him off. "You talk as if I'd be helpless to resist the Mighty Quinn if you decided I was your type." What was wrong with her? She knew better than to goad him, damn it! Even *knowing* she was playing into his hands, she couldn't seem to stop herself.

Amusement flickered in his warm cocoa eyes, and his fresh man-and-soap scent wafted up her nose. She gave herself an inner shake and reminded herself how everything about him irritated the hell out of her. Except he'd gone to special lengths to make sure she and Archer were well accommodated—hell, Sparky wasn't even a dog lover—not to mention how generous he'd been with her salary. He'd opened up his house to her, making her feel as though she belonged there. Crap, he'd even *thanked* her for how she'd been treating his mom, as if it were a big burden, which it wasn't.

With a shrug and a smirk, he plucked a trio of limes from a bowl on the counter and began juggling. "Lots of women seem to like the Mighty Quinn."

"Is that a pet name for your dick?" She let out an unabashed *bahaha*.

He ignored her.

"Just because you're a hotshot hockey player with a great smile doesn't mean you know what a woman wants in the sack."

Eyes trained on the limes, he broadened his grin, displaying his pearly whites. "You think I have a great smile?"

"Seriously? That's all you got out of that?" Her eyes followed the circling green mini-footballs, then came to rest on his handsome face, decorated in day-old scruff, as he concentrated on what he was doing. His tongue protruded, caught between his teeth. Yeah, add that sculpted body to the mix, and she got why women fell all over themselves for this cocky, class-A jerk. He'd be hard to resist once he pulled out all the charm stops. Well, not hard for *her* to resist because she knew who and what he was. That probably didn't apply to the rest of the female population, however—*especially* blond bimbos in danger of being dragged down from the weight of their boobs and lack of anything in their heads.

"No, I got the whole thing. But I gotta say—and not to brag or anything—if we're scoring by orgasms, I'm pretty sure I'm okay in the sack. The Mighty Quinn doesn't do anything halfway." He caught all three limes and leveled a devilish look at her.

Heat surged in her core, and she burst out with a laugh to mask it. "You do understand women fake orgasms. All. The. Time."

"Yeah, well, that may be …" He sounded mildly irritated, which made her smirk. Snatching up the limes once more, he tossed them in the air.

*Whoa! He's pretty damn good at juggling.* "How long have you been doing that?" She tracked the limes, letting them lull her.

He didn't take his eyes off the spinning fruit. "Juggling or having sex?"

She stifled the urge to reach out and snatch one of his stupid limes just to watch him screw up. "Juggling. I don't give a flip about your sex life."

"Since I was a kid. Mom got me started. It was one way to keep me distracted so I didn't drive her crazy." He smoothly caught the limes and flashed Sarah another grin. "Ask her sometime. I was a handful. She used to drop me off at the rink for hours at a time. She was trying to wear me out so she could deal with me."

"Like Michael Phelps, but on ice? Turned out well for MP."

"Yeah, I guess it turned out well for me too." His expression suddenly morphed into something akin to sadness. In that moment, his eyes reminded her of hot fudge sauce. Warm, dark, deep.

She gave herself *another* inner shake. "Was it a bad thing that it turned out well for you?"

"It was for my dad and my brother, Ronan." He stared at her for a beat, as if he had something else he wanted to say. Instead, he seemed to snap back from wherever he'd gone. "Welp, if I'm gonna get another workout in, I'd better hop to it and let you get back to your trashy novels." His teasing tone was back, and he winked at her. It should have annoyed the hell out of her, but something—she had no idea what—had temporarily dulled her desire to fire back an insult.

"I thought you were done working out?"

"I'm a little restless."

"Any luck with the TP?"

"No." He suddenly looked stricken. "Oh shit! I totally forgot about the flour."

"I'll go tomorrow."

His dark eyes narrowed. "Don't you have laundry to wrangle? I'll go. It was my screw-up." He turned and trotted away.

*What?* Somewhere in her addled brain, it occurred to her that the last few sentences of their conversation made up a rare civilized exchange between them since she'd moved to Denver.

They were cleaning up after dinner while Liz was engrossed in a romcom and petting Archer, who was, as usual, by her side in the family room.

Quinn stacked plates beside the sink for Sarah to rinse. "So. Wolf. Is that short for Wolfgang? Like the composer or Eddie Van Halen's kid?"

She whipped her head toward him but didn't see a telltale smirk. Still, her stomach clenched. "No. Just Wolf."

"That should've been your first clue the guy was a piece of work." He laughed out loud, and her clench turned to flaring white heat.

"Meaning what?" She shoved the rinsed plates at him and barked, "Dishwasher," not bothering to hold back her irritation.

Quinn flinched but managed to take the stack from her. "Meaning he's a tweeze because he was raised by parents who named him after a shaggy animal that howls. And if they're *not* the ones guilty of giving him the lame name, it means he named himself, which makes him an even bigger tweeze."

This brought her to an abrupt stop. She turned and faced him, fist on her hip. "As *usual*, you have no fucking clue what you're talking about. I think the name is incredibly strong and sexy."

"Yeah, well, you would." As he arranged the dishes in the dishwasher, he calmly added, "Jar, Sunshine."

"For what?" she whisper-screeched.

"You said 'no fucking clue.' That's a fiver."

A laugh from the family room startled them both. They peeked from the kitchen and spied Liz rubbing her hands together. She did that a lot whenever one of them tossed out a blue word. "This is by far the easiest job I've ever had! And the best paying!"

*Shit! What else did Liz hear?* A flush crept up Sarah's neck, and she tiptoed back to the sink, out of sight, stifling a groan.

Quinn retreated too. "Who says the money in the jar is for you, Mom?" He stabbed his finger toward the family room and whispered to Sarah, "Mom radar." Then he pointed to the back of his head, then at his eyes.

"She might be worse than *my* mom," Sarah mouthed back. They shared a snicker, which surprised her because she felt as though she'd just landed in the Quinn camp. Oddly nice.

"Well, then, what are you going to do with it all? There's a small fortune in those jars," his mother called back.

Without missing a beat, he yelled, "Thought I'd donate it to help out folks who are losing their jobs because of COVID."

Sarah's eyes shot to his, but he wasn't looking at her. *Is he serious?* A cursory sweep of his face told her he was. She could've been knocked over with a feather at *this* unexpected gesture.

"Oh, Quinnie, that's a wonderful idea. You're always so thoughtful like that."

"It's not that big a deal, Mom." There was a trace of peevishness in his voice. His cheekbones were flushed bright pink, and he fidgeted, seeming to avoid Sarah's stare. When he finally darted a glance at her, he tossed out an annoyed-sounding, "What? Don't you need to finish cleaning up?"

She opened her mouth automatically to hurl a barb as yet unformed but stopped herself. Why wasn't this egomaniac soaking up the compliment and growing even cockier? Instead, he seemed embarrassed, almost as if he'd been outed for a good deed.

Abruptly, he headed for his wing with a "'Night."

*Huh.* What other surprises was Quinn Hadley hiding?

Restless and unsure why, Quinn retreated to the gym for one more session once dinner finally settled in his stomach. Two hours later, his jolting energy somewhat dissipated, he walked into a deserted kitchen. He pulled a cold bottle of water from the fridge and placed it against his sweaty forehead while he caught his breath. The kitchen was dim, lit only by the under-cabinet lighting. Where was everybody? Even Archer was MIA.

A faint noise tickled his ears, and he paused to listen. It sounded like … high-pitched voices? He wandered to the French doors that led outside and peered through. The deck was submerged in darkness. Then a motion caught his eye, and he lasered in on it. Two dark shapes hovered by the hot tub. He'd solved the mystery of the noise only to ponder a new one. What the hell were his mom and Sarah up to?

A motion-sensor light came on—triggered, apparently, by Archer's madly swinging tail—and the forms froze. His mom's wide eyes were clearly visible as she lay across the edge of the hot tub. Sarah, whose back was to him, appeared to be helping her climb out. Though she was muffled through the thick glass, he distinctly heard his mother whoop. Then she burst out laughing, and Sarah folded over, bracing herself on the rim of the hot tub as her shoulders shook.

They couldn't see him, but he could clearly see them, so he paused to watch. His eyes had been pulled to Sarah immediately, to her wet skin glistening in the light. And there was a lot of skin to glisten because, Jesus, she was wearing very little: a bikini top tied with straps no bigger than skate laces and bottoms that barely covered the crack of her ass. What little fabric there was clung to her and outlined her contours. He needed little imagination to calculate how well her perfect ass cheeks would fit in his hands.

*Shit!*

He closed his eyes and shook his head, trying to dislodge the image from his brain. He did *not* need to be picturing himself fondling his buddy's sister's gorgeous ass. *Scratch that. Her ass is. Not. Gorgeous.* Too bad his stirring dick wasn't buying it. He willed it to calm the fuck down, envisioning a pissed-off Gage and how messed up their line chemistry would be if Quinn pulled anything.

And though he knew, *he knew*, he shouldn't be ogling Gage's sister, that's exactly what he continued doing. Couldn't tear his eyes away, especially when her movements caused her cute booty to jiggle enticingly.

The light winked off again, and more giggling followed. A thought pierced his lust-ridden brain. He should be helping because, at the rate they were going, Sarah was going to end up on that beautiful ass of hers while his mother slipped back under the water.

After rearranging his clothes, he flipped on the deck lights and stepped outside, leaning forward to disguise his obvious problem. Sarah's head jerked, and two pairs of wide eyes landed on him. Then they both dissolved in laughter again. His gaze bounced around the perimeter of the hot tub, taking in towels, an empty bottle of wine, and two glasses.

*They're hammered!*

"What's going on out here?" He was struggling to keep amusement from his voice. These two did not need *any* encouragement.

Sarah wheeled and faced him, and before he could stop himself, his eyes took a quick tour of her wet body, landing back on her grinning face. Jesus, the girl was smoking hot! Not that he hadn't suspected it, but here, with her facing him, her fully displayed ample assets would not be denied a starring role in his dirty mind. Sleek, toned legs, a flat stomach that hinted at a lady six-pack. Breasts bigger than expected—because damn if they weren't spilling out of her skimpy top—with beaded nipples imprinting the triangles of fabric laughingly called a swimsuit top. Everything was arranged in one hell of a perfect package.

He blew out a breath—praying she couldn't see the surging tent in his shorts—and willed himself to keep his eyes fixed on hers. Not wander anywhere below her chin. Yeah, he could do that. Absolutely. Maybe.

She smirked as if she knew *exactly* the effect she was having on him. "Your mom and I …" She paused to laugh some more while his mom snorted in the background. "Your mom and I decided to socially distance out here with a bottle of wine. We stayed six feet apart"—she slid her eyes upward as if pondering—"mostly. We also figured the heat would kill off any viruses."

Hysterical, his mom banged her hand against the hot tub's edge. Rolling his eyes, he crossed his arms over his chest. "Do you need my help to get her out?"

"Sure," Sarah giggled. "I've been trying, but …"

"She can't pull me out!" his mom hooted. "I'm too slippery!"

For Christ's sake, these two were drunk as skunks. Suddenly, Sarah began to shiver, so he darted to the towels, grabbed one, and awkwardly tossed it over her shoulders. "Here." He didn't dare touch her.

She wrapped it around her body—*thank fuck!*—and he proceeded to help his mom out of the tub. Her limbs were a little floppy, so he reached in and hoisted her into his arms. Seemed easier.

"Ooh, look Sarah," his mother said, "Just like Lord Lanternjaw in *The Lady's Lustful Lover*." Then she gave his shoulder a playful slap. "You're sweeping the wrong one off her feet. You should be sweeping Sarah off *her* feet."

*No, I really shouldn't.* He muttered a PG curse and took his mom inside.

After depositing her, he stuck his head out the door again, looking anywhere and everywhere but directly at Sarah. "Uh, you good out here? Need any more help?"

She materialized right beside him, nearly shooting him out of his shorts. "No, I'm good. But thanks." Her voice was on the breathy side.

He rolled his lips between his teeth and gave her a quick head bob before turning away. The energy he'd spent during the workout was surging through his bloodstream once more, and he loped down his hallway, chased by his mother's voice. "I think we scared him. Let's open another bottle of wine." More giggling ensued.

In his bedroom, he swiped the beanies from his nightstand and started tossing. Goddamn, this shelter-in-place crap was going to kill him. Couldn't go out, couldn't have anyone over. Bottom line: couldn't get laid. He definitely could use a good grinding fuck right about now. Maybe it would bleach the image of somebody's sister from his brain.

Despite his desire that Sarah stop messing with his mind, a picture of her in that nothing bikini played across his inner movie screen, and he missed one of his beanies. It hit the carpet with a soft thud, followed by the other two. He sighed as he picked them up and swapped them for his *other* phone. Facetime sex might keep him sane.

Closing and locking his bedroom doors, he toed off his shoes and plopped on the edge of the bed, where he turned on the phone and began scrolling through his contacts. He imagined each woman as her name glowed on the screen. Not a single one netted his interest. With a frustrated huff, he tossed his phone on the bed and yanked off his clothes. He headed for the shower, where he planned to kill two birds with one stone: jerking off and getting cleaned up.

He turned on both spray heads in his shower-built-for-many and soaped himself up as hot water peppered his skin. Sarah popped into his consciousness, so vivid he could've sworn she was standing in the shower with him. As if he could reach out and run his soapy hands over her slick, wet skin. Tease those tantalizing tits. Cup the softness between her thighs. Kiss her lips and plunder her soft mouth.

Though he told himself to knock it off, his dick would have none of it. The urge was too powerful, and it took over. Fueled by an image of Sarah's body in his brain, her lush mouth whispering erotic, dirty words in his ear, he came hard and fast.

Spent, he planted his palms against the shower walls to hold himself up, gasping in air. Jesus, what had happened? He couldn't remember jacking off and coming like *that* before. As if something potent had taken possession and moved through his body.

He shook his head. The *only* reason the vivid vision of Sarah had blazed in his brain was because she was the closest fuckable female. That had to be it. He could not, would not, let himself fantasize about her again. *She's off-limits. Just get her out of your mind now.* Problem was, he wasn't confident he could heed his own advice.

# Chapter 14

## Lockdown is a State of Mind

The next day, while Liz napped and Quinn was out for a run, Sarah had her nose in the fridge, humming to eighties music playing on her phone. She ran her eyes over the fridge's inventory. What could she make out of broccoli and ham? "Empanadas," she said aloud. "Crap. I don't have enough flour for the pastry."

"You have flour now," Quinn's deep voice rumbled behind her, and she let out a surprised yelp. She whirled just as he plopped an armful of brown paper bags on the counter.

"You went to the grocery store?" she screeched. "I thought you were running."

He flashed her an apologetic grin. "I was. After my run, I drove right by King Soopers and thought I'd check for you—"

"I was gonna go." She closed the fridge door behind her.

The smile faded, and a vertical crease formed between his dark eyebrows. "I was right there."

She cinched her arms over her chest, fighting the urge to acknowledge how sweet she found his gesture. "You've just screwed up my plan for the day."

His face dropped.

The crestfallen look gave her a surge of guilt, and she rushed on. "How am I supposed to trash-talk you when you do something nice?"

The grin returned with a triumphant twist. "Wait'll you see what else I got." Out came a humongous package of chocolate morsels that he laid on the counter. "In case someone feels the urge to make more cookies. Oh, and I went with paper bags because I read they're great for letting the cookies cool. Dual purpose."

She'd baked one batch of sugar cookies—one—since she'd arrived, and apparently he'd picked up on the fuss she'd made about how to properly cool them. Newspaper, her go-to choice, hadn't been available.

Suppressing her astonishment, she said, "I have bad news, Sparky. No flour."

He held up a finger. "But wait!" His delivery reminded her of a TV pitchman.

She watched his retreating back as he jogged toward the garage. Minutes later, he reappeared hefting a huge-ass bag of flour, and her mouth dropped open of its own accord.

He set it down. "I scored a twenty-five-pounder!"

Before she knew what she was doing, she flew to him and looped her arms around his solid neck. Oh God, his hard body felt even better than she'd imagined. Not that she'd looked that closely. Oh hell, who was she kidding? She noticed every damn time he was around.

For a nanosecond, he rocked backward, arms at his sides. Then he swept her to him and hugged her back. He fit her beautifully.

*What the hell am I doing?* Recovering her lost senses, she shoved herself away. "Um, thank you." Then she broke out in a smirk. "A little self-serving, isn't it?"

He looked dazed and stared at her for a beat before putting all his attention on the still-full brown bags. Keeping his head down, he began emptying them. "How so?"

She ignored the tingles racing up and down her limbs. "Well, you're the biggest cookie consumer in this house …"

"You noticed that, huh?" He raised his head, and a half-smile that managed to show off his dimples quirked. He patted his firm stomach "Since you started staying here, I've packed on an extra ten."

"Could've fooled me," she huffed. She was trying to sound annoyed, she really was, but her hip-hopping hormones got in the way. And honestly? He didn't look—or feel—as though he had an ounce of fat on him.

She swallowed. “Anyway, thank you. That was really thoughtful of you.”

His head dipped, and he returned to his unpacking. “I know, huh? Sometimes I even surprise myself.”

Without another word, she planted herself beside him and helped unload the bags. They worked side by side, putting away the foodie treasures. Finally, she said, “You really shouldn’t have gone. You’re exposing yourself to COVID every time you step into a store.”

He flapped a dismissive hand. “Pfft. I’m a big, strong hockey player, remember? I don’t get sick.”

“Yeah, well, *other* big, strong hockey players are getting sick, so don’t think you’re immune. Whatever happened with that tweeze-head reporter, by the way?”

“I didn’t tell you? The guy tested negative for the virus but positive for the antibodies. He’d already had it!”

“What? Is the team going to make him apologize publicly? He was a totally Twitter jerk about this whole thing.”

“Didn’t know you were paying attention, Sunshine.” He scooped a handful of nuts from a bowl she kept filled on the counter and popped them in his mouth.

Her cheeks heated. “I assume your teammates know. Are they talking to you again?”

“Mostly. I’ve been texting or talking with nearly everyone. They’ve more or less moved on, except Wyatt.”

She chuckled. “Well, what do you expect? He’s a goalie. They’re *all* temperamental. And superstitious. Well, all players are superstitious.”

He stopped chewing, and she hurried on, trying to fill the awkward silence. “Hockey’s my favorite sport by far. I love seeing the athletes’ reflexes, their strength, their bursts of speed. It’s breathtaking.”

She side-eyed him. His eyebrows had crawled up his forehead, and his mouth hung open. Evidently she’d shocked him.

He shook his head, seeming to recover, and smirked. “Who’s your favorite player?”

She didn’t skip a beat. “Gretzky.”

“No, I meant present day.”

Now it was her turn to smirk. “My brother, of course.”

“Damn.” He nodded. “But I totally get that. It’s the safe answer.”

“You honestly didn’t think I’d say *you* were, did you?”

A gleam lit his eyes. "You wouldn't be the first if you had."

She gave him her best eye-roll and went back to unpacking. "So fu—darn cocky."

A laugh rumbled through his chest. "Good catch, toots. So you making empanadas tonight?"

"Yeah, if that sounds good."

"Sounds great. Can you pack some with meat?"

"I'll see what I can do, caveman."

"Need any help?"

She narrowed her eyes at him. "Why are you being so nice?"

He shrugged. "I don't know. In a good mood, I guess. Don't feel like fighting." He broke out in Alabama Shakes's "Don't Wanna Fight," his voice possibly at a higher screech level than the lead singer's.

She stared at him for a few beats. Maybe he hadn't gone running at all. Maybe he'd gotten himself laid instead. The notion made her stomach sink a little, so she pushed it away. "I don't need help, but thanks."

"Better make lots." He waggled his eyebrows. "I'm going downstairs to work off the cookies I hope you're making along with the empanadas."

She was still gaping at the doorway after he'd left. Maintaining her dislike for him twenty-four-seven was becoming much harder.

Quinn couldn't take it anymore. Being cooped up just shy of two weeks with two nutty women was making him squirrely. That *had* to explain why Sarah Sunshine was on his mind. All. The. Freaking. Time. It would also explain what had motivated him to do something nice for her and why her reaction had made him feel like he could fly.

Not to mention what her commentary about hockey had done to him. His insides had cartwheeled at the possibility of carrying on an intelligent conversation with her about his sport. And goddamn, goalies *were* temperamental!

What he needed right now was to whack a fuck ton of pucks and work her out of his system—except she wasn't *in* his system. Was she?

He continued this debate with himself as he set up his shooting pad and dumped out a bucket of pucks in his driveway. Next he hung a screen that covered his garage door with an image of a goalie and five shooting targets. A few shots in, however, the very object of his frustration appeared.

"Hey, want some help with your drills?" Sarah stood to the side, hands in her back pockets, her eyes trained on the screen.

He stopped and straightened.

Her gaze swung to his. "I used to help Gage before he went pro. I'm not very good with a stick, but apparently I'm good enough to get in the way and be a pest, which was what he said he needed." She grinned.

"Why am I not surprised?" He grinned back.

He grabbed gloves and a stick for her—a shorter one from his juniors days—and soon they were marching through drills. She was better at stick handling than she'd given herself credit for, plus she had an uncanny ability to poke the puck away or get her body in the right place and impede his progress. Subtle, smart moves. In other words, she was a perfect drill partner. Plus, she could talk like one too.

"You really mix up your shots. Do you have a sweet spot?" she said as they took a water break.

"Top shelf, left," he replied without thought.

She gave him an approving nod. "Where Mama keeps the peanut butter."

A slow grin began to spread. "Exactly. Show me what else you know, toots."

And she did. He got so lost in the play that he zenned himself into a hockey zone. Unfortunately, it didn't eliminate the thoughts he'd been trying to displace—like the visual of her in her itty-bitty, wet bikini molded to her curves like a second skin. No, instead he kept picturing her working out beside him wearing nothing but *that.*

And who could blame him? Every time she was near, her scent drifted around him and beckoned him a little closer. He craved physical contact.

Jesus, he needed to get laid.

As quickly as the truism popped into his brain, he shoved it down. Even if he could indulge in a quick-and-dirty with someone *not* Sarah, that someone might pass on COVID that *he* could pass on to his mom. He wasn't *that* desperate—or that selfish.

While she stood to the side, he took a dozen more shots, trying harder with each pass for something fancy that would impress her—a spin-o-rama or between-the-legs move. Instead, he ended up looking like he didn't know how to score. To make matters worse, things below his waistband had perked up since they'd started their drills, growing into a wicked distraction.

Getting a boner around his buddy's sister should never happen. Yeah, he absolutely needed to get laid. It would solve everything.

They stowed the gear and headed in different directions inside. He wound up in the gym, where he picked up a trio of beanbags, trying to calm down his overactive imagination. Unfortunately, the damn thing wandered right back to Sarah and what a firecracker she'd be in bed. *Shit, don't go there!* He forced his wayward thoughts to this Wolf dude, and he tried to picture the man who'd breached her defenses and made it to her softer side. Some badass biker with colors, prison tats, and a bandanna? *Wolf* would fit the bill.

Wait. She didn't *have* a softer side. Who was he kidding? Of course she had one because he'd witnessed it firsthand whenever she interacted with his mom or Archer.

It was just *him* she didn't trot it out for. Although she'd trotted it out today, blowing the hell out of his mind when she'd hugged him for one stuttering heartbeat. Damn, she'd felt good against him. And she'd rewarded him with lively drill play. If only it could be more than *hockey* drill play …

*No, no, no, you perv!*

Maybe if he showed her more random acts of kindness, stopped goading her, she'd return the favor by using a little less acid on him. His mom had told him to use his charm. What did that mean, exactly? Use the same worn lines on Sarah that he used on women he picked up?

He practically laughed out loud at this idiotic idea. No doubt she would shred him into pieces so tiny they'd never be able to glue him back together again. No, that girl would need a custom approach if he were ever inclined to make a move, which he wasn't. No matter *how* many times he had to remind himself.

The loop in his ADHD-addled mind led him back to thoughts of Wolf and why Sarah thought his name was "strong and sexy" … and why the hell he was wasting so much time on Sarah Sunshine and Wolfman anyway. Frustration over his current train of thought had Quinn lobbing the beanbags across the room. Time to attack the rowing machine.

He definitely needed to get laid.

As he was in the grip of sorting his ping-ponging thoughts, his phone vibrated. "Dude, have you got ESP?"

"No," Nelson replied. "Why? Have you been dreaming about me again?"

"You're as funny as a broken skate blade, asshole. No, I was actually thinking about your sister and wondering about the douche she broke up with. They did break up, right?"

"Uh, yeah. Why?" Nelson's tone hovered between baffled and brotherly I'll-tear-your-head-from-your-body-if-you-touch-her.

"He called her the other day and seemed to shake her up. I offered her a phone, but she didn't want it. Your sister is stubborn as shit."

"You're just now figuring this out?" Gage paused to chuckle. "I knew about Douchebag calling her. I told her to come back here because Lily, Daisy, and I are clearing out for a while."

For some unknown reason, the thought of Sarah leaving gave Quinn a gut check. "Where are you guys going?"

"Beckett and Paige offered us their mountain house. Nobody's using it, it's bigger and more isolated than our place, and it has a full gym. With Daisy out of school, I took them up on it. We're about to head up. So Sarah's welcome to come back here—she'd have the whole place to herself—but she said she wants to stay at your place. I just thought I'd fill you in so you know that option's open. In case you get to a breaking point and are contemplating murder—or she is." He laughed as if this was the funniest joke in the world, which it wasn't.

Knowing that Sarah had told her brother she wanted to stay made Quinn's chest fill with something warm and gooey. Maybe she didn't hate him after all. "She like it here that much?" He tried to keep the surprise from his voice.

"Nah, I think she's more worried about Douchebag showing up at our place. He has no idea where to find her if she stays with you, so all in all, it's a smart move."

The warm goo cooled a few degrees, followed by a spike of anger. "Back up a sec. Is this guy coming for her?"

"She doesn't think so, but I suspect she's a little worried he might."

"Well, he'd better not try anything if he doesn't want to get his ass handed to him. Nobody messes with—uh, your sister."

"Sarah's more than capable of taking care of herself, but I appreciate you watching out for her, buddy."

After dinner, Quinn put his mom to bed, then retreated to his room and flicked on his TV. Bored as shit, he flicked it off, and his mind roamed to the fresh batch of cookies downstairs. A half dozen and a full glass of milk might put him into snooze mode, so he traipsed back to the kitchen.

He was surprised to find Sarah sitting in the mostly dark family room, knees drawn up under a quilt, Archer curled at her feet. A cozy scene. The dog raised his head and gave him a friendly chuff. Sarah turned her head toward him.

"Hey," she said softly. He liked the tone of her voice. No edge. Inviting.

"Hey. Why are you sitting alone in the dark?" He walked her way and dropped into an armchair perpendicular to the couch.

On her lap she held an illuminated iPad. "Just winding down now that everything's quiet."

He peered at her device. "Reading more smutty romance stuff?"

She shook her head. "No. I'm watching *Impossible Engineering*. Nerdy stuff."

"Huh. I like that show."

"So what are *you* doing? I thought you went to bed."

"No, it's not that late. I just wanted to check on you." Not exactly true, but what the hell?

"Check on me? Why?"

"I talked to Gage, and he said you're uncomfortable going back to his place." Entirely true.

Even in the dimness, he could see her eyes widen. "Oh. Do you want me to leave? I know we don't exactly—"

He put up his hand, palm out. "No, no. I'd rather you stay. My mom's … Shit, my mom's improvement is amazing. I can't believe what you've done for her already."

"It's not me." She shrugged, which drew his attention to a thin, stretchy, white strap under the oversized sweater that kept slipping off her shoulder. "She had the desire all along. She just needed a nudge."

Guilt washed over him. "Yeah, I should have tried harder."

"Don't beat yourself up, Sparky. Between moving into a new place and being on the road, your life was a little chaotic. It's amazing you pulled off what you did. I think it's sweet how concerned you are about her."

A tickle in his belly flustered him. He hadn't done shit and didn't deserve a compliment from Sarah Sunshine, no matter how much he craved it. The "fidgets," as his mother had called them when he was a kid, bumped through his body, making him twitch. He sprang up. "Well, uh, I just wanted you to know that if you're ever worried about Wolf, come get me. Day or night."

"Thanks."

He turned to leave.

"Do you play cribbage?" she asked.

"What?"

"Cribbage. You know, a game involving a board with pegs and a deck of cards?"

He scratched the back of his neck. Jeez, he needed a haircut. "It's been a while. I think we used to play as kids."

She tilted her head and smiled—a slow, subtle smile that curved her sensuous lips—and watched him as if waiting for something.

What she was trying to say finally got through to him. "What? You want to play cribbage *now*?"

"Why not? You got something better to do? Let's see if you can put your money where your mouth is." And just like that, the smirk was back. For a brief second, he wondered what it would take to bring that *other* smile back—the one that seemed alluringly private.

"Wait. My mouth hasn't claimed anything when it comes to cribbage."

Sarah twirled her hand. "Not specifically, but it sort of goes along with the whole cocky thing you've got going. C'mon. Let me beat your ass at something else."

"That's a buck."

"No, it's not. I thought we decided 'ass' is not a swear word."

"When you say it, it is."

"Why?"

"Because I wanted to give you shit."

"Two bucks!" she cried triumphantly.

"Fu—I totally walked into that one."

"C'mon, Sparky. Let's have some fun. Or are you chickensh—sherbet? The game *does* involve counting, after all."

"Chicken sherbet?" he chortled. "How about you and I make a deal?"

She quirked a suspicious eyebrow. "What kind of deal?"

"As long as Mom's not around, we forget the swear jar and say what comes naturally."

A long, slow nod. "I like it. I'm in."

Ha! They were on the same side for a change; it had only taken swearing. All of him suddenly sparked like he'd been dosed with caffeine. Even parts of him that shouldn't. What was wrong with him? Oh, right. He had a bad case of the fidgets, and he needed to get laid.

She eyed him. "So, cribbage? Or are you afraid the counting will tax your brain?"

Yeah, he could use Sarah Sunshine's stupid game—and her sass—as a distraction. What the hell could it hurt? "Hey, I can count. Otherwise, I wouldn't have a degree—"

"In engineering. Blah, blah. Yeah, yeah." One corner of her mouth curled up. "We all know how smart you think you are. Now stop bragging and get some cards. I'll grab my cribbage board."

Before he could toss back a retort, she was sashaying away, Archer on her heels. Quinn tried not to look at the way her hips swayed or the roundness of her ass in her yoga pants. Instead, he tried to imagine Nelson choking him out, but somehow his eyes lingered on Sarah's curvy backside and made him wonder—again—at the softness under the fabric.

*What the actual fuck is wrong with me? And how many more times am I going to ask myself that question?*

Her voice sliced through his fog, bringing to mind the sound of gnashing teeth. Nothing soft about it. "Cards, Sparky. Hop to it." He snapped right the hell back to the here-and-now and hustled in search of a deck of cards.

Three winless games and three beers later, Quinn hopped up to grab more brews while Sarah shuffled the deck. Gas flames danced in the fireplace, and mellow music played in the background with Sarah humming along. Either his fidgets had finally simmered down or he was beer-buzzed. Three shots of rum might have had something to do with it too. In the kitchen, he fished out two cold ones, popped them open, handing one to Sarah when he walked back into the family room.

Graceful eyebrows rose to her hairline. "*Another* beer? I haven't finished the last one you gave me."

He got caught in her gaze and quickly shook himself free. "Your eyes change color. Did you know that?"

"Yep. Depends on mood, lighting, all kinds of things. They're usually brownish-green, but they can vary from golden brown to gray-green and anything in between. They used to turn blue when I was a kid. They're also two different colors, just like Gage's." She paused a beat, taking in what must have been his confused expression. "Haven't you ever noticed Gage's eyes are two distinct shades of blue?"

"Uh, no. Then again, I've never stared into *his* eyes."

Apparently, she found this very amusing because—besides overlooking his slip about staring into her eyes—she snorted and doubled over. "Yeah, Gage might rearrange that pretty face of yours if you gave *him* the googly eyes."

*Googly eyes?* Nah, no way did Quinn give Sarah anything remotely resembling googly eyes. Okay. So maybe he wasn't the only one buzzed.

Sarah's head was swimming in a gurgling stream of happy bubbles. She dealt the cards and finished off the third beer before starting on the fresh one Quinn had brought her. Damn, she hoped she could count accurately during this round. The last round had been a challenge, but then again, Quinn wasn't doing any better because she'd whooped his ass three times in a row. *I don't do anything halfway.* No, he was losing *all* the way.

She began giggling uncontrollably. She should have felt self-conscious, but Quinn wore an amused look that broadcast it was safe to let herself go a little on his watch. He had such a nice smile. Why had she thought this guy was a jerk again?

"Are you trying to get me drunk so you can get into my panties?" she blurted.

A sly grin—complete with devastating dimples—slowly spread across his stubbled face. "Sweetheart, if I decided to get into your panties, I wouldn't need to get you drunk."

*Now* she remembered why he was a jerk. She hadn't had *that* much to drink. "Right. You'd have to knock me unconscious instead because that's the *only* way you'd score."

He let out a guffaw.

"What? You think I'm kidding?" she snapped.

"Not at all," he wheezed between chuckles.

"I forgot. I'm not your type." She gathered up the cards and began shuffling.

He pointed at the stack of cards in her hand. "Hey, you just dealt!"

*Whoops.* "I didn't like the look of that hand," she countered. He seemed to accept her explanation because he shut up and watched while she shuffled again. She dashed a look his way. "My brother says you like them young and dumb."

"Your brother should mind his own damn business. Seriously, do you guys tell each other *everything*?" He had a cute little smirk on his face.

"Ew, no." She slapped the stack of cards down and pointed. "Cut."

"Well, *you're* definitely not dumb." His pronouncement completely blindsided her. "And you're not exactly old either."

*What the hell does* that *mean?* She couldn't quite figure out what he was saying … if he was, in fact, saying anything logical. "I'm older than *you*, Sparky." Now she just sounded like a stupid kid. Damn it! Why did she care what she sounded like in front of him? A question for a more sober moment.

He cut the cards. "By five years. That's not *older*. It's just downright hot."

She couldn't hide her surprise when she flicked her eyes to him. "Excuse me?"

The smirk she expected was gone. Instead, he was fidgeting again, as if he were embarrassed. "You gonna deal?" He ran one of his big hands—with his long, strong fingers—through that thick head of rock-star hair.

*Why the hell am I noticing his hair? Not to mention his hands. At least I'm not focused on his broad shoulders or muscular chest. Probably because I memorized them already. Shit.*

Keeping her head down, she did deal, but she felt his eyes boring into her the entire time, watching her every move. Either his sudden intensity was making chills rush up and down her spine or she was coming down with COVID-19. Either option was bad, bad, bad.

They settled quietly back into the game, though she was having a hard time concentrating on her cards. *Shit. What do these numbers add up to?*

"So, uh, I'm curious what happened with you and Wolf that's got you worried he might come to Denver," he ventured. "If you're up for telling me. But you don't have to." He tipped the beer bottle to his lips and guzzled.

Sarah appraised him for a beat. "Gage didn't tell you?"

He shrugged. "Just said you guys broke up."

She let out a little hmph. "More like imploded. Detonated. A nuclear meltdown." She tried to imitate the sound of an exploding bomb.

Quinn chuckled. "You sound like something's stuck in your throat. This is how it's supposed to sound." He performed an epic imitation of an exploding bomb.

She clapped. "That's really good. Bet you do great car sounds too."

He nodded.

"I wish I could, but I think I need a penis. Being able to make realistic sounds is like a perk God throws into the package to compensate for men's … uh …" She had no idea what word to plug into the blank.

His eyes danced with mischief. "Charisma is the word you're looking for, toots. And it *complements*, not compensates."

"Does that pickup bullshit actually work? Please say it isn't so because I'm going to have to revoke my membership in the girl's club."

"And do what?" he laughed. "Join the boy's club?" He swept his eyes over her body, twice, lingering longer each time. "That would be a downright shame—and a waste of woman." His gravelly voice zapped her nerve endings, leaving her flustered. Between the timbre of his voice and the heated look in his eyes, her panties were about to go up in flames. He was giving off all the wrong signals, and her reactions were equally wrong. The alcohol merely added fuel to the fire. *Damn!*

She rose, teetered, shoved his rock-hard shoulder in the process of trying to balance, and swayed toward the bathroom.

"Wow! I try to be nice, and she pushes me."

She pivoted in time to see him throw his hands out to the side in mock outrage. "Because you're not being *nice*. You're being a self-serving dick who smiles too much."

He pointed at her. "Got it. I'll stop smiling."

Nearly tripping, she stumbled backward into the bathroom, where she untangled herself and turned around. Slammed the door behind her. Eyed her reflection in the mirror. "Sarah Sunshine, what the hell are you doing?"

# *Chapter 15*

## Let the Games Continue

Despite the five-alarm fire bells clanging in Quinn's head, he waited. Anticipated. When would Sarah emerge from the bathroom? Warnings—*run the hell away, as fast as possible!*—came roaring into his consciousness. But she'd been a bit unsteady, and he told himself he needed to be sure she didn't slip and hit her head on the sink. Didn't most home accidents happen in the bathroom?

"Arch," he hissed at the dog, "is your master—owner—mom—okay?"

The dog lazily lifted his head and gave Quinn an "I'm-sleeping-here" look, which should have clued Quinn that Sarah was fine. Archer would have been at the bathroom door if he had the slightest inkling she was in danger of keeling over onto the bathroom floor. That dog was damn smart. Unlike him.

When Sarah did come out, Quinn finally relaxed. She wobbled her way over to him—or maybe it was his eyesight doing the wobbling—and plopped her cute ass on the couch. *Damn it! She does* not *have a cute ass.* His eyes strayed and landed on her chest. Creamy flesh cresting over a bikini top popped into his head before he could stop it. He focused instead on her shoulder, bared by the slouching sweater, and the tiny strap that brought his mind back full circle to her in the bikini. *Killing me here.* Yeah, there were some mysteries under that sweater he was itching to discover. *Cut this shit out now!*

Peering at the cards, she began to hum. "Did you look at my hand while I was gone? I think we need to start over."

"What? No! Of course not. I don't do shit like that. I may be a lot of things, but I'm no cheater."

"Well, aren't you the rare one?" She picked up and arranged her cards, her eyes dancing just above them, mesmerizing him so he didn't register what she'd just said.

He dragged his gaze away and picked up his own cards.

They played in silence for a few minutes, the music soft in the background. Finally, he couldn't take not talking.

"Been reading more smokin'-hot romances to my mother?"

"Why do you ask? Want me to read to you sometime?" Her voice dropped low and husky on the last words, shooting straight to his groin, where a fire threatened to break out. *So not helping.*

He gulped down a groan, more aware than ever that he was harboring a boatload of steam that needed letting off. Time to change the subject.

"Speaking of romance … Are you going to answer me about Wolf, or should I just let it go?"

Mossy-green eyes snapped up to his, full of surprise. It took her a moment to recover, but her voice was soft when she spoke. "You really want to know?"

He gave his cards a quick once-over, though he didn't see a damn thing. "Yeah, I really do."

"I think I need more beer." She picked up the bottle and tipped it back, taking a long, hard swallow. He followed suit and waited. She didn't hold back when she launched into the story of how they met, how she fell—which stirred all kinds of other uncomfortable feelings in him he wasn't willing to examine—and how she later found out he was banging someone else.

He took a pull of his own beer. "So she was what, some piece of ass he picked up in a bar?"

She shook her head, and a sad, faraway look stole into her eyes. She folded her cards in her lap. "*I* was the piece of ass."

*"What?"*

Her gaze locked onto his. "He supposedly left for Sweden, and I was alone, so when some work colleagues asked if I wanted to join them at this new restaurant, I thought why not? It beat sitting home alone." She pulled in a huge breath. "So I'm having dinner, and who walks in but Mister-I'm-In-Sweden with a beautiful blond on his arm." Another tug on her beer. Quinn flicked his eyes to the bottle, satisfied it was still half-full. "He didn't see me at first, and I was … frozen in place. My mind couldn't wrap itself around what I was seeing. I kept thinking up excuses for why he was there with her—she was a client, a relative, a family friend—though it didn't explain why he was in Seattle."

Sarah set down her cards. "She was stunning." She whispered the last words reverently, like she believed this woman was far above her. It occurred to Quinn the woman couldn't have been, though he'd never set eyes on her.

"They were in my line of sight, all cuddled up. He kissed her, and I … Well, let's just say"—she pointed her bottle at Quinn before chugging the rest of her brew—"there was no mistaking the body language."

Her words slammed into his heart. They were raw, exposing her soft underbelly, and her vulnerability tugged at him. A voice whispered in his head that the finger point, the chug-a-lug—in fact her whole demeanor—were part of an elaborate defense mechanism she kept locked in place. She was giving him a rare peek behind her walls.

In an exquisite moment of clarity he might've missed had he been sober, he got it. He understood why she hated *his* guts. In her eyes, he was Wolf. Except he wasn't. Was he? The question dizzied his mind.

She wiggled her empty at him. "More beer?" Her voice came out choked, and her eyes were glossy.

All of him wanted to do *something*, but he had no clue what, so he simply said, "Aw, shit, Sunshine. Jesus," and drained his own beer before staggering upright to get more.

He returned with fresh bottles. She was sniffling, though he saw no tears. Archer's head lay in her lap, and Quinn felt a rush of affection for the furry mutt.

"Oh crap. I still need to throw down some cards," she muttered as her fingers tapped the small stack.

"Doesn't matter." Quinn fastened every iota of his attention on her. "Tell me what happened." He held his breath, praying she'd keep going, praying she didn't. Push, pull. This woman seemed to do that to him. A lot.

A huge intake of breath, an equally robust exhale, a pull on her beer bottle. "After I came out of my daze, I got up and headed toward them with no idea what I was going to say or do. He saw me coming, and he slid his arm from her shoulders and put on a cool-as-a-cucumber mask. Imagine my surprise when he introduced me as a *business associate* to Ingrid, his *wife*. I was so damn stunned I just stood there like an idiot. When I finally got my brain and my mouth connected, all I could say was, 'Nice to meet you, Ingrid.' Who does that? It turns out he'd been married for fifteen years—to the mother of two children I had no idea he had.

"I … I didn't know what to do, so I just walked away. I needed to go someplace where I could sort things out, make sense of them, think. It didn't hit me until later that my only refuge was the house I shared with *him*! No surprise, he showed up a few hours later—after no doubt filling *Ingrid* with a shit ton of lies—spewing all kinds of promises to divorce her."

She let out a mirthless laugh. "On top of it, he hadn't been anywhere in Europe for years. He's not even Swedish—he's as American as you or me. He'd been living in Seattle the *whole time* with his wife and kids! He led a double life, splitting his time between us under the pretext of traveling to Sweden for business. Not only did I feel like an utter fool, but I felt dirty. Ashamed. Like some cheap home wrecker. For fuck's sake, she's the mother of his children!"

The ridiculous thought that it was good they'd agreed on the new swear jar protocol blazed through Quinn's mind.

"I can't believe I'm telling you all this." She dropped her head in her hands. The confession baffled him yet filled him with pride in one breathless sweep. "Gage doesn't even know the guy was married. I couldn't bring myself to tell him that part, so I just said he had someone else. I can't … I don't want my brother to know."

"Your secret's safe," he soothed. "I'm not telling him."

She raised her head and zeroed beautiful, watery eyes on him. They had turned fern-green. "See, Sparky? Gage and I don't tell each other *everything*."

"I guess not," he agreed.

She guzzled more beer, and some leaked out of her mouth and slid down her chest under her sweater. A laugh spurted from her.

The scene sent his mind wandering to places it shouldn't. Wholly inappropriate places where she was naked, straddling him, or lying beneath him, wrapped around him, whispering that she wouldn't tell her brother as

Quinn buried himself deep inside her. His dick roused, suddenly eager to be surrounded in her wet heat. *Jesus! Gotta be the drinks.* Alcohol had a funny way of boosting sex to the top of his priority list. Couldn't be because he was finding her more and more attractive—even *without* the booze.

In need of yet another distraction, he blurted, "Do you have a picture of him?" *WTF?*

She eyed him skeptically. He didn't blame her. "You want to see a picture of Wolf?"

*No.* "Sure. Curiosity and all that."

With a swipe at her eyes, she picked up her phone and scrolled until she landed on what she was looking for. The heartbreaking look on her face nearly undid him, sending desire into a free fall.

"This is us right after I moved to Seattle." She handed him the phone.

Quinn took in the picture of a man with his arm around Sarah's shoulders, and two things struck him at once: First, Wolf looked nothing like a biker dude. He was a tall, lean, forty-or-fifty-ish man who exuded confidence and poise—in the regal style of one of Sarah's eighteenth-century dukes. In other words, Quinn's opposite. Second, the Sarah in the picture looked *way* different than the Sarah seated across from him. Seattle Sarah wore a green dress that hit her mid-thigh and molded to her mouthwatering curvature without making her look like she was trying to show it off. On the contrary, she was the epitome of class and femininity, and the contrast to her badass self was remarkable—not that he didn't find the badass Sarah attractive, but *this* Sarah was … Wow. Her long, dark hair curled in thick waves over her shoulders, and the smile on her face was dazzling. It conveyed pure joy while the man beside her, in stark comparison, looked as cold as a fjord. A pang of envy dug into Quinn. He found himself wishing *he* could put a smile of that wattage on her face.

"When did you cut your hair?" was all he could come up with.

"Couple months ago. I decided to cheer myself up while Wolf was … After he'd been away for a while. I cut it and did the pink for fun. He sort of freaked out over the change." A little chuckle escaped her.

Quinn handed the phone back to her. "I'm guessing he wasn't a fan of the nose stud either."

She shook her head no. "He's pretty straitlaced. Well, about *some* things."

"Do you think he'll come after you?"

She shrugged. "Doesn't matter. He lied, and I'm not going back. There's nothing to build a relationship on when trust has been turned into rubble. Without trust, you've got no foundation, no support to hold up the structure." Twiddling Archer's ears, she glanced at Quinn. "I hope you don't mind. I, uh … I'm not really in the mood for cribbage anymore. Think I'll go to bed."

"Yeah, of course." He stood when she did, waving at their mess. "I'll take care of this."

"Thanks, Sparks." She patted his arm in an affectionate move that surprised him even as it warmed him all over.

He stuffed his hands into his pockets to keep them from pulling her against him. "You gonna be okay?"

Closing her eyes, she nodded. "Yep. I'll be fine."

As he watched her walk away, he admonished himself. They'd had a great day together—best time he could ever remember having simply hanging out with a woman—and he'd had to push, had to know about Wolf. What had compelled him to ask? Curiosity. Competitiveness. Whatever it was, he'd made her talk about her painful past, which had made her cry. *Dumbass!*

Sarah definitely had a softer side. She'd exposed it, and Quinn liked what he saw. Now all he wanted was to make everything better. But how? He'd never been in this situation—whatever *this situation* was. Despite Gage's warnings, despite knowing better, Quinn couldn't deny his growing fascination with Sarah. Was it the same kind of draw he felt for other women? In other words, was it only because he was a horny fucker? No. This was different. He'd never wanted to know everything about another woman before. And he couldn't make heads or tails out of it.

# Chapter 16

## Socially Distanced Sex

As Quinn was heading into the gym the next morning, Sarah and his mom were heading out.

Sarah gave him a chin lift and a cool look that had him wondering if he'd dreamed last night. "Hey, Sparky. How'd you sleep?"

"Like sh—sherbet. You?"

She smirked. "Like a log."

His mom's puzzled gaze bounced between them, but before she could ask, Sarah herded her upstairs.

Sassy Sarah was back in all her glory and set the tone for the day, with her defensive systems solidly locked into place and bristling. Jonesing for a repeat of the night before when she'd opened up to him, he tried to rekindle the magic as they cleaned up after dinner.

In the family room, his mom was safely ensconced on the couch, and he ventured in a hush, "So what made you fall for Wolf in the first place?"

Sarah came to a complete stop and glared at him as though he'd committed some huge faux pas, like asking her to lick his hockey gear clean. "Why?"

He twirled a fork before dropping it into the dishwasher silverware basket. "Just wondering. He's a lot older." He bit back a remark about the guy being too old to get it up more than once a week. "Is that what attracted you?"

Her face went rosy with a flush, though he couldn't be sure if it was embarrassment or anger. Whatever the cause, it was a pretty color on her fair skin. "That was part of it."

"And then, of course, there's his 'strong and sexy' name." Why this irked him, he had no clue.

"Yes. It went along with that older-man mystique," she snorted.

"And I suppose *Wolf* was great in the sack." Though he tried to hold it in, snark laced words he shouldn't have even spewed. *What the hell is wrong with me?* A little voice blared that he was trying to knock Wolf down a peg or five, but he conveniently disregarded it.

"Oh God, yeah. Phew!" She fanned herself with her hand. "A very *skilled* lover, as only an older man can be. That's probably *the* main reason I fell for him."

Okay. Now she was just yanking his chain. Wasn't she? The conversation had taken a decidedly uncomfortable turn—his fault—and he was anxious to steer it in a different direction. "How about we work a puzzle after Mom goes to bed?"

"Too dark."

"Then let's play poker tonight." He waggled his eyebrows.

Her head did a little shake-bob thing like she was trying to get a bug out of her ear. "What?" Light flared in her eyes. "Oh, I get it. No, I am *not* playing strip poker with you."

He began buffing the counters to lock out the image of naked Sarah inviting him to explore all that skin—her wonderland. "I didn't suggest strip poker, Sunshine. Jesus, you think I'd want to play with my mom one short wing away?"

His mind lurched in a new direction: Was *he* as skilled as Wolf? Whatever that meant. Just as he wasn't sure exactly what made him successful at picking up women, he was equally uncertain about his bedroom prowess. Were his cocksure assumptions based on reality or on what his admirers constantly fed him—and what he wanted to believe?

Another mental segue, and he was questioning whether he was just as guilty as Wolf. Quinn had used a lot of women over the years. Except they'd used him too. It was mutual, consensual, honest. As for *Wolf*, what he'd done wasn't right. On so many levels. Dude was married, and he'd lied to Sarah. He'd sucked her into an affair while withholding facts she should have had in the beginning in order to make an informed decision.

Sarah twisting her head and peering up at him brought him back to the here and now. He must have still been frowning because her next words were, "Aw, is widdle Quinnie Winnie upset? C'mon. Don't sulk. Let's do this so I can beat your ass—ets in poker too."

"You're such a—" Flustered, he threw down the kitchen towel and stalked away. Behind him, Sarah's voice softened. "I'm sorry, Quinn. I didn't mean …"

*Whoa. She called me "Quinn."* He didn't register the rest of what she said because he was halfway down the hall and out of earshot, wondering how to stop comparing himself against Wolf. In his room, he stomped around the perimeter like a little bitch before he laced his hands on top of his head and blew out a series of lung-filling breaths, trying to blunt the spikes in his chest.

His phone vibrated—his *other* phone—and he checked the screen. *Dallas.* One of his favorite hotties. He answered with a "Hey, Theresa," before thinking through actually *speaking* with Theresa.

"Hi, Quinn," came her breathy voice. Only right now it bordered on squeaky. "Been thinking about you, lover boy."

His automaton self kicked into gear, and his lips tipped up in a half-smile. "Oh yeah? And what have you been thinking?"

"About you and me and—"

"You know I can't come see you right now, right? I mean, with the virus?"

"You can't fly down here for a day or two? I could fly up there. I *miss* you," she purred.

"Can't, sweetheart. Team rules." Not really, but she wouldn't know any different.

"Oh, I hate this virus!" Her voice had taken on a pouty quality. Pouty *and* squeaky. "I'm missing my favorite man. Guess I'll have to settle for talking to him—and doing other things with him on the phone. I'm wearing a special outfit. Want to see?" Her voice shifted into sexy mode. He pictured her in something sheer and small as she twirled her blond strands, but oddly, it wasn't doing a damn thing for him.

His mother's words about getting to know the women in his life ricocheted around in his brain. "Keep me guessing for right now, sweetheart." He plopped onto the edge of his bed. "What have you been up to?"

Her tone took on a surprised quality. "What do you mean?"

"I mean, what have you been doing? Are you working? Keeping busy?" *Seen any engineering shows? Done any 3-D puzzles? Read anything?*

"Well, the salon had to furlough all of us so, uh, I haven't been doing much of anything besides binge-watching *Friends*."

"Oh. Didn't know you were into that show." What else did he *not* know about her? So much. And that had always been fine with him.

She laughed—how had he forgotten her laugh sounded like a bray? "Oh yeah. This is like the fourth time I've watched the whole season from start to end."

*Huh*. "With all this free time on your hands, wouldn't you want to watch something different?"

"Like what?" She sounded genuinely mystified. "Why? What are *you* watching? As if I couldn't guess, dirty boy," she said slyly.

He ignored her inference. "Not exactly binge-watching, but I'm getting caught up on *Impossible Engineering*. I'm also enjoying *Shark vs Tuna*."

This seemed to blow her little mind because she didn't respond.

"Theresa? You still there?"

"I'm here."

Normally, their time on the phone was short and deliberate—to set up a meeting place. And they often did that by texting. He usually took her to dinner, but what did they talk about? He couldn't remember. Mostly, she talked while he sat, focused on getting back to her place, where conversation stopped and they got down to the real purpose for seeing each other.

"So, uh," he began, "what's the weather like down there?"

"Hot! And sticky. Hopefully, it'll cool off tomorrow." Another long pause. "What's it like where you are?"

"On the cool side."

As he hunted for a different topic of conversation, it struck him full force that all he had in common with this woman was sex. Not that there was anything wrong with that—it had been the reason he'd pursued her in the first place. Or had she pursued him? Didn't matter because, either way, stark ramifications were staring him in the face. Ramifications such as how conversation between them bumped and jolted, like people on skates for the first time.

He found himself anxious to escape what was turning into an extremely awkward phone call and hustle downstairs before Sarah turned in for the night. Maybe he could convince her to climb into the hot tub with him. *No, bad idea.* Maybe that poker game? A round or ten of cribbage? Parcheesi? He didn't care what the game was. Or they could curl up on the couch and watch something, anything, close enough that he could breathe her in.

"Quinn?" Theresa's voice jarred him back to the conversation he was *supposed* to be engaged in.

"Ah, yeah?" He cleared his throat.

"Did you hear what I said?"

*No effing idea.* "Which part?"

"Guess I tied your tongue, didn't I?" she tee-heed. "The part about showing you what I'm wearing and letting you watch me pull it off slowly—"

Something crashed downstairs. "Hey, Theresa, I gotta go, but it's been nice talking to you. Take care, okay?"

"Uh, okay. Bye, Quinn. Will I hear from you?"

Unbidden, a forceful "No" popped into his head. "Sure. Once we get back to normal, I'll be in touch."

He barely had time to chuck the phone on the bed before zooming downstairs. His heart hammered his rib cage as all sorts of bloody clips played through his head. When he got to the darkened kitchen, Sarah was frozen in place on the other side of the island, staring at the floor.

"What's going on?" he asked.

She lifted wide eyes to his. Then she covered her mouth, and her shoulders began shaking.

"Are you hurt?" He rounded the island. His gaze landed on what she'd been looking at, though he couldn't quite comprehend what he saw. As if she'd been trying to hold back a bursting dam, she suddenly let go, and peals of laughter rolled through her body.

Scattered at her bare feet were piles of bills and shards of glass from the now shattered swear jar. "I was … I was … trying … and then …" Her words came out in gasps, she was laughing so hard. "The whole … the damn thing …" She doubled over in hysterics, causing laughter to bubble up and out of him.

"Don't move until I clean up the glass. How did it happen?"

She finally caught her breath. "I was putting money in, and I knocked it over. Now we can swear all we want!" Another fit of laughter.

By the time he returned with a handheld vacuum, she was shaking splinters from money and setting it gingerly on the counter. Her body still shuddered with mirth.

"Where's my mom?"

Sarah stooped, reached, and plucked a bill off the floor. "She turned in. I'm surprised she hasn't come out to find out what the loud crash was all about."

Quinn motioned for Sarah to stand still while he sucked up shards around her feet. "She probably didn't hear it. Her bedroom's too far away."

Sarah inched out her big toe.

"Stop moving until I get this cleaned up!" he barked. "Where's Archer?"

"Outside." Her answer to his order was to dance in tight little circles, swinging her hips from side to side. She might as well have flipped him off.

He set the mini vac aside, trying not to laugh at her antics. "As usual, you're being a total pain in the ass. No more Mr. Nice Guy."

"When have you ever—" She let out a screech when he swooped her up. "What the hell are you doing?" She kicked her feet until he dumped her unceremoniously on the couch, where she promptly gusted with more laughter and rolled off.

He let out a few chuckles and wagged a finger at her. "Stay. Better yet, go find another vase. Maybe we can make this look like nothing happened."

She popped up, and as she walked away, his conversation with Theresa shot through his mind, along with the feeling of being off balance, unable to relax. By contrast, the tension that had had his insides wadded up was already melting away.

# Chapter 17

## Stud, Draw, or Strip?

Whatever had pissed Quinn off and sent him stomping away seemed long gone, and Sarah found herself breathing a sigh of relief.

In a huge room they called a butler's pantry, she rummaged around until she found the vases and selected the largest one she could find. What an idiot she'd been! Her baggy hoodie sleeve had caught when she'd been dumping in a few bucks, and when she'd wheeled, she'd pulled the damn thing with her.

Back in the kitchen, Quinn was crouched on the floor, finishing up, and she slid the vase onto the counter. "Excellent job, Sparky. You might have found your calling."

He looked up with a smirk. "Cleaning up *your* messes?" A hank of hair fell across one of his eyes, and he shoved it back.

Why the hell did that move cause her insides to bust a move, and why did he look hotter than he had before? As if he knew *exactly* what was streaking through her mind, a dazzling, dimpled smile overtook his features. *Oh hell. Don't go there, Sar.*

He looked down, returning to his work —and thank God because she was still checking for drool—when he said, "Wanna watch some *Impossible Engineering*? What season are you on?"

She gave herself an inner shake. "As usual, I'm light years ahead of you. I finished that up, and now I'm into *Jack Ryan*."

Even at this angle, she saw his smile broaden. "No shit? I just watched the first two episodes a few nights ago."

"I'm up to episode five." They spent the next half hour comparing notes on the characters, the storyline, the acting. Surprisingly, their opinions aligned.

"If I turn on episode three, would you be willing to watch with me so I can catch up?" he ventured.

She regarded him a moment, trying to ignore how handsome he was when he was earnest. "I thought you wanted to play poker."

"I did, didn't I? In that case, get ready to lose your panties, Sunshine." He gave her a wicked smile that sent a warm ripple through her body.

*He's kinda handsome when he's acting like a hotshot too.* When had that brash side of his—the one she usually disliked—suddenly become appealing? *Damn it!* "We agreed no strip poker."

"Goddamn. You're sucking all the fun out of this. Guess I'll have to take all your money instead."

She scoffed. "You're on, Sparky."

Quinn gathered up the cards while Sarah clucked with triumph. "Stop being so cocky, Sunshine. You're only up by one game."

He hadn't anticipated she'd be any good, but she'd surprised him. Again. Plus, conversation during play had ebbed and flowed naturally, seamlessly—even when they sparred. *Especially* when they sparred. Damn fun, and easy as gliding on a fresh sheet of ice. Even the silent lulls felt right.

For the first time since she'd destroyed the swear jar, he glanced at the clock, shocked that several hours had zoomed by. *Damn!* But he didn't want to stop, didn't want the night to end, so he bit his tongue about the time.

Sarah took a quick sip of her beer, giving him an appraising look. "Earlier tonight, in the kitchen, you got your undies in a bunch. What was that about?"

He still wasn't sure himself, though the exchange about Wolf—in the sack—had triggered it. Casting his gaze to the cards he was dealing, he gave her a noncommittal shrug. "Don't recall. Probably something snarky you said. You're always giving me such a ration of shit; I have a hard time keeping track."

"Well, if I offended you, I'm sorry."

Her soft, genuine tone had him snapping his head up. "What?"

Hazel eyes sparkled with mischief above her cute little smirk. She drew her bottom lip between her teeth, and his gaze dipped unabashedly to her mouth. God, she had nice lips. Sexy, deep pink, inviting him to nibble.

"I said, I didn't mean to offend you. *This* time." Her words jarred him right out of his ridiculous reverie.

A chuckle escaped him. "Duly noted. I'm sorry if I acted like a—"

"Tool? Jerk? Dickhead?" she offered helpfully. "No apology necessary. I'm used to it."

He shook his head with amusement. "*Anyone* being cooped up with you and my mom would be on edge."

"Maybe you're on edge because you've gone too long without doing the horizontal bop. Must be tough on a guy like you."

He jerked before he could corral the movement.

She reached out and shoved his shoulder playfully. "Sorry. That was mean. Let's get your mind off what you can't have and get busy with your next poker defeat." Her head went down as though she were studying the decidedly boring pattern on the back of her cards.

He stopped dealing. "What do you mean, 'what you can't have'?"

Her gaze lifted to his. "Uh, sex, dumbass?"

*Goddamn, does she really need to remind me? Especially when she's sitting over there looking all hot and cute and untouchable?* She'd taken off her hoodie, and he'd been checking out her T-shirt that read, "This Is Why I'm Hot," with a strategically placed drawing of a sun. Staring at her was like admiring something shiny and enticing that was locked up in a display case. Taunting and out of reach. He decided to have a little fun at her expense. "And why can't I have sex, exactly?"

Her smug expression was firmly back in place, and she added folded arms to strike a badass pose. "Unless you're having it with yourself, you're kinda screwed. Not!" She guffawed at her own joke. Her head swiveled dramatically. "After all, I don't see any potential playmates, do you?"

Now *he* smirked—and wiggled his eyebrows. "Thought for a sec I might be looking at one."

Surprise flashed through her eyes before she narrowed them. Arms unfolded, and she made a circling motion with her index finger. "Nuh-uh. No effing way. Let's see, how did you so eloquently put it? If we were on a deserted island together, I'd prefer offering myself up as shark bait."

He rubbed his jaw dramatically. *Guess I deserved that one.*

Sarah gave him a quick glance. "Something wrong with your face, Sparky?"

"Just trying to get feeling back after you busted my chops."

"Oh, good one," she snorted.

Just like that, there was that prickle from earlier jabbing at him when Sarah had gushed about Wolf's *skill.* Didn't matter that she'd probably been kidding; he couldn't keep his mind from roaming to how many more tricks a guy twenty years older had up his sleeve. Besides maturity and experience, what else did Wolf have on Quinn? Not money, that was for damn sure. But Sarah didn't strike him as the type who was all about the dough. There was a depth to her, multiple layers to be peeled back. Mysterious, intriguing. Unlike anyone he'd ever met.

*Damn, I feel like I'm looking at women through a different pair of binoculars.* He wasn't sure he was comfortable with the altered view. He shifted into stupid mode. "So the thought of having sex with me is that disgusting?"

She didn't answer at first, instead surveying him like a structural engineer searching for the weak spots in a building. *Yeah, that.* He began squirming and tried not to show it.

"Not exactly disgusting."

"So I've got *that* going for me. Gee, thanks." He blew out a gust of air.

"What I mean is, and forgive me if I tromp on your fragile male ego, you'd probably be fun for a night, but not for long-term."

This should have made him leap for joy. Hadn't "short-term" been his goal all along? Instead, her statement nearly knocked the wind from his lungs. "Why not?" Damn, it bugged him to know she thought that.

She stretched her arms above her head like a graceful cat, and her T-shirt rode up, exposing a narrow band of smooth, peach-flesh skin. An urge to kiss it, lick it, danced through his mind, but her next words shut down the flashing fantasy.

"You strike me as a one-trick pony."

Confusion must've shown all over his face because she gave him another eye-roll and an exasperated hmph. "You know, one and done.

Same routine with every woman. And if you're trading one puck bunny for another, you don't really have to try, do you? No variety, no spice, like when you're intimate with someone and you spend time exploring what really turns *them* on."

Uncomfortably aware that *he* was growing more turned on, he gawked at her. No words came. No coherent ones anyway.

"Cat got your tongue there, Sparky?"

"Yeah, the cat does got my tongue."

She laughed out loud. And who could blame her? He sounded like an asshat of epic proportion.

He gave his head a quick shake and blurted, "Have you ever dated a younger guy?"

She flicked up a forefinger. "Once. That cured me."

"How much younger?"

"Two years."

"What was wrong with him? Was he stupid?" *Like me?*

Her gaze swung to the ceiling, as though she were forming her thoughts, and returned to him. "Nothing was *wrong* with him, and no," she chuckled, "he wasn't stupid. In fact, he was scary brainy. He was just … young. Unsophisticated."

"In bed too?" Why was he even going there?

"He was meh in bed, although he made up for it in enthusiasm. He really enjoyed sex."

Quinn spluttered and laughed, relieving some of his pent-up tension like steam whistling out of a kettle. "And what's wrong with that?"

Cocking her head, she gave him a little grin. "Don't get me wrong. I have nothing against sex. In fact, it's one of my favorite things to do."

With the image of her creamy skin still emblazoned in his brain, her words bolted straight to his dick. As things rearranged themselves in his pants to accommodate his rock-hard shaft, he shifted in his chair and plastered on an "I'm-fascinated-by-what-you-have-to-say" look. While he *was* fascinated by what Sarah had to say, the growing distraction in his crotch was making focusing difficult.

Fortunately, she started talking again, saving him from having to find his missing voice, which would have no doubt come out strained anyway.

"The thing is, you can't screw *all* the time," she said matter-of-factly, which did nothing to alleviate his aching problem. "You have to be able to carry on conversations if you're going to spend time with someone. In fact, I think—for women at least—stimulating conversation is an aphrodisiac. A guy can be good-looking, have an Adonis body, and be able to swivel his hips like nobody's business, but the real turn-on is here." She tapped her finger against her temple. "You feel me?"

*Nothing I'd rather do than feel you.* His mind departed the cerebral world. He could have beat his chest and let out a carnal caveman yell in his current primal state. Instead, he cleared his throat, disguising a groan as he tried to get himself under control. "I think so." *Having a hard time processing here because all the blood in my body is in my swollen cock, where it'll stay until I do something about it.*

He needed another shower.

Quinn looked as though he was in pain.

"You okay over there, Sparky?"

"I'm good," he croaked. Another throat clear, and he barked out, "Have you ever dated a hockey player?"

"Ha! No." No need to even think about her answer before she spat it out there. She shook her head so violently she made herself dizzy. Or was it the beer? What time was it?

"Why not?" His still-strained voice held genuine curiosity.

"Because I've spent too much time around them, and I know what makes them tick. They're only interested in three things." She began counting on her fingers. "The game of hockey, their next meal, and their next lay. And most of them couldn't care less who the layee—or is that layer?—is. Is he interested in anything beyond her looks, like what drives her? Her goals? Things she loves and hates? No. His primary concern is how he can get his dick inside her."

His eyes popped wide, and he twisted in his seat.

*Yeah, I'm describing* you, *Sparky.*

"Toots, you've just described every male on the fucking planet."

She shot to her feet and shook her empty bottle at him. "Another beer?"

"No. I'm switching to rum."

"Ooh, then I will too!"

He grinned at her. "You *like* rum?"

"Well, I prefer bourbon. And Coke. Together."

"Yeah, they're usually together." He shook his head and gave her an indulgent smile.

They settled into their respective seats after he prepared their drinks, the next game forgotten for the time being. Which suited her just fine because she was feeling unusually chatty. Quinn was easy to talk to. No pressure, no judgment. She could say anything, blab whatever, and he accepted it with humor and curiosity. So liberating. And so different from talking to Wolf. Conversations with him had been stimulating, but she was realizing an undercurrent had always run through them, and the longer she'd been with him, the more guarded she'd become.

But with Quinn? He was an equal. A friend. A safe harbor. And right now he was giving her a quizzical stare.

"You look like you might blow a fuse over there, Sunshine. What's running through your head?"

She took a healthy sip of her drink. "What happened between your parents?"

She noted the surprise in his eyes. Yeah, she'd sort of blindsided him, and while that hadn't been the foremost thought in her head, it had been spinning around for a while.

He smoothed the back of his head. "Honestly? I wish I knew. They were together, and then they weren't. It's not like they lived separately, but when he left to coach in Poland, they might as well have divorced. To this day, I don't know why he left and didn't come back or why they're still married. Mom dressed it up as an opportunity"—he airquoted the last word—"but he's been there for years and acts as if we don't exist. I don't hear from him, I don't think Mom hears from him, and Ronan … Well, Ronan claims Dad calls him. But then, Ronan *is* the golden child." Brown eyes pierced hers, the pain evident in their depths. "It's totally jacked-up. I don't get it. You're lucky you've got a brother you like."

"I'm guessing you have one you don't like."

"Yes." He threw back half of his cocktail.

"Why don't you like him?"

"Because he's an asshole?"

She simply nodded.

"Okay. Because he's an ungrateful asshole who thinks his shit doesn't stink. How's that?" His voice held an edge she wasn't accustomed to.

Quinn's approach tended toward lighthearted, carefree. As though everything rolled off his back. Obviously, everything *didn't* roll off his back.

"Wow. I'm sorry. I don't know what I'd do without Gage. It was always him and me against my mom. But don't tell him I said so, or I might have to kill you." She gave him a little smirk in an attempt to lighten the mood. "You and I have father baggage in common, I think."

"Yeah? Tell me about your dad." He jerked his chin toward her drink in a "Need more?" gesture. When she shook her head no, he excused himself for a refill. "Hold that thought, Sunshine."

*Sunshine.* She'd hated the moniker at first, but now it sounded sort of nice rolling off his tongue, especially in that deep, decadent timbre of his.

He was back within minutes, sipping and gesturing for her to continue.

"Our dad didn't leave the country, but he might as well have," she began. "He took off and started a whole new family. We talk occasionally, but it's awkward as hell. It feels forced, you know? Like because we share the same blood, we have to stay in touch. Needless to say, we're not close with our stepmom or stepsiblings, which is sad. Mom's never explained what happened—I think he cheated on her—but whatever it was, it sure left a bad taste in her mouth for every human with a Y chromosome." She took a quenching sip of her drink.

"Is that why you're always giving me shit?" One corner of his mouth curved up.

"What can I say? I was indoctrinated at an early age." She let out a disgusted little puff of air. "But as I get older, I realize not everything my mom says is gospel. In fact, I often wonder if she didn't drive Dad away. Contrary to what she preached, I've had good experiences with past boyfriends—"

"Were there a lot?"

There was that earnest look again, as if the answer really mattered to him. "It depends on what you mean by 'a lot.' I'm sure the number of guys I've dated is nothing compared to *your* track record." She winked.

He seemed to wince, and she felt a twinge of remorse.

"Sorry. I'm not trying to be a jerk on purpose, but it's true, isn't it?" she said.

He pulled in a deep breath and exhaled slowly. His eyes slid to the side. "Yeah. Not gonna lie. I've treated it like a sport. But it's one thing to score goals in hockey. They're tangible. They count for something. And God, it's an unbelievable rush when that puck finds the back of the net. Don't even get me started on scoring a winning goal, especially in the playoffs." He paused as though gathering his thoughts. "But it's a different game entirely when you're scoring with the ladies, and it doesn't compare. Sure, there's a little rush at first and you impress your buddies, but you don't win a prize."

"I thought scoring in bed *was* the prize. Besides, you earn the right to swagger."

A laugh gusted from him. "Yeah, I guess there's *that*—for what it's worth, which ain't much." He fastened his eyes on hers. "This is gonna sound weird, but it's getting old. Same game, different night. Too easy. Like you're the only shooter on the ice, and the net has just doubled in size. And when it's over, I'm … I don't know. Disappointed, I guess. It reminds me of coffee."

She quirked an eyebrow. "Sex reminds you of coffee? Hot and bitter?"

He chuckled. "Not exactly. Think about how good coffee smells. The beans, the aroma when it's brewing. You're anticipating drinking it, and your taste buds get all worked up. But then you have a sip and … meh. Lots of promise, but the delivery is a letdown." He shook his head. "Maybe I'm just over it."

"Yet you continue the same behavior. Is it about scoring? Winning on and off the ice?"

"Maybe. I've never spent much time analyzing the motivation. One thing I do know: my libido doesn't have much of an IQ, but that motherfucker sure controls a lot of what I do." He gave her a smile that didn't reach his eyes.

*Whoa. Honesty alert.* He was laying himself open, and a need to soothe him surged inside her. "That's true of lots of people. Men *and* women."

"Yeah? I doubt yours pushes *you* around. In fact, I can't think of anything—or anyone—that *does* push you around."

"Oh good. The illusion that I've got my shit together is holding."

"You don't have your shit together?"

She busted out a laugh. "Hell no! If I did, I wouldn't be jobless and homeless right now."

"But you're neither. You have a roof over your head, and you're gainfully employed," he pointed out logically.

She saw no reason to remind her generous employer that her current caregiver position wasn't exactly her dream job.

He seemed to read her mind nonetheless. "I get that taking care of my mom isn't what you hoped to be doing, but it's just a temporary stopover. And when the time comes, you'll be kicking ass in Engineering World again." He paused a beat. "What is it you want, career-wise? Where do you see yourself in ten, twenty years?"

Had anyone ever asked her this question? She had a ready answer, though she couldn't remember sharing it aloud. "Honestly? I'd like to run my own show, which means I need to learn as much as I can in the meantime—about every aspect of the business—so when I get there, I do it right."

"Awesome goal. I bet you'll nail it."

Approval wasn't what she'd sought in telling him, but hearing it filled her with warm, floating fuzzies. "Thank you for the vote of confidence."

He nodded. "What's the hardest part of your job?"

"Dealing with prima donna architects."

"Didn't you say Wolf is an architect?"

"He is, but he's also a structural engineer, so he gets it. I think that's one of the reasons we connected. I appreciated his art, and he appreciated that a solid structure must support the art. We used to geek out on design and construction and talk for hours."

Hair hung over his eye, and he pushed it back with a grumble and raked his hands through it.

The alcohol she'd consumed seemed to crash into her in one powerful wave. "Is it a pain?"

His entire body, which had been on the twitchy side, came to a standstill. "Is what a pain?"

"The hair. All that beautiful, long hair." *What am I saying?*

Gorgeous brown eyes clouded with skepticism. "You *like* the hair?"

She rolled her eyes again. Jeez, if she kept it up, they'd get stuck in their sockets. *Thanks, Grandma.* "Not necessarily, but it's so … you. And honestly? I love the idea of your hair—on me."

His eyes widened, and he seemed to short-circuit.

"No, no, no, I don't mean *on* me, like we're so close physically you're dragging your hair all over my body. But like, I want your hair to be my hair." She flapped her hand at him as if this would make him understand her babbling. Only confusion—and that same pained expression—showed on his chiseled face.

Why her funny bone suddenly tickled, she had no idea, but she couldn't hold back the laugh-snorts. She didn't realize she'd needed the release, but it felt damn good. "I love your mom!"

He seemed to recover, an adorable smirk replacing the tortured, befuddled one. "Totally random, Sunshine, but I love my mom too!"

Now her laughs became so violent her side ached and tears sprang to her eyes, but she swallowed them whole when his expression grew wistful.

"Your hair was so pretty in that picture you showed me. Damn, you looked so beautiful. Not that you're not beautiful otherwise, but you had a special look. Because you were happy, I guess. I don't get how he could've … Shit, I'm sorry." His eyes caressed her with … Longing? Tenderness? She wasn't sure, but whatever it was, it stopped her heart.

And then she realized he meant Wolf. Just like that, a shroud folded itself around her. Suddenly, she was exhausted.

He flicked out a hand and brushed her arm. Tingles made her hairs stand up on end. "Hey," he said softly in his seductive, dark-fudge-sauce tone. "I shouldn't have said any of that." His hands came together and formed a T. "Timeout. Rewind. Tell me what you dream about besides running your own engineering company, Sunshine."

She narrowed her eyes. Well, she *thought* she did, though she couldn't tell. Her face was numb. At least the shroud had been nudged back a fraction. "How much have you had to drink?"

"Too much. Tell me what you dream about," he repeated.

"Whirled peas."

He blinked. Then one corner of his mouth climbed, and his dimple reappeared, like the sun coming out from behind a cloud.

*Oh. My. God.*

"You're not going to tell me, are you?" he said.

"Do you have any fudge sauce?"

"Say *what*?"

"Fudge sauce. Oh, never mind." Yeah, she probably shouldn't tell him what had just rocketed through her brain that involved fudge, his dimple, and her tongue. "I think I had a teeny-weeny bit too much to drink. I should go to bed."

He looked all kinds of disappointed. "We still have a game to play."

"No, I'm up by one, so I'm gonna fold and float away on my little contented cloud of victory." She sang a chorus of "We Are the Champions."

He chuckled. "Not half-bad. What happened to best of seven?"

"We *played* seven. You won three, and I won four."

"Well, shit." His hand shot to his chin and rubbed.

"How does it feel to be naked?" she blurted.

"Excuse me?"

"Your stubble. Where did it go? Don't you feel naked or cold or … hairless?"

His whole face transformed with a brilliant, panty-melting smile. *Oh shit.* That's *how he does it. Who can resist? He's like Medusa. No, she turned people to stone. He turns them into puddles of goo.*

"Yeah, I think you might be right, Sunshine. Time for bed."

Fortunately, she had just enough self-control in her tank that she held back the "Yours or mine?" on the very edge of her cottony tongue. She wobbled to her feet. "Whoa. Head rush."

He staggered upward and held out an arm to steady her. She leaned against it. God, he had a nice arm. She wanted to feel it around her again, so she nuzzled against his chest and was rewarded when his arms encircled her, gently at first, and tightened. Strong, warm, safe. So safe. She could fall asleep like this.

# *Chapter 18*

## COVID CALLING

*She feels incredible!*

Quinn stood rooted to the floor, afraid he might stumble backward. And he didn't want to stumble. No, he just wanted to stand here and hold Sarah forever. Inhale her floral, powder-fresh scent. Memorize the feel of her warm, soft curves pressed up against him and the perfect way she fit him. It hadn't taken getting drunk for her to look awful damn good—she'd already looked damn good—but now that he was totally buzzed? Jesus effing Christ, he wanted her like he'd never wanted anyone before.

She let out a little sigh and curled into him, her head snuggling against his chest. *Damn!* He laid his cheek on her soft hair, relishing the silky feel and the smell of her flowery shampoo. The move seemed to startle her, and she jerked in his arms. He loosened his hold. She stared up at him as if she'd just woken up. *KissmeKissmeKissme. Please.*

She shook her head. "We shouldn't be doing this."

"Maybe not, but it doesn't keep me from wanting to." *From wanting you.*

In a move that caught him completely by surprise, she shoved his chest with both hands—hard—and he staggered backward, clamping down on her wrists for balance and inadvertently bringing her with him. As he toppled to the floor, he yanked her so she broke her fall by landing on him.

Unfortunately, the move made him fall against a corner of the stone hearth. Something crunched, and bright heat raced through his shoulder.

"Oh fuck," he gasped. "Think I broke something." He raised his head and stared into her wide eyes staring back at him, all cat-gold and filled with something bordering on panic. Her body was draped over him, her parts lined up perfectly with his. Goddamn, it felt good! His dick agreed despite the pain radiating in his shoulder, and he began sliding her off of him so she wouldn't notice the little problem that was quickly growing into a bigger one. A sound escaped her that had his mind whipping to what she'd sound like if she were naked and riding him.

*Shit! Not helping.*

"You okay?" he croaked.

Somehow Archer had become part of the scene, part-sitting, part-crawling, whimpering beside them. Sarah shot up, hoisting her weight onto her well-toned arms, hovering her body so close Quinn could still feel the heat drifting off her skin. "Fine. But what about you?" To the dog, she said, "It's okay, boy."

Quinn reached for his shoulder. "Shit, I think I dislocated something."

She wrapped both arms around his good one, nestling it between her breasts. *Sweet Jesus!*

"Sunshine"—he winced—"you gotta let go of me." *Or I'm gonna flip you on your back and rip your clothes off.* How he could contemplate ravishing her in the midst of the pain, he had little idea.

She dropped his good arm like a linesman dropped a puck in a face-off—forcefully. "Oh. Sorry." She scrambled backward on her ass, bringing Archer with her, and plopped down on the floor out of Quinn's reach.

"No, no. I didn't mean to push you away." He brought himself upright. "Fuck! That hurts like a motherfucker!"

She rose in a crouch. "What can I do?"

"Nothing yet." He drew in and released three huge breaths, then hoisted himself to his feet. She followed suit, clambering to a standing position beside him. He side-eyed her. "Ever relocate a shoulder before?"

"What? No! I'll call 911."

"No! Those guys are around sick people all day, and I don't want them near Mom."

"What about a Blizzard trainer? They do this shit all the time, right?" Her voice had climbed an octave or two.

"No, they were exposed to the virus. Don't want them here either," he gritted out. "You can do it. I'll walk you through it."

Her eyes were owl-like, big and unblinking. "Have you done this before?"

"No, but I stayed at a Holiday Inn once." He managed a half-smile.

A ferocious frown pulled her brows together. "Not funny, Sparky. Let's try this again. Have. You. Done. This. Before?"

"I've seen it done. I know what to do."

She hugged herself, shifting her weight from side to side. All of him wanted to pull her in for a one-armed hug and comfort her. "Okay. Where do you want to lie down?"

He jerked his chin toward the hall. "My bedroom. Let's go."

When they reached the bedroom, she hovered by the door and broke out in a smirk. "Wow. So *this* is how you get women into your bed. You play the injury card. Clever, Sparky, but seems like a lotta trouble."

"Shut up," he snorted. "I'm gonna lie down. You'll grab my wrist—" He'd been rotating the shoulder, and something suddenly popped. The pain plummeted to a seven from fifteen on a ten-point scale. "Oh, thank fuck!" he panted and sat on the bed.

"What?" Her face was twisted with concern. Beside her, Archer, all smiles, did a happy dance, as if he knew the crisis had passed.

Quinn continued to work his shoulder. "Not dislocated after all. Just twanged, I think."

"What can I do?"

"In my closet, top shelf, there's a bin with braces and slings and shit. Pull it down. I want to immobilize the shoulder and ice it."

She spun and faced several doors. He motioned to the correct one. She stepped inside the closet and sucked in a breath. "What the—? This is a *closet*? I can see myself everywhere … and it's bigger than Lily's living room!"

"I call it the house of mirrors." He chuckled. Like everything else in the house, the master bedroom closet was over the top. A gaudy extravagance, every surface in the room was covered in mirrors—closet doors, drawers, built-in dressers. Apparently, the owners were gluttons for clothes and seeing themselves in them from every angle imaginable.

He directed Sarah to a high shelf. After pulling the box down—and nearly clobbering herself on the head with it—she brought it to him. As he was rummaging around, his phone vibrated. "Would you get that?"

Her eyebrows shot up. "Kinda late?" She picked up the phone and frowned at the screen. "Hello?"

A sick feeling, like when one accidentally hits "Reply All" in an email never intended for *all*, jolted him. *Oh shit! Wrong phone!* He could only watch in horror because she wasn't paying any attention to his wildly flapping hand.

"Well, who is *this*?" she snapped. Her eyes slid toward him. "Bunny? Are you serious? That's your *actual* name? Like, your parents *named* you that?"

He did a face palm, then feebly motioned once more for her to turn over his goddamn phone. She kept her eyes on him but didn't make a move. "Don't tell me, let me guess. Your first name is Puck," she chortled.

*That's the last I'll hear from Bunny.* He hung his head. In the blink of an eye, he'd swung from wanting to fuck Sarah senseless to wanting to throttle her senseless. The shoulder was simply a sidebar. As he rose and came toward her, she hurriedly said, "Well, he's a little indisposed right now. Some extracurricular acrobatics that didn't go as expected, and he'll be laid ... up—"

He plucked the phone from her hand. "Bunny?"

"Quinn? What's going on?"

"Uh, well, it's a long story—"

"No doubt it's a fascinating one." Sarcasm dripped off every word. "Look, I—"

He dropped his hand holding the phone to his side. He couldn't hear what she was saying, but he *could* hear the squawk.

Meanwhile, Sarah was tiptoeing toward his door. "You're not going anywhere," he warned.

While Bunny's voice yammered on, Sarah dashed to the door. "Actually, I am." Archer darted through, followed by Sarah, who closed the door nearly all the way, leaving only her nose visible through the crack. "'Night, Sparky. It's been real."

The door snicked shut, and he stood staring after it, the phone still cradled in his hand. He brought it to his ear. "Bunny?" No answer. "Uh, Bunny? You there?"

With a sigh, he sank onto his bed and awkwardly wrestled with the phone until he deleted her contact information. It occurred to him he should have felt bad about it, but he hadn't thought of her in weeks. A twinge of guilt poked him. The level of alcohol in his system might have explained why his self-examination sharpened, but for whatever reason, he saw himself through Sarah's eyes. He *was*, in fact, Hunter McMurphy. And he didn't like it one damn bit.

As he lay in bed a while later, he replayed his evening with Sarah, briefly wondering why the hell she'd shoved him in the family room—likely because she'd had more sense than he had. His mind meandered to Sarah's exchange with Bunny. *Is your first name Puck?* In spite of the cringe-worthy conversation, laughter spurted from him.

Later, as he bumped along on a wave of uncomfortable, restless sleep, the most important takeaway of the night was how Sarah had smelled and felt in his arms.

Sarah brushed her teeth—twice—scoured her face, and let Archer back inside from his foray out in the yard. One glance toward her bedroom door confirmed she'd locked it—not that she expected anyone to come crashing through it. Especially an anyone with a broken shoulder. But she was tipsy and couldn't trust herself to push Quinn away if he got close again.

*Damn hormones!*

Staring at herself in the mirror, she debated slipping on one of her newer sexy cami sets. In case her room combusted and firemen came to the rescue, of course, she had to look her best. Which was why she spread a dab of foundation over her face, slicked on a little gloss, and plumped her hair. There. Now she was ready for firemen to break down her door … or anyone else who happened to wander by.

Had Archer been capable of an eye-roll, he'd have given her one as he curled up on his bed.

She slid between cool, crisp sheets, clicked off the lamp, and stared at the shadowed ceiling.

*Omigod, what did I almost do tonight? And with Quinn Hadley, Ladies' Man Supreme, of all people!* She sighed and ran her hand over the silky cami, then heaved herself out of bed to change into a more practical pair of knit shorts and a tank that read, "I Drink and I Know Things."

*It should read "I Drink and I Know Squat."*

Her limbs were lead-like and achy, no doubt from the spill she'd taken with Quinn earlier. Despite her fatigue, a persistent cough prevented her from settling in. Within an hour, the cough had brought on nausea and drove her into the bathroom. Why did she drink so damn much tonight? Shit, she hadn't gotten sick from overdrinking since college.

After she emptied the contents of her stomach, she cleaned up and dragged her butt back to bed. Soon she was shivering so hard her teeth clacked together. She piled on a few sets of sweats and wool socks, wrapped her shoulders in a blanket, and padded to the kitchen in search of herbal tea. Her head pounded. The short walk left her so exhausted she had to lean on the counter and catch her breath.

"What's going on, Sunshine?" Quinn's low voice behind her nearly launched her into the ceiling.

She wheeled, twisting herself in the blanket and almost tumbling over. In the gloom lit by a mere refrigerator door light, she took in his hulking presence, clad in only shorts and his arm in a sling. In his good hand, he held an ice pack.

"Oh damn," she squeaked. "Can you play hockey?"

Confusion crossed his face. "Not tonight. Are you okay?"

She shook her head. "I don't think so. I think … I drank too much."

He pointed at a barstool. "Sit. I'll be right back."

It seemed as though he was gone forever, and she folded her arms on the counter and laid her heavy head on them. Her skin was hot. A gentle hand brushed the hair from her forehead, and something firm passed over it. A sharp intake of breath followed by, "Shit! You're burning up." Apparently, the something firm had been a thermometer.

Quinn grasped her jelly arms and somehow tugged her upright. But she was so, so tired. All she wanted to do was collapse and sleep.

"Sarah," he said softly. "When was the last time you had anything to drink?"

"Bourbon and Coke," she mumbled.

"Nothing after that? No water?"

She began to shake her head, stopped, and winced. "Ow. No, nothing."

"Sweetheart, we need to get some fluids in you."

A little snort escaped her. "You call everyone 'sweetheart.' I'm not everyone. I'm Sunshine."

He frowned at her as he twisted a cap off a bottle and poured clear yellow liquid into a cup.

"Are you mad at me?" she whimpered. God, she must have been really wasted. Her emotions were on the point of a pendulum, swinging wildly from side to side. She felt more drunk now than when they'd been drinking.

"No, Sunshine. I'm not mad at you. Here, drink this." He pressed a cool cup to her lips.

She took a few sips and pushed it away. "Blech. What is that?"

"Gatorade. Be a good girl and take a few more sips for me. Then I want you to swallow some ibuprofen."

"Since you asked so nicely." Her words came out in a slur.

She couldn't remember drinking any more Gatorade, but she was vaguely aware of being carried in steely arms and placed gently on her bed. The blanket had been taken off her shoulders, and Archer was pressing his wet nose against her hand. Cold. She was so cold, and her body felt as though her joints were being separated on a rack. Covers were tugged over her. Thick, warm fingers raked through her hair, pushing it off her forehead, before settling on her cheek. "Hey," a deep voice whispered, "you get some sleep. I'll check on you in a bit, okay? In the meantime, if you need *anything*, you call or text me. Got that?"

"Mmph."

She slipped into a dark, chilly whirlpool.

*Damn it to hell!* Why had he gone to the grocery store? The liquor store? He could have had that shit delivered, but no, he just had to get out. Quinn had no doubt he'd brought COVID home and given it to Sarah. Icy tendrils of fear wrapped around his spine like bindweed. If he'd given it to Sarah, who looked all kinds of sick, he'd exposed his mom too.

He paced his room, his head pounding and his chest tightly banded. Four thirty in the morning. His mom would be up soon. He jogged into the kitchen and tore through every cleaner in the utility room, grabbing anything that blared "disinfectant" or "bleach." Then he went to work cleaning, scrubbing, scouring—no easy feat for a guy with an arm in a sling who'd never been any good at cleaning in the first place. He stopped long enough to check on Sarah, who slept under Archer's watchful eye. Her fever had dropped a few degrees, and Quinn breathed a sigh of relief.

"You'll come get me if she needs anything, won't you, buddy?"

The dog nodded once. Actually nodded. Quinn didn't question the phenomenon anymore, he simply believed. And honestly, leaving Sarah in her room was easier to do with Archer on duty.

Back in the kitchen, he brewed coffee and went to work disinfecting light switches, door latches, handrails.

"What are you doing?"

He whirled to find his mom, in a robe, giving him a puzzled look. "Son, you don't look so good. And what happened to your arm?" She started toward him, and he backed away.

He held up a warning hand. "Six feet, Mom. Sarah's sick. I'm pretty sure I gave it to her, and I don't want you catching it."

His mom stopped and gawped at him. "Sarah's sick? Just what did you give her?"

"I'm pretty sure I brought COVID home. She came down with it last night. Cough, fever, chills. She's sleeping last I checked, but she didn't sound so good. Right now I'm disinfecting everything. I'll take care of you while Sarah's under the weather, but you and I need to stay away from each other."

His mother folded her arms across her chest. "I can take care of myself." She held up her own warning hand when he began to protest. Funny, he hadn't noticed it before, but they shared similar mannerisms. "I'm not just saying that to be stubborn, Quinnie. I'm moving much easier, and I'm capable of getting my own meals and helping with yours. I'll make sure Archer gets outside and has what he needs. Your job is to take care of Sarah." This is when it struck him his mom was standing, *not* sitting in her wheelchair, and had been for the last week. His good shoulder dropped an inch or two as some of his tension lifted.

"Now tell me what happened to your shoulder," she said.

He gave her the condensed, family-friendly version of last night's fall—the one with no mention of him holding Sarah or her pushing him away.

"I'm going to get Archer," he said.

She nodded. "Good. I'll let him out and get him fed."

When he went back to Sarah's room, she was struggling to sit up. Her covers were thrown back, and her sweats were in a pile beside the bed, leaving her in a skimpy tank and shorts.

"What are you doing?" he barked.

Wide eyes darted to his. "Getting up? I need to pee."

"Why'd you take your clothes off? Why aren't you covered up?"

She blinked at him. "I'm burning up, that's why." Another beat, and she added, "If I felt better, I'd laugh at the irony of this situation. Sparky wanting a girl to put her clothes *on*."

He responded with an aggravated "Hmph," though he was all sorts of happy she felt well enough to get her snark on. He leaned down to help her sit up.

She swung smooth, bare legs over the edge of the bed and planted her feet. "I've got it from here," she said. Then she folded over and began coughing.

"Aw, shit. I'll get you some cough medicine." He beckoned Archer to follow and zoomed back to the kitchen, where his mom was pouring herself a cup of coffee.

She turned slowly. "There's my Archer man."

Quinn left to plunder medicine cabinets. When he reached Sarah, she was back in bed, her eyes hooded and her breathing wheezy.

"Hey, you okay, Sunshine?"

"Yeah, just exhausted from my short trip to the bathroom."

"Lean forward," he ordered.

She complied.

He punched and arranged her pillows, then leaned her back gently so she was in a reclining position. She still hadn't put her clothes back on, and her skin was cold. Resisting the urge to throw something over her upper body, he picked up her half-full glass of Gatorade and thrust it at her. "Drink."

"I don't like that stuff." She sounded like a pissed-off two-year-old. He expected her to thrust out her lower lip at any moment. Despite how disheveled and uncomfortable she looked, she was adorable, and his heart might have bumped against his rib cage a little faster.

"Well, tell me what you *do* like, and I'll get it for you." He handed her two gelcaps. "In the meantime, take this cough syrup and drink." He raised his eyebrows for emphasis. She grumped, but she did as he asked.

After arranging her sweats on the bed so she could easily reach them, he returned to the kitchen and poured his own tall mug of coffee. God, he needed caffeine. His phone lay on the counter beside him, and after downing half his brew, he thumbed a text to Nelson.

Nelson's response was swift: *You'd better take good care of my sister.*

Quinn could practically hear his growl. But then again, Nelsy had the right. Nonetheless, Quinn rolled his eyes before replying: *On it. What does she like to drink? Definitely not lemon-lime Gatorade.*

Gage: *IDK. Orange juice? Beer for sure.*

Quinn resisted the urge to type, "Beer's not gonna help, dumbass." Instead, he went on the hunt and found a six-pack of apple juice. Watered-down juice and ibuprofen in hand, he traipsed back to her room. She'd put on her sweats again and was snuggled under the covers. He rousted her, grateful when she gulped the juice and took the pills without a fight.

"Want something to eat?"

She shook her head.

He picked up the remote from her nightstand. "Can I put something on for you?"

"As long as it's not the critically acclaimed *Big Boobs on the Beach*."

He let out a chuckle. "Glad to see you still have your sense of humor, Sunshine." He quickly located one of the science channels, where they were broadcasting a series about the universe. His eyes fastened on the screen. "Does it bend your mind thinking about all the stars out there and what lies *beyond* the universe?" he said almost to himself.

"God, yeah. And I love it. I love this show," Sarah mumbled before turning her head to the side and drifting off.

"Me too," he whispered.

She started making cute little snoring noises, and he stretched out on the bed beside her, the show droning in the background.

When he woke up, there was drool on the pillow he'd apparently commandeered and a pair of different-colored hazel eyes fixed on him.

"Wakey, wakey, Sparks. You were out cold."

"Hmph?" He sat up on his good elbow and looked around. "What the hell? How long have I been out?"

"Long enough that they moved on to a series about the Bermuda Triangle."

He scrubbed his hand over his face. "Is it any good?"

"Meh."

He dropped his head to one side and looked at her. "Then why didn't you change it?"

She gave him a chin lift. "Because somebody hogged the remote."

He glimpsed the remote still locked in his grip. "Oh shit. Sorry." He pushed it at her. "How you feeling?"

"Like dog pooh, but the meds are helping with the chills and aches. How's the shoulder?"

"Glad to hear it. Shoulder's fine." He sat up and gingerly stretched what he could of his upper body to keep from setting off his sore shoulder. He glanced back at her. "Need anything?"

"I'm good for now. Is your mom doing okay?"

Huh. She was sick yet still thinking of his mom? "Mom's doing great. We've got it all worked out, so don't worry your pretty little head. Just get better."

"Think I'll fall back asleep for a bit."

"Good. Holler if you need anything." He stood and blinked sleep out of his eyes.

"Hey, Quinn?" she mumbled.

"Yeah, babe?" *How—and why—did* that *slip out? I've never called anyone "babe" in my life.*

"Thanks for taking care of me."

And hearing that was another first.

# Chapter 19

## But It Was Catch and Release

Sarah got worse before she got better. For nearly four days, she toed the line labeled "delirious," drifting in and out. Quinn had been in touch with the Blizzard's medical staff about his shoulder and about her. They declared her not sick enough to be taken to the hospital and discouraged him from trying. If he took her in, they said, the hospital might keep her and she'd be isolated from family and friends. *Screw that.*

So Quinn took charge of her care. She needed him, and he realized he liked being needed by the tough little badass with the sharp tongue. Meanwhile, he made sure his mom kept up with her therapy and had whatever she needed.

He'd also started walking Archer. Who else would do it? Besides, it got Quinn out of the house, in the fresh air, without having to don a hazmat suit. So here he was, on an early April afternoon, taking Archer for a stroll along a green belt in his neighborhood, soaking up unseasonably warm weather at the leading edge of an oncoming snowstorm. He wasn't the only one needing a fix of fresh air, though. People were everywhere, on paths and on the grass, though keeping their distance from everyone else.

As he and Archer wandered along the trail, he let his thoughts roam a different sort of path. He pondered how caring for his mom and Sarah made him feel useful. Helpful. Valuable. Like he felt when he played for his team. A giver instead of a taker. He'd been a taker his whole life, and right now he could have been performing some sort of cosmic balancing act to offset those times. Not that the little he was doing could truly put everything on a level playing field, but it was a start. He liked that.

"Quinn?" A voice behind him pulled him from his mind's meanderings.

He stopped and turned. A woman he didn't recognize was jogging toward him in tight running clothes, though she was apparently missing a sports bra because her tits bounced jauntily in time with her jarring steps. As she drew closer, alarms tripped in his head.

"I thought that was you!" she panted. "What a coincidence. I happened to be out for a run, and you're—I didn't know you had a dog."

*Coincidence my ass!* "Dory, how've you been?"

She bent over to pet Archer in an obvious play to flash her impressive cleavage. Archer backed up and flung his head, as if avoiding her touch. *Whoa!* That dog loved everyone; Quinn had never seen him back away before.

Dory shrugged and straightened, giving Quinn a flirty smile. "I'm doing well. Except for being sad a certain someone hasn't returned my calls." Striking a pouty face, she placed her index finger against one corner of her mouth and tugged it down.

He stared at her while a shit ton of detritus swirled through his head. *This chick looks way better in the dark after I've consumed a fifth of rum. Sarah's got beautiful skin and even prettier eyes. Is Dory stalking me?*

"Sorry. I've been, uh, busy … The virus and all. I haven't checked messages lately." *If I had, I'd have blocked you.*

Dory crossed her arms over her chest, pushing her boobage upward and outward. He hadn't meant to dip his gaze there, but the motion had been dramatic enough to catch his attention. His eyes shot back up to hers. She sported a little smirk. *She knows exactly what she's doing.*

"But your team's not playing," she complained. "I thought with you having more time on your hands, we could be together more." The flirty smile transformed into a downright scary one—probably her failed attempt at cagey.

*I fucked this girl—twice—why? Liquor. Libido. Lunacy.*

He snaked his fingers through his hair. "Well, actually, I've been spending lots of time with … with my mom and …"

She shot out a hip and perched her fist on it. If she was going for sexy, she'd failed at that too because her posture resembled a gimpy flamingo.

"Who *else* have you been spending time with?" This came out in a decidedly possessive, less friendly tone. She narrowed her eyes on Archer. "You still haven't told me where you got the dog."

"Well, he's not really my dog."

"You son of a bitch!"

He rocked backward as if she'd slapped him. She closed the distance. "No closer than six feet!" he blurted like a total idiot.

She ignored his dumbass declaration. "You have a new girlfriend, don't you?" Her voice had soared upward by a few decibels.

He threw out a hand in an apologetic gesture. "Dory, I'm sorry. I shouldn't have—"

"Don't you touch me, you, you … two-timing prick!"

Heads turned. Quinn tried to duck his. "I wasn't trying to touch you."

Archer gave off a series of sharp barks and shifted his weight from leg to leg. Whatever the dog was doing, it diverted Dory's attention from Quinn for a moment, and he took in the audience surrounding them like spokes arranged at six-foot intervals.

Dory lasered her focus back on Quinn and wagged a finger at him. "We're done, Quinn Hadley! And don't think you can call me and smooth this over!"

Before he could protest that he *hadn't* called her—*wasn't that what she was just griping about?*—she pivoted on her heel and stomped away. Quinn blew out a relieved breath and tugged on Archer's leash. The dog seemed as anxious as he to get away from Dory, the green belt, and its clustered spectators.

*God, I hope no one caught that on camera.* In the next breathless instant, he understood being taped might be the least of his worries. Minutes later, when he and Archer were safely ensconced at home, he texted Paige Miller, who'd helped him find this rental house in the first place: *About the defunct security system. What would it take to fire it up again?*

Sarah tossed and turned. She fought demons escaping out of a hole in the ground she couldn't seal up. They were coming for her, snatching at her to offer her up as a meal to a pack of hungry wolves. Sometimes it was one lone wolf.

Quinn hovered on the edge of her nightmares, concern etched in his oh-so-handsome features as he force-fed her fluids. She had a blurry recollection of him saying her fever was one-oh-two and that she was *not* sick enough to be taken to the hospital. Good, because she liked her room; the bed was big enough for her to thrash in while she went from hot to cold and back again.

She didn't care that her clothes were sweaty, she was sweaty, and her hair was pancaked to her head. Quinn would hand her fresh, oversized T-shirts that smelled like him, mumbling about wearing his stuff because he didn't want to rifle through hers. Everything he said came out garbled, as if he spoke in tongues, but the distinct word "babe" sometimes pierced the veil of her consciousness. She might have even let out a little sigh at hearing it.

Archer seemed to be bedside at all times, stalwart that he was, holding a canine vigil. Even in her fever-addled brain, Sarah recognized humor in the fact that Quinn and Archer were sharing caregiver duties.

She'd settled in after an especially restless doze, finding that just-right spot where she could breathe through her nose and not cough. She floated, dreaming she was in this bed and flat on her stomach. The covers were pulled down to her butt, and big, rough hands were under her tank top, gliding over her skin, rubbing something greasy into her upper back.

*Oh God, yessssss! A sex dream! But what's with the greasy shit on my back?*

The "shit on her back" wasn't just greasy, it was mentholated. She raised her head. The hands stopped. She glanced over her shoulder. *Not a dream.* "What are you doing?"

Quinn peered at her. "You don't remember me asking just now if you wanted me to spread this on you?"

"No. What is it?"

He held up a jar that appeared ridiculously small in his meaty hand. "Tiger Balm. Some Chinese stuff Mom uses everywhere, for everything. She thought it would be good for your congestion. I swear to God, I asked and you said, 'Go forward,' or 'Go for it,' and rolled on your stomach and pulled the covers off. That wasn't me."

*I did? Damn, I'm definitely out of it. I'd have remembered giving an okay for a back rub, if for no other reason than I wouldn't have wanted to miss it.* "Did you do my front too?" Her voice came out in a squawk.

He looked genuinely affronted—it was kind of a cute look on him. "God, no. I thought I'd do your back and leave the rest to you."

"Are you done?"

"Not quite. There's a little more to—"

"Thank *God*!" She flopped back on her stomach with a noisy sigh. "Carry on, Sparky."

A rumbly laugh reverberated in his chest. "Yes, ma'am." His fingers worked over her back, her shoulders, her spine, kneading and digging as he teased up her top inch by inch. She adjusted so he could push it higher, clearing her shoulder caps. Then she moaned; she couldn't help herself. What he was doing felt soooo damn good. Maybe she should stay sick.

The more she moaned, the deeper he massaged, until her upper back was reduced to warm jelly.

"Lower back," she croaked when he stopped.

"You sure?"

"I'm sure. Just keep it above the panty line."

"I'll do my best," he chuckled. "There's not much room to maneuver." He splayed his warm hand over the small of her back. "You don't have a lot of real estate. My hand reaches almost all the way across your back here." His voice was gravelly and low. Sexy as hell. He hadn't bothered to pull her top back down, nor did she urge him to. Air moving over her mentholated skin sent tingles from the follicles on her head to the tips of her toes. Or was it his touch causing that sensation?

He leaned down and whispered beside her ear. "That's a very fine pair of dimples you've got there, toots. Nicest I've ever seen." His warm breath caressed her skin, turning it all goose-bumpy. She might have let out an errant moan that had nothing to do with his fingers kneading her back. This was followed moments later by a shameful whimper when his fingertips brushed just below the top of her panties. She longed for them to slide down farther. For him to drag her panties down, slowly, slowly. Down to her ankles. Off her ankles. For him to explore and massage her ass, her legs, and slide a calloused hand between her thighs and creep higher, higher, doing wickedly wonderful things with his strong, thick fingers.

But he behaved—*damn him!*—and she bit back her frustration.

Yeah, she *had* to be sick if these lustful thoughts were chugging around in her head. Obviously, she'd moved from the delusional to the hallucinating phase of the virus's progression.

With an extended sigh, she let her body melt into the mattress, and she floated away with the incredible, sensual sensation of Quinn's powerful hands all over her bare back.

Sarah's soft snuffling noises signaled she was asleep, and Quinn reluctantly withdrew his hands from her smooth skin and straightened. Other parts of him were pretty damn straight too, and looking at her naked back and her perfect ass jiggling beneath her thin panties every time she moved only added to the ache. Her arms were crossed over her head, and white half-crescents of soft flesh where her bare breasts were pressed into the mattress taunted him, urging his fingers to touch and stroke and caress.

*She's sick. She's sick. She's sick.*

Archer was staring at him staring at Sarah. Quinn stood, and the dog's gaze traveled to the wood on full display in his gym shorts. *Yeah, I'm the sick one, Arch.* He glanced back at Sarah's form longingly. *And now I have a new image for the spank bank.*

He kept his eyes fastened on her exposed back. Lack of blood in his brain meant only a skeleton crew was at work in the processing department, which left him bewildered about what to do with her top. Leave it the way it was? She'd get chilled. Pull it down? That might involve reaching underneath her body and fondling—er, fumbling—until he secured it in place. He felt his enthusiasm rising at the prospect of option two; unfortunately, the visual turned his wood into granite. Maybe he should do nothing—stand and stare until she rolled over—

*Covers!*

He pulled the covers over her instead and scrambled from her room. The problem in his pants wasn't going away, and he was anxious to hit the shower and take care of it—if he could make it that far.

A battle raged in his head. Every admonition his saner self had thrown at him, every logical argument to *not* picture his buddy's sister when he rubbed one out, flew out the window because damn it! She was the only woman currently on deposit *in* his spank bank.

How that had happened, he couldn't be sure, but even an image of her pissed-off brother was no longer a deterrent.

His vibrating phone gave him an iota of control. Reading the text calmed his libido down by reminding him of a different, unsettling problem.

Paige: *There's some confusion over the security system. Landlord claims it's owned outright, but the alarm company that installed the equipment claims it's leased. The dispute may take a bit to resolve, but I'll keep working with them to iron it out.*

Quinn: *Meaning?*

Paige: *Meaning they won't activate the equipment, so for now no monitoring and no alerts. Are you having security issues?*

Quinn: *Not yet. Just prepping.*

Paige: *COVID zombies or crazy female fans?*

Quinn: *One potentially crazy female fan.*

Paige: *Being married to Beckett Miller, this is a risk I understand. She's prolly harmless.*

Quinn: *Prolly.*

Paige: *Got backup until I can sort this for you?*

Quinn: *Backup?*

Paige: *A dog? A gun? Hermione's magic spells placed around the perimeter?*

Quinn: *LOL. Dog and his badass owner.*

Paige: *Sarah and Archer. You're safe, then.*

Quinn wasn't so sure he agreed.

# Chapter 20

## Read to Me

Sarah awoke to her phone buzzing. What time was it? How long had she been out? Her eyes focused on the incoming call, and she picked it up.

"Sar!"

"Hey, Bro." Her voice came out thick, groggy.

"How are you feeling?"

"I have no idea. Just woke up."

"Shit. Sorry. Quinn's been keeping me up to date, and he thought it'd be okay if I called."

"It's fine. It's nice to talk to a friendly voice."

"Is Quinn not being friendly?" Gage's voice held a puzzled tone.

"No, he's been great. Beyond great. This is going to sound really strange, but besides Grandma—in her heyday—I couldn't ask for a better caregiver." *A less smothering one, perhaps, but it's sort of cute the way he worries and hovers.* Sarah smiled at the ironic twist that had switched caregiver roles. And yeah, she was surprised by Quinn's attentiveness. She never would have guessed the guy had it in him.

As he'd been doing since she'd first moved in, Quinn Hadley was canting her view of him.

"What *kind* of care?" Gage growled.

"Knock it off, would you? Nothing's happening. He's been a perfect gentleman, and I've been sick."

The attitude evaporated. "Oh. Sorry, Sar. You'll let us know if you need anything, right?"

"Of course." *If Quinn doesn't beat you to it.*

They talked a while longer, and when they hung up, Sarah was exhausted. She flopped backward on the pillows. *God, I wish this would end already!* She rarely got sick, *hated* showing weakness, and was an impatient patient.

Archer suddenly flew into the room, all wags and tongue. "Buddy! Where were you?" She dropped her hand on his head, and he smiled while she stroked his fur.

A breathless Quinn wasn't far behind. "Hey, Sunshine. We were shooting pucks in the driveway. Well, I was shooting and he was retrieving. Were you just on the phone?"

"Yeah. Gage called. He's convinced we're having wild monkey sex twenty-four-seven. He's ready to swoop down from the mountains and whisk me away."

Quinn's liquid brown eyes grew round. "Was he serious?"

"About the monkey sex or whisking me away? I guess it would be both."

He blinked.

Sarah chuckled, which led to coughing, which led to wheezing, which made her chest tighten and her ribs ache.

He dropped onto the edge of the bed, making the mattress dip. She rolled against his hip and tried to extricate herself while coughs racked her body. He gently picked her up and placed her against the pillows. "Something to drink? Cough medicine? What do you need?"

"How about a bottle of bourbon?" she croaked.

"Not on your meds list, babe, but nice try."

*Babe? There it is again. Does he call them all that?* The endearment should have bugged the hell out of her, but oddly it didn't. It sounded … nice.

*Crap! I'm regressing back to the delusional part of the sickness.*

As if he realized what he'd said and it bugged the hell out of *him*, Quinn vaulted off the bed and ran both hands through his hair. "I'm heading to the kitchen. Can I get you anything?"

"No. But how about you come back and watch *American Ripper* with me?" Shit, she sounded pathetic. Sick and pathetic. But as fascinating as the show was, it scared the stuffing out of her, and having Quinn there would make it less frightening. Go figure. Now she was turning the guy into a virtual knight in shining armor. *Yeah, I'm sick all right.*

"Maybe in a bit. I need to check on Mom and take care of a few things." He was fidgety, twitchy as hell.

She tilted her head. "You're always asking how I'm doing. How are *you* doing? Everything okay, big boy?"

His look verged on panicky. "Why wouldn't it be?"

"I don't know. You're acting a little off." *Or maybe it's that delusional thing I've got going on.*

"Am I? Guess I need to spend some time in the gym."

"You do that. And work out for me while you're at it, okay?"

"Sure will. And Sarah?"

"Mmm?"

"If you see, or hear, anything weird—like someone working in the yard—you let me know, okay?"

"Why? What's going on?"

"Nothing. Just … strange times right now."

"'Kay." She sank into the billowy pillows. Something niggled at her, but she was too tired to unravel it, and soon she was drifting into slumber again.

Rustling at the French doors woke her up. It was twilight, and her room was dark. She raised her head, but she was alone. No Quinn, no Archer. She glanced toward the uncovered glass doors but saw nothing beyond. Probably just her imagination.

She texted Quinn and got up to take a shower, overjoyed that she had the energy to get herself shampooed and washed. When she stepped out of the bathroom, Quinn was lounging on the other side of her bed, hands laced behind his head as though he belonged there. A vague recollection of him doing that the last few days hovered like a mist.

"What are you doing here?" she blurted.

"Your text said you heard a noise, and I thought I'd take a look outside."

"I think my imagination caused it."

He shrugged. "I didn't see anything. But it's pretty windy out there."

She took him in, all long and stretched out on the bed in jeans, bare feet, and a Henley that molded to mouthwatering muscle. "Have you been sleeping next to me?"

He looked startled but quickly recovered. "Sometimes when we're watching a show together, I doze."

"What have we been watching?"

"All kinds of shit. We've watched everything from science to biographies to ancient pyramids. Is there anything you're not interested in?"

"Not really."

"Do you remember watching past hockey games and talking about the plays?"

"Vaguely."

"You know your stuff."

"So do you."

He laughed. "As I should. Hungry? Thirsty? Is there anything I can do to make you more comfortable?"

God, he was sweet. She lowered herself on the bed and sighed into the mattress before lowering her lids. "I'm good. I feel about fifty pounds lighter after my shower."

"You smell really, really good."

Pleased, she rolled her head toward him. "Yeah?"

"Oh yeah."

"Good, but I think the shower wore me out. My eyes burn too much to read or watch TV. Would you read to me?"

He cleared his throat. "Uh … read what?"

She leaned over, swiped her e-reader from the nightstand, and switched it on. "Here."

"It isn't the romance crap, is it?"

"Is the big, bad hockey player chicken?" Her toes started to tingle just thinking about that deep voice of his reading some of that "romance crap."

"Of course not," he scoffed. She could have sworn he blushed.

"Maybe you can score the characters on their … prowess. You know, like at the Olympics?"

A chuckle rumbled through him, and she grinned.

He started to read. He got through one sentence before he fell into hysterical laughter. "I can't do this!"

"Embarrassed?"

"Yes! Happy now?"

"No. You've only read one fucking sentence."

"Okay. Are there some non-sex parts I can start with? You know, like foreplay, so I can build up to the more graphic shit? You sort of threw me into the deep end here, Sunshine. We already have hard-as-wood cocks going into wet folds. And why the hell aren't they using protection?"

A laugh spurted from her. "It's the eighteenth century, you nut."

"They had STDs back then."

"Of course they did, but they didn't have Trojans … or Durex … or …"

He cleared his throat. "Okay. Let me try this again." He man-giggled through half of the scene, until he finally dissolved in guffaws. "Oh my fucking God! This is … this is … porn!" he wheezed.

"You're taking all the romance out of this, you know."

"That's what *she* said!"

"C'mon, Sparks. I know you can do this. And if you can't, I'm kicking you out of my bed."

"That's *also* what she said!"

She turned her head to the side and cracked open an eyelid. "You've been kicked out of bed before?"

He nodded. "God, yeah."

"Don't take this the wrong way—like letting it go to your already oversized head—but I'm having a hard time picturing it."

"Like I said, toots, I don't do things halfway. When I piss off a woman, I *really* piss her off."

Now it was her turn to chuckle. "Now *that* makes sense."

He laid the e-reader between them. "How about I read from the latest issue of *Structure*?"

"You read my magazine?" Her tone broadcast her surprise.

"Cover to cover. Fascinating stuff. I'd forgotten how much I like it."

"*I* haven't even read my magazine," she groused.

"So this is perfect. There's this great article about anchored wall systems."

"Meh."

"Okay. There's a different issue on evaluating historic stone bridges."

She blinked a few times. "How many of my magazines have you read?"

"I've read them all. I hope that's okay."

"Of course it's okay." She closed her eyes and snuggled into her pillow. "I like the sound of the bridges, but don't read it to me. Just tell me about it."

He did, his voice lulling her into a warm, floaty place. When he grew quiet, she opened her eyes and peeked at him. He was staring at her.

She frowned. "What are you looking at?"

"You." He tapped the end of her nose. "I like your nose. And the bling."

When she crossed her eyes to look at it, he laughed. "You have long eyelashes," he said in a reverent tone that fired something in her tummy. "Did you know they flutter when you dream?"

*Oh wow! That's either super creepy or really, really sweet.* Judging by the tender look on his face and the soft tone of his voice, she was going with the latter.

She swallowed around a sudden lump in her throat. "No. I don't usually record myself when I'm sleeping."

As if he hadn't heard her quip, he reached out and swept her hair back. "And your hair … It's so silky it constantly falls across your face." She closed her eyes, relishing the feel of his fingers as he tucked strands behind her ears. It was such a gentle, intimate gesture that she was both moved and completely stunned. Two warring emotions welled inside her.

He snatched his hand back, the sudden movement popping her eyes open.

He shrank away—as much as a man his size could. "Sorry … Hey, can I get you some soup?" His abrupt businesslike tone was completely incongruous with the lover's sensuous voice he'd used when he'd touched her. Sick as she still was, she found herself yearning for the lover to return—and equally appalled that she craved it.

The next day, Sarah sauntered into the kitchen, and Archer hopped up to greet her. Two heads swiveled in concert; two pairs of eyes riveted on her. She raised her hand in a self-conscious little wave. "Hey, Liz. 'Morning, Sparky. How is everybody?"

"What are you doing out of bed?" Quinn barked.

She went for a nonchalant shrug that ended up resembling a shoulder jerk. "Don't blow a fuse, Sparky. I'm feeling better and decided I was tired of being lazy. How's your shoulder?"

He gave her a blank stare.

"The one that was in a sling?" she added helpfully.

Recognition dawned in his cocoa eyes. "Fine."

Liz broke out in a broad grin. "Welcome back to the land of the living, doll. You've been missed."

Sarah stole a glance at Quinn, who surveyed her over the rim of his coffee cup as he took a sip. His dark brows were knotted together. *Not so sure Sparky missed me. He looks like he wants to choke me out. What happened to that really sweet guy?* She smoothed her T-shirt that read, "Zombies Eat Brains … Don't Worry, You're Safe." The shirt had been too tight to wear before, but apparently she'd dropped some weight because it fit snugly over her long-sleeved tee.

When she lifted her head, she caught Quinn reading the slogan—and looking rather embarrassed about it, judging from his bright burgundy cheekbones. "Nice T-shirt," he rasped.

"Thanks."

He cleared his throat. "So. We're glad you're feeling better, but until you're symptom-free for two weeks, you have to stay in—"

"I figured as mu—"

"And you have to socially distance from Mom." He tilted his head toward Liz.

Her heart sank. "How am I supposed to do my job?"

"You're not. She and I have this."

Dread bloomed in Sarah's chest. "Oh. So I guess you won't be needing me anymore?"

Liz and Quinn glanced at each other, then both spluttered at once. They were so emphatic Sarah couldn't understand either one, but it gave her a lift. Quinn took the lead. "No. I mean yes, absolutely, we—Mom needs you. I'm the temporary replacement, and I'm pretty sure she'll be glad to have you back." Liz nodded. He broke out in a deep-dimpled smile that instantly put Sarah at ease. Honestly, she'd missed that smile. *God, what a sap!* "Another One Bites the Dust" blared in her brain. *One more woman blinded by Quinn Hadley's brilliant smile.*

"And," Liz added, "you're still on the payroll." She slid her eyes to Quinn, who turned slowly, deliberately, and gave her a frown that might have looked real if not for one corner of his mouth twitching. Liz shot back a twinkly smile.

He rolled his eyes dramatically and refocused on Sarah. "What she said."

"No, I couldn't! I'm not doing anything except sucking up your food and—"

"Sunshine, you've barely sucked anything." Something flashed in his eyes, and his cheekbones flushed a deeper shade, if that were possible.

Uncomfortable—for so many reasons—Sarah shifted her weight. "I have a hard time accepting, um, other people's kindness"—*and letting them pay me for doing squat*—"but I want to thank you both … so much for looking out for me."

"Don't look at me." Liz jabbed her pointer finger at Quinn. "Sparky here is the one who took care of you—and me. And he might've been more protective of you than Archer."

Archer's ears perked up at the mention of his name, and he trotted back to Liz and parked his fuzzy butt beside her.

Sarah was overcome with a weird shyness, and she cast her gaze to the countertop. "Well, thank you."

"I guess now's the time for me to announce my apology to the world," Quinn rumbled.

Sarah raised her head. "Apology for what?"

"For making light of the virus. I had no idea … You were so sick. And Mom could have come down with it. Thank God she didn't."

Behind his back, Liz mouthed, "He was very worried."

"Anyway, I'm glad you're back. You'll have to take it easy because I've been reading about people who think they're better but it doubles back on them, and voila, they're sick again."

Sarah snickered. "Showing off your command of the French language again?"

He stared at her for a few beats, then broke out in a grin. "I can't believe I'm saying this, but I missed your witty repartee, Sunshine."

"I think I missed fencing with you too, Sparky."

Judging by the heat blazing up her neck and over her face, she was pretty sure she'd just gone an even darker shade than Quinn's cheekbones. Meanwhile, Liz's eyes bounced between them, and her smile widened with what could only be described as mischief.

# Chapter 21

## You Can Do That Virtually Too?

One week later, Sarah hummed along at nearly back-to-normal speed. Quinn still wouldn't let her do anything beyond lifting a fork to feed herself, and he was positively militant about enforcing it, a polar opposite to his easier-going side. She found it sorta sexy in an alpha I'm-the-boss-of-you kind of way. Not usually a masculine style she cozied up to, but he had a way of getting behind her defenses. Probably those damn dimples.

Late afternoon one day, they were seated at opposite ends of the couch. She was on her laptop, and he'd commandeered the all-COVID-all-the-time TV from Liz while she soaked in the hot tub. *Thank God!* Sarah had had enough of COVID-19 to last a lifetime.

Quinn was currently engrossed in an episode of *Engineering Disasters*. "So what do you think, Sunshine? Did the engineer call out the wrong rebar?"

Sarah squinted at the screen. "Sorry. I tuned out the show." She glanced between him and her computer screen several times. "How big are you?"

His head whipped toward her. "What, now?"

"How big are you?" she repeated.

A slow, sexy smile spread over his face. "Why don't you slide on over here and find out?"

"Oh, for fuck's—I'm talking about your height and weight. I already know about your ..." *Oh shit. Did I really almost just say that?* By the look on his face, he was finding what she had to say way more interesting than the twisted metal carnage on TV.

"My what?"

She stared at her laptop, wondering if she could be absorbed into it. "Nothing."

He shifted so that he faced her, and he leaned in, his voice low and melty and hypnotic. "What were you about to say?"

Eyes still glued to her computer, she blurted, "I heard some of your groupies talking about your … a certain part of your anatomy in the bathroom the night of the team dinner."

In her peripheral vision, his spine went ramrod straight. *"What?"*

She flapped a dismissive hand at him. "Don't worry. It was complimentary. Your ego would have inflated at least another two dress-shirt sizes."

"What did these supposed *groupies* look like?"

She turned and met his gaze. "Like the ones you usually go for. Blond, heavy in the boob department, slut—er, slinky. I think one of them was a repeat lube-and-tune customer."

He gave her a look that broadcast he was processing the information—in overload mode. "What, uh, exactly did they say?" he coughed.

"Really? I don't want to repeat it. It's embarrassing."

"I find it difficult to believe *you* could be embarrassed by anything, Sunshine. But this is important. Did you catch any names?"

The tone of his voice set a few alarm bells ringing. "Why? Did you lose her number?"

He threw himself back against the couch and dragged his hand through his hair and over his face. "You are so frustrating sometimes!"

"Me? I thought you missed my witty repartee. And jeez, I had no clue you were so desperate for a blow-by-blow—literally—about your dick. Maybe you should shoot video of yourself and watch it. That way—"

"Jesus Fucking Christ on a cracker, don't even go there," he snapped. The back of his head rested against the couch, and his eyes were closed, giving him a relaxed appearance. But the rest of him totally contradicted his calm affect. His hands were laced across his stomach, and his thumbs circled one another like accelerating propellers. One leg was bouncing to some ridiculously fast and out-of-sync rhythm. "You have no clue how *not* funny that is, toots."

*Whoa!* This sounded serious. Gage had had some unpleasant experiences with "overzealous" fans, and while he'd never shared the deets of what had happened, he'd often taken Sarah to events as his plus-one for protection—before he met Lily, of course. "Hey, Sparks, what's going on?"

"First tell me what they said. Please."

She put the computer aside and wiggled in her seat. "Well, it went something like, 'He's soooo cute. I get why you screwed him in his truck,'" she said in a high-pitched voice. When she looked over at him, Quinn's eyes were shuttered, and he had a pained expression on his face. He made a rolling motion with his hand, indicating she should go on. *Talk about uncomfortable!* "Um, there was more discussion about your dimples and hair and how funny you were. Then the one … Her name was—" Sarah snapped her fingers. "What's the name of that fish in *Finding Nemo*?"

He groaned. Not a good kind of groan. "Dory."

"That's it! Dory. Well, Dory squeezed her tits and told her friend how much you liked them."

Another long, low groan. "I can't believe women talk about that shit." Another hand drag over his face. "Fuck me."

"Wasn't that the whole idea?"

He rolled his head toward her and opened his eyes. "Would you just …?" he gritted out before looking away again.

"Okay. But consider yourself warned. There's more, and it doesn't get any less graphic." She paused a beat and continued cheerfully. "But you might actually enjoy this part. I think most guys would like hearing how, uh, well-endowed a woman thinks they are."

"Sunshine!" he yelled. "What. Did. She. Say?"

A few weeks ago, her sadistic side would have enjoyed toying with Quinn Hadley the way a cat toyed with its prey, but that was before she'd gotten a glimpse of the *other* Quinn Hadley—the one who was fun to talk to and who cared about his mom. The one who'd sat with Sarah and nursed her through her sickness without complaint. The one who took Archer for walks. The one who was giving his swear jar money away.

So despite her misgivings about him, it was with no joy and a whole lot of cringing that she sped through her narrative. "She said you were so big she choked when she went down on you and that she wasn't putting out in the backseat anymore and that you needed to either take her to your house or a nice hotel with room service because she wasn't a slut."

Deafening silence hung in the air between them.

At last, he let out an extended, strangled breath. "Shit. Fuck. Goddamn."

"Yep. Those would be the top three I'd go with too."

He turned his head back to her and smiled. Not his full-on, dimpled smile, but one that was achingly lovely because it seemed so special and genuine and … private. "Thank you," he said. "I know that wasn't easy—even for a sassy potty mouth like you—and I'm sorry you had to hear it *and* repeat it."

"Is she giving you a bad time?"

He shook his head. "Not really. I bumped into her the other day when Arch and I were out for a walk, and it was awkward as hell. But that's what I get for being an idiot and hanging with her in the first place."

*Hanging? Yeah, that's one way to put it.* The thought of Quinn and the buxom blond made Sarah a little queasy. "Do you want to hook up with her again?"

Despite his fidgets, he gave her a swift, emphatic reply that calmed her a fraction. "Hell no. That was a mistake I wish I could do over."

"What would you do if you could?"

"Run the other way."

"Is everyone here?"

A chorus of feminine yeses sounded through Sarah's laptop as she relaxed against her pillow-packed headboard and fisted a bourbon and Coke. After last night's epically embarrassing conversation with Quinn, she was stoked for her first ever virtual Girls' Night Out. Lily, Natalie, Paige, and Paige's assistant, Katie, raised their adult beverages in a toast, and Sarah joined them.

"Here's to Paige's Pussycats," Natalie chortled.

"I can't drink to that," Paige scoffed.

"Just drink, Paige. It'll get better. I promise," Katie urged.

Sarah was already on the verge of laughter.

"How about Paige's Pixies?" Lily suggested, but she was shot down immediately.

"No," declared Katie. "That's Beckett's exclusive moniker for his wife."

"Why do we have to be Paige's anything?" Paige protested. "Couldn't we be the A-Team?"

"The P-Team!" someone shouted, and they all had another drink.

Then the names started to fly, accompanied, of course, by more toasting and drinking. No surprise, the names got sillier by the turn.

"Paige's Pants!"

"Paige's Peaches!"

"Paige's Page-turners!"

"What the hell's a page-turner?"

"Who cares? It's a suggestion, so we drink!"

From there, the conversation segued to what the women were doing during quarantine—working, naturally—what their husbands or boyfriends were doing during quarantine—getting in the way, coaxing the women into the bedroom more than usual, naturally—and how happy they'd be when the men got out of the house—naturally.

Sarah listened to their hilarious stories, an outsider, though not on the outside.

Finally, Lily said, "How's life with Quinn Charming, Sarah?"

"Different than I expected, especially after I got sick."

"How so?"

"He's a regular mother hen, clucking over me." After Lily's loud laugh, Sarah added, "I know, right?"

"Sarah," Katie interjected, "you should totally do Quinn."

Sarah spluttered. "Why?"

Katie raised her glass and batted her lashes. "Because he's hot, that's why. Can you imagine tugging on that hair like a set of reins while you're riding him?"

"Katie!" the other women sang in a chorus.

"You've *got* a boyfriend," Lily reminded her.

"What? I don't actually *want* Quinn. But Sarah could tell us what all the fuss is about."

"There's fuss?" Sarah was suddenly uncomfortable, reminded—again—how Quinn attracted women like sharks to blood. Moreover, why did this bother her?

Katie's eyebrows bounced. "There's always fuss over a guy like him."

"You mean a player who's fucked half the women in the northern hemisphere?" Sarah scoffed.

"He's not *that* bad," Lily chimed in. "Is he?"

"Puck bunnies on speed dial." Then Sarah told them about the call she'd taken on Quinn's *special* phone.

"But Quinn's so nice," Lily protested.

"Which is *why* he's fucked half the women in the northern hemisphere!" Natalie declared triumphantly.

A knock sounded on Sarah's door, and the women all went silent. "Uh, hello?" Sarah said to the door.

"You decent?" came Quinn's voice. Over her laptop's speakers, the women could be heard laughing.

*Oh shit! Did he hear that?* A twinge of guilt bit her. "Um, yeah, but I'm kinda in a virtual meeting here."

He cracked the door and stuck his hand through—a hand holding a fresh bourbon and Coke. "Thought you could use a refill for your *meeting*. If you want to hand me your empty—"

"How did you know?"

"ESP."

Sarah traded out the drinks, and the door snicked shut. When she returned to her laptop, everyone else had fresh drinks too.

"Oh shit," said Natalie. "You know what this means, right?"

Paige nodded solemnly. "Yep. The menfolk are conspiring."

Sarah was confused. "Conspiring?"

"They're talking to each other," Natalie said. "Which means they're working *like a team* with the ultimate goal of getting that winning score."

"Which is?" Sarah felt like she was one step behind.

"They want to score tonight," Lily offered helpfully.

When Sarah didn't respond, Natalie added, "Score *off* the ice. Like, they're looking to light the lamp? Taking aim in hopes of putting the biscuit in the basket? Using their hard sticks to—"

"Got it!" Sarah interrupted. "I don't need any more metaphors to understand the gist of … being in the crease."

They fell over howling. When they recovered, Paige was still giggling. "I'm afraid. *Very* afraid."

The party paused. "Why?" Lily asked.

"Are you kidding? I'm Fertile Myrtle, and Beck's got superpowered swimmers. All I want is some good, old-fashioned, down-and-dirty sex *without* what comes nine months later!"

A man's voice boomed in the background. "I heard that! Ready whenever you are, pixie."

"Omigod, now they're eavesdropping!" Katie yelped. Sarah cringed. They all burst into a fresh round of laughter.

"Okay. Okay," Natalie dropped her voice between her snort-giggles. "We still have to get poor Sarah hooked up."

Sarah mocked in a haughty tone, "'Poor Sarah is just fine, thank you very much."

"No taking Quinn for a spin?" Katie asked.

Sarah sputtered. "Definitely not! Don't get me wrong. He's nice to look at, but he knows it. Not interested in that type."

"Hmm. What would you say to a *different* dark-haired, dark-eyed guy? One who's a little more mature and loves dogs?" Natalie suggested.

"Oh, I know who you're talking about. Your brother, right?" This from Lily. "He's a cutie."

Sarah feigned indifference. Not that she was interested in the brother. Just the opposite, and she didn't want to offend her newfound friends.

"Yep." Natalie took a slug of a red cocktail.

Lily picked up the slack. "Tall, lean, dark brown hair, big brown eyes, and funny. He's kinda like Quinn, only Drew doesn't know he's good-looking."

"What do you say, Sarah?" Natalie poked.

"I'll think about it." She wouldn't, of course, and hopefully the idea would just fade away.

The party progressed for another hour until the women said their good-nights, leaving only Paige and Sarah.

"Thanks for including me, Paige. I had such a great time tonight."

"I'm so happy you joined in. You're a great addition to the group." Paige paused. "While I've got you, I wanted to ask if I could send over some blueprints for a project I'm thinking of, and since we can't get together in person—"

"Yes! Please!"

Paige chuckled. "Okay. I'm glad you're on board."

"Well, you know what it's like, being cooped up twenty-four-seven with—"

"Oh yes. And I also know the 'type' you're cooped up with. Intimately."

What had Sarah missed? "I'm not sure I follow."

"Beck was a total player. I tell people he changed girlfriends as often as he changed socks, and the man changes his socks at least twice a day."

Sarah rummaged around in her memory bank, coming up with limited images of Beckett doting on his wife and his baby daughters. "Seriously? He's like Mr. Mom."

Paige chuckled before heaving her eyes to the ceiling. "Yeah, well, things are different now. *He's* different. If you want a look-see at the old Beckett Miller, I'm sure you can still get an eyeful on YouTube. I just hope like heck that when our girls are old enough, the evidence is completely wiped from the planet. I don't need them seeing footage of their half-naked dad dancing with completely naked women or getting his drunk self tossed from strip clubs."

Sarah's eyes popped wide. "Whoa! I had no idea."

"Good!" Paige smiled, her dimple on full display. "Then there's hope. Seriously, though, I didn't want to give the man a chance. I had my own trust issues, but then I got to know him and realized what was hiding under all that bad-boy behavior."

"How did you get past it?

Paige shrugged. "I decided to trust what was in front of me and ignore the stuff from his past. After all, people change. They grow up. I believed with all my heart that he was—we were—worth taking a chance on. And I haven't looked back. No regrets." She tilted her head, her expression taking on a dreamy quality. "He's incredible. He's … Let's just say I'm so glad I looked beyond the hype and saw the man. I can't imagine life without him."

Paige's voice cracked on the last words, and Sarah felt a tug on her heartstrings.

When she hung up, her mind was a rolling cement drum, churning a slurry of thoughts … and they weren't about the blueprints she'd been excited about.

# Chapter 22

## I'M NOT WITH STUPID

One morning a week later, after Sarah had worked out in the gym with Quinn's mom and helped her into the hot tub, she thrust a brightly wrapped package at him. "I got you something."

His breath stuttered for an instant as surprise rocketed through his veins. A gooey feeling followed, settling in his chest as soft and sticky as warmed toffee. "Like, a present? What is it?" He pointed. "Is it going to explode?"

"Guess you'd better open it and find out." A devilish gleam brightened her hazel eyes, making things in his southern hemisphere perk up like they seemed to whenever he was within eighty feet of her.

He gave her a devilish look of his own and inspected the flat box. It was neatly wrapped with a shiny blue bow. He shook the package next to his ear. "Is it sexy lingerie you're going to model for me?"

She cinched her arms over her chest. "In your dreams, Sparky."

*Yeah, that scenario's* definitely *in my dreams.*

Presents weren't something he was used to getting, and he hated to destroy such a pretty one. "Did you wrap this?"

She nodded.

"Wow. Another talent I didn't know you had. Wonder what else you can do?" He scanned the package, trying to find the easiest, least destructive way in.

"Wouldn't *you* like to know?"

"As a matter of fact, yes, I would." He was rewarded with the eye-roll he was after, accompanied by a loud snort. Were they doing this? Were they flirting? His hopes found a toehold somewhere above his head and climbed.

Gingerly, he unstuck the tape and was carefully peeling back the paper when she snatched at the gift. "Jeez, you're slow!"

He yanked it from her grabby fingers. "Hey, hey, hey! This is *my* present."

"Then open the da—darn thing!" She rolled her eyes—again. God, she did that a lot, but he had to admit he got a wicked kick out of pushing her buttons, especially when she rewarded him with a quirk of her pretty lips as she was doing now. Yeah, she thought it was funny too.

Slowly, deliberately, he opened the box and pulled out its tissue-wrapped contents. Nestled in the folds was a T-shirt, which he pulled out and held up. On its front were emblazoned the words, "Sorry, Girls, I Only Date Models."

"Uh … thanks?"

A shit-eating grin split her face. "It's a good one, huh?"

"You do realize this is for guys who actually *don't* date models?" Too late, he realized how arrogant and ridiculous he sounded.

She swung her gaze toward the patio door. "Good. Your mom won't hear this." Her gaze swung back to him. "Oh. My. Fucking. God! You are so damn full of yourself!"

*Can't disagree there, but I* do *date models.* Did *date models. Wait. Why am I* not *dating models anymore? COVID-19. But is that the only reason?* He stared at her. "I don't know what to say."

"Easy. Say, 'Thank you, Sarah. You're such a thoughtful person.'" She batted her eyelashes.

"Uh, thank you, Sarah. You're such a thoughtful person." He ran his eyes over her face. No malice. No evil lurking in her unmatched, mossy-green eyes. Just something like happiness dancing in them. Because she'd given him a present?

She was proud of this gift, and he was being an asshole. He should be telling her how much he appreciated the trouble she'd gone to, even if he wasn't psyched about the gift itself.

"You didn't have to do this, Sunshine." He wrapped the T-shirt back up in the tissue and crammed it in the box.

Her face fell, disappointment etching her strangely delicate features. Strange because he hadn't thought them delicate when he'd first met her. Had she always had that soft curve at the base of her neck? The perfectly shaped eyebrows that accentuated her big eyes? Smooth skin that reminded him of fresh cream?

The next words that came out of her mouth nearly undid him. "It was just my way of saying thanks for everything you've done. But you don't like it, do you?"

Smoothing the hair at his nape, he said, "No, I love it. I can't believe you did this for me. It's just that …"

"Oh. Is it too small? I got you an extra-large tall."

He tore his gaze from her. "No, I'm sure it'll fit. I was just thinking it'd be nice if we could change the word 'Models.'"

"To what? Porn stars?" she snickered.

He shook his head and looked her straight in the eye. "I was thinking 'Engineers.'"

"Oh." Hyperspeed calculations seemed to take place behind her eyes. "Oh!"

For such a badass, she was letting her emotions play all over her face. Maybe because her walls were made of papier mâché—a flimsy facade to disguise the fact that what she hid behind them was, in fact, pretty soft and vulnerable. Right now he could see right through her, though it didn't help him understand *what* he was seeing. Was she pleased by what he'd just revealed? Terrified? Disgusted?

Her eyes shuttered. "There's something I should tell you." She gusted out a breath. "I'm … I have a date tonight."

*WTF?* "Excuse me?"

"I have a date."

*She's kidding, right?* "You said that. When?"

"I said that too. Tonight."

"With who?" he snapped.

"Whom."

"Damn it! With whom?" His insides were curling in on themselves, his world spinning off-axis.

"You sound like my brother, you know that?"

"I don't care who—whom—I sound like. How the hell can you go on a date? Wait. Time-out. Tell me you're going to get dressed up, sit in your room, and do a virtual date on your computer. That's it, right?" *That still sucks.*

She shook her head. "No. I'm out of quarantine now—it's been over two weeks since I got sick. In fact, you can be out too, I think, so if you wanted to date some of your models …"

Why did it bother the shit out of him that she was okay with him dating *anyone*? Shaken to the core, nothing made sense to him right now, and he didn't have the time or temperance to unravel it. Eyes closed, he shook his head. "Wait, wait, wait. Hold up a minute. Where are you gonna go? No restaurants are open."

"Um, he's cooking dinner. Or ordering takeout. I'm not sure which."

His eyes flew open and fixed on hers. "You're not kidding, are you?"

She seemed to size him up warily. Slowly, she shook her head.

He cinched his arms across his chest and tried to puff it up a few sizes. "Who is this guy? How did you meet him?" he blurted, unable to stop himself. Holy crap, was he really going there? Yeah, because he had first dibs. She was his.

*Goddamn.*

When had he started thinking of her as *his*? And was this ownership of the she's-my-sister variety? Or was it of the caveman she's-my-woman variety? While he didn't know that he had a right to the first scenario, he sure as hell didn't have a right to the second one, and the buzzing in his brain wouldn't help him sort it out anytime soon. This was brand new territory for him, and he didn't like being here. He wanted back on familiar ground where he didn't give a shit what a woman he was lusting after did in her spare time. He vaguely registered that when it came to Sarah, though, this whatever-it-was went way beyond lust.

Sarah casually brushed at her sleeve. "I met him online."

Now the buzzing in Quinn's head erupted, shooting his blood pressure into the stratosphere. Control slipped from his grasp. "*What?* Don't tell me you used a dating app!"

Amused eyes pierced his. Clearly she was enjoying herself. "Okay. I won't tell you I used a dating app."

*Fucking fuck!*

He mustered his best authoritative voice. "Sarah. This is *not* a good idea."

In a move that totally flustered him, she patted his cheek. "Don't worry, Sparky. He's Natalie's brother, Drew, and it's a blind double date. Well, my part—and his too, I suppose—is blind, but not the double date part. Natalie and T.J. will be there." She beamed at him, looking entirely too pleased with herself.

This just got better and better. Goddamn Shanstrom was *still* pissed about the press conference, wasn't he? And this was his jacked-up way of getting even.

Quinn narrowed his eyes. "I thought you said you met him online?"

"I did. Natalie introduced us, we had a FaceTime session, and I decided, what the hell? Voila! Blind double date." When he didn't respond, she smirked. "Voila is French for 'ta-dah!'"

As he watched her sashay away, it occurred to him that she'd been right. He'd been totally full of himself, deluded by the ease with which he'd picked up random women in bars for far too long. Because when it came to *this* particular woman, not only did "pick up" sound far too crass, but he had absolutely no clue how to move the puck to the goal line.

Sarah smudged smoky eyeliner under her lower lashes and stood back from the bathroom mirror. "Meh," she said to her reflection before she applied lipstick. While she wasn't going for knock-'em-dead, it was sort of fun to get dressed up after spending months in sweats, workout togs, and T-shirts. The dress-up clothes made her feel pretty, feminine, sexy, and she'd make the most of tonight. Drew seemed like a nice guy, but the date wouldn't go anywhere. Tonight would simply be a welcome diversion. She'd get away from Quinn Asshat Hadley, the cocky bastard. *So damn full of himself.*

"This T-shirt is made for guys who actually *don't* date models," she told her reflection in a snippy voice. "Well, good for you, Romeo!"

Maybe she'd picked the wrong slogan, but jeez! He didn't have to be such a jerk about it. *At least show a little appreciation.* And what was with that "Let's change 'models' to 'engineers'" quip? Nothing like taking an extra dig at her.

*Asshole.*

After dabbing perfume behind her ears, she slipped on her skyscraper heels and wobbled to Liz's room. Archer followed, watching her with canine concern, as if he were angling for the best spot to catch her when her ankles folded and she came tumbling down. Heels had been a regular accessory for professional garb, but lately? Flats all the way, and she was out of practice.

A muffled "Come in" sounded behind Liz's door when Sarah knocked, and she let herself in. Liz was propped up in her bed, legs stretched out in front of her, an e-reader in her hand. She set it down, lifted her glasses onto her head, and let out a loud whistle. "Look at you! Sarah, you are smoking!"

Sarah perched on the edge of her bed, suddenly self-conscious. "Is it too much?"

"Oh no, doll. You look fantastic. You're gonna have that guy eating out of your hand—as soon as he stops drooling." She let out a little sigh. "And Quinn's gonna be eating his heart out."

"No, he's not!" Sarah scoffed a little *too* loudly. Why did Liz's words set off a little flare of heat at Sarah's core that rushed to her cheeks? "He won't even know I'm gone. He'll probably be catching up with his girlfriends. That'll take all night."

Liz shook her head. "I doubt it. He's never been one for relationships. I have a feeling his family is partly to blame for that."

"What do you mean?" Quinn rarely mentioned the rest of his family.

Liz patted her hand. "Long story—stories—silly family squabbles."

Sarah laughed. "In other words, none of my business. Sorry. I shouldn't have asked."

The older woman seemed to appraise her. "No, doll. That's not what I meant. Every family has its skeletons, and it didn't occur to me that you'd be interested in ours."

"Well, you know about mine, so it's only fair. If you feel like sharing. I'm running early anyway."

Liz stared up at the ceiling. "It's complicated. But I guess what family isn't? I think it all started to derail right after the accident."

Sarah leaned back on her hands. "Accident?"

"Quinnie didn't tell you?"

"No. He's never mentioned it."

"Interesting. Well, Mike, Ronan, and I were coming back from a tournament in Minnesota. Ronan was in an elite league, like Quinn, only Quinn was a few years behind."

"Quinn wasn't with you?"

"No, he was competing in a different tournament, and he was billeting with a family in Portland, so he went with them." She shook her head. "Thank God he *wasn't* with us. Anyway, it was late, we were all exhausted, and we were smack in the middle of a winter snowstorm. I told Mike we should get a motel, but he was anxious to get home. We went round and round, and I lost that battle." A wistful smile played over her features. "So we drove. Mike and I were supposed to share the driving—Ronan didn't have enough experience for the road conditions. Mike agreed to wake me for my shift, and I fell asleep. When I woke up, it was long past time we were supposed to switch, but Mike was still behind the wheel. I could tell he was tired, and the snow was coming down in heavy, hypnotic flakes.

"When I suggested we pull over and trade, he just shook his head. I think some of that macho bravado was at play. 'I'm the man. I'll drive.' Ronan was asleep in the backseat, and I tried not to, but I dozed off again. And then it happened."

Something—the memory—passed through Liz's bright eyes, dulling them. She appeared as though she watched a movie playing only in her head. Before continuing, she drew in a long, shuddering breath. "I woke up to the car hitting a guardrail—Mike had fallen asleep and the car drifted. It felt as though we spun forever, smashing and bouncing and scraping against that guardrail. It was horrible. I was terrified. My husband and my boy were in that car, and I thought we were all going to die."

Sarah sat in stunned silence, wanting to reach out and take Liz's hands, but they were firmly twisted in her lap. Instead, she rested her hand on Liz's ankle, trying to suffuse her with strength and caring.

"Obviously, we didn't die," Liz chuckled mirthlessly. "But in some ways, we did. Ronan's leg was fractured in three places and had to be pinned together. I suffered injuries, including head trauma the doctors think might have triggered the Parkinson's. Mike didn't get a scratch on him, and I think that was a worse fate. He couldn't forgive himself for hurting me and for ending Ronan's dreams of making it in the NHL, so he shut down. When he was offered a one-year coaching job in Poland, he jumped at it. I think the guilt was eating him up inside, and he wanted to leave the memories behind for a while, so I went along with it.

"One year turned into two. When he wanted to stay through a third year, I felt as though he'd given up on us, and I told him he was a coward." She paused, hauling in a breath. "I was angry, hurt, and I told him not to come back. We've been in this strange limbo ever since. Right before I came to live with Quinn, I asked Mike for a divorce."

Sarah's eyes widened. "Does Quinn know?"

Liz shook her head. "No. I haven't told either boy. Until things are settled between Mike and me, there's no point. They don't need the extra heartache.

"My poor Quinn took the brunt of his father's guilt and his brother's rage. *Especially* when he got drafted into the NHL. He and his brother had pushed each other, but then they'd been friends. That was shattered after the accident. Whether Ronan would have made it or not is something we'll never know. But instead of enjoying Quinn's success, Ronan became more jealous and Mike more guilt-ridden. Quinn was surrounded by a broken family through no fault of his own, and he took flak he didn't deserve, so he put up his own walls. We're all like individual guard towers, built out of the same stone, close in proximity but wholly apart. I wish it were different.

"I'm proud of what Quinn's achieved. He's smart, he's determined, and when he makes up his mind about something, he's tenacious. He goes all in. The fame and fortune came, and having no one to give him a reality check, he threw himself into a new lifestyle the same way he does everything. Wholeheartedly."

"He doesn't do anything halfway," Sarah said almost to herself.

Liz laughed. "No, he most certainly does not. As a mother, I'm not terribly proud of some of his behavior, but I'm hopeful. I think you're a good influence."

Sarah's surprise at this statement came out in a squeak. "Me?" In that moment, all she could picture were the overflowing swear jars.

"Yes, you. Usually, he surrounds himself with women who … Well, let's say they have their own agendas and they tell him what he thinks he wants to hear, and he buys into it. Maybe it helps him forget. I don't know. But these women aren't the type he can build anything with. They won't sustain him through the long haul.

"I think being around you grounds him in a way they won't and I can't. It's good for him to know there are strong, intelligent women he can't make swoon with a wink. That have far more substance than the bimbos he takes up with."

Sarah bit back a chuckle. Liz seemed not to notice, and she continued. "He respects you. He listens to you. I see it. What you do and say matters to him. And though he acts devil-may-care, it was a charade until you showed up and the real Quinn—the genuine, lighthearted one—re-emerged. I thought it had been lost."

As she absorbed the details of Quinn's family, Sarah's head reeled. No way was she what Liz played her up to be, but still, she was touched.

She swiped at an errant tear on her cheek. "I'm so sorry about what happened, Liz. But at the same time, I'm glad you told me. It explains … Well, that insight helps me understand your family dynamic a little better."

Liz sighed. "It's a rather ugly dynamic. And my heart aches for us all. Especially Ronan. He's turned this tragedy into something even more twisted by being vengeful. Did Quinn tell you about Jennifer?" When Sarah shook her head, Liz followed up with, "No, that doesn't surprise me. It's just one more unpleasant memory. Would you like to hear it?"

Did Sarah want to hear it? A surprising tug of jealousy said no. But curiosity, and a desire to understand, won the argument. "Yes, I would."

"Quinn had just started dating Jennifer, a lovely girl. It wasn't serious, but Ronan, for reasons known only to Ronan, pursued her behind Quinn's back. I guess he wanted whatever he thought belonged to Quinn. And he got her."

"So Ronan's wife … the kids …"

"Yes. That's Quinn's Jen."

*Quinn's Jen.* Sarah realized her mouth had dropped open. "He must have been devastated." Even as her head spun with everything Liz had stuffed into it, she tried to picture this girl Quinn had dated. It didn't seem right to ask to see a picture of the happy family just to satisfy her perverse curiosity.

She realized Liz was talking, and she tuned back in. "It wasn't as though Quinn was ready to marry the girl, but the idea that his brother—who'd once been his best friend—would hate him so much that he'd do such a thing … It was a blow, you know?"

Sarah recoiled. Where in the narrative was the blame to be laid at Jennifer's feet? Ronan betrayed his brother by going after her in the first place, but it took two to tango, and Jennifer's betrayal was just as stomach-turning as Ronan's.

Liz seemed to remember herself. "Oh my gosh, Sarah. You have a date to get to, and I'm holding you up." She made a pushing motion with her hands. "Go enjoy yourself!"

A bit dazed, Sarah left Liz's room and wandered to the kitchen, only to face Quinn, who stood like a massive tree, his arms crossed over his chest. As he looked her over—with an expression she couldn't read—she looked *him* over. Through yet another entirely different facet of the same crystal she'd been looking through. Who was this man?

# Chapter 23

## Sparky Blows a Fuse

Quinn tried to hold his jaw in place so it didn't swing open and smack him in the chest. Because goddamn! Sarah cleaned up really, really well. Not that he'd suspected she *wouldn't* clean up or that she wasn't gorgeous in her natural state. But still, seeing her like this stole the breath from his lungs. And he hadn't counted on that.

Women who caught his attention were typically either beautiful or hot. Sarah was beautifully hot. Or hotly beautiful. He couldn't decide because he couldn't put two words together, let alone muster a coherent string. So he just stared at her. And stared at her.

"What?" she snapped, bringing him out of his fog.

"I just … You're not wearing one of your goofy T-shirts."

"No, Sparky. I'm going on a grown-up date."

"Dressed like that?" *Oh Christ, could I sound any stupider?*

Glancing downward, she ran her hands over her flat stomach and curvy hips, smoothing her clothes. He covertly made a thorough perusal of his own while her attention was drawn to her self-examination.

*Fuck. Me.*

He stood rooted in place by indecision. Should he follow her? Not let her leave in the first place? Throw her over his shoulder caveman style and haul her … into his bedroom? Or let her walk away?

She raised her hazel gaze to his, which was when he noticed she'd gone to the trouble of putting on makeup. Not a lot, but enough to brighten her eyes and skin. "What's wrong with how I'm dressed? I thought the outfit was rather classy."

Classy. Yeah, that was one way to describe the silky, form-fitting purple top and dark skinny jeans. Though it was modest, as in it covered everything, something about the outfit was also incredibly sexy. Maybe it was the way it made her smoky eyes pop. Or maybe it was because the fabric draped what it covered and put it on display, hinting at the skin beneath without revealing it. Maybe it was the damn stilettos. Really high, really shiny, really black. With a little bow on them.

He was grinding his back teeth so hard his jaw ached. He plastered on a fake smirk. "Isn't that a little over the top for a guy you don't know?"

Those beautiful eyes flashed and narrowed. "What are you? My second brother now?"

He tilted his head side to side, faking indifference. "I told Gage I'd look out for you."

She snorted. "I don't need him doing that, and I certainly don't need *you* taking over for him, Junior."

*Junior?* How could such an innocent word sting so badly and reduce him to a squawky-voiced, barely shaving punk?

He'd ponder that later. Right now, he was fixated on Sarah and her *date*. He'd done his intel on Drew. He knew the guy was a few years older than Sarah—one of those *mature* men she was so fond of. Not to mention he was some sort of damn consultant in the tech field, which made him smart. *Fuck!* And the guy played hockey—strictly beer-league stuff, but still, he had to be in shape, right?

"What time will you be home?" He sounded like his mother.

Sarah narrowed her sexy-as-fuck eyes at him. "What's it to you?"

He mustered all the nonchalance in his arsenal, barely keeping his voice in neutral. "Things are a little crazy in the world right now, Sunshine, and I want to be sure I know what to expect in case … Well, I just want to know when to start worrying if you don't come home."

Now her sexy-as-fuck eyes widened. "Oh my God! *Now* you sound like my mother."

*I know*. But he wasn't about to back off. "So? When do you think?"

"I can't believe we're having this conversation," she grumbled. Her eyes slid to the ceiling, and she seemed to count off. "Eleven? Midnight? I guess it depends on what we do after dinner."

*WTF?* A flare ignited in his stomach. "What do you mean, 'what we do after dinner'?"

"Like if we play a game or watch a movie or … whatever. Do you want me to text you when I'm on my way home so you know I haven't been captured by aliens or slave traffickers?"

"Yes. Yes, I do."

"Okay, Sparks. You got it. Now if you'll excuse me." She bent down to rub Archer's head and cooed, "You take care of Sparky, okay? He looks like he's about to detonate." As she leaned over, Quinn caught a flash of creamy flesh being held in place by a black bra. Yeah, he was about to detonate all right.

After she'd left, he couldn't scrub the image from his brain. Hopefully, she wouldn't be giving Drew the same view when she bent over to pet T.J. and Natalie's dogs, which brought to mind her bending over for Drew in an entirely different way. His heart rate skyrocketed.

He paced, thoughts and emotions colliding and wreaking havoc inside him. He waited all of about half an hour after she'd left before he texted her. *Did you get there OK?*

When she didn't answer right away, he texted T.J. *Sarah get there OK?*

T.J.: *Yep.*

Quinn: *So what are you guys doing?*

T.J.: *Talking. Chilling. Drinking beer. The orgy hasn't started yet.*

Quinn resisted the urge to tell T.J. what he could do with himself. Instead, he typed: *Gage wanted me to keep an eye on her since he's in the mountains.*

T.J.: *She's in good hands tonight.*

Quinn chuffed, looked at his phone wondering *whose* hands, set the device down, picked it up, chuffed some more. *Are you still pissed at me?*

T.J.: *About what?*

Quinn: *Press conference?*

T.J.: *WTF?*

Quinn: *Sorry, man. Thought you were still mad.*

T.J.: *No, but if you apologize for that little stunt one more time, I will be pissed. Same goes if you keep texting me. I want to enjoy myself tonight. Later.*

Quinn let out a growl of frustration. Maybe he should drive over—

"Quinn?"

His mother's voice startled him. She was leaning against a wall, giving him a tentative look. "Everything okay, son?"

A long, slow breath deflated him. "Yep. All good, Sassy. Ready for me to make you some dinner? A cup of tea?"

Her face lit. "And play Parcheesi?"

He chuckled. "Yeah, but you'd better not cheat."

"I *never* cheat."

"Pretty sure you do."

"Quinn Anthony Hadley, I swear, if I could put you over my knee …"

"No swearing, Momster." Without thinking, without knowing what he was doing, he walked toward her and pulled her into a hug. She sighed against him, and his arms wrapped around her frail frame. As natural as you please. Like they'd been doing this forever.

She disentangled herself and, with a tender smile, ran her slim fingers through the hair hanging in his face. As she pushed it back, her light blue eyes sparkled. "She's just out to have some fun. We're all a bit frayed around the edges right now, and it'll be good for her. And you."

"Uh, yeah. Sure." He didn't want to delve into understanding what his mother was implying, and it seemed easier to play along. He ran his hand over the shaggy hair at the back of his head.

Her eyes darted there. "I can give you a trim, if you like."

The floppy strands had been driving him crazy. No visits to the hairdresser's meant they'd gotten long and unruly. "Actually, yeah, that'd be nice."

They gathered up what she needed, and he obediently took a seat on a stool in his bathroom. Like old times.

"How short?" she asked.

He stared at himself in the mirror, and for some reason the word "junior" played tricks in his mind. "I'm ready to ditch the flow, Mom."

Her eyes widened. "You sure?"

"I've been wearing it this way to impress the ladies, which suddenly seems like a really stupid reason, especially since it's a royal pain in my a—rear." He nodded at her in the mirror. "Yeah. Let's do this."

"Okay, son," she giggled. "No more lettuce for you."

He winced with the first few snips, watching each strand float to the floor, but then he relaxed. He was a little kid again, and he reveled in the feel of her fingers working over his scalp. "You like your blue hair, Mom?"

She paused to check herself in the mirror. "Yes. It's fun. Like Sarah. She's fun. I like having her around. How about you?"

Confusion swirled inside him. *Did* he like having Sarah around? She made him crazy in so many ways—some good, some not. He merely hmphed in response.

After several beats, his mother said, "You two remind me of your father and me."

The scissors nearly flew from her hands when he swiveled his head to look at her. Somehow he managed to avoid getting his eye poked out. "What does that mean?"

"Trying to out-challenge each other. It was the same for your dad and me. Never knew a man who could push my buttons so easily. I loved it."

"So why aren't you together anymore?"

Her eyes stayed focused on her work. "We're just taking a very long break." A wistful smile curved her lips. "But oh, I miss the teasing! He gave as good as he got, and we fed off each other. It was exhilarating for a long time."

Quinn cleared his throat. "So why did you guys … Why the long break? Could he not deal with the Parkinson's? Was he …?"

She caught his eyes in the mirror. "Unfaithful? Not before he left. Since then? I hope not, but I don't know. Three years is a very long time."

Her tone told him the separation had been a long one for her too. "Yeah, but *you* haven't …"

"No, I haven't." She flashed him an unreadable look. "I think our being apart has more to do with how convoluted our lives became after the accident, how little we communicated, and how hurt and angry we both were. Between our demanding lives, my disease, the trouble with Ronan—" Her eyes went wide, and she came to a standstill.

Suddenly, she had *all* Quinn's attention. "What do you mean, 'the trouble with Ronan'?"

"Nothing. Forget I said anything." She bent back to her work.

"No, Mom. What about Ronan? I know he's your favorite—it's no secret. Dad wanted *him* to break into the NHL, but then he got hurt. I know Dad was disappointed it ended up being me instead, so you won't hurt my feelings by talking about it." *I'm a big boy now. I think.*

She stopped again, and he wondered if she was going to get through the entire cut or if he'd end up with lopsided locks. Then she laid a hand on his shoulder. "Is *that* what you think? Oh, Quinnie. Ronan is *not* the favorite."

A few silent beats went by before he screwed up the courage to ask his next question. "Then why all the special treatment for him? Is it because I was too much to handle and you couldn't deal?" In Quinn's memory bank, his parents had thrown all their attention at Ronan, letting Quinn fend for himself, *especially* after Ronan's hockey hopes had come to a screeching halt.

Now his mother rested both hands on his shoulders and her chin on his crown. "Quinnie, trust me when I say Ronan needed … help, even before the accident. You didn't. Yes, you were high energy and drove me crazy at times, but you were capable of standing on your own, unlike your older brother. You have a good head on your shoulders about most things. And your dad and I … Well, let's just say it was all hands on deck, and that deck was almost always Ronan. And then the accident. Your dad …" She let out a little sigh. "Well, I always worried we cheated you, but you were so good-natured and seemed to roll with whatever … Gosh, Quinnie, I'm so sorry."

And she was. He could read it in her misty eyes.

He sat in stunned silence while she finished cutting his hair. Finally, he spluttered, "So Ronan's *not* your favorite?"

She offered him a wry smile. "No, honey. I don't have any favorites, but if I did, it wouldn't be your brother."

Blown away couldn't begin to describe his state of mind after her revelation. He'd have to chew on it a while before digesting it. In the meantime, his chest felt about a hundred pounds lighter.

His mom grasped both sides of his head and squared his face to the mirror. "What do you think?"

Though it wasn't the professional job he was accustomed to, and the short length would take some getting used to, he gave her his honest answer. "Best haircut I've ever had, Mom. Thank you." And it had nothing to do with his hair.

Sarah removed her heels from her pinched feet and quietly slipped inside the house from the garage. Quarter after eleven, and everything was dim. Good. Liz and Quinn were in bed then, which was where she would head. After an evening of polite conversation, she was exhausted. But where was Archer?

She padded the length of the hallway that led to the kitchen, and her question was soon answered when Archer rounded the corner, his tail swiping back and forth at full throttle.

She dropped into a crouch to pet him. "Aw, I love how you say hello. But you're not much of a guard dog, are you? I could've lifted the family jewels by now and—"

A figure loomed out of the dimness, startling her, and she fell on her ass.

"You okay, Sunshine?"

She stared up at Quinn's silhouette. Something didn't compute, but the voice was definitely his. He reached down and clamped a big hand on her arm, hauling her upward. A glow from the kitchen illuminated his face. "Have fun tonight, toots?"

"Oh my God! Where's your hair?"

"My bathroom floor," he quipped and took a few steps back.

"Why?" The question came out plaintive, whiny.

He shrugged his rock-hard shoulders. "I was tired of it. Why? Thought you didn't like it?"

"It's not that … It's just … It was your *hair*. Your identity was wrapped up in that hair."

"Not really." He walked into the family room, where the TV flickered. She followed. The volume was so low she barely heard it, but she recognized the show about ancient aliens.

"So you're like Samson now," she blurted.

He picked up a mostly full beer bottle and tipped it to his lips. "I'm what?"

"Samson. Delilah cut off his hair, and he lost his strength. Not good if you're a hockey player."

Cocking his head, he stepped closer. "Are you drunk? You shouldn't drink and drive. I would've come—"

"No. Just in shock." She kept her eyes fastened on his face, scanning, taking him in as she adjusted to the gloom. Solid cheekbones seemed more prominent, and his clean-shaven jaw appeared a little more squared off. The youthful, I'm-all-that persona had retreated, eclipsed by a confident … man. A powerful, mature man. Could a haircut be responsible for the transformation? No. Thoughts of the accident—how it had impacted Quinn's life, his entire family's life, how his father had left, what Jennifer and Ronan had done—had been running roughshod in Sarah's brain all night, and once again she'd found the axis on which she'd pinned her opinion of Quinn Hadley tilted. In fact, it listed so far to one side she was considering scrubbing her initial impression and rebuilding what she knew of him from scratch.

Quinn arched his eyebrows. Even *that* was a different look—far more rugged and appealing.

Sarah blinked a few times, then swallowed, trying to coat her suddenly parched throat. *Is the hair having this effect?*

"You're making me nervous here, Sunshine." His honeyed voice was low, and it resonated inside her, skittering delightful shivers along her spine and limbs. Arm and neck hairs lifted, electrified, standing at attention.

"Sorry. Your new look might take some getting used to."

"What's your initial verdict?" he said casually.

"You remind me of a grown-up instead of an overgrown, messy kid. Does it feel weird?"

"Having you stare at me like that? Yeah. Really weird. Wanna beer?" Without waiting for her answer, he turned and went to the fridge, fished out a bottle, uncapped it, and brought it back to her. He stood at arm's length—just close enough to hand her the bottle—and frowned. "Did something happen tonight?"

*Yeah. Someone grew up and got a whole lot sexier while I was gone.* She took a long, cooling drink. "No. We just sat around, had dinner, and talked. I haven't spent that much time around T.J. The guy's hilarious."

Quinn hmphed and muttered something she didn't quite catch. He raised his bottle to her. "So you had a nice time. Good." He took a slow pull, watching her intently over his bottle. "What did you think of Drew?"

*Wait. Is that what this is about? Is he … jealous?* She answered as honestly as she could, in a sudden and inexplicable rush to put him at ease. "He's a nice guy. We had a good time, the four of us. It just felt like friends hanging out. Which it was."

"You gonna see him again?"

"I doubt it. Unless it's at a big get-together. We're not … He's interesting, but not my type. I don't think I was his type either."

Quinn was wearing the T-shirt she'd given him, and it hugged the hard planes of his shoulders. Those shoulders visibly eased. "So what *is* your type?" Another tip of his beer bottle. As he swallowed, she was transfixed by the ripple of muscle along the column of his neck.

His hooded eyes were watchful as he waited for her answer. The air had been sucked out of the room, and electricity crackled between them. Without warning, she'd grown jumpy, parts of her igniting as her nerves danced.

She took another sip of her beer to calm her somersaulting tummy. "I don't know that I have a type."

*But if you keep looking at me like that,* you're *gonna be my type.*

# Chapter 24

## Things That Go Bump in the Night

"How about a poker rematch?" Quinn heard himself say. And he was lucky he had enough brainpower to come up with that much. He'd been out of his fucking mind the entire time she'd been gone, imagining things she might be doing with another man. On a skate's edge, watching, waiting in the formal room at the front of the house, anticipating the sweep of her headlights ever since his mom had gone to bed.

When he'd finally seen the yellow beams illuminating the long drive, he'd blown out a gust of relief. The fact that it was only a little after eleven had made him relax even more. From there, it had been a matter of beating feet back to the family room and arranging everything so it looked as though he'd been sitting there the whole time and couldn't have cared less whether she was home or not. And now that she was facing him in that purple top and jeans that caressed her curves? He didn't want to let her go. Playing poker with her wasn't his top choice, but he'd settle for it.

Sarah perched one hand on her hip, her heels dangling in her other hand. "You're ready for me to beat your ass again? You *are* a glutton for punishment."

"Hardly. I've been holding back. Now I'm ready to take the gloves off and beat *your* cute little ass."

Her head rocked back slightly. Yeah, he'd said it. But it was true—she *did* have a cute little ass. If she had a problem with it, she got over it, and soon they were seated at the coffee table. And she was beating him again.

"This is a stupid game." He threw down his cards, fully aware how much he resembled a bratty five-year-old.

Sarah made a big show of collecting them, sass quirking her mouth and shining in her eyes. "Not so sure it's the game, Sparky."

She was probably right. His mind wasn't on poker. At. All. He rose, intending to grab their empties. "Want more?"

"What? Beer or ass beating?" She rose too and parked her fists on her hips.

"You're funny," he chuffed. His eyes locked on hers. Dark green pools caught and reflected the light glowing from a table lamp. Shimmering, mesmerizing, pulling him into their depths. Green-gold fire glass. The most beautiful eyes he'd ever seen.

*Stop. Just stop.* He tore his gaze from hers but didn't move.

"Hey, are you okay?" Her voice drifted toward him, laced with concern but soft and musical at the same time. So feminine. She took a step, then another, and reached up to brush her fingertips over his bicep. Her touch electrified, and his hands shot out and cradled her face. Astonishment flashed in those eyes, but she didn't resist, and he took it as the invitation he was craving, pulling her mouth to his with urgency. That one burst, that one swift movement, and the hunger that had been building up inside him uncoiled in a cascade. His lips were on hers, moving, exploring, tasting. He couldn't recall a kiss that had ever started like this one, and it caught him by surprise. She responded instantly, sweetness and tenderness on the surface, but beneath it ran an undercurrent of passion that he longed to delve into.

While his libido might be impulsive, his body was not. He controlled it, leashed it on the ice and in the bedroom, but something more powerful was taking control of him, like a fast-moving wave about to swamp him. When his tongue met hers, it took every fiber within him to hold himself back from the edge, to keep from plunging in. *More, more, more* screamed in his brain as he froze on the brink of devouring her mouth. Much as he wanted to lose himself, to plunder at will, one last tether held him back.

He tore his lips from hers and peered at her, his hands still holding her face, his breathing ragged. Wide hazel eyes peered right back, and her hands slid along his forearms. Her voice came out choked. "Why did you stop?"

*Oh hell yes!* Of all the things she *could* have said, she'd said what he wanted to hear … before he knew how desperately he'd wanted to hear it.

He tried to keep the shallow breaths from his voice, pausing to swallow. "Because I'm not so sure it's a good idea to go down this road." *Because I won't be able to stop myself.* "Your brother won't be happy."

Her lips tipped up. "I won't tell if you don't," she murmured. Her words rocketed to his already stiff cock.

The space between them became charged, as if an invisible microburst of energy pulsed, propelling them into one another. He leaned in, and she matched him inch for inch as his gaze held hers. When their lips touched, gently at first, he didn't close his eyes—simply kept them trained on her face, every exquisite detail clear as he drank her in. Her skin was smooth, silky, flawless.

Her lips brushed his. "You're staring," she whispered.

"Because I can't take my eyes off you."

She pulled back with a giggle. "I bet that's what you say to all the girls."

Her words hit him like shards of ice, and for the first time in his life, he regretted the casual hookups that peppered his past. He shook his head. "No. I've never said that before in my entire fucking life."

"Oh."

He was still leaning, his face tilted so his mouth lined up with hers. With a boldness he didn't feel, he said, "So are you gonna kiss me, or what?"

"You're not afraid of my brother?"

"Fuck yeah, but he's not here right now, and all I can think about is kissing you so you'll shut the hell up."

With a smirk, she snaked her arms around his shoulders and drew close. "Wow. You are the romantic one." Her mouth teased his right before she sucked in his bottom lip and softly sank her teeth into it.

*Goddamn!* Time for gentle was over. He sealed her mouth with his, and she opened, inviting him ever deeper, slicking her tongue over his. Within seconds, they were feasting on each other. She gave as good as she got, and sweet Jesus, she tasted like something he could get addicted to. Apples, cinnamon, wine, a trace of her fruity beer, and something sweetly and uniquely her.

Once again, control dissolved faster than sugar in boiling water. Normally when he kissed a woman, he steered them where they'd go and how they'd get there. But this was … He couldn't keep a straight thought. Tingles raced one after another through his body, each more powerful than the last. It was all primal sensation as he took in Sarah's fragrance, the feel of her soft, wet mouth on his, the little mewling sounds at the back of her throat, and how her body molded itself against his like a custom-fit leather seat.

Kissing Sarah was like walking into a candy store and putting every possible flavor, every possible texture, every possible color in your mouth at once. An explosion. A kaleidoscope. A full-on, all-sensory experience.

Their tongues entwined and danced together. He swept her mouth, relishing the feel of her moist, warm depths. She pushed back, invading his mouth, and he gave himself over to her to pillage at will, losing himself while she took control of the kiss. *Holy shit.*

Her arms banded around his shoulders, her fingers plowed through his hair, and her body stretched and shaped itself to him. Pillowy breasts pressed flush against his chest had his hands trembling in anticipation of touching, exploring, learning what made her gasp. Fingers glided to her narrow waist, the top of her ass, caressing as he pictured her enticing dimples, before moving to cup her cheeks and yank her against his steely length. He skimmed his hands upward, under the hem of her blouse, and his fingertips played across her smooth skin until they reached their target. He cupped her breasts, strumming her beaded nipples through lace before working the material down and caressing her flesh. Her nipples tightened into pearls he longed to roll around on his tongue and taste and tease and suck. She let out a moan and dropped her hand between them, stroking him through his jeans. An involuntary low groan rumbled through his chest, and a new thought muscled its way in. *Don't come, don't come, don't come.*

Sarah was like no one he'd ever felt before. All fire and raw passion, responsive to every touch and shift, chasing her pleasure even as she bestowed it. She had him grinding against her hand like an eager teenager. The dim realization dawned that if he didn't get himself under control, he'd go up in flames. And he hadn't even been inside her yet.

Reluctantly, he uncoupled his lips from hers. He was swimming, gasping, and he needed to wrestle back the helm on this ship or he'd drown. His hands still beneath her blouse, he stroked and kneaded, delighting in her soft contours while he trailed kisses down her silky neck, grazing her collarbone with his teeth. She moved her hand from his swollen cock, gripped his shoulders, and dropped her head back with a sighing moan that had him wanting to sink his teeth into her throat. Restraint was a thin, shredded curtain he took swipes at and fleetingly grasped. He switched directions and licked a trail to her ear, where he nibbled and nipped her earlobe, trying to catch his breath.

Just as his hands were working her blouse up, the storm of the kiss ebbed for an instant, and she pulled back and stared up at him as if she'd just realized who the hell he was and what the hell he was doing to her. He paused his fondling as he waited for a signal, a glimmer that she wanted him to keep going.

"Should I stop?" he panted. *Say no, say no, say no.*

"I don't know. What are we doing?"

He dropped his forehead against hers. One corner of his mouth quirked. "You honestly don't know?"

A laugh bubbled out of her. "I *know* what we're doing, but what are we doing? Gage is going to kill us."

Two questions struck him at once: Was she looking for an escape because she wasn't into him? Or was she into him and, unlike him, was thinking ahead? If they took this further, where he longed to go, it wouldn't be casual—not for him—and Gage *would* find out. As bad for his health as that might prove, all of him wanted option two.

He straightened, slid his hands from under her blouse, and placed them on her shoulders. "I thought you said we wouldn't tell him." Now he sounded like a stupid kid again, which pulled some of the wind from his lusty sails. His cock didn't get the message, though. It just wanted Sarah, and it was begging for release, pushing so hard against his fly it might split the zipper momentarily.

To his chagrin, she pulled away and straightened her clothes. His mind wandered to whether her breasts were still exposed under the blouse, and he stifled a groan along with the urge to get his hands back on her and find out for himself.

"Maybe we shouldn't have started this." Her voice held a small quaver he tried to decode.

"Even if your brother finds out and beats my ass, it's totally worth it."

She smiled, and he took it as a sign and drew near once more, snaking his hands around her waist and snugging her to him. She didn't resist, melted against him, and he took her hand and placed it back on his crotch. "Maybe we shouldn't have started it, but how do you want to end it?"

She drew her bottom lip between her teeth and dipped her gaze to where her hand rested on his dick. Unabashedly, she stroked him again and raised her molten eyes to his. He nearly lost it. "Maybe we can help each other out," she murmured.

His hands moved under her blouse of their own accord. The thrill of discovering the lacy cups weren't back in place made his shaft dance. She blinked, and a slow, lazy smile curved her lips. Teasing her breasts, brushing her nipples, he cocked an eyebrow. "Help each other out how?"

She leaned in to his ear, increasing the friction outside his fly. His eyes might have rolled back in his head and stayed there. "Well," she whispered, "I think it's been a while for you, and I know it's been a while for me, and if this is just sex—"

He froze. Went completely still. His brain, which had been floating in and out of a sex-induced daze, suddenly came on board at full capacity. Why did the words "just sex" leave him a little chilled? They were the same damn words *he* would have used, so why were they balling in his chest, ready to flare into heartburn?

*Just sex.* Was that it for her? The question surprised and confused the hell out of him. More questions raced through his head. Compared to Wolf, would Quinn disappoint? Was Quinn capable of living up to what she was used to? What would it take to capture her heart?

Answers were as fleeting as his control had been mere moments before.

He withdrew his hands and glided them up and down her arms—on top of the fabric. "Don't take this the wrong way, Sunshine, but—"

With a growl, Archer hopped up, alert, his body straining toward the French doors leading to the deck.

Sarah removed her hand from Quinn's fly and hissed, "What is it, Arch?"

Glass crashed. Archer barked. Sarah's eyes popped wide, a mirror to Quinn's own.

He spun in place, adrenalin speeding through him like a dam bursting—unlike the pleasurable dopamine rush he'd been enjoying. In the shadows by the French doors, something glimmered on the floor. He glimpsed his hockey stick propped against a doorframe. Another pivot, and he faced Sarah and squeezed her arm. "Go to my mom's room and stay there. Make sure you keep your phone on you." Archer whined beside him. "And take Archer."

Sarah called the dog, who looked torn between her command and wanting to investigate with Quinn. Quinn waved a hand at him. "Go take care of your mom."

The sight of Sarah and Archer trotting away gave Quinn a gust of relief. He grabbed his stick and headed for the glass doors. Before he reached them, glass crunching beneath his shoes brought him to a halt. He dropped into a crouch and ran his fingers over a rock sitting among scattered shards. Cold air blasted him. He glanced at the door, not surprised to find its pane shattered.

*Someone threw a fucking rock through the door!*

He flicked on the deck lights and stepped through a different French door. Were those footsteps coming from the pool surround below? Oddly, the motion sensor lights didn't come on. All his senses sharpened. Cautiously, he worked his way down the steps that led from the deck to the pool level, his eyes sweeping the darkness that enfolded the landscape around it. Normally, the area was illuminated by timed lights, but when his feet hit the bottom landing, he was plunged into eerie inkiness.

He peered at the darkened gym windows. In a murky corner, he thought something moved. He inched toward it, stick gripped. When he found nothing, he methodically walked the length of the floor-to-ceiling glass and came up empty.

Faint, indistinct noises pulled his attention to the depths beyond the pool. He crept around the perimeter, his neck hairs standing on end. *Why didn't I grab a flashlight? Because everything's supposed to be lit up right now!*

The farther he went along the pool's edge, the more the cold, gloomy night closed in around him. His heart was a jackhammer in his chest. The sensation was familiar, though one he experienced on the ice. Not like this.

A rustle on his left startled him. *Something, someone, is there.*

He pushed a cleansing breath through his lungs, counted to three, and deliberately put one foot in front of the other. He raised his stick and plunged into darkness.

# *Chapter 25*

## SAMSON AND SARAH

Sarah ran for Liz's room. A little unnerved by the crash moments before, being with Liz was probably as much for her own comfort as for Liz's.

While the sound of breaking panes had startled her, the look on Quinn's face had really spooked her. His usual smirk, the cocky-casual look, had morphed into downright alarm. The flutterbugs that had set flight during their no-holds-barred lip-locking had been zapped by his sobered demeanor.

As she and Archer navigated the hall, however, her mind detoured to how Quinn had practically dived into her mouth. *Omigod! Soooo hot!*

Her hormones kicked up, and the tummy tickles blossomed once more despite the mystery back in the family room. She couldn't stop her panties dampening at the recollection of his mouth and hands on her, adding to the moisture already there. If he kissed everyone *that* way … Jesus, no wonder women wanted him!

The thought turned her quivering insides leaden, like someone had lassoed her dragonfly wings, and his words floated through her lust-riddled brain. *Don't take this the wrong way, Sunshine …* Fuck! He had been about to tell her he wasn't interested, hadn't he? And that was with her proposing no-strings sex, something a guy like him should have jumped at. She'd offered up her hussy self on a platter, but he'd kissed her and said, "Thanks for the sample, but no thanks." Maybe he'd decided older and brunette were an interesting walk on the wild side, but he'd stick with blond and busty. Except it hadn't felt that way. No, it had felt like he was ravenous and couldn't get enough fast enough.

Telling herself to knock it off, she lightly rapped on Liz's door and pushed it open. The soft light from a bedside lamp revealed Liz reclining on pillows, her arm flung to one side and an e-reader just beyond her grasp. Her eyes were closed, but she stirred as soon as Archer found his way to her side.

"Oh! How did you get in?" Pulling herself up, she rubbed Archer's head. Confusion crossed her face when she saw Sarah. "Sarah? Is everything all right?"

Sarah clasped her hands behind her back and took a short breath to even her voice, choosing her words carefully. "Everything's fine. Quinn heard a noise outside and went to check it out, so I thought I'd look in on you before heading to bed. Do you have everything you need? Anything I can get you?"

"No, doll." She patted the bed beside her. "But tell me about your date. Did you have fun?"

*Date? Right. Seems like weeks ago.* She perched on the edge of the mattress and filled Liz in, which took all of two minutes.

"Quinn was beside himself after you left," Liz laughed.

Sarah frowned. "He *was*?"

"Oh yes. Fidgeted and cussed and paced like he had a bur stuck up his butt. It was kinda cute. I'm not sure I've ever seen him do that before. But then again, he hasn't had to since he went from college to the big league. If you have people taking care of your every need, padding your life so all you have to do is show up—oh, and sycophants telling you how great you are all the livelong day—well, lack of maturity and basic checks and balances will do funny things to someone's brain."

A giggle bubbled inside Sarah. "I'm having a hard time picturing it." The image of Quinn pacing with "a bur up his butt" and the fact that he'd cared enough to be agitated in the first place made her a little giddy. God, she was acting like a starry-eyed teenager.

Her mind zigzagged to him heading toward the noise, his tightly gripped hockey stick to hand. Surely he wasn't in any danger, was he? He'd come give them the all-clear any minute, wouldn't he?

Minutes ticked by, and though Liz was talking, Sarah struggled to focus on what she said. Where was Quinn? She glanced at her phone. A half hour had already passed with no word from him.

She rose and headed for the door. "Think I'll go see what's keeping Quinn. Is it okay if I leave Arch here with you for now?"

"Sure, doll."

As Sarah reached for the lever, the door *whooshed* open. She jumped when Quinn loomed in the doorway. "Hey," he said softly.

She scanned his eyes but couldn't read anything there. His expression was blanker than his poker face. Noticeably missing was the hockey stick, though his hand twitched. "Hey. Everything check out okay?" she ventured.

"Yep."

Something in his bearing set off a few alarm bells in her head. He pushed his way inside, apparently eager to get to his mom, and Sarah stood back. Intruder syndrome had her softly calling Archer and leaving mother and son behind.

In her own room, she flung herself on the bed and stared at the ceiling. *Shit!* What had he discovered? What *could* he have discovered? This was a gated, safe community for Denver's elite, wasn't it? The same unpleasant thought—that he'd regretted the kiss—stabbed its way into her musings, delivering a nasty sting. If he had, she found herself hoping they hadn't shifted into an irretrievably awkward zone that meant the loss of his friendship—a friendship that had snuck up on her and grown into something precious.

Forty minutes later, she was still in her date clothes, stretched out on the bed, staring at the ceiling, her thoughts bobbing atop an endless whirlpool. A knock so soft she almost missed it sounded. Archer's raised head confirmed what she'd heard, and she got up and opened the door. There stood Quinn, straight and sober. She almost shook her head—to clear the cobwebs—because she wasn't used to the short-haired, serious look on him.

"Can I come in?"

Shit. He was being serious *and* polite. She swept her arm to the side. "Of course."

His hand—that masculine hand that had heated her skin—smoothed the back of his head. "You okay?"

She blinked. “I’m fine. How about you? What did you find?”

He let out a big gust of air. “The glass was broken out of one of the French doors.”

“How?”

His eyes drilled hers. “A big-ass rock was launched through it.”

A chill ran up her spine. “Kids?”

“I don’t think so. Listen, can we talk?”

Another chill, and she began rubbing her arms. “Yes. Should I be sitting?”

He closed the door and motioned toward the seating area. “Let’s both sit.”

“You’re being awfully cryptic, Sparky.” She curled up in one of the armchairs, tucking her legs beneath her, while he took the other seat.

He leaned forward, his elbows on his tree-trunk thighs. The T-shirt stretched over his broad back, displaying his sculpted shoulders and biceps. As his hands dangled between his knees, his thick wrists rotated and his forearms flexed. Veins corded with enough definition to be sexy, but not ridiculous, crisscrossed their surfaces, hinting at the power contained there. He reminded her of a big cat, every muscle taut, ready to spring. God, he was a sight, with layers and ridges and planes that called to her.

She needed to get herself under control. “So what’s on your mind?”

He cleared his throat. “You remember the blond that you, uh, overheard in the bathroom? Dory?”

“Yeah?” She couldn’t muster any snark about Dory—only bewilderment edged with dread. The blond’s words rolled around in Sarah’s head, along with an image of her taking Quinn in her mouth while he fondled her double Ds.

Bile rose in Sarah’s throat.

His next words weren’t what she’d expected, and they erased the awful vision. “Well, I might have a little problem of the ‘I’m your favorite fan’ variety.”

“I don’t understand.”

He dragged a hand over his face. “While you were sick, I was out walking Archer in the neighborhood, and she came out of nowhere, pretending she was running, but I think it was—I’m not trying to sound conceited here—but I think she set it up to run into me.”

“What makes you say that?”

"From the, ah, outfit, her makeup, and how she didn't *look* like she'd been running … like she'd been lying in wait instead. Anyway, she kind of lost her shit in front of some people, and I got a really bad feeling—like I might be dealing with someone who's a taco shy of a combo plate. I called Paige to see about getting the security system fired up, but that hasn't happened yet." He offered a weak smile.

Sarah swallowed, her throat sticky. "How many times were you with her? Dory, not Paige."

Another huge breath moved through his lungs. "Look, I'm not proud—this is *not* how I want you to see me—but besides the night in my truck, I brought her back here the night of the team dinner."

Sarah's heart caved. "Oh."

She could feel Quinn's eyes on her, intent, searching, but she felt sick. This wasn't like finding out about Wolf's marriage. She and Quinn … there was nothing romantic between them. They didn't really know one another. Hell, she'd done her best to avoid getting to know him. And yet she realized with exquisite clarity that had all shifted.

"Sarah," he said gently, "this is uncomfortable as hell for me to talk about. Nevertheless, I'm not going to hide anything from you. I'll tell you whatever you want to know, and if it means you hate my guts, I get it. This … incident … is one blaring example of why I'm not man enough for you. But I want you to know as much as possible about her in case … Well, I don't want to see you get hurt."

*Not man enough? What the hell is he talking about?* She shoved the thought aside and latched on to another. "Why would she hurt me?"

He leaned toward her and held out his hand. Sarah looked at it and hugged herself instead of taking it. He let it dangle in the space between them. "I don't know that she could, but if she's crazy …"

"Did you call the police? About the rock?"

He straightened. "I did. They didn't sound too concerned. 'Oh, you think a woman you slept with hurled a rock through your window? You realize we've had gusts up to sixty miles an hour tonight, don't you, Mr. Hadley? Board up the window. Have a nice night.'" He scrubbed a hand over his jaw. "This may sound unreal coming from someone like me, but it tears me up to think I might've brought a problem home to you and Mom. Especially when it was well within my control."

She stole a glance at him. Fatigue and remorse were carved in his chiseled features, and they tugged her heartstrings. "Do *you* think she did it?"

"I don't know. Ask me if I think she's capable, and my answer is yes. I hope I'm just being paranoid." He leveled a hard gaze at her. "I want you to be alert, don't go out, and keep Archer with you and my mom at all times."

The hair prickled along Sarah's neck and arms. "Planning on going somewhere?"

"No, but this is a big place. Without a working security system. And if you want to … if you want to go back to Gage's, I understand. Just say the word, and I'll help you move back."

A charged silence hung between them until Quinn dropped his head against the back of the chair. "There's nothing quite like coming face-to-face with the consequences of my actions to realize how stupid I've been." He gave her a sidelong glance. "Sarah, I'm sorry for being such an asshole. I—"

She held up her hand. She didn't want to hear him confess to kissing her because she'd been handy. The humiliation would simply add one more sad fact onto the heap. "Got it. No explanation necessary." She rose. "Tonight was the culmination of a series of mistakes. It happens."

He shot to his feet, confusion and hurt clouding his expression. "Do you wish tonight hadn't happened? Not the rock. I'm talking about between us."

It occurred to her they were like parts of a train on two different tracks. Her head spun, and she couldn't untangle the contradictions coming at her, including those forming in her own head. Did she wish the kiss hadn't happened? No. And yes, because she'd had a taste and wanted more. Did she wish she'd gotten more, that they'd gone farther? Yes. And no. "Look, Sparks. It's after one. I'm tired, you're tired. Let's just get some sleep and talk about it after breakfast, okay?" She ignored his crestfallen expression as she ushered him through her door.

# Chapter 26

## How Did I Miss That?

Sarah woke the next morning shocked to discover it was past ten. When her head had finally hit the pillow in the wee hours, the thoughts chasing their tails in her brain had come to a standstill. Lights out. Surprisingly, she'd gotten a solid seven hours. When was the last time she'd slept so late? And why hadn't Archer woken her up? As she looked around, she realized it was because he wasn't there.

She showered, pulled on last night's jeans and a T-shirt that read, "I'm Kind of a Big Deal," and made her way to the kitchen. Quinn sat at the counter, cradling a coffee cup, facing her as she walked down the hallway. At his feet sprawled Archer, without a care in the world. Quinn straightened his hunched shoulders and lifted bleary eyes to hers. His gaze drifted over her chest. The hint of a smile played on his lips. "Good morning, Sunshine—what's left of it anyway. I was just contemplating rousting your *big deal* lazy ass."

"Did you let Arch out?"

"I did. You looked like you were sleeping peacefully, so I took pity on you and didn't wake you up. You're welcome."

The thought of him peeking in her room should have bothered her, but somehow it didn't. Instead, the intimate act filled her with unexpected warmth.

She poured herself a cup of fresh brew. "Not my fault I was out. I had to catch up on my beauty sleep after someone kept me and my *big deal* lazy ass up late last night."

"You don't need beauty sleep," he murmured.

Was that a compliment? A feather danced in her stomach. "Looks like you could've used some beauty sleep yourself, Sparky. You look terrible this morning."

"Gee, thanks. Maybe that's because I haven't been to bed yet." She arched her eyebrows, and he sipped his coffee. "While you were snoozing the morning away, the cops came and took a look around."

"What did they say?"

"Nothing, except they found nothing conclusive. There could've been footprints, but everything was too mashed to tell."

"And the rock? They took it for fingerprints, right?"

He shook his head. "Nope."

"What? Do they think it hurled itself through the window?"

"Basically. They claim a human would have had to park outside the estate, climb the fence, then cover a lot of ground to do the deed, and they don't think anyone would go to that kind of trouble just to smash a window. However, they *did* find it plausible the wind whipped over the deck and tossed a six-inch river rock through a triple-pane window, laws of physics be damned." He sighed.

"Not only did they forget their physics, but they've obviously never studied engineering," Sarah snorted.

"Yep."

"Where's your mom?"

His chest heaved on an exhale. "Lying down. She's not feeling well."

Sarah's stomach plummeted. "Oh no! Did the rock incident upset her?"

"No, she says it's a flare-up in her leg, and she just wants to stay off her feet." He twirled the cup bottom on the counter. "So I've been thinking . . ."

*Uh-oh.* "That's always dangerous for a pretty head like yours." Sarah popped up to grab a yogurt from the fridge.

"It might be a good idea if you moved back to Gage's," he said softly.

Her head was in the fridge, her back to him. She felt as if she'd just taken a punch to the gut, and she paused to catch her breath. With slow, deliberate movements, she closed the fridge, turned, and walked back to the island, where she took the stool opposite him. Not looking at him, she peeled the lid off her yogurt and fought to keep a tremor from her voice. "Why do you think that's a good idea?" She couldn't decide if she was mad, hurt, or both. Nor in what proportions.

"Look, Sarah—" The chirp of a text interrupted him. "Fuck!" He slid his phone from the counter. "It's Mom. I'll be right back." He hauled himself upright and jogged away.

Sarah blew out a breath. From a world-rocking kiss last night, they'd submerged into some kind of swampy no-man's-land. She didn't know where they were, how to navigate it, or how to keep her head above water. Against her better judgment, she liked Quinn—a lot. Maybe more than liked, and it scared the shit out of her. Then again, maybe her better judgment was operating correctly, and she was—as Paige had suggested—looking beyond the flashy veneer.

Her feelings for Quinn had bordered on fuzzy, but last night they'd sharpened when she'd been with Drew. The entire time she'd been wishing he were Quinn. She'd hated to admit it to herself, but there was no point in hiding the truth, was there? Why deny herself something, someone, without exploring the possibilities first? Of course she couldn't help but wonder why, among all the men on the planet, she'd been drawn to a professional flirt. Was it a COVID consequence? After all, in the last six weeks, he'd been the lone male humanoid within reach. The fact that he was a force of nature and made her hormones sing could have also clouded her judgment … along with his sense of humor, his intelligence, and his huge heart.

Muddled though her insight might be, there was no denying he challenged her, kept her on her toes—and *that* was sexy as hell. So what if he also happened to be a hockey player?

Even playboys fell, and the fact that she was so different from the Dorys he was used to had her thinking that yeah, maybe there was something worth exploring with him. Should she choose to. And the choice was entirely up to her—how deep, how far. She'd never let herself be duped again. Her vision was clear, her eyes wide-open.

If the rock hadn't thrown itself through the window and interrupted them, it's certain they would have ended up in his bed or hers. Would she have let it go that far? Hell yes. And that, surprisingly, wasn't just her crazy hormones talking.

But the fact that he had stopped them—hadn't it been right after she'd suggested they have no-strings sex?—dug at her. He'd been on the verge of telling her something she wasn't going to want to hear. She'd learned over the years that when someone told you not to take something the wrong way, inevitably you *would* take it the wrong way—or you'd take it the way it was intended, which hurt like hell.

Crap! She drew in a breath and steeled herself for ramming headlong into clearing that question out of the way. As cozy as staying in her semi-bubble of bliss was, it would be less painful to pop it now before she could drift away.

Quinn returned to the kitchen barefoot, entranced by the sight in front of him. Sarah, her back to him, was having a lively conversation with herself, complete with gesticulations. The words weren't so loud he could pick them all out, but he caught a few—something about clearing him out of the way.

Shit! Not what he wanted to hear. He pulled in a silent breath and braced himself.

"What are you doing there, Sunshine?"

She wheeled. Embarrassment, hurt, and anger waved through her features. Those big hazel eyes narrowed and fastened on him, turning icy. "How long have you been standing there?"

"Long enough to know you're having some kind of argument with yourself."

She perched a hand on her hip. "Yeah, about that."

*Get a grip. Here it comes.* He could practically hear her say, "You might be an interesting boy toy, but beyond that, I like a guy who's waaaaay more mature, Sparky." In another bracing maneuver, he crossed his arms over his chest and planted his feet. What he was bracing for—besides her telling him to get the hell out of her life—he had no idea.

"So last night," she began, "you started to say something—"

"And you said we'd talk after breakfast. Guess what? It's long after breakfast—because someone slept in late while someone else waited, I'd like to point out. So hit me with it. Let's get it over with."

"You go first," she ordered.

"What? That's not how this works. The duke certainly wouldn't go first."

Sarah snorted. "With the chambermaid he would. Just not with his true love, Millicent."

Quinn arched his eyebrows. "So you go for two-timing dukes?" The words were out before he realized what he was saying. "Oh shit, Sunshine. I didn't mean—"

She waved him off. "It's okay. I'm a big girl." With an expelling breath, she continued, "Last night you started to tell me … You said something about not taking things the wrong way after I suggested, uh, we help each other out. I've been filling in the blanks and waiting for the emu egg I think you're planning to drop on my head—"

"*That's* what this is about?" He smacked his palm against his forehead. "No, no! God, no! What I wanted to tell you, what I was trying to say … Look, I haven't had any practice at this, so bear with me. I was *trying* to tell you that for me, this"—he motioned his index finger between them—"isn't about sex. Well, not that I'd *object* to sex with you because I'm a huge fan of that idea. But I get it if that's all *you* want out of it because … Let's face it. You think of me as a kid who's—"

The hard look in her eyes softened. "Wait, wait. Back up a sec. You weren't about to say that kissing me was a big mistake? I mean, between me not being your type and my brother—"

She could have knocked him over with a hockey sock, but he recovered and moved so fast she had no chance to protest. Grasping her arms, he pulled her to him and kissed her hard and quick.

Now it was her turn to be confused—and dazed—and she reared back. "What did you do *that* for?"

"To show you kissing you was no mistake. And because I'm happy. Apparently, you care."

"About what?"

"Me." He shrugged. "Go on. Admit it."

Those glittering eyes narrowed on him again. Yeah, he'd better not push his luck.

He plopped down on a stool and yanked her onto his lap, but she vaulted upward. Spreading his legs wide, he encircled her in his arms and anchored her in place.

She pushed against his hold. "Let go, you big lug."

"Not a chance. And what's up with the emu egg analogy?"

Rigid as a goal post, she turned her side to him, leaned away, and crossed her arms when she realized he wasn't letting go. "Emu eggs are big and make a mess when they break."

He tried not laugh. "Okay, Sunshine. No emu eggs, and no more interruptions. Let's clear the air. First of all, circling back to your question about that kiss being a mistake, the answer isn't just 'No,' it's 'Fuck no!' I want to do *more* of that. A lot more."

Tugging her closer, he placed his index finger under her chin, guiding her face within a breath of his. She didn't resist, her warm body growing pliant. He dropped his voice. "Let me be absolutely clear. Sarah Nelson, I want you. More than I've ever wanted anyone. And I don't mean for one or two nights. I think about you all the time, I dream about you all the time—no one else. Some of those dreams, by the way, wouldn't make it past any censorship board I know of.

"I don't care what your brother thinks, what my mother thinks, what your dog thinks. I only care about what *you* think"—his finger tapped her chest—"and about what *you* want. Understood?"

Her mouth formed an adorable little O. "But I thought—"

"I know what you thought, and you were wrong." *Even your badass self is wrong once in a while.*

A long, slow breath escaped her, followed by, "Oh! I didn't understand."

"No, but now you do. So there's something I need from you."

She cocked an eyebrow.

"Go out with me."

She laughed. "Go out with you where?"

"You'll see. Then after that, I want to take you to dinner. What do you like to eat? I should know that already, shouldn't I, since we've eaten nearly every meal together? Do you like champagne?" His insides were fizzing like a freshly opened bottle of the stuff—from nerves or excitement, he wasn't sure. Didn't matter. Right now he was revved and ready to go, the fatigue from his sleepless night forgotten. God, there was so much about her he didn't know, and he couldn't wait to learn it all.

"When were you thinking of doing this?"

"Today. This afternoon."

She frowned and smiled at the same time—the look broadcast she thought he was nuts. *Smart girl.* "You're kinda wound up there, Sparky." Her fingers raked his scalp. She'd moved in a little closer—or he'd pulled her in—and her breasts brushed his chest tantalizingly.

He resisted the urge to let his head fall back and his eyes roll into the farthest reaches of their sockets. "Sorry, babe. Guess I'm a little distracted."

"No, it's sorta cute."

"Cute?" *Shit. Is that a good thing or bad thing?* "As in 'you remind me of an Ewok,' or 'you're a five-years-younger punky kid'?"

"If those are my only choices, I'd have to go with the Ewok. They're cuddly. Actually, though, I don't know if you're the cuddly type."

"If you're a really good girl, you'll find out." *So will I. Never been the cuddly type before, but once I get Sarah in my arms?* Before she could utter another word, he cupped the back of her head and covered her mouth with his, swallowing the rest of her words. His tongue became a heat-seeking missile, zeroing in on the seam of her lips, probing, pushing, demanding entrance. With a sighing moan, she opened and let him in, let his mouth take hers as she wrapped her arms around his neck and let out little whimpers that fired straight to his very hard cock.

*Oh, sweet Jesus!*

He loved tasting her, couldn't wait to explore and taste more of her, and he deepened the kiss but kept his hands strictly in the PG zones. A chuckle rumbled through him, and Sarah pulled back, her lips a little puffy and a crooked smile on her face. "Something funny about that kiss?"

"Nothing funny about that kiss. That kiss was *hot.* I was just thinking I'm twenty-five, and I'm worried about getting caught by my mom." He lightly touched the tiny diamond on her nose.

Mischief twinkled in her eyes. "You might want to double-check your curfew with her."

"Why is that? Planning to keep me out late?"

She started twiddling the hair at the back of his head. Shivers raced along his spine. It felt so damn good! He wanted her small fingers all over him. "Or up late," she murmured.

*Hell yeah!* His stomach turned a few flips, and he had to swallow before he could rasp, "Doing what, exactly?"

"If you're a really good boy, you'll find out."

*I want to find out right this goddamn minute. But I can wait.*

He stared deep into her gold-green eyes, hoping she could read how much he meant his next words. "We can take things as slowly as you say. We're on *your* timetable. Nothing has to happen tonight, tomorrow night, or next month. I want to get to know Sarah Nelson. Has she ever had a T-shirt with a bolt pattern force distribution calculator on it? Does she think the episode about building the Golden Gate Bridge was as cool as I do? Does she want kids someday while she's running the world?" Had he ever said anything like this before in his life? Absolutely not. But he'd never been so fascinated by a woman before. No, everything was different with her, and he was barreling ahead with everything he had.

He never did anything halfway.

# Chapter 27

## The LBD Never Fails

Sarah's head floated somewhere above her shoulders as she padded down the hall. Quinn was insane—in a fun, light, catch-you-up-on-high-spin-cycle sort of way. A mix of energy and spark and whimsy, and it was infectious. She grew giddy wondering where he was taking her.

A few hours later, she was cursing her hair as she raked her fingers through it. Why wouldn't it cooperate? And why did she care? She was merely having dinner with a man she'd shared many meals with. Except she'd never gotten dressed up to eat with him before. Not to mention the man in question had morphed into someone who made her heart race just thinking about him. One with surprising layers she wanted to peel back, who was open, earnest, eager to please. A human version of Archer. Yeah, there was that charm factor, but Archer was charming, and she didn't mind that about *him*. If Archer hadn't been neutered, he'd probably hump every girl dog he could get his paws on. So all in all, Quinn and Archer shared many of the same characteristics. She laughed out loud at her own convoluted justifications.

"Admit it, the man said. You like him," she told her reflection.

She gave herself another appraisal. Was the little black dress overkill? Didn't matter. It felt good on, and she looked good in it. The modest halter affair showed off her bare shoulders—one of her best assets—and the fabric graced her slight curves, amplifying them. A row of simple pearl buttons adorned the front from her collar bones to the hemline that skimmed her knees. Simple, classic, and hopefully whistle-worthy.

Maybe she was being silly, but all of her wanted to wow Quinn. She wanted to know she still had that effect on a man when she put her mind to it. Besides, the poor guy had been subjected to her sloppy, bitchy side since he'd met her, and it was time to flip the switch and show off the feminine version of herself that had been MIA for far too long.

One last look in the mirror, and she pulled on her strappy black high-heeled sandals and snagged her leather jacket. As she came out of her room, Liz and Archer were waiting for her. Liz's eyes danced with delight.

"Oh, doll, look at you! You are *stunning*!" She wrapped her hands around Sarah's arms and pulled her in for a better look. "It'll be a miracle if *your date* can keep his tongue in his head."

Sarah grinned. "You heard, huh?"

"Yes, and I told Quinnie I need rest and some 'me' time. I'm turning in early tonight, so you kids will have the house to yourselves." She sent Sarah a conspiratorial wink.

A blush raced up Sarah's neck and spread from her cheeks to her scalp. She felt like a seventeen-year-old going to the prom with the school's hockey team captain.

"Thank you, Liz. Um, do you need anything?"

"All set. Don't you worry about me. Just enjoy yourselves." Liz pecked her cheek, catching Sarah by surprise. Sarah hugged her back, then headed for the family room, where Quinn was waiting for her, rocking on his heels, his back to her, his hands in the front pockets of his black dress slacks as he looked somewhere beyond the newly repaired glass. She paused for a moment, taking in his broad back in a fitted white shirt before her gaze roved over the rest of him, appreciating all she saw—down to his mouthwatering tush. Her feet hit the stone floor, and the click-clack of her heels had him pivoting toward her. And dropping his jaw. A most gratifying reaction indeed.

He swallowed, and his eyes swept over her. "Hey, uh, you look … you look … amazing."

She could feel the blush intensify and heat her face. "Thank you. You cleaned up rather nicely yourself. So I didn't overdress?"

His short hair was combed back, and he was freshly shaved. The combination of the dressy-casual clothes and the impeccable grooming made him devastatingly handsome. Did he do this for all his dates? He hadn't for Dory. Sarah put the thought out of her head because it didn't matter. Tonight, he'd done it for *her*, and that's what counted.

A slow smile spread over his face, brightened by his dimples. "Not at all. You're perfect." He held out his hand to her, and she took it. The warmth of his big hand as it captured hers was reassuring, like coming home to a safe haven. Interlacing their fingers, he drew her beside him. "This way."

In the garage, he pulled the cover off a dazzling white Mercedes AMG GT coupe, opened the passenger door, and got her settled before sliding behind the steering wheel.

Her eyes took a spin around the sleek interior. "Nice jalopy."

"I only drive it for special occasions." One corner of his mouth quirked, and his dimple deepened.

Traffic was light, and they glided north up I-25. Sarah soaked in the sights streaking past her. How long had it been since she'd been beyond the confines of Quinn's neighborhood? The skies were clear, the temperature hovering at a pleasant seventy-two, and the approaching skyline seemed to sparkle in the late afternoon sun.

When Quinn exited on Colfax heading east, she gave him a puzzled sidelong glance. "Where are we going?"

He lowered his sunglasses and side-eyed her. "Be patient. We're almost there."

Another turn, and he nosed the car beside a parking meter across from the Colorado Convention Center.

"We're going to a convention?" She was truly puzzled.

"Nope. No conventions right now. It's something better." He helped her out of the car and into her jacket, fed the meter, then took her hand and crossed the street. "Ever seen Denver's Big Blue Bear in person?"

Her eyes lit on and traveled up a towering lapis bear sculpture that seemed to be peeking through the convention center's windows. "No," she whispered reverently, "but I heard a lead engineer give a talk on it once, and I've always wanted to see it." She kept her wide gaze riveted on the colossus as they approached.

Quinn gave her hand a squeeze. "It weighs ten thousand pounds and stands forty feet high. The steel structure holding it up inside is nearly two-thirds the height of the bear."

The closer they drew, the more she gawked. "Amazing."

Quinn released her hand, and they circled the sculpture. "Think of the size of the footings that are holding this thing up," he said. "I wish I could've gotten us inside so you could check out the support structure, but with the COVID restrictions, it wasn't gonna happen."

She glanced at him, his expression like a hopeful kid, and something warm bloomed in her chest. Tears unexpectedly stung her eyes, and she quickly averted her gaze to the bear. "No, this is perfect. It's beautiful."

A few more turns, and they plopped on a stone bench at the bear's feet. Her neck muscles began cramping from looking up.

He took her hand and cradled it on his thigh. "When you've had your fill, we can stroll to Sculpture Park and check out the Dancers."

Soon they were walking around the tall, lithe statues, their white bodies in stark contrast against Colorado's blue vault. The sun was dipping behind buildings, throwing long shadows. Soon the sky would turn a deeper shade, and Sarah felt a chill in the spring air.

Quinn dropped an arm around her shoulders and pulled her against him, his body hard and full of heat. "You cold, Sunshine?"

"Getting there, but I'd like to see the bear one more time."

He grinned. "Absolutely."

After one last lingering look at the bear, Sarah said she was ready to go, and Quinn took her arm and led her back to the car.

She inhaled a deep breath. "Thank you. That was … really special." A simple outing, but the thought behind it touched her deep inside.

"I'm glad you liked it. Hungry?"

She laughed. "I could eat. But I thought restaurant dining rooms were still closed?"

"I have a special restaurant lined up." Mischief danced in his mocha-brown eyes.

When Quinn pulled back into his own driveway, Sarah shot him a bewildered look. "Are we getting changed before we eat?"

"Nope." He parked the car and helped her out. A smile played on his face, but he said nothing as he guided her inside the house.

A few twists and turns, and they stood at the entrance to the dark solarium. Quinn flipped a switch, and soft light winked on. Sarah gaped at what had once *been* the solarium. The 3-D puzzle projects had been moved out of sight, and the space had been transfigured into a fairyland. A table for two sat beside a floor-to-ceiling window, and plants had been rearranged to give it a cozy feel. Overhead, strands of twinkly lights were suspended like stars.

She turned her head, taking in the sparkling curtain above. "This is beautiful! Did you do all this?"

"Yep." He seemed embarrassed, which turned her heart into softened butter. His hand still held hers, and he gave it a tug, leading them toward the table.

"Where'd you get the lights?"

He smoothed the back of his head. "I ducked into a Super Target."

She stared up at him. "*Today?* I thought they were only selling food right now."

"They are, but I talked a clerk into—"

"Don't tell me," she laughed. "Was the clerk a woman?"

"Uh, kinda. I think she's got a few years to go before she qualifies." He pulled out a chair for her, but rather than take a seat, she took in the beautifully decorated table before her: white linen, votives and sprigs of greenery, stacked plates flanked by varying sizes of silverware, just like in high-end restaurants. At each place setting was a wine goblet ready to be filled.

*I'm a little blown away here.*

"You really outdid yourself." She paused a moment to catch her breath, hyperaware of his body beside hers, not quite touching, but so close she could feel the heat radiating from him. "You enlisted your mom's help with all this, right?"

He scoffed. "This was me and Pinterest all the way. I have talents beyond hockey player playboy, you know."

"You looked at Pinterest boards?" *I'm a lot blown away now.*

"Yep. I had no clue what I was doing—this is a first for me—so I researched. Pinterest is great." He shrugged. This is when she noticed his silverware placement was ass-backward, which warmed her all over. He really had done it on his own.

"Yeah," she said dumbly, "Pinterest *is* great." A wild tickle in her belly suddenly annihilated her appetite. A thought pierced her romance-addled brain. "Are you cooking?"

He shook his head. "No. I ordered a dinner from Elway's that got here just before we did. Mom knew it was coming, so she stashed it in the warming oven and texted me."

Blown away *and* bowled over. She slid her hand from his and gazed up into those soft brown eyes that were roaming over her face. Overcome, she infused her voice and her expression with every emotion swelling inside of her, hoping he'd understand the unformed thoughts she was trying to communicate. "The bear, this beautiful setting … It's all so incredibly thoughtful. I'm overwhelmed." She pulled in a breath. "Would you be offended if we put off dinner for a little while?"

Confusion played across his face.

"It's not that I don't *want* dinner," she murmured. "I do. Very much. But right now, my mind's moved on to … other things." *Like jumping your bones.*

His mouth and eyes went round as understanding seemed to dawn. Another smile formed, and he dropped his gaze to her mouth.

She turned, facing him fully, and rested her hands on his chest.

He swallowed, then rasped, "Whatever Sunshine wants." Wordlessly, he drew her in, his eyes never leaving hers. He cupped her face, dipped his head, and anchored his arms around her, cinching her against him, igniting small blazes deep inside her. An instant later, his mouth was on hers, moving languidly, as if he were savoring morsels. She locked her knees to keep them from buckling.

The kiss heated quickly, their mouths and bodies merging together in a frenetic bid to meld into one. He felt so good under her hands, so powerful, so *right.* He engulfed her, surrounded her, and she surrendered herself to him.

He broke the connection, trailing nibbling kisses along her jaw and neck that radiated out like miniature shock waves. "I'm happy to keep doing this here, Sunshine," he mumbled against her skin, "but how about someplace a little more private?"

A laugh rose in her throat. "Not my room. It's too close to your mom's."

He pulled back and grinned. "Mine, then?"

When she nodded her answer, he drew her away from the wonderland with urgency. Like a couple of naughty kids, they raced to his bedroom, giggles spilling from them both. But when they burst into the room and he locked the doors behind them, he spun her and pinned her in place so fast she lost her breath. The teasing, the lightheartedness screeched to an abrupt halt, transforming into unbridled passion. Eager mouths feasted on one another, hands rushed to tear at clothes, bodies moved in sync toward one overriding purpose.

And she was utterly, joyfully lost.

Quinn had been ready to fly when he realized how happy he'd made Sarah. Now he bracketed her against the door, reluctant to shift should the swirling storm of magic binding them diminish. But she was right there with him, caught up like he was, and he could let himself go. Lines blurred. He didn't give a damn about age, her brother, or their pasts. Their differences dissolved into a buzz he pushed to the back of his mind.

He'd never been here before, standing on a precipice and ready to lose himself. In *her*.

Between tongue-filled kisses, he became aware she was unbuttoning his shirt. He pulled away to tear it from his body, then landed back against her, groaning with the feel of her fingers digging into his back and shoulders.

"Your turn," he growled against her mouth. Faint light from somewhere illuminated the tiny buttons on her dress, and his fingers were on them, fumbling to get them undone. The buttons seemed to go on and on, and when he thought he'd reached the last one, he yanked and heard fabric rip.

Wide-eyed, he jerked backward. "I'll get you a new one," he panted. If the tearing bothered her, she didn't show it. No, she was panting too, and her heaving chest yanked his eyes to her burgundy-and-black lace bra and the sweet little bow between the cups, right where he wanted to plant his mouth. Creamy flesh crested the tops and peeked enticingly through the lace. He cupped one breast and kneaded it with a little more roughness than he'd intended. She let out a provocative sound that made his rock-hard dick throb painfully against his fly. Slowly raising his eyes, he was momentarily trapped in her molten hazel gaze.

She wanted this as much as he did—a fact her hands were making abundantly clear as they worked at loosening his belt.

His mouth took hers again, and he pushed the dress from her shoulders, letting it slide down her body and drop to her feet. Lips and tongues locked in a torrid tango, he pivoted their bodies again, moving toward the bed.

God, he wanted *all* her clothes on the floor. Now.

He unclasped her bra and didn't bother taking it off before filling his hands. *So damn soft, so …*

She got his belt unfastened and shoved his pants and boxer briefs over his hips, but the briefs got hung up on his shaft, as hard and erect as a flagpole. Wordlessly, they switched, him getting untangled while she yanked off her bra.

For a moment, they faced one another, frozen in place. The sound of their ragged breathing surrounded them. His eyes blazed a path from her face to her stiletto sandals and back up again, and unbearable need consumed him. He dropped on the edge of the mattress, taking pants, underwear, socks, and shoes off in one wild flourish, then tugged her to him and wrestled her panties down her legs. She bent her leg behind her, reaching to undo one of her shoes, giving him a glorious view of her body gilded in the soft light.

She was utter perfection, a masterpiece, and his slim hold on patience dissolved. He wanted all of her.

He grasped the hand loosening her shoe, and she gave him a curious look. "Leave them on," he said as he fell back on the bed, pulling her on top of him, eliciting a lusty giggle from her. Soon he'd rolled them onto their sides, his arms encircling her, her hands laced behind his neck and her silky thigh draped over his hip. Her pointy heel grazed his ass.

Flipping her on her back, he bent his head and sucked a nipple into his mouth, hard. Meanwhile, his free hand massaged her other breast, strumming her nipple, and she arched her back off the bed with a throaty moan that scattered his coherent thoughts, letting them fall among the discarded clothes on the floor.

What remained in his head was unformed, primal, carnal.

Her tongue traced the seam of his lips, and he opened, letting her dance in and explore. He might have let out a long, thunderous sigh when she dragged the edge of her heel across the back of his thigh. While she kissed him, her fingers plowed through his hair, shooting tingles to his blazing groin. Her nails raked his shoulders and arms, pain and pleasure entwined together, and he rode the explosion of sensations like a white-water kayaker.

Fuck, she felt good! What she was doing to him, how she felt beneath him. The real Sarah blew his fantasy Sarah out of the water.

He ran the tip of his tongue along her throat, over her collarbone, pausing to suck on her sweet skin, then latching on to a breast, licking, nipping, suckling, tasting. The more pressure he used, the more her body seemed to spark and hum to some erotic rhythm he could actually *feel* coursing through him too. He was transported, moving without strategy, simply tuned into her cadence like he was part of an amorphous, heaving sea without boundaries.

He trailed a free hand over her smooth flank, digging his fingers into her contours, relishing the silky skin along her inner thighs as he worked his way up. She was all wetness and heat, and when his finger entered her, her body bowed again and she gasped out, "God, yes!"

He lost what was left of his mind.

Her fingers were on him, his were inside her, their mouths locked in a blazing kiss. A connection like an electric lasso bound him to her, its twisted strands made up of need, desire, and impassioned desperation.

What could have been seconds or minutes later, he was tearing open a packet and rolling on a condom without recalling taking it from the nightstand. No words were exchanged between them—just sensual susurrations and the undulations in her body spurring him on. As he paused between her legs, she clung harder, urging him inside.

At first graze, her hips rose to meet him, and her legs wrapped around his hips, her heels prodding his ass while her nails bit into his back. He eased inside her, inch by inch, struggling to hold himself back. She took all of him in with stuttered moans. Measured strokes at first, barely controlled, quickly transformed into powerful, penetrating thrusts. As he slammed into her, heat flashed and pooled at the base of his spine, and he fought the wave overtaking him.

Her body seized. She clenched and shuddered and shook around him, and he toppled over the edge and followed her with a thundering release.

# Chapter 28

## I'VE NEVER BEEN TO THIS RESTAURANT

Sarah's legs slid off his hips, which was when Quinn realized he was still buried deep inside her, his hands tangled in her hair, and he was panting against her neck as he floated down from unparalleled nirvana.

His synapses began firing in sync once more.

*Hoooolу shit!*

The only way he could describe their coupling was by visualizing a space missile launch. Fire, detonation, a climb to a stratospheric height, an unimaginable explosion, ending with a softly rocking parachute ride back to the earthly plane.

One of her hands caressed his head while the other soothed his back, her touch featherlight, a counterbalance to her clawing and the heated, untamed sex they'd just shared. Fuck, he'd come faster and harder than he could ever remember—not what he'd wanted to do his first time with Sarah. He'd planned to take his time bringing her to the brink and reeling her back, making her come again and again, showing her he was capable of being a good lover, but those fantasies had been hijacked by a force he couldn't comprehend.

Suddenly aware all his weight pressed her into the mattress, he prepared to roll off, but she held him in place and hummed, "A few more minutes."

He obliged, sagging back on top of her, memorizing the feel of her skin against his, her body aligned with his in some wonderful kind of carnal harmony.

*We're just helping each other out* started looping in his brain, followed closely by *It's just sex*. His heart grew heavy.

The idiot in him wanted to ask, "How did I do?" as though he awaited some kind of ranking calculated by a panel of judges. He winced inside as he pictured how low those numbers would be and how Wolf would top him on the leader board. Fortunately, restraint was taking hold once more and saved him from opening his mouth and embarrassing himself further.

When he'd caught his breath, he planted tiny kisses along her neck and shoulder and nuzzled her hair. "I should go clean up," he murmured, and she released him with a sigh. One look over his shoulder as he headed toward the bathroom nearly stopped him dead in his tracks because, holy fuck! She'd rolled to her stomach, knees bent and ankles crossed above her perfectly rounded ass, her stilettoed feet suspended midair. His well-used cock managed to twitch in response.

The vision was branded in his brain, and all of him hoped he'd have endless opportunities to collect more images.

"Can I take the shoes off now?" she called after him, a giggle lacing her voice.

*Nuh-uh, no way!* "Anything you want."

After he'd disposed of the condom and cleaned up, it dawned on him she might want to clean up too, and he soaked a washcloth in hot water. In all the years he'd been sleeping with women, not once had this thought occurred to him.

He exited the bathroom, surprised and delighted to find Sarah hadn't covered up. Instead, she reclined in her full naked glory, one knee up, and unabashedly tracked him as he walked toward her.

Her eyes flicked to his hand. "What's that?"

He sank onto the mattress beside her, untwisted the cloth, and brushed it between her thighs, along her seam, over her mound.

She closed her eyes. "Oh God, that feels sooo good. Don't stop."

He continued his ministrations, eating up her sensual sighs. Jesus, he could get used to this. Did he have a chance?

A quick throat clear, and he blurted the unthinkable. "Did you enjoy … I mean, were you … Did I …?"

Her eyes fluttered open, and she sat up, a mischievous grin playing on her features as she pushed her fingers through his hair. "You know, you're pretty damn cute sometimes. Like right now."

Fuck. Now he felt like an even littler little kid—with a super-hot, naked, one-hundred-percent woman running her fingers through his hair. "You're not answering the question I shouldn't have asked," he muttered and dropped the cloth on the floor.

She scanned his face as if she were assessing him, and her lips curved into a broad smile before she pulled his head to hers and planted a languid, breath-stealing kiss on him.

Rubbing her nose against his, she purred, "Let's put it this way: I've been asking myself what took us so long and how soon can we do it again."

No lie, his heartbeat went from limp to anaerobic, and his dick was hoisting itself back to full mast—which didn't escape her attention. Her hand raked a light path up his thigh and teased his stiffening cock. "Soon, it would appear."

He let out an involuntary moan.

"Too much, Sparky?"

He grabbed her hand, yanked her against him, and went to work devouring her sensitive neck and earlobe, gratified when her skin erupted in goose bumps. "You're *almost* too much, Sunshine, but I'll catch up. I'm a quick learner."

Soon she couldn't stop giggling, and he had her pinned beneath him, unable to hold his own laughter back. He rose above her and leveled his gaze at hers. The light in her eyes had shifted, transforming them into dark liquid pools that communicated more desire than mere words ever could. In that moment, he saw himself reflected in her, and he soared to ten feet tall.

In an achingly tender move, she reached up and brushed the hair from his forehead. Another smile—a secret one for only him—and his heart squeezed.

"What are you thinking?" He'd never asked a bed partner that question in his life. He'd never cared enough. But with *this* woman, he wanted to know her most intimate thoughts.

She played with his hair, sending pleasurable chills down his neck and spine. "I'm thinking that we still have a dinner to eat."

His stomach silently rumbled. "Hungry?"

"Mm-hmm, but I'm not feeling very motivated to get out of bed just yet—"

"Don't move." He pushed her back against the pillows. "Sit back, relax. I got this."

Sarah watched Quinn pull on his boxers and leave the bedroom. She could watch that body move every minute of every day. Lying on the bed, she stretched her limbs like a contented cat in a patch of sun. All of her still tingled from their combustible, animallike lovemaking. Oh my God, when had it ever been like *that*? Never. Ever.

*Wow!*

The tempest that had been the joining of their two bodies reminded her of makeup sex on steroids—except they hadn't had a fight and they'd never had sex before. She swung her legs over the side of the bed and surveyed the messy piles of clothing. The scene mimicked the explosive quality of their whole encounter. Sarah had always been aware of the passion simmering below her surface, but she'd never unleashed the beast before—not completely anyway. Never had she felt safe enough. But Quinn had not only tapped it, he'd released it and matched it. And then some. He'd taken her hard and fast, and her body had climbed to new heights she'd never known existed.

*You underestimate your power, Sparky.*

She picked up his crumpled white shirt and slipped it on, pulling in the scent of his aftershave and him while she haphazardly fastened buttons. Her eyes caught on the cockeyed placement of her discarded sandals, and she giggled aloud at the memory of his blazing eyes when her heels were the only thing she wore. She slipped those on too and headed to the bathroom.

When she emerged, Quinn was nudging the bedroom door open. "Dinner?" In his hands was a huge tray piled with plates of mouthwatering food. Tucked between them were silverware, napkins, and wineglasses … and two lit votives.

"God, yes! I'm suddenly starving." She scrambled toward a large table that occupied a sitting area, cleared it, and he set the tray down, which was when she noticed he wore a barbecue apron with the picture of a man's body in a loin cloth—à la Tarzan—showing off a cartoonish muscly chest and abdomen.

"Um, what's with the wardrobe change, Sparks?"

He yanked two wine bottles from roomy pockets and held them up with a wide grin. "Had to improvise so I could bring everything in one trip."

"Is that … *your* apron?"

"Nah. Found it in one of the pantries."

She stifled a laugh. "Well, you need to take it off. This cartoon's got nothing on the real deal."

Waggling his eyebrows, he put the wine down and took off the apron, then scanned her from head to high-heel-sandaled foot. His eyes lit, and his dimples deepened. "I like *your* look—a lot—but maybe you should take yours off too."

With a chuckle and a head shake, she began unloading the tray. "No, I'd get too cold."

He came up behind her and snaked his arms around her middle, pulling her close, placing a shiver-inducing kiss at the base of her neck. "I can keep you warm." His voice was dark and sexy and flowed over her like the filling in a hot lava cake. Sinfully delicious, gooey, warm.

She melted against him. "I know you can, but we'll never eat. Which would be a shame, by the way, because this all looks incredible."

He released her with a butt pat. As she arranged the plates, he pointed. "I took a chance on what you'd want and ordered a few appetizers to start. That's tuna tartar, steak tacos, shrimp cocktail—"

She barked out a laugh. "Is there an appetizer you *didn't* get?"

He quirked a smile and walked her through the salads, entrees, and sides. He'd ordered enough to feed an entire team, though after witnessing him massacre plates of food for the last few months, she had no doubt he'd polish all this off too.

"White wine okay to start?" He began pouring. "I thought we'd pair different wines with the different courses."

*Wha—?* Yet another surprise from the man, and she found herself entranced. "I didn't know you were a wine connoisseur, Sparky."

"There's a lot you don't know about me. And I might have taken a crash course at the liquor store today." After filling his own glass, he raised it to her. "To Sunshine." He clinked his glass to hers, and they each took a sip.

"What do you think?" he asked after she'd had a nibble of shrimp cocktail. "Did my wine coach do a good job?"

"As far as I'm concerned, he gets an A plus-plus." *And so do you, you overachiever.*

He paused between bites and pointed his fork at her. "Glad to hear it."

Dinner conversation flowed easily, naturally, and she bubbled with laughter as he regaled her with stories. He talked with his hands, and she found herself fascinated with his expressions and gestures. A megaphone blared in her head: "Quinn Hadley, man of many talents: wine expert, interior decorator, storyteller, passionate lover."

She'd quit eating a while ago, but the passionate lover was in the midst of a foodgasm over a rack of lamb. The groaning reminded her of the guttural noises he'd emitted while they'd been burning up the sheets.

An unpleasant memory meteored into her head. *The man is packed*, Dory had blathered in the bathroom. Yeah, Sarah had to agree, but damn it, Dory had been there first, and the realization jabbed at Sarah's soft spots. And how many others besides the fish? How many women in his *other* phone was he in touch with? In a breathless instant, she was brittle and wobbly, and not from the wine.

Could she handle the cavalcade of colorful characters decorating Quinn's past? No way would she be anyone's substitute player. Never again.

He seemed to tune into her shift. "Anything wrong? You're thinking so hard I'm afraid you're gonna blow a gasket. Oh shit. I'm sitting over here eating like a pig. Mom would be appalled. Is that it?" He laid his fork down and leaned back.

"No, no. You're fine. Keep eating." She flapped her hand at him.

He gave her a skeptical look. "Then what just slammed into you? Something I said? Did?"

Damn. He wore a forlorn look. *Might as well just throw it out there. No reason not to be honest here, especially since this probably isn't going anywhere anyway.* "Ah … I'm not sure why, but my mind detoured to your phone."

When he gave her a quizzical look, she added, "Your hookup phone."

He didn't miss a beat. "It's been off for weeks."

"Aren't you checking messages?" she blurted.

Confusion must have shown all over her face because he leaned forward with an indulgent smile. "No, and I'm not going to. Because I don't give a fuck. Before I shut the damn thing off, I sent everyone a text saying I was off the market."

Her body turned boneless and nearly slipped off her chair, though her insides were jumping for joy. "Why did you tell them that?" She tipped the wineglass to her lips to have something, anything, to do and realized too late it was empty.

Attentive host that he was, he refilled her wineglass. Then he took her free hand in his, twining their fingers. The feel of those calluses on her skin made her belly dance. "Because it's true. I'm choosing to be unavailable." His voice was low, earnest, and his eyes, all warm chocolate, held hers. "Though there's one person—she's the only exception—I'm completely available for. But even if she doesn't want me, I'm done playing the field. That okay with you?"

Sarah downed another sip of wine, willing her short-circuiting brain to begin firing on all cylinders again. *Who says you're not good at this stuff, Sparky?*

His thumb caressed the back of her hand. "You know, of course, that *you're* that person. I have no idea when or how it happened, but it did." He shrugged as if this needed no further explanation. Truth was, she wouldn't comprehend if he *did* elaborate because her mind was reeling. In the midst of her twisting thoughts was the notion she had no business starting up a relationship with anyone new.

"But I just broke up with … And Gage … And …"

"Yeah, I get it. I've thought about it a lot. I don't want to pressure you, so if this is too much too soon, just tell me to back off. But I plan on sticking around until you *are* ready. In the meantime, feel free to use my bod as much as you'd like." He gave her a devilish, dimpled grin.

She couldn't say anything because an inferno began raging inside her, ready to combust in her core and burn her into an ash heap.

# Chapter 29

## WHO INVENTED MORNING AND WHY?

Sarah's eyes shifted back and forth. Had he gone too far, revealed too much? Too bad he couldn't have taken a crash course from the fictional duke in how to say the right things in the right order. He'd have been the first to sign up because, Jesus, he didn't want to fuck this up, but her expression told him he probably already had.

He continued stroking the back of her hand. She hadn't told him not to, hadn't flinched under his touch, and her skin felt too good to stop. "You okay over there?"

She straightened but didn't pull her hand away. "Fine. Just … processing."

An inner sigh of relief eased his shoulders. "Well, while you're processing, I'm going to clear these dishes and get dessert."

He rose and began stacking plates on the tray. Following suit, she stood beside him, her shimmering hazel eyes riveted on his. "I don't know what to say," she whispered.

He leaned down and kissed her. "You don't need to say anything. Except maybe, 'What's for dessert?'"

She wrapped her hands around his arm, rested her head against his shoulder, and laughed. This version of Sarah was *not* the prickly porcupine he'd been sidestepping these past few months, and he stood still, taking her in. It occurred to him she was letting down her barriers, showing him her well-guarded, well-disguised, innermost self. And damn, he loved it. He wanted more.

"I don't think I can eat another bite right now, but tell me what's for dessert." Her voice held an amused lilt.

*You.* "Something I can't pronounce, but it's chocolate."

"That's all that matters."

He hoisted the tray, hovering it at his midsection to hide the very obvious effect her touch, her voice, her scent had on him. His boxers did abso-fucking-lutely nothing to contain the problem, but still, he had to chuckle inside as he veered toward the kitchen. What was a first and should have been all kinds of weird—the two of them, nearly naked, eating a romantic dinner in his bedroom—*hadn't* felt weird. Instead, words like comfortable, simple, and nice came to mind. He pictured the cleaned-up version of the story he and Sarah would tell their kids one day when they asked about their parents' first date.

*Whoa.* Where had *that* come from? Quinn had never given any thought to a family before, but somehow that didn't feel weird either—which *was* weird. Maybe with the right partner … What the fuck was going on with him? Lost in unraveling the answer to that particular question, he unloaded the tray and stacked the dishes in the sink.

When he returned to the bedroom, Sarah lay on her side in the middle of the bed, facing away from him with her eyes closed and the sheet tucked under her arms. Missing were the few clothes she'd had on during dinner, and her smooth back was exposed to the flare of her hips, giving him an intriguing peek at those dimples. He paused a few beats to soak in the sight, and his cock sprang to life, declaring its appreciation.

In the past, with any other woman, alarms would have been screeching in his head by now, and he'd be calculating the most expedient way to escape. But Sarah belonged right where she was, and when she stirred and let out a sweet little sigh, he stripped off his underwear and slid between the sheets, his front to her back.

He gathered her in his arms, all warmth and silk, and she hummed, "You're finally back." She wrapped one arm around his. With the other, she reached behind and started playing with his hair, sending little shock waves racing along his spine, straight to his aching cock.

"Miss me?"

"I can't believe I'm saying this, but yeah, I missed you." Her voice was dozy and cute, and it touched something deep in his chest.

He kissed her shoulder. "I missed you too." And he meant it.

She rolled over, her soft breasts squashed against his chest, and sealed his mouth with hers. With long, slow slides of their tongues, the kisses grew deeper, then messier as hands glided and explored and skin blazed against skin. His last lucid thought was of the yearning to climb inside her and never let go. He'd cut away his anchor, and the slim tether of control he'd clung to his entire adult life had gone with it. In that moment, he was lost. He might drown, washed away in a sea of Sarah, and he didn't care.

Sarah drifted out of a sleepy fog and blinked. On her back, she scanned the dim room to get her bearings—as if the overgrown koala bear wrapped around her wouldn't have been reminder enough. Quinn's head was on her chest, his heavy arm and heavier leg pinning her in place. Steady breathing—and the weight of his head—told her he was asleep.

She pointed her toes—the only part she could move for being trapped—stretching, triggering soreness in parts that hadn't been exercised for a long while. It felt wonderful.

His hair tickled her chin, but trying to nudge him off her was as futile as trying to break free from a determined boa constrictor. He gripped her like his own personal body pillow.

*What time is it?*

A quick glance at a shuttered window brought a surprise. Was that daylight leaking through? *Oh shit! Is Liz up? Where's Archer?*

As if in answer, a soft scratching sounded on Quinn's door, followed by a whimper. Shoving at Quinn's arm, she bucked in panic. He shifted with an "Mmph," only to double down on his hold. She blew out an exasperated breath.

"Quinn!" she hissed. "Let me up!"

He rubbed his head against her chest as if he were trying to adjust said body pillow. *Ooh, that feels kinda good.* As she was admonishing herself for getting distracted, he raised his head, planted his chin, and gave her a sleepy smile. "You're still here," he mumbled. His hands began gliding up her sides, each one targeting a breast.

"Of course I am. Someone's got his Death Star tractor beam locked on me, and I can't escape."

His eyes opened fully, and he slid off of her. "Shit. Sorry. My bad."

A pang of remorse jabbed her. "It's not that I don't like it. It's just that it's morning, and Archer's on the other side of the door trying to get in."

Realization seemed to dawn, and his eyes grew wide. "Oh shit! Mom can't be far behind."

If last night had been all deep, velvet sensuality, this morning was its antithesis. Sarah scrambled from one side of the bed, Quinn mirroring her movements, and both of them frantically snatched at clothes, tossing them between each other in a scene straight out of an old slapstick movie.

"You stay here," he whisper-shouted as he dragged on his boxers and a pair of jeans he pulled from his closet floor. "I'll take care of Archer." He began hopping in place to get his second leg in.

Panties on, she wrangled with the bra clasp at her back. She engaged one hook and called it good before pulling on her torn dress and getting it stuck on her head. Quinn was beside her, yanking the garment over her shoulders.

"Quinnie?" Liz's voice floated from behind his door. "You awake, son?"

He and Sarah came to a grinding halt, exchanging round-eyed looks. "Oh shit!" they mouthed at the same time.

"Almost, Mom," he called back.

Now came Liz's muffled chuckle. "It's nearly eight. I guess that's why Archer's trying to wake you up. I'm not sure where Sarah is, but I'll go look for her."

"Uh," he yelled, "I think she was going for a run this morning. I'll take care of him."

"Odd that she'd run without him."

He buttoned his jeans, grabbed a T-shirt from a dresser drawer, and winked at Sarah. "'Odd' sounds just like Sarah, Mom."

Sarah returned her best glittering glare. He stepped over to her and planted a kiss on her mouth that fired up her insides and left her nearly speechless.

"I'll make up an excuse and keep her distracted so you can get back to your room," he whispered. "Then change your clothes and get your cute little ass to the kitchen. Act like you just finished a run or got out of bed. Piece of cake."

She stifled a laugh. "Depends on whose cake!"

After dodging her way back to her room like a curfew-breaking teen trying not to get caught, Sarah took a quick shower. Much as she hated to wash away Quinn's scent, she didn't need Archer—or Liz—sniffing it off of her.

Rather than her usual ratty pair of sweats and a sloppy T-shirt, Sarah pulled on a pair of butt-hugging jeans, topped with a red tank that read, "Blink If You Want Me."

Heart pounding relentlessly against her ribcage, she faked a casual air and sauntered into the kitchen, where Liz and Quinn huddled at the counter drinking coffee. Archer charged her and buried his nose in her crotch. *So much for washing the scent off.*

She moved the dog away. "Hey, now. Stop that."

Quinn raised his head at the sound of her voice, scanned her T-shirt, and blinked. One corner of his mouth quirked, and he blinked rapidly so many times she lost count. A flush ignited on her chest and spread northward. Why hadn't she thrown something on over the tank?

Liz turned slowly and smiled. "Well, there you are. I swear Archer was nearly frantic when I got up. I think he thought you were hiding in Quinn's room because he insisted on going that way." Liz seemed to realize what she'd implied—no doubt alerted by the deep pink staining Sarah's exposed skin by now—and quickly pressed her lips together as though stifling a laugh.

Sarah ruffled Archer's neck. "Crossed signals, I guess. I wasn't hiding." Not a lie, not a confession, but not much of an answer either. Hopefully, Liz didn't notice. Meanwhile, Quinn's eyebrows bounced with amusement.

Several awkward moments later, Sarah had settled down with a cup of coffee and was asking Liz when she wanted to hit the gym.

"Not today, doll. I think I'll head back to my room for a while."

*Okaaaaay.* Sarah's nerves danced along a knife's edge. Was Liz feeling all right? Did she know what had happened in Quinn's bedroom? And did she disapprove? Maybe she'd been stifling a scolding instead of laughter.

"Are you feeling all right this morning, Liz?" Sarah ventured.

"Yes, of course." Liz's voice was high, tight, strained. "I just need some quiet time away from … Well, just some quiet time."

After she'd left the kitchen, Sarah gaped at Quinn. "What's going on with your mom?"

"No idea. She's been acting sketchy since I got up."

A renewed flush heated Sarah's face. "Do you think she knows about last night?"

"I don't see how she could." He shrugged. "Although I wouldn't put anything past her."

Sarah suddenly felt small and cheap.

Quinn rose and rounded the counter, surrounding her in his strong arms as he came up behind her. He laid his cheek on her head. "I can guess what you're thinking, and you're reading it all wrong."

She leaned against him, feeling snug and safe in his hold. "So Sparky's a mind reader now?"

"You're not as good at hiding stuff as you think you are."

"And you're an expert at reading women?"

He kissed the top of her head and gave her a little squeeze. "No, though I'd like to become an expert at reading *you.* How am I doing so far?"

A few simple words had her sighing and returning to an even plane. How did he do that? "Not too bad, but you've got a way to go." *Even* I *can't read me sometimes.*

He chuckled, his warm breath ruffling her hair. "Can't wait for you to start teaching me."

And there it was, that zing that hit her core and dissolved into a puddle of heat. Lord, how was she going to keep her hands off this man—and keep his mother from catching on?

All of Quinn wanted to haul Sarah back to his bedroom, and he busily tried on one excuse after another to get her there. *You left something behind. We tore up the sheets, and I was hoping you'd help me make my bed. Have I shown you my shower?* Nothing passed muster as plausible, so he went with honest, leaning down to nip her ear and whisper, "I didn't get near enough of you last night. What do you say we duck back into my room?"

She craned her head and gave him an eye-roll so huge he thought her eyeballs might disappear in their sockets.

"Trying to read your signals, Sunshine. Is that a 'Take me now, you hot stud,' or an 'I want you so bad, but later'? I couldn't tell."

Her shoulders started shuddering with laughter. "I gotta hand it to you, Sparky. You do see the beer bottle half-full."

Before he could ask her what she meant, her phone buzzed. "It's Gage."

He stepped back so she could answer.

"Hey, Bro. What's going on?" Her eyes slid to Quinn's, a question mark flitting through them. His body tensed, primed to run interference for her.

A quick head bob, and she said, "No, it's gotten better. Either he's not being such a pain in my ass or I'm getting used to him. He's standing right here, by the way."

Quinn's muscles uncoiled a fraction, and to Sarah he mouthed, "Haha. Don't tell your brother."

She mouthed, "Don't tell your mother," right back at him, a mischievous glint in her eyes. Another head bob. "Sure. I can do that. How soon?" A pause. "You got it. How are Lily and Daisy?"

Quinn idly picked up coffee mugs while Sarah chatted with her brother. When she finally hung up, he turned and asked what Nelson wanted her to do.

"Their house has been empty the last six weeks, and he wants me to go check on it." She shrugged.

Protectiveness surged inside him. Where it came from and why, he didn't know. It was just *there*. "Let me know when you're going, and I'll go with you."

She shook her head vigorously, and her hair shifted in glossy layers. A vision of her tossing her head side to side, moaning incoherently as she'd orgasmed underneath him last night rocketed straight to his crotch. His dick hadn't exactly been asleep, but now it woke right the hell up, raring to go.

"No, you won't," she argued. "Someone needs to be here for your mom."

*Mom. Right.* He sidled up to Sarah's back once again and bent his head to kiss her shoulder, pulling her tank strap out of the way so he could kiss her there too, and moved slowly up her neck.

"Quinn, stop!" she hissed, but the giggle in her voice contradicted her words.

He didn't stop. Instead, he kept kissing, adding soft sucks and nips as he went, and snaked his hands around to knead her breasts. "Whatever you say, Sunshine."

She shoved at his arms. "Your mom might see us."

"She might," he mumbled against her earlobe right before licking the shell of her ear. "I'll stop as soon as you say you'll have dinner with me again tonight."

"In the sunroom or your bedroom?" Her voice came out breathy.

Lick, nibble, fondle. "Well, we could *start* in the sunroom … or not." Kiss, suck. He started grinding against her ass slowly, pausing when *his* phone buzzed. The name on caller ID surprised the hell out of him. "I should take this."

She adjusted her tank, slid off the stool, and walked toward her room. A sigh escaped him as he watched her.

He answered the call. "Wyatt! Where you been, man?" Wyatt hadn't acknowledged him since the press conference nearly two months ago. Yeah, this was a call he'd needed to accept.

"'Sup, Hads?" Not the most enthusiastic of greetings, but Quinn would take it.

They shot the breeze for a few minutes, discussing when the NHL might start back up, what they were doing to keep in shape, and how glad they were they'd been paid out their salaries for the season, though it sucked that they'd miss out on the revenues the league normally generated.

"So you know that blond you were seeing the night of the dinner?" Wyatt said when they'd run through the regular bullshit.

"Which one?" Quinn quipped—out of habit—then looked around, feeling guilty as hell. What if Sarah had heard him? Not cool.

"The hot one. Dory."

Quinn's wacko antenna shot up and began a sweep of the area. "What about her? We're not seeing each other."

"I know. That's why I'm calling. I, uh, sorta, um, I started hanging out with her. Is that cool with you?"

Quinn's first reaction was, "Take her! Please!" but he held it back. "Yeah, no problem." Then he leapt to how the hell Wyatt knew Dory. He almost laughed out loud. She'd probably slipped her number to every guy on the team. For a puck bunny, sleeping with a player was about the conquest. Bragging rights. He pictured them swapping score cards and stories over pink cocktails, and it soured his stomach. Why had this never bothered him before now? Because he hadn't given a fuck, but Sarah changed all that.

Should he warn his buddy that Dory was a potential nutjob? Maybe Quinn had blown it out of proportion. Besides, Wyatt was no stranger to crazy chicks. "How'd you two meet anyway?"

More hemming and hawing from the other end, then Wyatt broke out in his nervous giggle-laugh. "Uh, I ran into her at the same place the night after the dinner."

"Have you been seeing her since?"

"Uh, not really. Until a few days ago. I ran into her again at the grocery store in Breckenridge, and we, uh, spent some time at my place in the mountains."

*Wait.* "What?"

Wyatt started backpedaling, tossing out excuses like strip joint patrons threw out money. "Well, we might have started seeing each other a little sooner, but she said it'd be cool with you. It *is*, isn't it?"

Quinn's mind began calculating. "So you and she weren't in town a few nights ago?"

"No, man. We just got back yesterday." Wyatt sounded as confused as Jake from the State Farm commercial.

Could Dory have left Wyatt's place, driven to Quinn's to lob a rock through his window, then driven back? Quinn shook his head to dislodge the ridiculous idea. *No way. No one's* that *crazy.*

"Yeah, it's totally cool with me." Quinn would worry about how awkward a team get-together might be in the future. Wyatt with Dory, him with Sarah, Nelson there too. He flinched inside. "Go for it. Happy for you, man."

Quinn hung up, an uneasy feeling creeping up his spine. If Dory hadn't launched the rock through his window, who had?

He texted Sarah. *Workout with me in the gym in 5?*

Sarah: *Thought we already worked out?*

Quinn: Different kind of workout, although I'm UP for a repeat of the last workout.

Sarah: *Cute.*

Quinn: *Is that a yes or a yes?*

Sarah: *See you in 5.*

He puffed out a breath he didn't realize he'd been holding, and his mind meandered away from the rock to being in bed with Sarah this morning. Despite his mom's jarring wake-up call, there'd been no weirdness between him and Sarah. No awkwardness. Just a natural progression that felt so right.

By the time he'd changed into gym shorts and a T-shirt, excitement was percolating in his veins. He couldn't wait to be with her again. Somewhere along the way, he'd convinced himself the wind or kids had been responsible for the rock toss after all, and he shoved the incident to a far corner of his brain.

# Chapter 30

## Did Not See That One Coming

The next two days unfolded in a surreal limbo. COVID-19 had turned the world nonsensical a while ago, but Sarah had floated contentedly between her usual daily role in the Hadley household and a totally different, unforeseen role in Quinn's bed at night. There, they spent covert hours talking, exploring one another, and making love.

Lurking at the back of Sarah's mind were two inescapable perceptions: First, Liz had been acting strangely distant since Quinn and Sarah's first "date," and while no one pointed to the elephant in the room, Sarah was convinced Liz knew what she and Quinn were doing after lights-out. Second, while Sarah enjoyed her intimate time with Quinn, she questioned whether their fledgling relationship would wither on the vine. Was it merely a COVIDism, a consequence of being forced to shelter in place together, or something more that could outlast whatever their "new normal" would be?

These thoughts drifted in her head as she prepared to check on Gage and Lily's house. Maybe getting out of her pleasant bubble, driving across town and seeing firsthand that the world still spun on its axis, would infuse her with a sense of reality and force her to plan for what came next. She couldn't live with Quinn and his mom forever.

Quinn walked her and Archer to the garage, stealing a kiss before he helped her into her Jeep. "You sure you don't want me to go with you, babe?"

Sarah shook her head. "No, I'll be fine. I've got Arch, and he'll save me from any big, bad bogeymen. Besides, my lips could use the break."

Dark eyebrows shot to his hairline. "Is this your not-so-subtle way of telling me you want me to stop kissing you?"

She chuckled. "No. Just seeing if you're paying attention."

He leaned in and laid a knee-melting kiss on her. "When it comes to your lips," he murmured, "I'm always paying attention." He pulled back and shut her car door. "You're back in an hour, right?"

She gave him an exaggerated eye-roll. "Yes, Sparky. And if I'm running late, I'll text or call you."

"How about you text me when you get there and again when you leave?"

She nodded her agreement, stifling the exasperated sigh lurking in her chest.

"Okay, then. You may leave." He followed this with a royal hand-roll.

"Why, thank you, benevolent master."

Winding along the drive, she peeked at her rearview mirror, where Quinn's big frame stood by the open garage door. One last wave, and he disappeared from sight. Overprotective and overattentive were adjectives she never would have imagined using for Quinn Hadley, nor could she have envisioned herself *enjoying* either. They should have chafed her independent self, but oddly she liked it. He had a way of making her feel special, important. The way he treated his mother, but different. Sarah doubted any of his puck bunnies had burrowed that far into his world, and she would take in whatever she could and savor the ride as long as it lasted. Eyes wide-open.

She turned down the alleyway behind Lily's house and pulled in front of the detached garage. Before exiting the Jeep, she sent Quinn a quick text letting him know she'd arrived. With a flip of the picket gate's latch, she let herself and Archer into the backyard. The dog took particular interest in a flower bed beside the back door as she fumbled with the key. He snuffled and pawed at the ground where some early spring blooms lay broken atop the soil, as though they'd been trampled. Probably some neighborhood cat using the bed as its outdoor litter box.

"Arch, stay out of the dirt."

Sarah unlocked the door, and Archer wedged his nose in the crack, flinging it wide in his eagerness to get inside.

"Jeez, Arch. What's the big rush?"

While Archer ran from room to room, Sarah closed the door behind them, dropped her keys and phone on the kitchen table, and started a sweep of the little house. Nothing out of place, no strange smells, everything buttoned up tight. The place looked as though the family had been living there all along and had just stepped out to run an errand.

Sarah headed toward the two bedrooms, and Archer streaked past her, tongue and tail wagging in time.

"Wow, Arch. I had no idea you liked it here so much."

In the master bedroom, a gust of cold air took her by surprise. Checking the windows turned up nothing. When she reached the bathroom, the air grew colder, and soon she spotted the reason why: a small window above the toilet was open. Only a few inches, but enough to let the chill in. Was it always open like that? She'd ask Gage when she texted him at the end of her inspection.

Another quick look-see, and Sarah made for the kitchen to lock up and leave. The low sound of a male voice sent shards of ice shooting from the base of her spine to her neck. She stopped in her tracks. Was she hearing things? Was someone merely talking outside?

"Archer?" she whispered.

She crept toward the kitchen and called his name again. Though she couldn't see him, he returned an excited little whimper. Every alarm in her body went off at once, and she glanced over her shoulder at the front door. Run outside? What would she be running *from*? And then what? Her keys and phone were in the kitchen. Besides, Archer was her warning system. Had someone been there, she told herself, he'd have barked or growled instead of emitting the one happy cry.

Somewhat mollified, neck hairs nevertheless at full attention, Sarah shuffled a few more steps and caught sight of Archer's backside. He was sitting, almost dancing in place, his tail sweeping the floor like an animated dust mop. There couldn't have been a threat.

Several more steps, and she got a full view of the kitchen … and realized how sadly mistaken she'd been. Her keys and phone were gone, and there stood Wolf, blocking the back door, patting Archer's head while the dog scarfed down chunks of meat littering the floor. *No wonder he didn't bark!*

Wolf raised icy blue eyes to hers, and one side of his mouth curled into a thin smile. "Everything comes to he who waits."

Quinn glanced at his phone. Again. Ten minutes past when he'd expected Sarah home, but he told himself to chill the fuck out. *It's only ten minutes.* Except she'd sent only the one text when she'd reached Nelson's house. She'd promised to text when she left, but he hadn't gotten that message yet. Sarah was many things, but she wasn't flaky—which was one among countless reasons why he'd fallen for her.

He tapped her a message and eyed his beanbags. Funny how he hadn't had the urge to juggle lately. But he sure as hell needed to now, so he picked them up and started tossing them in the air, one ear cocked for an incoming text.

*She decided to run an errand and forgot. She got caught up talking to neighbors. She found a problem, and Gage is talking her through it.*

"Quinnster?" his mom said from across the kitchen. "You look agitated."

"Hi, Momster. Didn't see you there."

"Because I just got here. Sarah still out?"

He caught the bags and blew out a frustrated breath. "Yep."

"Is that why you're worked up? She's not on another date, is she?" Soft crinkles of amusement appeared around his mother's mouth and her bright blue eyes. Another time, he might have let her teasing slide off his back. Instead, he found himself shaking his head, stifling the urge to bark, "No!"

"Well, maybe it's best she's not here right now. I need to talk to you."

He straightened and gave his mom his full attention. "About?" *Is this the part where she tells me she's heard us through the ventilation and to stop fucking the staff?* Except Sarah wasn't staff. And they'd been pretty damn discreet. And he wasn't just fucking her—they were learning about each other, physically *and* mentally. Totally different.

His mother crossed the expanse and pulled a bottle of water from the fridge. With some effort, she hoisted herself onto a stool.

"Are you hurting?" Quinn frowned, not masking the concern in his voice.

She flicked her hand. "A little bit. I've had a tiny setback, but I'll be better soon. How's your shoulder?"

*Nice divert.* "My shoulder's *been* fine. Back to you. I haven't seen you stretching or soaking in the hot tub much lately. Maybe you should get back to it?" She gave him a gimlet eye that had him backpedaling. "You tell me or Sarah if you need *anything.*" He paused a beat and braced himself. "So what is it you need to talk to me about?"

He could not have prepared himself for what came out of his mother's mouth. No matter how much steel he willed into his spine, it folded like an overcooked noodle.

"Well," she cleared her throat, "You might have noticed me acting strangely lately. That's because I, ah, asked your father for a divorce. Apparently, it shook him up, and he started calling … and emailing. We've been talking. A lot. He wants to … He's asked that we spend some time together—alone—and see if we can work through our differences."

Quinn sat in shocked silence for a beat, finally blurting, "Why would you do that, Mom? How's he going to deal with your Parkinson's any differently now than he did back then, which was *not* dealing with it?"

She picked at the hem of her shirt, her gaze cast down. "That's some of what we plan to explore. He's making his way home now, through Serbia or something. I expect to see him in a day or so, after he's had a chance to settle in and get over his jet lag." With a wan smile, she raised her head and met his eyes. "Well?"

*Well what? What am I supposed to say?* "You expect him *here.* Where's here?"

"In Denver. A friend's letting him use his patio home while he's away. I've agreed to stay there for a few days with your dad."

Bands constricted around Quinn's chest. Irony slapped him across the jaw: he didn't want his mom to leave. "Why doesn't he just stay here?" He realized he was clenching his jaw as he said it. So only the threat of a divorce got his dad's sorry ass in gear? Totally jacked-up. All of Quinn wanted to protect his mother from having her heart trashed again, even if he had to protect her from his dad.

"This place may be as big as a hotel, but it's hard to miss anything that's happening under this roof." She winked, and he began stammering a protest. If *that* didn't give him away, the flush heating his cheeks certainly did.

"Your father and I have years' worth of dirty laundry to air, and I expect the volume will get loud. I'd like privacy when I blast him," she added.

Despite his constricted heart, Quinn let out a laugh. "I hope you hit him with both barrels!"

The sly smile and twinkling eyes returned to his mother's face. "Oh, I fully intend to! Three years is a long time to keep things bottled up." She sighed. "But being married to someone twenty-some-odd years is a long time too, and as your dad correctly points out, we've had far more good years together than bad."

"Why didn't you tell me this was going on?"

She shrugged. "I don't know. I was reluctant to give him so much as a hello when he first called. In fact, Sarah caught us on the phone, and I hung up quicker than a kid about to get busted doing something naughty." A little chuckle bubbled up, then her tone sobered again. "I wasn't sure—I'm still not sure—if there's anything left between us that's salvageable. I don't know what the future holds for your dad and me, but after giving it a lot of thought, I have to do this. Besides, I have nothing left to lose by talking to the man."

*Yeah, you do. Your heart.*

"I know what you're thinking, Quinnie. Yes, your father walked out on me—on *us*—once before. But I'm a little wiser, a little more independent now, thanks to you and Sarah. I know what I want and what I don't want. Just because I'm prepared to hash things out with him doesn't mean all's forgiven and we're getting back together again as if nothing happened." She covered Quinn's hand with hers. "So? What do you think?"

"Does it matter what I think?"

"Yes. Very much."

A warm spot had been pulsing in his chest when she'd said he and Sarah had helped her become more independent. Now it downright thrummed. "I guess … if this is what you want, Mom, I'm behind you. I just want you to be happy."

Tears glossed her eyes. "You've grown into a good man, Quinn, and I'm proud of you. Adulting isn't for the faint of heart."

He laughed to keep his own tears at bay. "Does this mean I finally graduated?"

She patted his hand. "With honors."

Suddenly, his thoughts detoured to Sarah, and a thought struck that made his heart wobble. "If you and Dad decide to patch things up, you won't need Sarah anymore." *And I won't have a reason to keep her here.*

"I think you're getting ahead of yourself. Let's keep the status quo until I have a better idea how things with your dad are going to play out. In the meantime, Sarah can continue staying here. You two will have the place to yourselves." Another conspiratorial wink.

Mom totally knew what he and Sarah had been up to. Oddly, his shoulders eased with a modicum of relief. Then his mind leapt to him and Sarah having the run of the house. Alone. Or would she want to return to Gage's?

A bolt of awareness jarred him. "What time is it?" He snatched his phone from the counter. "Fuck!" *She's an hour late!*

His mother gasped. "Quinn Anthony Hadley, you've been so good lately—"

He corralled his galloping heart. No texts, no calls. "Swear jar. I know. I'll take care of it later," he mumbled. He rose, found his socks and shoes, and began pulling them on while his mind scattered in a dozen different directions. *Keys. Jacket. Mom.* "Will you be all right on your own for a little while?

"Yes, of course. But where are you going?"

Not wanting to worry her, he tossed out the first thing that came to mind. "I forgot I promised Sarah I'd … get her a new 3-D puzzle since I finished her last one. I want to have it here before she gets back."

"But the stores aren't—"

"Governor Polis said they can reopen with a limited number of customers." He ignored the bewildered look playing over his mother's face, giving her a kiss on her cheek before jogging to the garage.

"Don't forget a mask," his mother called.

In the truck, he hit Sarah's number. After one ring, it went straight to voicemail. He hit the number again and listened to the same damn message as he threw the vehicle into reverse and backed out. He slammed the truck into drive and tore out to the street.

During the frantic trip to Nelson's, he tried Sarah's number repeatedly. "Come on, come on! Pick up!" he hissed, but Sarah didn't answer. He left her a few messages, telling himself her phone might have died and she didn't have a charger. Why hadn't he thought of that before? But she would have been home by now, dead phone or not. *Maybe her car died too.*

He hit Nelson's number, trying to keep his voice casual when his buddy answered. After the obligatory greeting, he got down to it. "Sarah was gonna head over to your house at some point today, but I don't remember when. Have you heard from her?"

"Not yet. She said she'd text me once she was done checking things out."

"So the last time you heard from her was—"

"Yesterday afternoon sometime?" A note of suspicion was creeping into Nelson's voice, so Quinn gave him a quick, "No big deal. Thanks, man," and hung up.

He pulled in front of Gage and Lily's house behind a gray Mercedes SUV. Parked cars crowded the narrow street, but Sarah's Jeep was nowhere in sight.

"Fuck!" He pounded the steering wheel. "Where are you, Sunshine?"

Maybe she'd driven the Jeep a block away because there hadn't been any spaces open. In the meantime, he'd check the house. What if she fell, was hurt inside? He switched the truck off and grabbed his phone. Leapt out and slammed the door. Rounded the hood. Ran up the walkway and peered in a window. Jogged the perimeter of the house, peering in more windows.

There were no signs of Sarah or Archer.

Panic welled inside him. Where could she have gone? Metro Denver's population was over three million. Where the fuck should he start looking?

He stood at the back corner of the house, absently scanning the yard while he grasped at possibilities. A picket fence and building framed the back edge of the lot. *A garage!* He raced along the outer line of the fence until he reached the detached building. A flash of teal caught his eye, and he slowed his steps.

Sarah's Jeep was parked off the alley, stashed behind the garage. He approached cautiously, peeking in the windows, trying the door handles. Locked up tight, and still no signs of Sarah or Archer.

A sound like a low *whoof* drifted toward him, but he couldn't tell where it came from. He circled the detached garage until he found the service door. He turned the knob, poised to open it, when a shriek from the house wrenched his attention that way. His blood turned cold.

He lunged through the gate and ran across the yard to the back door.

# *Chapter 31*

## WOLF REINTRODUCTION PROJECT

"There's nothing more to say, Wolf! Now give me back my keys!" Sarah kept the rising panic from her voice by channeling frustration, anger, and dread into a screeching forcefulness she didn't feel.

Wolf had been lying in wait—for her to show herself, for a chance to plead his case, for one last shot. And it had paid off because now he had her cornered, her phone and keys held hostage, her dog tethered by a short leash to a refrigerator foot that immobilized him. All Archer could do was vocalize his distress.

At first, Wolf had invited her to sit at the kitchen table while he declared his promises, while he'd tearfully begged her to return to Seattle, while he'd listed the reasons she belonged to him. He'd been carving the same hopeless circle around the same futile conversation. When she'd had enough, she'd told him so. Since that moment, his tenuous hold on reality seemed to slip, his voice taking on an eerie, icy calm that unsettled her with each passing minute.

Was Wolf capable of violence? She'd never seen it, but the man across the table wasn't the one she'd once loved. He'd always been lean, but now he resembled a cadaverous collection of skin-encased bones. And his face, once sharp, proud, and patrician, was a gaunt version of its former self, lending his glacial eyes a sunken, haunted look. The overall effect was that of someone unhinged—and fucking dangerous.

For Sarah, what began as outrage over his audacious ambush—and impatience with his unending pleas—had morphed into cold, congealed fear. For over an hour, he'd denied her the right to leave, the use of her phone, and the ability to take care of Archer.

She couldn't gauge the level of Wolf's crazy, and she had no clue what he planned to do with her and Archer. Nor did she intend to find out.

He was regarding her with an empty, hollow stare. Frantically, she searched for ways to defuse him and convince him to let her go. Nothing she'd tried so far had worked.

She dropped her voice, hoping Wolf didn't pick up on her telltale quaver, and injected fake concern into her tone. "You look tired. Why don't you go back to your hotel, get cleaned up, have a rest? We can have dinner later and talk."

His eyes blinked on, like someone had thrown a switch. Then he began cackling, and frosty needles shot through her veins. "Oh, that's rich!" he wheezed. The laughter stopped, and his voice dripped with ice. "If I leave you to go back to the hotel, you'll bolt. No, Sarah. It's not going to work that way. Wherever I go, you go."

"Wolf, I have people counting on me. I need to—"

"*I'm* counting on you, Sarah. No one else matters. Just me."

She calculated the distance to the back door. Could she make it? Not with Wolf blocking her way. And what about Archer? Their best chance was her escaping. If she could get to the front door …

Rising swiftly, she pivoted toward the living room. A chair clattered behind her, and Wolf was on her before she was halfway to the door. One hand squeezed her arm so hard her fingers tingled. His other hand was in her hair, jerking her head back.

"You're hurting me!" She tried to shake him off, but he clamped down harder and dragged her backward, away from freedom. Archer began barking. Heart pumping like a runaway locomotive careening down a mountain, she twisted in Wolf's grasp. With her free hand, she swung at his head, but her hand glanced off his bony shoulder. He tightened his iron grip on her hair. Her scalp was on fire. Any more pressure, and it would tear. She gasped.

As they scuffled between the kitchen and living room, she caught her breath and screamed in protest, but he didn't let up. Kicking at his legs, his ankles, she nearly lost her balance. Once more, he ratcheted up his hold. The only thing holding her up was his hand in her hair.

Wild eyes bored into hers, his mouth twisted in a tight, cruel line. Over his shoulder lay the kitchen, and she eyed the curtained half-window back door longingly. *Too far.* Her eye snagged on a shadow outside. *I'm seeing things.*

Wolf scanned his surroundings and growled something about a bedroom. He began dragging Sarah out of the kitchen, heading for the hallway. She slapped at him, clawed at him, spat at him. He stopped and raised his fist. She braced herself, anticipating the blow. Before she could process what she was seeing, the back door exploded. Glass shattered and rained down like drops of crystal. Archer barked. Wolf cursed.

A huge figure loomed with a roar. Soon she was being shoved backward, spinning, windmilling. She landed on her hip with a bruising thud that expelled the breath from her lungs. The room tilted. She dragged in air. Everything slowed. Shoes squeaked. Men grunted and snarled. Archer's barks climbed in pitch. The noises seemed muffled, far away.

The sound of skin smacking skin jarred her, and she looked up just as Quinn's fist connected with Wolf's jaw. A pop, a crunch, a groan, and Wolf sagged to his knees. Quinn towered over him, hands balled and ready, his chest rising and falling with each labored breath.

One well-placed foot, and he shoved Wolf sideways. Wolf crumpled into a heap on the floor. The distinctive sound of sirens wailed, growing louder until they seemed to be right outside the door.

Sarah sat frozen in place, gaping at Wolf's unmoving form.

Two strong arms enfolded her, pulled her to her feet and against a hard, still-heaving chest. *Quinn.* She buried her face against him and pulled in his reassuring scent. He smoothed her hair while he held her. "Did he hurt you? Are you okay?"

Numb, she nodded weakly. "I'm okay," she croaked. "Archer?"

"Let me let the cops in, then we'll take care of Arch."

It struck her that in Quinn's arms, she was safe. Her knees wobbled and gave out. "Don't let go," she heard herself plead.

"Not a chance, Sunshine."

Hours later, Quinn finally had Sarah tucked safely in the passenger seat of his truck, and he drove them home, hands firmly on the wheel. Sore, skinned knuckles reminded him of the altercation when he gripped too hard, and he smiled to himself as he shook that hand out. *Totally worth it.*

He'd called Nelson once he and Sarah had buckled in, and she was talking animatedly with her brother over the vehicle's sound system.

"So he broke in and was waiting for you inside?" Nelson sounded incredulous. Quinn didn't blame him.

"No, he didn't *break* in. I didn't lock the door behind me, and he was watching the house, so he slipped in after me."

"Why didn't Archer tear into him?"

"Because Archer knows him, and Wolf came prepared with raw meat and a leash. While Arch was busy scarfing up the goodies, Wolf anchored the leash to the fridge." She went on to describe, as she had to the police, how Wolf had taken her keys and phone and kept her there against her will. Quinn bristled at the memory of Wolf's hands on her. The back door window wasn't completely obscured, and he'd gotten an eyeful of what was going down before he crashed through it.

"Sorry about destroying your back door, dude," he said when Sarah paused for a breath. "It's secure now, but you'll definitely need a new one. Just let me know what the damage is. I'm good for it."

Nelson laughed. "Hey, forget about the damn door. I'm just glad you were there to take care of my sister."

Quinn side-eyed her with pride. "I'm not sure how much taking care of she needed. She was holding her own pretty well until the son of a bitch about tore her hair out."

Sarah rubbed her head gingerly and slid him a hooded look. "Don't let Quinn fool you. He was like the cavalry, riding to the rescue in the nick of time. Wolf got the first shot in, but Quinn dropped him with one punch, and that was all she wrote."

Quinn fidgeted, his cheeks heating, while Nelson guffawed. "Maybe you should start dropping the gloves on the ice, Hads."

"And ruin this pretty face? No way. T.J. can keep his job," Quinn retorted. Sarah beamed him a smile, and his chest expanded a few coat sizes.

"So what's next?" Nelson asked.

"They've got him locked up"—*for now*—"on a laundry list of charges, including felonies. They've taken Sarah's and my statements, and they'll be contacting you and Lily too. But it ain't over. Not by a long shot."

"He'll get out on bail, right? Then what?"

Sarah's hand trembled, and Quinn covered it with his and squeezed. "Because of the seriousness of the charges, they'll set a bail hearing first to determine the amount, so he's not getting sprung just yet. I'm taking Sarah home with me, and she'll be safe there. Wolf doesn't know where I live, and he's not going to find out. Grims and one of his buddies are picking up Sarah's Jeep as we speak and bringing it to my place, so there's no chance for Wolf to follow and figure out where she's stashed. But just in case, I'm in the process of getting the security system fired up. And if those precautions fail and he shows up—"

"He's a fucking dead man," Sarah growled.

*There's my little badass!* He lifted her hand to his mouth and dropped a kiss on it. He couldn't keep the grin from his face.

They hung up, and Quinn pulled up to the house, surprised to see a dark Buick SUV parked in front. Inside the garage, he helped Sarah down from the truck. Without thinking, he crushed her against him, burying his nose in her hair and breathing in her flowery vanilla fragrance. For about the hundredth time that day, he sent a thank you upward to whoever was in charge of the universe. A thank-you for letting no more harm come to her; a thank-you for putting him in the right place at the right time; and a final thank-you for being able to save his girl from a fucking nutjob. *His* girl.

For the second time that day, hot tears stung his eyes and clogged his throat. He held her close, cradling her while he blinked them back and got himself under control. They clung to one another like a pair of drowning people who had just found life preservers. And they would have stayed that way if Archer hadn't barked to be let out of the truck.

Quinn released Sarah, taking a quick swipe at his eyes, and grabbed the door handle to let Archer out. At the same time, the door from the house flew wide, and his mother stood framed in the doorway. "Quinn? Is Sarah with you?" He'd called his mom to tell her he'd be late and why, and to be sure she was all right. He'd offered to send someone to stay with her, but she'd scoffed and flat out refused. *Of course she did.*

Sarah threaded her way toward his mom. "Right here, Liz."

His mother threw her arms around Sarah and, with a sob, pulled her tight to her body. "Oh, doll! I was so worried about you."

"So you're not mad at me?" came Sarah's muffled voice.

"No, of course not. I've just been distracted, dealing with … other things."

Quinn hadn't had a chance to fill Sarah in on his earlier conversation with his mom.

To his surprise and chagrin, both women burst into tears. He stood rooted where he was, Archer by his side, and man and dog glanced at each other as if to say, "What the fuck do we do now?" Normally, when faced with a combination of women and waterworks—not that Quinn had much experience, having deftly avoided it most of his life—he'd have run the other way or given them a Titanic-wide berth. Instead, he approached and embraced them, kissing each one on top of her head, gratified when they both hugged him back fiercely.

"Hey," he said softly, "maybe we should move this party inside?"

His mom's watery blue eyes widened. "Before we do, there's something you need to know."

Nothing could possibly top what the day had already brought, could it? His answer came a moment later when a familiar, disembodied male voice asked, "Liz? What's going on?"

Quinn looked up as his father rounded the corner. Locking on eyes the same color as his, he choked.

"Dad?"

# Chapter 32

## Swinging from the Family Tree

*Surreal.* What other word could describe today? Quinn stood in his kitchen, opening a bottle of water, trying to act as if his father standing beside his mother at the counter was the most natural thing in the world. He failed miserably. He pushed a cleansing breath through his lungs and took a swig.

Sarah had ducked out after introductions to shower and rest, which was exactly what she *should* be doing. As much as his mind was occupied with the scene in front of him, a chunk of it was stretched out with Sarah on her bed. Was she okay? Was she freaked out? Did she need his help? Should he check on her?

His father cleared his throat, yanking Quinn front and center. "This must be a shock, me being here."

Quinn infused his voice with as much casualness as he could muster. "A little. Mom said it'd be a couple of days before you showed up."

"I landed a few hours ago." Slightly strained, his father's voice was no less commanding than it always had been. "I'd planned to lay low for a day, but I changed my mind and came straight from the airport instead." With a smile that crinkled the corners of his eyes, his dad glanced at his mom. "Your mom said it was okay."

His mother nodded her agreement, though her face was unreadable.

Quinn tipped the bottle and gulped, surreptitiously studying his dad. His hair was thinner and grayer, his face creased with more lines, and his complexion was pastier than the healthy hue Quinn remembered. The vigorous, stern, stoic father of his boyhood had been replaced by a bowed, middle-aged man.

Minutes that felt like hours of awkward silence ticked by. *Fuck it. Cut to the chase.* "So what's the plan?" Quinn kept his voice even and his eyes on his dad.

To his surprise, the unyielding knot that usually bunched his father's brows loosened, softened even, and he dipped his head and shook it. The simple shift in posture seemed to shrink his stature. He raised his head and pinned Quinn with an open gaze. "Your mom wants a divorce. She has every right, but I'm here to talk her out of it."

Anger rose from Quinn's gut. "And *that's* what it took to get your attention? Pretty pathetic, Dad." Had he ever spoken to his dad so boldly? No, but then it hadn't mattered before.

Frozen in place, his mother darted wary eyes between him and his father.

His dad blew out a breath. "You're right, Quinn. It *is* pathetic, and I'm not proud of it, but I'm here to fix it if I can. I understand that I've got a lot to answer for, to make up for. Believe it or not, I've been wanting to reach out to your mom, you, and your brother for so long, but I didn't know how. This pandemic was a wake-up call. It's driven home how much I've missed all of you and how selfish I've been with the people who matter most to me." He let out a sigh. "Your mom asking for the divorce, well, I guess that was the final kick in the pants I needed to take a hard look and ask myself what the hell I was doing. I decided life's too short, and I've squandered enough." He shrugged, and his shoulders dropped.

*Whoa!* Quinn had never heard his dad say so much at once so candidly. Taken aback, he blurted, "You say you wanted to reach out and didn't know how, but you were in touch with Ronan regularly."

His father's brows drew together in puzzlement, the vertical pleat between them deep. "Did Ronan say that?"

"Yep. He made it sound real cozy."

The puzzlement turned to sadness, and his dad shook his head. "No. Didn't happen."

Thoughts collided in Quinn's head, and he couldn't separate them. Uncomfortable as someone skating with a broken blade, he nodded and contemplated his beanbags. From behind him wafted a familiar, comforting smell he wanted to sniff clean out of the air. *Sarah.*

"Hi." Sarah stepped beside him and bumped his arm with hers. Craving her touch, he dangled his sore hand, letting it brush her side. She seemed to understand what he needed and inched a little closer, her fingers flitting over his. The simple contact, though not obvious to his mom or dad, puddled warmth in his chest and steadied him. And there was her fragrance, stronger now that she was close, swirling around him like a protective cloud.

"How you feeling, Sunshine?"

"My head's a little sore, but otherwise I'm fine."

He cast her a side glance. She was wearing a T-shirt that read, "I'm Not Short, I'm a Hobbit!" His lips quirked as he pondered asking her about her fuzzy feet, but then he noticed a band of bruises circling her upper arm, and his blood began boiling.

"Jesus fucking Christ! Look what that bastard did to your arm!"

Sarah craned her head to look, and his mom snapped, "Quinn! Swear jar!"

His father gaped at his mother. "He's a grown man, Liz … and a professional hockey player! You're making him feed a swear jar?"

*He's a grown man.* Quinn liked the sound of that rolling out of his dad's mouth.

His mom wagged a finger. "Don't butt in, Mike."

Quinn chuckled—actually chuckled—and it felt damn good. "It's okay, Dad. Gotta let Mom think she's in charge of *something*."

"Ha! Amen to that."

His mother shot Quinn an exaggerated glare that she then transferred to his dad. "You're *both* skating on thin ice." His father had the good sense to look contrite.

"That may be, Mom, but I'm a lot more concerned about Sarah's arm." Quinn scanned the bruises, afraid to touch them.

His dad wasn't afraid. He rounded the counter and took Sarah's arm gently in his hands. "May I?" She nodded. As he examined the bruises, he said, "The paramedics checked these out, right?"

"And my head. They said I'd be tender in a few spots, but that I was okay."

"All the same, you need to take it easy." His dad gave her a smile that reached his eyes, then sidled back beside his mom.

Quinn jabbed his forefinger toward his dad and spoke to Sarah. "What he said."

She smirked. "Oh goody. Does this mean you're going to wait on me, Sparky?"

"Don't push your luck, Sunshine."

"Aren't they cute?" his mom whisper-shouted to his dad.

His dad's eyes bounced between Sarah and him, a hint of amusement tipping his lips, though he didn't say a word.

Sarah couldn't tear her gaze from the Hadley father-and-son combo as they cleaned up the kitchen after dinner. Similar features, similar movements, similar builds, except for Quinn's extra twenty pounds and two inches. After meeting Mike, Sarah understood where Quinn got his brown eyes and dimples, though his father didn't seem to wield them with his son's easy charm.

She also understood why Quinn had distanced himself from his parents. Right now she sat in a front-row seat, watching a family flailing for some semblance of normalcy.

Tight-lipped, stoic, stiff. Mike looked as though he were holding back a swell of emotions, his eyes betraying a longing when he watched his wife and son. An outsider by choice, he wanted back in, and Sarah couldn't help but feel sorry for him.

Dinner had been strange yet ordinary at the same time. They'd sat down like a family, but watching Mike and Quinn floundering for common ground had been excruciating. No amount of cajoling by Liz had smoothed the path. No, only time and grace would help these two work things out. Mike took tentative steps during the meal, making feeble offerings of a skinny olive branch, while Quinn dug in with a surliness that made Sarah flinch at times. While he might argue he was looking out for his mom, Sarah suspected the reasons were more complicated. Vulnerable, wounded

Quinn was striking out like an injured bear. And how would throwing Ronan into the mix change the dynamic?

Quinn continually shot her concerned glances, and she responded with reassuring smiles. He didn't need to add worrying about her onto his heap. So she tried her damnedest to project a calm exterior while inside she still quaked like an aspen leaf in a howling wind.

He must have seen through her flimsy facade because when they were alone, he tipped her chin up so she looked at him. "I'd guess by the dark circles under your eyes that you're exhausted, Sunshine. We need to put you to bed."

Yeah, he was right. She'd been too bone-weary to change into a suit when Liz had invited her to soak in the hot tub with her and Mike. She was almost too bone-weary to go to bed—or maybe she was reluctant because tonight of all nights she didn't want to sleep without Quinn's arms wrapped around her. Had she been able, she'd have crawled into them already and snuggled there for the duration.

"Am I going there alone?" She managed a light, almost playful tone.

"Afraid so to start, babe. Until I can get rid of the PUs—"

"PUs?"

"Parental units?" He kissed the tip of her nose. "You've never heard that one?"

"Can't say as I have. Maybe because I only had the one."

"That reminds me. Have you told your mom about today?"

Sarah's eyes widened. "Hell no! That would mean telling her the whole sordid story. I'd be handing her ammunition—"

"You never told her about Wolf?" His voice rose with disbelief.

She shook her head. "I only told Gage."

Quinn chewed on his bottom lip.

"What's zooming through that brain of yours, Sparky?"

His eyes lasered in on hers. "Just wondering if you'll ever tell your mom about *me*."

She opened her mouth, but nothing came out. Her brain was in flux, thoughts cascading in a torrent, rendering her speechless.

He rubbed his forehead, and his mouth turned down as though melancholy tugged at it. "I'm guessing not, by the look on your face." A pause and a head shake. "Forget I said anything. Besides, we have to be practical. Telling your mom would mean telling your brother too." He let out an extended, lung-emptying sigh that plucked her heartstrings.

When she climbed into her own empty bed, she was more confused than ever. A solid night's sleep. That's what she needed, and she'd sort out the meaning behind Quinn's words and her tangled feelings with fresh brain power. Liz had promised to let Archer into Sarah's room on her way to bed, and Sarah drifted off.

Sometime later, she woke when the door opened and Archer padded in. Consciousness winked on just enough to remind her she'd fallen asleep troubled, that she had questions to resolve. With a grumble, she settled back into her pillows, chasing oblivion. A rustle of clothes, and the covers were lifted. As alarms began sounding in her head, a familiar scent she loved and the big body it belonged to slid against her back. Strong arms banded around her, pulling her close. Quinn's warm breath ruffled her hair.

"What about your mom?" she whispered in the dark.

"Don't care," he whispered back. "I need to hold you."

A long, contented sigh escaped her, and she relaxed in the warm cradle of his arms. A thought rocketed to the surface, where it bobbed. "Wolf must have thrown the rock," she mumbled.

"Mmm … but the cops said he wasn't in town then. Plus, he didn't know anything about me or where I live."

*That's true.* But she wanted the whole mess tied up with a neat little bow so she could descend into untroubled sleep. "Kids."

"Or the wind," Quinn agreed in a voice thick with fatigue.

When she next stirred, light seeped through the windows and Archer whimpered softly to go out. She slid from Quinn's hold, let Archer out, and hit the bathroom. Quinn's hulking frame had barely moved when she slipped back under the covers and faced him. Eyes shut, a dozy half-smile on his face, he wordlessly encircled her and drew her against him. Heavy and hard, his shaft pressed against her abdomen.

"Someone's happy to see me," she purred.

He hummed his agreement.

She dropped her hand between them, and her fingertips traced the head cresting the waistband of his boxers. He let out a growl, and she slipped her hand inside, wrapped it around his thick length, and began a slow, sensual pumping.

The growl became a long, low groan.

"Do you want me to stop?" she whispered.

"Fuck no," he muttered.

A knock sounded on her door, followed by Liz's voice. "Sarah? You awake, doll?"

Another groan, and Quinn flopped onto his back. "Great timing, Mom," he grumbled under his breath.

"Just getting up, Liz," Sarah called, trying not to giggle. "Be out in a minute."

"Okay. I'll make some coffee."

Quinn blinked at the ceiling, then turned his head to Sarah with a devilish smile. "Morning, Sunshine. How'd you sleep?"

She propped up on an elbow and leaned her head into her palm. "Much better after someone climbed into my bed."

His look turned tender, and he ran the back of his hand along the side of her face. "Me too. I didn't like you being so far away."

"A little risky with your mom next door, wasn't it?"

"Yeah, but totally worth it." He rolled to his side and mimicked her pose. "Let's just tell her already."

Sarah darted her eyes to the ceiling and fixed on a wrinkle in the texture. "Too soon, I think. Gage might find out."

"From my mom? How?"

"I don't know. Besides, she's got a lot on her plate right now."

He tapped Sarah's nose. "Okay. But I want to tell her soon. I'm tired of sneaking around."

Sarah feigned shock. "I thought sneaking around added to the excitement."

"I can think of waaay more exciting things we could be doing if we *weren't* sneaking." He waggled his eyebrows.

A series of tingles raced up from her core and puckered her nipples. "Such as?"

"Guess you'll have to find out." With that, he hoisted himself out of bed, plucked a T-shirt from the floor, and pulled it on. His morning wood hadn't diminished, and the tenting in his knit boxers left little to the imagination—a fact Sarah wholly appreciated.

He picked up a pair of sweats and smirked at her. "See something you want, Sunshine?"

She shrugged a shoulder. "Meh. Maybe."

"Well, if you're not sure, stop ogling me."

"Or what?"

He dropped onto the mattress, crawled to her, and kissed her stupid. "Or," he whispered against her lips, "I'll shake the peaches from your tree so hard that my mom *and* the whole fucking neighborhood will know exactly what's going on." He nipped her bottom lip and retreated to pull on his pants. She resisted the urge to tackle him.

A moment passed before she caught her breath and squeaked, "Promise?"

He sent her a wink as he cracked open the door. "Oh yeah. That's a promise."

Quinn wasn't able to keep that promise over the next few days. In fact, they had little time alone together to even sneak kisses. The house had exploded with activity, from police follow-up to Mike's presence early every morning until long after dinner. Sarah didn't mind him being there, though she couldn't say the same for Quinn, who kept an emotional distance from his parents while he watched guardedly. Sarah had warmed to Mike, who'd relaxed enough to let loose an easy laugh as they talked. He avidly studied the routines she and Liz practiced and joined them in the gym, gently inserting himself into Sarah's role with unexpected grace and humor.

"I'm working on earning the backup spot on the roster," he said to Sarah one day, "so when you're taking time off, it's a seamless transition. And maybe, eventually …"

Sarah laid a hand on his arm. "What about her Parkinson's? She'll never be cured."

His eyes quickly misted over. "I know. Which is why it's so important I spend time with her now—these are the good years. I just wish I'd figured that out sooner."

Her own eyes brimming, Sarah whispered to herself as he walked away, "I hope you earn that spot." From there, her mind wandered to the near future. If Liz and Mike reconciled, there was little need for Sarah. There'd be *no* reason for her to live under Quinn's roof. She'd find her own place, ramp up her job search in her chosen career, and submerge herself in her new reality. Quinn would move back into his beloved condo and resume his old lifestyle. Everyone back on track after the disruptive pandemic's derailment.

Maybe it was time to send out more resumes and check into rentals.

Her heart sank.

Later, as she was sharing a soak with Liz in the hot tub, Mike appeared wearing trunks and a grin. "May I join you ladies?"

Sarah didn't miss the twinkle in Liz's eyes. "Of course," Sarah answered, shifting so Mike could sit next to his wife. "Have you seen Quinn? He started working out when Liz and I left the gym, and I haven't seen him since."

Mike nodded. "As a matter of fact, I have." A smile lifted a corner of his mouth. "He's working out his frustrations by smoking a bucket of pucks in the driveway."

"Frustrations?" Liz echoed. "What's he frustrated about?"

"Oh, probably a combination of things. He can't play, he doesn't know *when* he'll be able to play, he's stir crazy, he doesn't know how to handle his old man hanging around, and"—his eyes darted to Liz—"he's none too happy about our family get-together. Not to mention it's eating at him that the slimeball who hurt Sarah is free on bail."

Sarah tried not to contemplate Wolf on the loose. She told herself she was safe, that he didn't know where she was, that he wouldn't hunt her down. But when she was back on her own? A shudder rippled through her.

In a bid to distract herself, she focused on one glaring question and blurted, "What family get-together?"

"Quinn didn't tell you?" Liz said. "We're having a virtual family, um … We're Zooming." Her eyes landed on her husband. "Is that the right term, Mike?"

"I think so. We're video-conferencing with Ronan and his family. I guess we're doing a cocktail hour."

"When's this taking place?" *And why didn't Quinn say anything?*

Mike shrugged. "In a few hours. We hope you'll join us. Archer too." He winked at her.

When Sarah exited the hot tub, she threw on some clothes and went in search of Quinn.

# Chapter 33

## ZOOM

Quinn was bagging up pucks when Sarah stepped out of the garage on the driveway, her wet hair plastered to her head and her feet bare. He arched an eyebrow. "Going somewhere, Sunshine?"

She shook her head. "Looking for you."

"Aw, you missed me." He opened his arms, and she walked into them, huddling close. The smell of chlorine wafted up his nose. When she didn't say anything, he added, "You *didn't* miss me? Well, I missed you, and if I could get my fucking family to leave, I'd show you just how much."

She looked up at him, a little smirk on her flawless face. "Promises, promises. Speaking of family, I hear you're having virtual happy hour with them today. Why didn't you tell me?"

Quinn's jaw clenched. "If I did, then I'd be admitting it's happening and I'm going to be part of it, neither of which I *am* willing to admit at the moment."

"That bad?" Hazel eyes searched his.

"Dad's back, and now we're all supposed to come together in some big kumbaya moment. I'm having a hard time swallowing it. Besides, Ronan's a tool. I have no use for him." A twinge of guilt flared as he recalled his mother's stricken look when he'd told her he wanted no part of their get-together.

Sarah kissed his chin. "I get that. Your dad invited me, you know."

This caught him off guard. "Really? Are you going?"

"Yeah, I think I will. I'm curious about this pain-in-the-ass brother of yours. But it'll be really weird if you're not there."

He threw his head back. "Fuck me!"

"I'd like to."

He leveled his gaze at her, trying not to laugh and trying to ignore the twitch in his shorts. His mind leapt to—and immediately backpedaled from—dragging her into the truck's backseat and fogging up the windows. Maybe a pantry? A laundry room? "Did they send you out here to coerce me? Sex with you, by the way, is an awesome form of coercion. For the record."

She giggled. "I'll remember that."

"Good." He touched the tip of her nose.

Thoughts ricocheted in his head as he regarded her. Maybe he could tolerate *family time* if she were part of it. She'd be his backup, his defense. He'd certainly score points with his mom—and his dad, which shouldn't have mattered, but somehow was starting to.

While he'd bristled earlier when his dad had appeared in the driveway, arms crossed—watching with what Quinn assumed was a critical eye—Quinn had relaxed when he'd realized his dad wasn't going to tell him what to do and how to do it. Instead, to his utter surprise, his dad had done nothing but compliment his play and his shot, citing one highlight-reel goal after another. Even Quinn hadn't remembered the ones his dad described in minute detail. Apparently, Dad *had* been paying attention.

"Good thing I wasn't your coach," his dad had joked. "I'd have probably ruined you. You have an innate talent, and you had the right coaches at the right time. I've noticed a lot of your goals come off that wicked wrist shot of yours. It's precise, and it's deadly. A thing of beauty. Your timing, the way you transfer your weight back to front, the flex in your stick … No wonder goalies can't stop you. I'm proud of you, son." The last bit his dad had said so softly Quinn wasn't sure he'd heard him right.

Sarah's voice brought him back to the here and now. "It doesn't bother you that I'm curious about your brother, does it?"

Quinn grunted. "As long as you limit it to curiosity."

She answered with an eye-roll.

Hours later, Quinn found himself at the dining table in front of a laptop, sipping a beer. He and Sarah flanked his mom and dad, and Archer sprawled at their feet. Ronan and Jen anchored the screen while a niece or nephew bobbed into view from time to time, interrupting in their munchkin voices. The conversation revolved around his brother and his family—with the occasional detour to Mom's rehab with Sarah or Dad's stint in Poland. This suited Quinn fine. Less attention for him to devote, less for him to say.

When the conversation wound up, Ronan declared he wanted to "catch up" with his little brother for a few minutes, so Quinn took the laptop to his office, where he began tossing a trio of beanbags.

"'Sup, Ro?"

Ronan smirked. "Sounds like you have your hands full."

Quinn wouldn't allow his brother to goad him into admitting *anything* he took on wasn't a cakewalk—especially now that he had a better grasp of where Ronan was coming from. "Not sure why you say that. You saw for yourself it's all good here. Mom continues to improve, thanks to the regimen Sarah put her on." He added an extra dose of smug to his tone. "Mom's been getting around like a champ on her own two feet. She hasn't used the wheelchair in months." *Unlike when she was with you, dickwad.*

Had Ronan *ever* thought to work with their mom to increase her mobility? No. He was too damn selfish.

Before he could get carried away, Quinn's logical self reminded him he hadn't thought how best to help his mom either—except to hire caregivers. His mom had been right about his previous picks. Glorified babysitters. She'd made little progress until Sarah arrived. Could Quinn take *some* credit for hiring Sarah? *No, dumbass. Mom picked her and nagged you until you hired her.*

His mind meandered to how different life would be without Sarah. Yeah, that had worked out well for his mom *and* for him.

Ronan's scoff yanked Quinn's attention back to the screen. "The timing was lucky, that's all. Mom would've gotten there had she stayed with us."

Ronan was doing it again, pushing Quinn's buttons, but surprisingly the buttons weren't engaging. "Sarah's the one who came up with the program. All on her own."

"You've got a thing for this girl, don't you?" Ronan's chuckle held an evil note. "Can't say as I blame you, though. The girl's smokin'. You tappin' that yet?"

Quinn sipped his beer. "I always forget just what a prize fuckwad you are. Sarah's here because she works for Mom."

"You've always been an idiot, Quinn, but you're an even bigger idiot than I figured you for. She's there. She's convenient. She's hot as hell. You're not going to be getting it anywhere else. If I were you, I'd be *all over* that."

"Yeah, you totally would."

"What's the fuck's *that* supposed to mean?"

Quinn pulled in a breath and lined up his thoughts. "It means even though you're married to a hottie of your own, you still have to screw everything that moves. Why is that?"

Ronan cackled. "Well, well, Mr. High and Mighty himself, ladies and gents." Now his voice took on a snarling quality. "My relationship with Jen is none of your fucking business. It never has been."

Quinn's voice remained calm. "You've been telling me how to run my life for as long as I can remember. Let me return the favor and give *you* a little piece of advice, Bro. Free of charge. Someday this shit's gonna come back and bite your ass. Jen's going to find out—not from me, but probably from one of your hookups—and you're gonna wake up and she'll have taken the kids and cleared out. That day, you are going to be one sad mofo because it doesn't matter how many women you fuck, you'll never find another one who cares about you enough to put up with your bullshit.

"You're my role model for what happens when you pull the trigger and get married too soon. And by too soon, I mean you haven't grown up. You've always been a self-centered prick who doesn't give a rat's ass about anyone but himself. You think what you're doing is between you and whoever you're hooking up with, but it's not. You have a wife and kids who are part of the equation, no matter how much you try to ignore that fact, and you're opening them up to potential crazies without them knowing it. You keep going the way you're going, and it's only a matter of time before you hurt them."

The blood had drained from Ronan's face, and he went a sickly shade of pasty. "Fuck you!" he spluttered.

"Your brilliant comeback tells me I hit the nail on the head. You chew on that for a while, Ro. Later." Quinn hung up and pushed a cleansing breath through his lungs. For the first time in his life, he shrugged off his brother's taunts. A huge weight lifted from his shoulders, and calm settled in.

Later, while Sarah spotted him at the bench press, he told her about his conversation with Ronan.

"Wow. Wonder if we can nominate him for Husband of the Year? Just watching him during that session …" She paused to shake her head. "I don't get it. His wife's gorgeous and sweet, and he treats her like he's doing her a favor. Why does she put up with that?"

He puffed out, "Don't know."

Sarah helped him guide the bar onto its stand. "I feel sorry for her and the kids, but I feel sorry for him too."

Oddly, so did Quinn. "Why?"

"Because he's driven by one-upping you. How does a person focus on anything meaningful when they're obsessed with outdoing someone else? If you were married with three kids, he'd have four. You buy your tenth car? He'll run out and buy his eleventh. You sleep with a hundred women? He'll bang a hundred and one. It's one big competition for him. It's gotta be exhausting."

Quinn winced inside. Did she really think he'd slept with a hundred women? Whether he had or not was irrelevant—it was her perception that mattered to him.

"Think I'm done. Thanks for your help." He sat up and looked into clear hazel eyes that held no judgment—only warmth that nearly stole his breath.

"Anytime." She placed her hand on his shoulder and bent to kiss his cheek. "And by the way? No matter how long or how hard he tries, your brother will *never* outdo you in heart." With that, she turned and walked away.

*I love her. I fucking love her.*

Back in the kitchen, Quinn was mixing up a protein drink when his mother came up behind him. "Quinn?"

He downed some of the drink. "Yeah, Mom?"

"Thank you for today. The virtual family Zooming thing. I know that wasn't easy, especially with your brother acting like a complete dolt. But you kept your cool, and I'm so proud of you. You've definitely earned your Adulting degree."

He had no idea what to say, nor could he talk in case he choked up. His mom seemed to sense it. She opened her arms wide. "How about a hug for your mom?"

He set his drink down and fell into his mom's outstretched arms, wrapping his own around her fragile frame. He realized with a start he didn't want to relinquish her—they were a family, she and he. But if he had to let her go, having his father step into the role somehow softened the blow.

# Chapter 34

## House of Mirrors

Three days later, Quinn was stowing his mom's suitcase and wheelchair in his dad's SUV while she exchanged good-byes with Sarah. The late afternoon sun cast a golden hue on budding trees and brought out a touch of dark red in Sarah's glossy hair. Though his mother only planned to be gone a few days, and only across town, she sniffled as though she'd never lay eyes on Sarah or Archer again.

*This is what being part of a family feels like.*

She clutched both of Sarah's hands. "You'll stay here with Quinn, right? Where it's safe? With that crazy man out on bail, I don't want to worry about you being all alone at your brother's house." A shudder shook her shoulders.

Sarah exchanged a knowing look with Quinn before giving his mom an indulgent smile. "Don't you worry. I'm staying put."

"And I'll sit on her if I have to." Quinn was about to have Sarah all to himself for the first time since she'd come to live with them. Possibilities of the naked variety ran an endless circuit in his imagination, making his insides pop and fizz as he contemplated the hours and places and ways they could—

"I'm *really* going to miss Archer," his mom lamented, turning forlorn eyes on the dog. Archer wagged and pranced; he had to know he was the subject of their conversation.

Sarah about blew Quinn out of the water when she said, "Why don't you take him for tonight? He can help Mike get accustomed to your meds and some of your routines. I'll come get him tomorrow, and that way I can bring anything you might have left behind."

*What?*

His mother's eyes widened. Quinn's probably did too. "But won't you miss him? Don't you want him here for security?"

Sarah ruffled Archer's furry neck. "Of course I'll miss him, but I'll manage one night. As for security, I think everything finally got worked out with the alarm service." She darted her eyes to Quinn, who flinched. Paige had resolved it, but Quinn had missed the last step: activating his own account. *Damn it!* With the insanity of recent days, he'd completely spaced it, though he wasn't worried—he'd hired a security company to track Wolf's whereabouts. Through them, Quinn had learned that the jerkoff had engaged a Denver defense attorney and immediately split for Seattle, holing up in the house occupied by his wife and kids, no less. Inwardly, Quinn shook his head, bemused why this woman would let her cheating, lawbreaking husband move back in. Oh well. Not Quinn's problem. All he cared about was that Wolf was states away from Sarah.

After the Buick disappeared down the drive, Quinn took Sarah's hand in his and led her inside. He gave her a devilish grin. "Gee, we have the place to ourselves. What do you want to do, Sunshine?"

She flashed him a sultry smile. "Oh, I don't know. Reorganize the kitchen? Catch up on laundry? Play hide-and-seek?"

His eyebrows inched up his forehead. "Hide-and-seek? Sounds interesting."

Inside the foyer, he locked the front door and hit a keypad that closed the front gate to the estate. *Safe and secure. No interruptions.* Then he tugged her to him and ran his hands up and down her sides. "What are we hiding, Sunshine?" His mind zipped to hiding his favorite body part inside her.

She giggled. "I hide, and you have to find me."

"And what do I do with you once I find you?" Fire traveled from his abdomen south.

"Anything you want." She nipped his neck and danced out of his hold. "You count to twenty—no cheating—while I hide."

"Wait! This place is huge. I might not find you until next week. We need some rules."

"Such as?" She bounced in place, her grin spreading and eyes twinkling. Today the weather was warmer, and she was dressed differently, in a short denim skirt and a top that tied behind her neck. It was made of white, flowy material that swayed with her movements. The top bared her shoulders, but she'd thrown on a short navy sweater that covered them. What she couldn't hide was the fact she wasn't wearing a bra. The top was made up of layers of sheer material that obscured but were nonetheless flimsy. He licked his lips. Maybe if he lunged at her right now, he could shorten the time it took to get his hands on her.

Instead, he reined in his libido. "Such as you can hide anywhere inside two wings—yours and mine. The rest of the house and outside are off-limits."

"Deal," she squealed. "Now go lock yourself in a pantry and count." She pivoted, glancing between entries to the two wings.

"One …"

"Not until you're in the pantry!" she laughed.

He spun away and headed toward the butler's pantry. "One and a half …" A covert glance over his shoulder told him she was poised to duck into her own wing. "Two …"

When he hit twenty, he set off toward *his* wing. She'd probably tried to throw him off, the little minx. His logic paid off when he entered the ridiculous huge-ass walk-in-closet and spotted one of its many mirrored doors ajar. A flash through the gap had him grasping the handle and opening it wide. Anticipation danced in his veins.

Sarah nearly fell out of the closet compartment in a fit of laughter when Quinn whipped it open. He smirked, not looking the least bit surprised. She hadn't wanted to make it *too* tough on him—she wanted to be found after all—but she'd hoped to make it more of a challenge than she had.

He tugged her out and closed the door, and she twirled in place slowly, taking in the garish finishes. "Holy … I still can't get over the size of this room!"

"Yeah," Quinn agreed. "Totally impractical."

"Unless you have thousands of clothes and shoes." The space reminded her of a lavish ladies' fitting room from an old movie—one where the guy relaxes in a cushy armchair and drinks a martini while the woman he's buying a wardrobe for models every piece of clothing he's selected.

Surrounded by one mirrored surface after another—even the drawers and end panels were covered in mirrors—the space boasted a white marble floor shot through with gray veins and covered in furry white area rugs, decadent crystal chandeliers suspended from high ceilings, and a white leather ottoman large enough for two people to lie side by side. *Wow!*

Quinn looked around the closet—scratch that—salon. A slow, sly smile curved his lips. "Since I found you, I get to do anything I want with you, huh?"

Nerve endings fired, and she suddenly felt shy. "What did you have in mind?"

He reached for her and turned her in his arms so they both faced their reflection in a mirror. Oh so languidly, he slid her sweater off her shoulders and down her arms. "You know," he began in a deep, thick, chocolate-syrup voice, "I thought this closet was an architectural eyesore and an extravagant waste of space." He pulled the sweater completely off and tossed it on top of a mirrored dresser.

He ran his fingertips lightly up her arms, his gaze holding hers in the mirror. Goose bumps erupted under his touch, and tingles shot to every extremity like a haphazard cluster of exploding fireworks.

"And now?" she rasped.

"Now I see the *real* reason they built it, and I think it's the best room in the house."

She paused to clear her throat, but it betrayed her when it came out in a breathless quaver. "What, do you suppose, is its *real* purpose?"

His hands glided to her hips, hiking her skirt up a few inches, his fingers teasing her hem, and he nuzzled her cheek. Darkened with lust, his espresso eyes shimmered in the reflection. "Watch, and I'll show you," he murmured.

Then his hands slowly worked their way over her ass, up her spine, pausing to caress her bare upper back before unzipping her halter and loosening the tie at her nape. Like the sweater, he drew the top down leisurely, exposing her inch by inch. Cool air and heightened sensation puckered her skin. She exhaled.

The top hung up on her hips, but he abandoned it, instead cupping her exposed breasts, his eyes tracking his movements. "Now *that* is what I call architectural perfection," he rumbled, his mouth beside her ear, feathering warm breath along her neck.

Her nipples had already compressed into hard peaks. His thumbs began circling them slowly, and they tautened into tighter beads. He dropped his mouth to the base of her neck, trailing moist, open-mouthed kisses along her shoulder, his eyes now trained on hers in the mirror. Caught in his gaze, she couldn't look away.

One big hand traveled up, wrapped around her throat, and turned her face toward him. They were surrounded by mirrors, and she caught a glimpse of their bodies from a side angle, adding more flutters to her topsy-turvy tummy. Then his lips were on hers, his tongue sliding into her mouth, the kiss slow and sensual, mimicking his fingers exploring her contours as they moved from one breast to the other.

Mewling noises rose from her throat, and she couldn't contain them. When she tried to turn her head away to catch her breath, his hand held it firmly in place while his tongue probed and swept her mouth. Lips and tongue then moved across her cheek, her jaw, her ear, her throat, sucking, licking, grazing his teeth over her skin.

One fluid movement, and he was suddenly in front of her, sinking to his knees. "Watch," he repeated. "Keep your eyes on the mirror."

The back of his head blocked her view until he shifted, and one side of her body came into view. She watched in fascination as his hand covered her breast. On the other side, still blocked from view by his head, he latched onto the other breast, sucking it into his mouth hard. She gasped, and her knees jellied. While he suckled and licked and nipped, his fingers rolled her other nipple, tweaking and pinching. She kept her eyes trained on what he was doing, fighting the temptation to let her head fall back.

*Oh. My. God!* Her body was transforming into a blazing Roman candle, her senses on overload. Her breaths came fast and shallow. Whether it was from his touch or the erotic charge she got from watching what he was doing, she couldn't say. And she didn't care.

Reflected in the mirror, her slim white fingers tunneled in his soft brown hair. He switched breasts, his mouth inflicting the same tortuous treatment on the other side while his fingers toyed with the one he'd just released.

Gently, he bit down on her nipple while his hands glided to the top of her skirt. The button was quickly released, the fly unzipped, and the skirt forced apart. His mouth still working over her breasts, he pushed the halter and skirt over her hips, down her legs, until they puddled at her feet. She shot out a hand, steadying herself against the dresser. His hands returned to her breasts, massaging, kneading, squeezing. She noted dully that her skin looked pale compared to his and that his big hands on her made her body look small. His mouth moved across her stomach, sending shivers dancing along her spine. He ran the tip of his tongue along the top of her panties, then trailed kisses after.

A moment later, he rose up and was behind her once more, his unmistakable erection pressing against her ass. Mouth on her neck, eyes on hers, his hands roved over her breasts, her rib cage, her stomach, her waist, her hips. They landed on the straps of her lace panties. He hooked his thumbs in the stringy bits, and just like her other clothing, he pulled them down in one long, deliberate motion. Dropping into a crouch, he dragged them down to her ankles. She still wore flats, and she toed them off, kicking them to one side.

He took his time standing upright, running his hands and tongue over the backs of her knees and thighs, covering her ass with soft bites and wet licks, lingering at the dimples he seemed so fond of, and finally up the channel of her back to the base of her neck. She leaned her head against him and let out an extended sigh.

His hands skimmed her body and dove between the tops of her thighs, where they stroked and squeezed. His thumbs, those talented thumbs, feathered over her mound and joined together to trace the length of her entrance, down, up, down, up, circling, teasing, supercharging the carnal chills racing through her body. Bowing her back, she reached behind and buried her fingers in his thick strands.

"You're not watching," he whispered against her ear right before he nibbled her earlobe.

She blinked and focused on his eyes staring at her in the mirror. Elbows in the air, arms behind her head as her fingers played with his hair, she reminded herself of a stretching cat. His gaze wandered to his hands between her thighs, and hers followed. Strong fingers nudged her legs apart. One hand cupped her while the other feathered its way up her body, pausing to tweak her nipples, until it reached her chin.

"Open," he demanded softly.

Lost in a sex-filled pleasure daze, she opened her mouth. He inserted his middle finger, and she sucked on it—hard—tongued it, hollowed her cheeks as he slid it in and out of her mouth. His eyes blazed as he watched her in the mirror. Her tongue flicked his index finger, and he ran it over her lips before inserting that one too.

"Killing me, Sunshine," he groaned.

*Good! Because you've reduced me to a quivering mass of nerves.*

Out came his fingers with a wet pop, and he dropped them between her legs. One finger entered her, slick and warm, then the other. His free hand returned to her breasts. She closed her eyes and moaned as he slid his fingers in and out, in and out, her body humming with the sensations of his slow, steamy seduction.

He nipped her neck. "Open your eyes, babe."

Her gaze landed first on his eyes, traveling to his calloused hand toying with her breasts, and finally to his fingers moving in and out of her. She arched again and began grinding against his hand at a leisurely tempo.

"Fuck, what a gorgeous sight you are," he said reverently. "I could watch you every hour of every day and never get tired of it."

She was on the verge of falling apart, and she didn't want to go there alone. Wordlessly, she dropped her arms to her sides and slid a hand behind herself to his waistband, inching inside his gym shorts, running her fingers along the length of his engorged cock, spreading moisture over its head with her thumb. In the mirror, his eyes widened, then fluttered closed for an instant. With her other hand, she caressed her breast, her eyes drilling into his as she pinched and rolled her nipple.

"Goddamn, Sunshine. You are so fucking sexy."

He stepped up the pace between her legs. *Oh … I … Oh!* Her mouth parted, and her eyes glazed over, but she kept them fastened on his as she wrapped her fingers around his steely shaft and pumped in time to his fingers.

A look that was part-pain, part-pleasure twisted his features. He huffed out an "Oh God!" then seemed to get himself under control, determined fingers curling and sliding and tormenting. "Come for me, Sunshine," he breathed. She dropped her hand from her breast to the dresser to steady herself.

Now it was her turn to toss out an "Oh God," but it came out as a cry as she climbed her climax. Loosening her grip on him, she closed her eyes while she chased the top of the pinnacle and shattered into countless shards.

As she drifted back down, he corded his arms around her waist, his hands soothing her skin, his mouth plying soft kisses along her neck and shoulders.

She stared at herself in the mirror, then at him, bringing herself back to earth and the hall of mirrors. Her skin was flushed pink all over. "Oh my," she muttered.

A low chuckle rumbled through his chest. "I'm liking this closet a helluva lot."

She nodded her approval, then twisted in his arms. His hands cupped her ass, and his eyes darted over her shoulder. "This is a nice view too."

Craning her head, she caught a glimpse of her bare backside, followed by different views in other mirrors as she swiveled her head. "Can't say I've ever done this in a closet before. Definitely not one covered in mirrors."

"Me neither." He tucked a strand of hair behind her ear and looked down at her, his eyes deep pools of desire.

Gripping the hem of his T-shirt, she lifted it up his torso, running her hands over smooth, carved muscle. "No? I would've thought this wasn't new for you."

He yanked the shirt over his head and pinned her with a bemused look. "No," he said softly. "This is a first for me. *You're* a first for me. Everything's new with you."

*Oh.* Tingly warmth puddled in her gut and spread up her chest, down her legs, ringing her middle. She tugged on his shorts, and he pulled them down along with his boxers, freeing his very heavy, imposing erection. He kicked off his clothes and his flip-flops and stood before her without a stitch on. Now it was her turn to view *his* beautiful body from all angles, and she sucked in a breath. As if her hands had a mind of their own, they began caressing him, and her eyes trailed after. The man was fucking gorgeous. She walked a circle around him while he stood ramrod-straight, her hands never leaving his body. While her fingers played over his skin, tracing scars, exploring, fondling, his eyes tracked her in the mirrors.

Taking his hands in hers, she walked backward, bringing him with her, until her knees bumped the ottoman. She dropped on her seat and peered up at him. "Watch."

His lips quirked in a smile, but it slid off his face when she took him in her hand and guided his thick length to her mouth. A kiss, a lick, a flick of her tongue, and she closed her lips around him while she kept her eyes fastened on him. To her delight, he let out a loud hiss. His hands dropped to her shoulders, moved to her head, fingers burying themselves in her hair, his grip tightening as she sucked and nipped and swirled. She fisted him in one hand while the other played with his balls.

Eyes closing, he dropped his head back and moaned. She stopped what she was doing. "Watch," she purred.

"Yes, ma'am," he choked. His eyes roamed around the mirrors but didn't close. Instead, he muttered and gasped and cursed as her hands and mouth worked him. He thrust into her mouth with short, controlled strokes while he held her head in place.

His chest heaved, and his breathing grew more erratic, his thrusts more intense. Mutterings turned to low groans and grunts. His knees buckled and swayed. His balls tightened. He was close.

He clamped down on her head, stopping her. "If you don't stop, I'm gonna come," he warned in a guttural rasp.

"I know," she murmured.

Liquid brown eyes darkened by desire widened, then fastened on hers. She kept pumping and sucking and cupping. His fingers dug into her scalp, his knees dipped, and he surged into her, his body convulsing as he came, his mouth moving but nothing coherent coming out. She swallowed, drinking him down. Tense muscles eased, then he lifted her chin with his forefinger. "That was … that was …"

She blinked up at him.

"Fuck!" was all he could say.

"Is that 'fuck' in a good way or a bad way?"

He lowered himself onto the ottoman, tipping her over and dragging her beside him as he lay down. "Fucking amazing," he sighed.

"Oh good. You had me worried for a sec, Sparky." She held back a giggle and nestled against him. His arms encircled her; he adjusted her head so it rested on his heart. One hand held her in place against him. He was solid and hard-planed, and God, his warm, smooth skin felt like heaven against hers.

"You have *nothing* to worry about. Fuck, I'm not sure I've ever come so hard." His thumb traced lazy patterns on her arm. "Your skin is so soft."

His mind seemed to be bopping from one thought to the other, and she realized how much she loved following it—when she could keep up, that was. She craned her head to look at him. "There you go being adorable again. Now knock it off, or I won't be able to give you your daily tongue-lashing."

"Is that what you call it? A tongue-lashing? And I get one daily? Sweet! I promise to stop being adorable right now."

She swatted his chest playfully. "That's not what I meant, and you know it, you perv."

"How does thinking of you with your mouth on my dick every single day make me a perv?" He laughed out loud. "I think it makes me normal."

They lay quietly for a few minutes, and he seemed to drift off, so her eyes took a tour around the glittering space. A tickle in her tummy made her squirm. "Yeah, the mirrors definitely add to the eroticism," she whispered to herself.

His chest rumbled, surprising her. "Mm-hmm. Wherever I live, I'm having one of these built."

"For you and your—"

Looking down at her, he put a finger to her lips. "Would you stop? I'm not sharing a playroom with anybody but you."

*Oh.* There came that warm, gooey sensation again.

His hand played with her hair, then drifted down her shoulder, her arm, coming to rest on her hip. It slid to her ass and stroked, tickling her. He cleared his throat. "Have you thought about all the different things we can do in this room?"

She let out a laugh. "Apparently, *you* have. Tell me what scenarios you're picturing in that wicked brain of yours."

He propped himself up on an elbow. With the back of his free hand, he caressed her cheek. Soon that hand was roaming over her chest, her belly, her inner thighs. "How about I show you instead of tell you?"

# *Chapter 35*

## When Mom's Away

If Quinn ran the world—or at least *his* world—he'd stay with Sarah in the house of mirrors and never come out. They'd never wear clothes, and they'd spend their days and nights rolling around, taking each other to new heights while they watched themselves catch fire. They'd collect into white-hot flames and detonate—in every goddamn mirror. Of course, they'd have to eat to keep up their strength, so he'd pay people to leave food outside the door and take it away when they'd finished. How awesome would that be?

Anything involving Sarah and sex was awesome, though. And as for new highs? That's all he'd been climbing since they'd first slept together. Yeah, things had been subdued after that first night when they'd ripped each other's clothes off, but they'd had to be careful to keep their relationship on the down low. Today had made up for the cautious encounters and then some—and the day wasn't over. As he considered the possibilities, his cock twitched to life.

She was stretched out on her back on the ottoman, and he ran his hands and eyes over all that soft skin of hers. He loved touching her. Staring at her. Kissing her. Making her back arch. Being inside her. Listening to the throaty noises she made when she came. Feeling her soft, wet mouth on him. Watching her in a hundred mirrors as she fell apart all over him.

Watching her in the same mirrors as she took him in her mouth and drove him out of his fucking mind.

"Mmm," she purred when he twiddled her nipple. He loved how easily it tightened into a hard ball when he toyed with it. He'd never been with anyone so responsive, so completely *there.* Her body seemed to hum and sing under his touch.

Unable to stop himself, he squeezed her breast into a peak and dipped his head, sucking on her nipple and flicking it with his tongue. A little moan, and her back bowed. Yeah, she liked it when he tortured her like this. He bit down none too gently and rolled it between his teeth. She gasped. She liked this torment too. He slicked his tongue over her peak in a soothing motion and blew gently.

"Oh, mmm," she sighed. Goose bumps erupted, and he let a satisfied smile lift the corners of his mouth. Learning what turned her on was his new mission in life.

Now her fingers were plowing through his hair again—he loved *that* too—and he repeated the process with the other side, rewarded with more soft moans, gasps, and languid writhing.

He lifted his head. "Are you watching?"

She shook her head and gave him a sleepy smile. "Should I be?"

"Oh yeah. Watch yourself in the mirror when I do this." He clamped down on her nipple again.

"Ohhhh," she gasped.

Contented she *was* watching, he dallied a little longer before sliding his hands under her ass. He moved down her smooth body, his tongue tracing the faint lines of her abs, garnering him more stuttered exhales. Her back bowed so hard he thought she'd lift off the ottoman. God, she was so damn hot!

His eyes moved from her to the mirrors while he kept up his slow advance. When he reached her mound, he buried his nose in her curls and pulled in her scent—a scent that drove him all kinds of crazy. He swore the way she smelled and tasted meant she'd been made just for him.

With a nudge of his head, she opened her legs. "Drop your knees to the side, babe. And watch." He chuckled to himself. She complied, and his mouth was on her, sucking, tasting, kissing. He flattened his tongue and ran it up and down her seam over and over, flicking her sensitive spots. Her hips pumped and gyrated, setting him on fire.

*God, I fucking love this!*

It was as pleasurable for him as he hoped it was for her, and he lost himself in the sensation. Only with her had he ever felt this way.

Her lower body twitched off the ottoman, and she squirmed all over. Moans rolled through her. He looked up to find her watching him in a reflection. He winked at her, slid off the ottoman onto a fuzzy rug, dragging her ass to the edge with him. Then his hands were splaying her wide. In the surrounding mirrors, the sight of himself poised between her legs trapped in his hands—knowing what he was about to do—stiffened his cock and sucked the breath from him.

"You're absolutely beautiful," he murmured before lifting her to his mouth. She made a high-pitched gargling noise and bucked. He gripped her thighs so she couldn't escape his onslaught. Then he feasted on her, driving her to the brink and back, again and again. Her cries climbed higher, she babbled incoherently, and her writhing grew more spirited, making his rock-hard dick throb with need.

She let out a little wail, and he heard his name falling from her mouth in breathless gasps. One last lap at her, and he released her. Panting and whimpering, she rolled to her side. In one mirror, the entirety of her front was on display. In another, her back. A pink flush made her skin glow. She was the most beautiful thing he'd ever seen.

He hoisted himself beside her and covered her mouth with his, kissing her long and deep, letting her taste herself while he stole the last of her moans. After he released her lips, he caressed the side of her face. "Hey, Sunshine. How you doing?"

A satisfied sigh escaped her. "I think I can feel my fingers and toes again." She slipped her hand between them, her fingertips feathering along his length. "Which should come in handy for what you need."

His swollen cock rose to her touch, and he couldn't hold back the groan that thundered through his chest. "What I need is you," he growled.

"I can tell," she giggled.

She toyed with him, her touch sometimes light and sometimes not, and he grinded against her hand, craving release. Fingers that weren't occupied with torturing his dick tugged at his hair, skimmed over his shoulders, his back, his flank, his butt, tickling the back of his thigh. Her hands felt incredible on him.

Her mouth landed on his neck and trailed soft, sucking kisses to his ear, where she sank her teeth into his earlobe. "No one's ever made me feel the way you do," she murmured.

He raised his head and looked at her. A tentative smile curved her lips, and her eyes were open windows to her heart, where he saw himself. An arrow pierced his chest, a sensation so sharp yet so staggeringly sweet he couldn't breathe. In that moment, her defenses were down, leaving her exposed and vulnerable. The urge to protect her, to make sure nothing ever hurt her again, overwhelmed him. But he was exposed too, and she could have led him anywhere—he'd have been helpless to do anything but follow at her whim.

Gently, he pushed her hair off her face and kissed her eyes, her forehead, her nose. Her lips. Soft, slow kisses that grew heated as pure emotion surged and spilled over, melding with desire in a whirlpool that couldn't be contained. He was a drowning man. He'd never felt anything like it.

Mouths and limbs tangled in a frenzy, and she rolled over him, slid off of him, and landed on her hands and knees on the ottoman. "I want you inside me. Now." Her throaty voice was low, demanding.

His pulse shot into overdrive. He stood, snagged a condom he'd stashed in his shorts, and sheathed himself. With one knee digging into the ottoman, he pulled her hips toward him. Holding onto one hip, he braced his weight on his other arm and leaned over her, his tip prodding her seam, while he nipped her ear. "Is this what you want, Sunshine?"

"Oh yes," she exhaled in a breathless rush.

He brought himself upright and looked at their reflections. The sight of her naked, on all fours, him poised to enter her, nearly ended him right there. Her eyes, smoldering green-brown pools, flew to the mirror, catching his. He grasped her waist. One long stroke, and he sank deep inside her. She gasped. He stilled.

"Don't stop," she hissed, her glittering eyes piercing his in the mirror. Her back was bowed, making her round ass stick up, and he saw it from every angle. Saw her tits sway enticingly. Saw himself withdraw and thrust back inside her, harder this time. And again. Saw the pleasure on her face with every stroke.

She let out a long, sweet moan.

Consciousness dissipated, and he was flexing his hips, driving into her, in and out, while he held on to her. She pushed back against him, undulating her hips, chasing his cock and her pleasure. His grunts and groans mingled with her moans and cries, filling the room. Their coupling, primal and raw, was on display in every mirror. He watched himself take her, watched himself plow into her over and over, watched himself make her his.

*Mine.*

She watched too, her head canted at a different set of mirrors. The sight unleashed something toothy and wild deep down, and he became a pile-driver. White heat raced down his spine, pooling at its base. With a shudder, she cried out and contracted, surrounding him in a tight, wet clench. Her mouth was open, her head thrown back, her features a study in carnal bliss. And he couldn't stop. He hit the precipice at full speed and flew over with a shout, his release long, hot, and hard.

His knees were pudding, and he collapsed against her. She went down on her stomach with him draped on her back, both of them sucking in air. When he'd caught his breath, he looked up to see her gazing at him in one of the reflections. She smiled, and he nuzzled her neck.

When his limbs worked again, he got up and disposed of the condom. Back in the house of mirrors, he glimpsed her curled up on one of the white fuzzy rugs, and he stretched out beside her, his front to her back, gathering her to him—where she belonged. Eyes closed, she wiggled closer and hummed contentedly. He blinked at their reflections, loving what he saw. She fit him perfectly, in so many ways. As he drifted off, the words, "I love you, I love you, I love you," wound through his head.

Sarah stirred to Quinn wrapped around her, the sight reflected unendingly in the shimmering silver mirrors. Physically, her heart rate and breathing had returned to normal, but mentally she was still trying to catch her breath.

A chorus of *Wowwowwow's* buzzed in her head, leaving her at a loss for words to describe their soul-penetrating lovemaking. *Lovemaking*, however, was too gentle a term for the passionate connection that had ignited them both. Whatever else it was, it went light-years beyond a physical joining.

Something deep, visceral, and powerful had passed between them. This most definitely was not *just sex*.

When had she ever been so aroused, so moved? *Never*. The delicious burn in the muscles of her thighs and stomach, her sensitized skin, told her she should have been sated, but instead she craved more.

She studied his reflection. A broad, tanned forearm draped her middle, a dark contrast to her peach-tinged skin. His large hand splayed across her chest, covering one breast fully while his fingers grazed the other. His other arm was pillowed under his head, thick chestnut locks resting on his elbow. A calf dusted in dark hair nestled between her legs. Rhythmic breaths fell soft and warm on her neck. The way he cradled her, infusing her with his heat, comforted her every nook and cranny. How ironic that the man whose mere presence once had her spitting insults now evoked equally powerful feelings of an opposite nature. When, and how, had that happened? It had been a gradual shift, an erosion of walls she'd built from anger and bitterness after her humiliation at Wolf's hands.

But what about the blond babes Quinn drew into his orbit? The same worn questions circled inside her brain. Once COVID restrictions were lifted, would he revert to his old ways as a free-wheeling, high-scoring hockey hunk who trolled bars and clubs for hookups? A little voice piped up in her head. *No*, it insisted. She wanted to believe it, but only time would tell. *Eyes wide-open.*

Behind her, the hockey hunk stirred, mumbling under this breath. His leg bent hers back, and cool air soothed her tender parts. Still half-asleep, he kissed her neck while his arm and hand tightened their hold.

"Mmm, Sarah, smile." He hummed a few bars of a familiar tune.

His eyes opened, and he stared at her staring back at him. "I *really* like this room," he said in a dusky voice. "We might have to lock ourselves in and never leave."

She twisted in his arms and faced him. His hand slid down her back to cup a cheek.

"Not sure how practical that is. We'll need food, showers … And speaking of showers, I'd like to clean up."

He planted a kiss on her forehead. "How about a swim first?"

"A swim where?"

His eyebrow quirked. "In the big, heated pool outside the gym?"

"I stuck my toe in there. I'm not sure how *heated* it is."

"That was late in the winter, when it was still cold. It's much warmer now." When she eyed him dubiously, he added, "Where's your sense of adventure? Let's go find out just how warm it is. Besides, I can always heat you up." Now his eyebrows bounced.

"You do have a talent for doing that."

His lips tipped up in a happy, dimpled smile.

"All right," she sighed. "I'll get my suit."

"No suits," he scoffed. "We're skinny dipping."

"We are? But—"

"No one can see us."

Before she could think of another argument, he was on his feet, hauling her up with him, a very determined look on his face.

A few giggles escaped her. "Can I at least wear a robe out there?"

He looked her up and down, and she nearly broke out in a blush. With a shrug, he began opening mirrored closet doors. "There are robes in here somewhere." He went from one door to another.

"Aha!" he cried triumphantly, holding up two plush terry robes like the ones luxury hotels offered their guests. Blue for him, pink for her.

They covered up and made their way to the gym, where they grabbed oversized towels.

Quinn opened a glass slider, and they were out in the brisk night air. At the edge of the pool, he shucked his robe and tossed it on a lounge chair. She was clinging to the warmth of hers, but he stripped it off her, and it joined his. Then he pushed her in, making her gasp, and dove in after.

After the initial shock of the plunge, she began adjusting to the water temperature. Sort of. Quinn was underwater, and he broke the surface, sucking in air and doing the man wet-hair-fling move. The end result had him looking like he sported a cockeyed fin on his head. He swam toward her, his body cutting a big shadow in the ghostly blue glow of the pool lights. Beyond the pool, the backyard melted into a solid curtain of black.

Quinn gathered her up in his arms and flung her through the air. She landed with a *Slap!* With fake outrage, she lunged, wrapping herself around his back while she tried to haul him underwater. He laughed. "I think I have a flea on my back." Strong hands peeled her off him and dunked her.

And so it went. They splashed, spluttered, raced, tackled, whooped, always with the same outcome: their bodies bumped together, wet skin sliding against skin, limbs entangling. Lingering kisses and fondling ensued.

During a moment of calm, Sarah wrapped her legs around him and gazed up at the star-freckled sky while he twirled her on the surface of the water. They were plunged in quiet. Chilly air puckering her exposed skin, she righted herself and looped her arms around his neck. He swam backward with her clinging to him. Movement in the dark snagged her attention, and she strained, trying to pick out what it was.

He turned his head, peering in the same direction. "What are you looking at, babe?"

"I thought I saw something. Probably just a prowling cat or a raccoon."

"There are probably all kinds of critters out here every night we never see."

A devilish gleam lit his eyes, and he was wrestling her again, trying to toss her through the air. She managed to kick his legs out from under him and escape his grasp, squealing as she scrabbled out of the pool. Shivering, she snatched the towels and raced up the stairs to the main deck and the hot tub, shouting, "Last one in the hot tub has to make dinner!"

Loud splashes and squishing sounded behind her, but she slipped into the hot bubbles before Quinn reached her. With a loud, satisfied "Ahhh," she sank until the water touched her chin. "Much better."

Grinning like a madman, he clambered in after her. Their horseplay continued but transformed into tongue-filled kisses, roaming hands, and bodies melding together.

"We should go inside," he panted.

"Why?"

"Because I don't think what I want to do to you is going to work in a hot tub. Besides, I need another condom." Her nipples perked up.

Soon they were wrapped in towels, dashing into the warmth of the family room. Quinn locked the door behind them and guided Sarah to the couch, where he sat and pulled her on to his lap so she straddled him. The towels came off, a condom went on, and she impaled herself on him.

*Heaven.*

After adjusting to his girth, she began moving, her hands anchored on his shoulders. His eyes devoured her, and soon he was thrusting up into her. Their voices and breathing gathered speed. Sarah was lost in the feel of him deep inside her.

An outside light came on, flooding the deck in brightness. Quinn stilled, pulled her off him, and rose to investigate. Her bubble of bliss popped. He stood at the French door, stark naked, scanning. The memory of shattered glass cooled her, and she gathered a pillow to herself. "Do you see anything?"

"Nah. It was probably that cat or whatever you saw. It must have come up on the deck and triggered the motion sensor lights." He tugged on the door handle. "All locked up." Then he turned with a shrug and headed back to the couch. His swollen shaft seemed to be pointed right at her, and it bobbed as he walked. Her face must have given away her amusement *and* her appreciation because he glanced down at himself and gave her a wide, dimpled grin. "Heat-seeking missile."

She toppled over in laughter, but humor was swallowed up in greedy kisses as he pushed her on her back. He lowered himself on top of her, his knee parting her legs. Then he entered her, slowly, and eased out. His feet found purchase against one end of the couch, and he surged back into her. And again, over and over, his pace steady and relentless. Wrapping her legs around his flexing hips, she met his powerful thrusts with all she had. He rocked her hard, shooting her beyond the stratosphere—twice—before reaching his own climax with a roar.

# Chapter 36

## I'll Take Steak Over Fish Anytime

Quinn was sated, utterly wrung out, and he floated on a cloud of ecstasy. After their couch antics, they'd both been ravenous, and they scarfed down a throw-together meal of omelets, bacon, and pancakes.

Sarah wanted to wash off the chlorine, so Quinn went to retrieve the robes they had left poolside. He jogged downstairs to the gym, discovering he hadn't locked this particular slider because he'd chased Sarah up the stairs to the hot tub. Once outside, he aimed for the lounge chair. It was empty. A quick spin revealed the other chairs were empty too.

Baffled, he smoothed the back of his head and scanned the perimeter of the pool. Nothing. As he was about to give up the search, something pale caught his eye. It lay motionless in the shadows, just beyond the edge of the glow cast by the pool lights. He headed toward it, slowing his steps the closer he got. A noise like a hiss stood his neck hairs on end.

*It's a cat. Calm the fuck down.*

Another few steps, and the object came into view. He crouched and brushed his fingers across it. A pink robe. How had it wound up there? Picking it up, he peered into the dark, looking for the second robe, but the yard was plunged in inky blackness. A chill chattered along his spine, and he hustled back to the house, locking the gym slider behind him.

Walking into the master bedroom, he glimpsed the curve of Sarah's peachy-pink back as she fiddled with the shower controls, and he forgot the robe in his hand.

When she saw him, she turned and smirked. "I guess I need a coach to show me how to operate this contraption."

His eyes traveled over her body, and he gave her a wolfish grin. "I'm your man."

Her eyes dipped to his hand. "What's that?"

"Oh. Your robe. Couldn't find mine." He held it up to show her, and her eyes went as round as an owl's. She let out a squeak. He craned his head and nearly squeaked himself. The robe had been slashed repeatedly from just above the hem to the shoulder, rendering it a collection of wide terrycloth ribbons joined at the top and bottom. "What. The. Fuck?"

She pointed. "You found it like that?"

He explained how and where.

She blinked—several times. "I don't think a cat would do that."

*Neither do I.* "Maybe a mountain lion is prowling the neighborhood? I hear animals are bolder now that the pandemic's got people sheltering in place."

"You're not serious!" She shivered and rubbed her arms.

"How do *you* explain it?"

"Not a mountain lion. Maybe a bobcat?"

By the time they'd showered and fallen into bed, they'd exhausted logical explanations and agreed to put the whole thing aside until morning. As Quinn gathered her close, pulling in the scent of her freshly shampooed hair, he ran his hands over her silky bare skin. With a sigh, he drifted off to sleep in a euphoric fog.

Quinn awoke with a start, his heart hammering in his chest. He was on his back, and Sarah's warm weight nestled against his side as she slept in the crook of his arm. He scrubbed his hand over his face, trying to orient himself. Outside, it was still pitch-black.

Had he had a nightmare? He couldn't remember.

He thought he heard a rustle and lifted his head to stare into the shadows surrounding the bed. Something moved. He blinked, convinced what he saw was a hallucination brought on by being jarred out of a deep sleep.

Then he felt a shift in the air. Something—or someone—was breathing heavily, and it wasn't him. He glanced down at Sarah, but her inhales were soft, slow, a different cadence from what he *thought* he was hearing.

A flash in the dark, and every alarm bell in his head tripped at once. Blood whooshed in his ears. Adrenalin flooded his veins. An unearthly scream fired every nerve, and he shoved Sarah from the bed. He rolled just as something punched into the mattress beside his head, a harsh ripping sound following after.

"He's here, Sarah! Run!" he bellowed.

Scrambling from the bed, Quinn's feet became entangled in the covers. Whatever had slashed the mattress was yanked out. It rose up and sliced through the air. Little grunting noises mixed with keening. Quinn heaved his body to the side, his shoulders and head thudding to the floor. Another blow struck the mattress, puncturing it scant inches from his hip. The rest of him was still twisted in the sheets, and he kicked.

A light snapped on.

A wild-eyed woman stood at the foot of the bed, bathed in light, struggling to free a kitchen knife. She froze, distracted by the light. Blond hair escaped a black cap.

*What …?*

Dory's eyes burned into his and jerked the blade free. She double-fisted the handle, drawing it up in what seemed to be slow motion.

"You called her 'babe'! I heard you!" she shrieked. "You couldn't keep your hands off her—in the pool, the hot tub, and you fucked her on the couch right in front of me! I hate you!" She raised the knife above her head, aiming it at Quinn. He curled away, but not enough to escape the trajectory of the plunge. He threw up his arm. A sudden thump, an impact, and Dory flew to the side. The knife tumbled from her grasp, landing beside Quinn's thigh. He kicked the covers off and seized the blade. Then he was up, moving.

He rounded the foot of the bed. Sarah was crouched over Dory, one knee digging into Dory's back. Dory had lost her breath but was rousing. Spitting, hissing. He nudged Sarah off her and took over, his knee now wedged in Dory's back. His weight drove the breath from her again, and he clamped down on her wrists and held them behind her back.

Sarah grabbed her phone from the nightstand where she'd clicked on the lamp, and her wide eyes traveled from Dory to Quinn as she dialed. She put the phone on speaker and tossed it on the bed. "Nine-one-one. What's your emergency?" crackled through the room.

"A crazy woman broke into my boyfriend's house and tried to stab him." Sarah wrenched open the closet door and darted him a look. "Tape? Rope? Laces?" She jerked one of his shirts from a hanger and wrestled it on.

*What's she asking me?* A klieg light flashed on in his brain. *Smart girl.* "Gear bag, middle of the right wall. Should have laces *and* tape."

The operator asked questions, and Sarah answered, her voice shaking as she rifled the closet.

"And the woman is still there?" the operator asked.

"Yes!" Sarah screamed.

Underneath him, Dory kicked, cursed, yelled. Her strength took him by surprise. She bucked his knee off. Then she rolled and twisted, and he lost his grip on her hands. Screeching like a banshee, she scrabbled, hopped up, and rushed toward Sarah. On his knees, Quinn lunged and caught Dory's ankle. She thudded to the floor, her free leg swinging wildly. Her heel glanced off his shoulder, but he held on, adrenalin pumping furiously through his body. Lunacy might have fueled her strength, but it was no match for his.

He caught her other ankle, hauled her in, and jerked her back on her face. Her back was too small to fit both his knees, so he rammed one between her shoulders and pinned her with his weight.

"Sarah," he panted, "the cops need to unlock the gate to get in." He rattled off his code and location of the exterior keypad.

Sarah relayed it and dropped beside him with two rolls of hockey tape and a handful of tangled laces. Still talking to the nine-one-one operator, she dove for Dory's legs, sat on them, and ripped a length of tape she handed Quinn. Getting it wound around Dory's wrists, however, proved futile. Determination blazing in them, Sarah's eyes met his in a silent exchange. He nodded. While he held Dory's hands, Sarah wound tape around her wrists. In sync, they worked quickly and bound her ankles too.

Quinn gulped in breath, and sweat dripped off his forehead. Sarah slid off Dory and leaned her head against the bed, her chest heaving. Then she was on the move again, snatching his T-shirt and shorts. She tossed them at him and sat on Dory while he dressed.

The doorbell gonged just as the disembodied voice of the nine-one-one operator announced the police were at the front door.

Sarah leapt up. "You stay here with her. I'll let them in."

He kept his knee, and his weight, firmly in the center of Dory's back, who now sobbed uncontrollably.

The officers appeared in the doorway, Sarah right behind; one had drawn her weapon. Quinn put up his hands and backed away in a crouch. The male officer's eyes bounced between Dory bound on the floor and Quinn.

Questions, answers, more questions. The female officer looked at Quinn as though she were trying to work out a puzzle. Finally, she said, "You're Quinn Hadley. You play for the Blizzard."

He nodded and pointed at Sarah. "And that's my girlfriend, Sarah Nelson."

Dory shrieked. "*I'm* his girlfriend! I caught him cheating on me with that ugly bitch!"

Hours later, after Dory had been hauled away, the cops had sorted the situation enough to leave Quinn and Sarah in peace for a few hours until they were due at the station for formal statements. Though the officers didn't elaborate, they'd arrested Dory on other charges besides those she'd racked up at Quinn's.

As Quinn closed and locked the front door, he sagged against it, fatigue seeping into the marrow of his bones. Sarah put her arms around his waist, rubbing her cheek against his back, and tugged him toward her room. "C'mon, Sparky. Let's sleep in my room tonight."

*If I can sleep.*

He flopped into her bed and tucked her under his arm. "I thought Wolf had broken in. I never imagined it was Dory. But she was outside, watching us the whole time. When we were in the pool, the hot tub. She spied through the windows when we were on the couch and set off the lights. She must've sneaked in through the gym door before I locked it."

Still wearing his shirt, Sarah snaked her arm around him and nuzzled his shoulder, soothing him. A shiver ran through her body. "I saw *her* out there, not a cat. And she must have shredded my robe."

The cops had found his robe, intact, stashed in some bushes.

"She threw the rock," he said.

"How? I thought she was with Wyatt."

"I don't know how she did it, but she did." He shuddered with the recollection of his shredded mattress and how close Dory had come to burying the knife in him. And if she'd immobilized him? He had no doubt she'd have gone after Sarah. "Jesus, Sunshine. What the fuck is wrong with people? We know how to pick the crazies, don't we?"

She parked her chin on his chest. "I guess that's one more thing we have in common."

He tweaked her nose. "How about we just stick with each other from now on?"

Her eyebrow dipped. "Except we're crazy too."

He ran his fingers through her hair. "A good kind of crazy. And your crazy matches mine perfectly. I think we make a good team."

"You think?"

"I know."

The next day, Quinn called Wyatt, keeping the shit-shooting to a bare minimum before he launched into the reason for his call. "So I wanted to ask you about Dory."

On the other end, Wyatt was uncharacteristically quiet.

"It's not like that, man," Quinn explained. "I wanted to know if you're still seeing her."

A throat clear. "Haven't seen much of her. She's been acting strange lately, and last week she went dark. I'm guessing I pissed her off, but I'm not sure why. Or maybe … Is she, ah, back with you?"

Quinn kept himself from barking, *Hell no!* "No, she's not, and when I tell you what went down last night, I'm betting you'll be relieved she's not with you either." Quinn filled Wyatt in, leaving Sarah's name out of the narrative. He referred to her simply as "a lady friend I've been spending time with."

"Are you fucking kidding me?" Wyatt spluttered. "This is a joke, right? You're making this up."

"Wish that was the case, buddy. But don't take my word for it. Her arrest should be public record, so check for yourself."

Quinn lost count of how many times Wyatt muttered, "My fucking God!"

"Do you remember when you first told me you were seeing her? You said you'd been at your place in the mountains?"

"Yeah?"

"I'm just trying to wrap my head around some of the dates." Quinn told Wyatt which dates.

"No, man. She was here the whole time. She drove up separately, but she didn't go anywhere."

"You're sure?"

"Positive. In fact, McMurphy, his date, and a few other friends joined us. They saw her here too." Wyatt laughed. "Though one of them wishes they hadn't."

"What do you mean?"

"I don't know what set it off, but McMurphy's date got into it with Dory one night when we were all pretty wasted. What a shit-show! Told Dory she was nuts. There was no shortage of claws. Dory got so pissed, she … Oh shit! I totally forgot she *did* leave. But it was only for a few hours, I think. Not the whole night."

When Quinn pressed him, Wyatt said, "Shit, Hads. I don't know how long she was gone. I was hammered. I just know she showed back up, and everything was cool again. But—here's something else I totally spaced—I found out later two of Hunts's tires were slashed. He had a hell of a time getting new ones, and his date ended up missing some important work thing. He told me all about it afterward."

"Which night, Wyatt?" *This is really important.*

"Let me think. Had to be the last night we were there."

The same night the rock sailed through Quinn's window. By the time he hung up, Quinn was slicked in a fine sheen of sweat.

Over the coming weeks, Quinn and Sarah learned far more about the woman who'd attacked them from Officer Easton, the policewoman who'd been at the scene that night.

"You were lucky," she told them over coffee at Quinn's one morning. Liz and Mike were there, and Archer pranced around Officer Easton as if she were feeding him Beggin' Strips.

In between stroking his head, she ruffled his neck and crooned that he was a good dog. "Good thing this handsome boy wasn't around that night."

"He was with us," Liz blurted.

The officer gave her a nod. "That saved him. We investigated a similar case about eight months back. One of our pro basketball players was being stalked by a woman who tried breaking into his house. There are lots of similarities between the two cases. Unfortunately, in the basketball player's case, the gentleman had a dog. That dog was fed a poisoned meatball right before the attempted break-in. The suspect in your case is facing animal cruelty charges in addition to everything else."

Sarah gasped. "What happened to the dog?"

The officer just shook her head, and something pointy dug into Sarah's heart.

Quinn put his arm around her shoulders and squeezed, and she dropped her head against his chest, drawing comfort from his warm strength. "How do you know it's the same person?"

"The evidence lines up," Officer Easton answered.

Sarah looked up at Quinn. The blood had drained from his face, and his mouth hung open. "Thank you for being here that night, Officer," he finally croaked.

She stood to leave and sent him a wink. "Couldn't let anything happen to my favorite left-winger."

That night in bed, Sarah shivered as she snuggled close to Quinn. "Thank *God* Archer was with your mom and dad. Who could do something like that to a defenseless animal?"

"A wacko named Dory, apparently. Hopefully they lock her up for the rest of her life," he replied.

"Amen to that." Sarah rolled over and rested her chin on his chest. His fingers tunneled through her hair, and she relished the feel on her scalp. "Gotta hand it to you, though, Sparky."

"Hmm?"

"Yet one more woman falls under the Hadley spell. I think you have a new admirer in Officer Easton."

He flashed his full-dimpled smile. "I promised her some tickets. And speaking of the Hadley spell, how come you're immune?"

She grinned. "Who says I am? Those impressive hockey reflexes of yours kept me safe—twice—and kept you from getting stabbed." She tried not to gush, she really did, but it was hard not to. Truth be told, she went a little weak-kneed every time she thought about how he'd dropped Wolf and how he'd shoved her out of harm's way while twisting his own big body away from Dory's lethal knife. Power, action, speed—heady attributes that drew her like metal to a magnet.

"Speaking of impressive, your quick thinking saved our asses. *You* knocked her down before she could carve me up, you're the one who called nine-one-one, and you thought of tying her up. And you held it together under a shit ton of stress. Courage and grace under fire, Sunshine. I'm awed by you." He picked up her hand and kissed every finger.

His unabashed admiration heated her neck and face. "But I fell apart afterward."

"So what? So did I," he laughed. "As I recall, we *both* had a serious case of the shakes after the police left. What matters is you were sharp when it counted."

"Like you said, we're a good team." She kissed him long and deep.

# Chapter 37

## Back to Reality, Whatever That Is

As weeks passed, Colorado loosened more COVID-19 restrictions, and the NHL announced its Return to Play Plan. Teams would begin training camp in mid-July—what would normally be smack in the middle of the off-season. After training camps came team qualifiers and round-robins for playoff seeding, with all games being played in Edmonton or Toronto.

Sarah stood in Quinn's kitchen, staring ahead vacantly, sipping hot tea in a bid to settle her jolting tummy. Spread out on the counter were Paige's blueprints, and while the project had held Sarah's attention earlier, her mind was too far adrift to finish her notes.

Archer let out a yip and took off toward the garage. *Quinn's home.* Sarah's jolting stomach positively galloped … with excitement and dread.

He burst from the hallway, Archer dancing at his feet, tossed his gear bag on the floor, and strode toward her.

"Hey," he said before he leaned down, cinched his arms around her, and kissed her silly.

She gave him a little shove when they came up for air. "You're all sweaty!"

"No, I'm not. I took a shower after practice just for you so I'd smell good and you'd want to jump my bones as soon as I walked through the door. Now kiss me and jump my bones already." He leaned in for another kiss, but she slipped out of his grasp.

A nervous laugh escaped her, and she took another swallow of her tea. "I *jumped your bones* before you left this morning."

"So?" He winked at her, and his eyes shifted to the blueprints. "What are you doing with Paige's drawings?"

"Wrapping up."

He grabbed a sports drink from the fridge and twisted off the cap. "What did you find?"

Engineering talk was a welcome segue, and she pounced on it. "They're going to need more piers for that foundation, and the HVAC system has to move."

"I get the foundation—it looked a little suspect to me too. But why the HVAC?"

"Because a support column needs to go there." She blinked. "You studied the blueprints?"

He grinned. "Yeah. You know what I do for my work, so I thought I'd check out what you do—in your *other* job."

*My* real *job*. "Yeah, about that." Another swig slid down his throat, and she stared in awe as it moved along the thick column of his neck.

"About what?" he asked.

"I've been sending out resumes," she blurted. "In fact, I have a virtual interview tomorrow."

"That's great they want you, but aren't you getting on it a little soon?"

She rushed into her prepared speech. "I don't think so. Your mom doesn't need me anymore; she's doing great. In fact, she and your dad are looking for a service dog. She's hardly ever here, so I've had a lot of spare time." *And I'm bored!* "While you've been attending your meetings and small-group trainings, I've ramped up my job search again. I figure with your full-on training camp starting in a few weeks, you'll be really busy, and then you're off to Canada for the playoffs for God knows how long. It's a good time for me to get on with—"

"So which Denver firms are hiring?" He crossed his arms and leaned against the counter, pleats between his knotted eyebrows.

Crap! Why hadn't she just told him what she was doing at the beginning? Because it had seemed easier not to until she had something solid.

"I'm not just looking in Denver." She held her breath, waiting for this statement to sink in. Applying for the out-of-state openings had been driven by one factor: the positions were in prestigious firms like the one in Seattle, and she wanted to find out if she could land a coveted job on her own merits. Whether she'd take it was a different matter altogether.

Quinn's mouth hung open, and astonishment flashed in his brown eyes. "Where are you looking?"

She tried to keep her voice light. "Mostly in the western states."

He seemed to measure her. "And tomorrow's interview? Where's that company located?"

Inwardly, she cringed. Why was this so hard? "Texas. Not so far away." No reason to tell him she had interest from North Carolina, Illinois, and Virginia, which had been a huge confidence booster. Now that boost didn't seem to lift her as much.

He threw out an arm. "How's that supposed to work? You live in Texas, I'm in Denver, and we see each other every few months? Unless I'm traded to Dallas, which won't happen if I can help it." The better part of wisdom made her hold back that Texas wanted her because of her Spanish, and working there would mean long stints in Mexico. A long shot, and even if they offered her the job, what would she do with Archer?

Quinn's eyes bored into her. Her mouth opened and closed. "We never talked about life after the caregiver job ended, and I just assumed—"

His frown deepened, and she hurried on. "The pandemic has twisted everything. Hasn't it occurred to you that this … attraction"—she waved her hand between them—"only happened because we were stuck together? And that once we were unstuck, everything would go back to the way it was?" *Like Cinderella … who had a happy ending.* "Maybe this is a good time to take a break and see if this thing we've got is going to survive outside of a forced shelter-in-place." These arguments had been churning in her head, and they made perfect sense. Surely Quinn's logical brain would see it, too.

Instead, his volume climbed. "*Attraction?* That's what you call what we've been doing?" He ruffled his short, damp hair. "Where do you see yourself living if you stay in Denver? And where do you see me living?"

"I assumed you'd move back into the condo you miss so much, and I'd stay at Gage's until I find my own place here or …" *Move away.* Except she didn't *want* to move away, but she owed it to herself to look at *all* her options, damn it! It didn't mean she and Quinn wouldn't see each other.

"You're doing a hell of a lot of assuming on your own. Did you assume we'd go our separate ways? Is that what you want? You haven't once mentioned living in my condo with me, so I can only *assume* that option's off the table," he huffed.

She gawped at him. Living with him hadn't crossed her mind, and if it had … Well, she'd made that mistake with Wolf, and she didn't intend repeating it. "We never talked about me living there!" she spluttered.

"Because I didn't see this freight train bearing down on me." He paused to pull in a breath. "Why not just stay with me? We're so good together."

Emotions tightened into a twister inside her. The plea in his eyes reached into her soul, but she needed to do this. For her. For them. Somehow, she couldn't find the words to explain.

In a resigned tone, he said, "So when are you planning to move in with Gage?"

"The governor lifted the restriction on real estate closings, so Gage and Lily close on their new house next week," she answered lamely.

"Meaning you're moving in with them next week. Were you going to tell me or just let me come home to an empty house?"

"That's not fair!" God, he could be infuriating!

"Neither is putting everything into play without talking to me!" A storm brewed in his expression.

"I don't need your permission!" Her voice pitched high.

"No, you don't, but I *thought* people who were in love discussed big decisions with each other. I classify picking up stakes and moving halfway across the goddamn country a big fucking decision. Instead, you've been laying your own plans that you're just now springing on me. You're not in a vacuum, Sarah. This shit matters to me. It affects me too."

*People who are in love?* He was in love with her? Was she in love with him? She pushed the questions aside because damn, she needed to do a better job explaining.

"When I moved to Seattle, I uprooted everything for a man I never would have started a relationship with in the first place had we not been forced to work together, and look how that turned out."

A fire kindled in his eyes. In a low, dark voice, he said, "Have you told Gage about us?"

This was not going the way she'd hoped. When she'd played it out in her head, they had an objective conversation where she laid out her doubts, the reasons behind them, and her plans moving forward. In turn, he would say he understood where she was coming from and that he was behind her. They didn't fight or rip apart at the seams. Instead, they fell into bed and loved each other like they always did. "No," she said in a small voice.

"Why not?" A challenge tinged his tone.

"Because he knows about my Wolf disaster," she shot back. "If I tell him about you and me, he'll say it's too soon, that you're the wrong guy for me. Worse, if things don't work out between us, I'll have to admit one more screw-up to him. It has a compounding effect."

"Goddamn it, Sarah, I'm not Wolf! I haven't hidden a fucking thing from you, good or bad. Want to know who I am? Open your eyes. I'm the same guy I've always been, and I'm standing right here."

"I didn't say you were Wolf!"

The tempest in his chiseled features gave way to hurt that nearly tore her heart in two. "But you're judging me based on him. How the hell *can* this relationship work if you think of us as a 'mistake,' a 'disaster,' or a 'screw-up'? The way I see it, 'taking a break,' running to Texas for a job—or wherever the hell you wind up—is codespeak for 'This is my way out.'"

Her anger started to rise. "You're putting words in my mouth! First of all, I never called us a mistake—"

"Not directly." He heaved out a sigh. A lock of soft sable hair brushed the tops of his eyebrows, and she had to stifle the urge to push it back, to touch it. Something told her she was about to give up that right, and her heart thumped heavily in her chest.

"Am I supposed to let you support me? Sit around the house all day, building 3-D puzzles, waiting for 'my man' to come home so my purpose is fulfilled by fawning over him like he's the center of my universe?" He took up the crossed-arms pose again, his dark eyebrows inching toward one another, deepening the vertical creases between them. "Quinn, I need to prove to myself—and my family—that I can stand on my own two feet and that I'm capable of providing for myself." Her plea leaked out in her voice.

"But you already have! That's exactly what you were doing long before Wolf derailed you."

*Stubborn man!* "Why can't we just move everything to the back burner for a bit and let it simmer while we figure us out?"

"You mean while *you* figure us out. I don't need to figure out a damn thing, except whether this was just a fling for you all along. 'Meh, a younger hockey player might be a fun way to pass the time.'" He paused a beat and gusted out a breath. Her brain was firing like an ignited pack of firecrackers, and before she could process, he said, "All right. You want a break? You got it."

With that, he pivoted and trod toward his room without a backward glance. Stunned, all she could do was watch him go.

Quinn went from drawer to drawer, an automaton yanking out clothes and stuffing them into a duffel. "This is your own damn fault, you stupid fuck," he muttered to himself. "*You're* the dumbass who told her to use you any way she wanted." But he'd never expected her to take him up on it. No, cocksure as he'd been, he'd believed she was in as deep as he was. His mother's words slammed him relentlessly, like the Hulk beating Loki as though he were a dust-filled rug: *She'll give you a run for your money because she'll be the only woman you can't impress with just your smile.*

*Fuck me!*

His duffel was overflowing—with what, he wasn't sure—and he hadn't touched his closet. He needed at least one suit and some dress shirts and shoes, didn't he? But going in there, seeing himself reflected in the mirrors, without her … *Fuck it!* She'd be gone next week, and he'd come back and get the rest. By then, maybe his wounds wouldn't cut so deep and he could move around the space with a detachment that eluded him at the moment.

He snatched the beanbags from his nightstand—resisting the urge to stop and juggle—threw them in the duffel, and zipped it shut. Relief washed over him when she was nowhere in sight—he wasn't sure if he'd rail at her like an ass or beg her to stay with him like a pathetic dweeb.

But Archer, the all-seeing, all-knowing wonder dog was there, and Quinn gave him an extra-long scratch.

With his duffel over his shoulder, he grabbed his stick and gear bag and hustled to his truck. As he backed out of the driveway, he wondered what he'd left behind. Besides Sarah. He'd sort it—all of it—at the condo, where he could think without smelling her perfume or seeing her diamond-bright, gold-starburst eyes he'd want to drown in.

An hour later, Quinn stood in his condo alone. The tenants had been on a month-to-month and had moved out weeks before, but he hadn't done a thing to get it back into the rental pool. Fortuitous procrastination, as it turned out, since he was moving back in. The concierge had met him to inspect the unit, and she'd departed with a breathy, "It's good to have you back, Mr. Hadley. You know where to find me if you need anything." Emphasis on "anything."

*Yeah, no thanks.*

Now that she was gone, he ran his fingers over the polished, monolithic white island and let his eyes wander to the two-story wall of glass. He'd always loved that view, but now, as he took it in, it left him … cold.

He turned toward the hand-forged stainless-steel-and-glass stairway that led to a spectacular master suite. The staircase had always awed him because it seemed to be suspended in air. Suddenly, he saw it through a new lens. Sarah's lens. His focus sharpened on a series of cables and bolts he'd never noticed, and he gained an entirely new appreciation for the structure. But like the wall of glass and the counter, it left him cold. The big-ass house he'd never liked flashed in his mind's eye, filling him with color and warmth. Was it the house or the beings in it? His mother, Sarah, Archer.

A reminder from the concierge beeped on his phone. *Rooftop party in ten. Practice your social distancing.* A sign that more pandemic restrictions were being lifted, but he didn't give a flying fuck. He pictured pretty people clustered in small groups, engaged in a familiar mating dance he wanted no part of. A pang dug into his chest. God, he already missed Sarah.

He couldn't do this.

With a sigh, he eyed his phone and dialed Paige. She picked up on the first ring. "Security system running okay?"

"Uh, yeah. It's great. I was just wondering about the lease. It was for six months?"

"Yep, so you're up at the end of next month, but you have an option to extend for another six."

"I'd like to exercise that option. Can you set that up? I was also wondering if you could come by the condo and have a look. I'm thinking of putting it on the market."

"Yes to both questions. I'd be delighted. By the way, I just went over Sarah's recommendations on my build-out. She says you helped her. I had no idea you were an engineer too."

He couldn't hide his surprise. "She said that?"

"Yep. She was very complimentary. So I guess when your hockey career's up, I can call on you too?" She let out a lilting laugh.

"Nah. She was just being generous. Anything I contributed—and I say that laughingly—was blown out of the water by her expertise. You've got a good structural engineer on your team. She knows her stuff."

"I wholeheartedly agree. So will she and your mom be staying too?"

"Not sure yet. Still working out those details."

"Well, no matter. Yours is the only name on the lease, so I'll get the extension ready for your signature."

He thanked her and hung up. A text blinked, and his pulse bumped up.

Sarah: *Archer and I are back at Gage's permanently. Mansion's all yours.*

His thumping heart sank to his stomach.

Quinn: *You didn't have to leave.*

Sarah: *I know. Just thought it would be easier on everyone.*

His mind reeled. All he could think to text was, *Do you think it's safe?*

Sarah: *Yep. We're Wolf-proof.*

Whatever the hell *that* meant. At least Gage was there to protect her, though from the most recent report Quinn had received, Wolf was too busy juggling new trouble in Seattle to come Sarah-hunting. Accusations of fraud—brought by his wife, no less. *What goes around* … Quinn couldn't think of a more deserving candidate.

Quinn: *So you're back in the Pepto-Bismol room?*

Sarah: *Just for a few days until we move and I have the guesthouse to myself.*

His fingers hesitated over the keyboard. What could he say? *Killing me here. Come back. I love you.* No. She didn't want him. She'd walked out. Instead he typed, *Hope the move goes well. Thanks for letting me know.*

He got a thumbs-up emoji in response. That was it, then. His heart constricted, on the verge of imploding.

Needing a lifeline, he dialed a different number.

"Mom? You and Dad busy? Can I stop by and say hey?"

His anger and hurt retreated a fraction when she said, "Of course! We'd love to see you."

Quinn patted his belly in the tidy eat-in kitchen at his dad's place. "Dad, that was great! Didn't know you could cook."

"Neither did I," his dad chuckled, "until I had to live on my own. Your mom did make the potatoes." His dad threw his mom a smile, and she beamed.

Quinn was surprisingly gratified by his dad's efforts to please his mom, treating her with the reverence she deserved. Not to mention he was highly amused observing his dad trotting out a domestic side Quinn had never seen before.

Father and son worked side by side cleaning the kitchen while his mom lounged on the couch out of earshot. They talked about Quinn's return to play, then Quinn asked his dad about his plans.

"I'm not sure yet."

"But you'll still coach, right?"

His dad shook his head. "It's probably time for a change." Pausing what he was doing, his dad turned and looked him dead in the eye. "I'm no good at it."

Astonished, Quinn frowned. "Since when?"

An extended, cheek-puffing sigh. "Never had a winning season in Poland."

"Because you didn't have the right talent."

"No, it goes way back. Started with you and your brother. I … I've needed to say this for a long time, but it isn't easy, so bear with me." His father's voice shook, and Quinn could have sworn his eyes glazed. He swallowed around a lump in his throat and stood still as his dad continued. "I recognized you and your brother's talent, so I pushed both of you. Too much, too hard. I thought Ronan had the better chance at The Show, and … In the end, Ronan didn't make it, and that was my failure—on so many levels, especially with the accident. In the meantime, you were on the rise, and you were doing it without my help. Maybe that ate at me too. Bottom line, I messed up royally, and then I ran. Ran to Poland to lick my wounds and forget, I guess.

"I've regretted it every single day. If I had it to do over again, I would've stayed and confronted my demons like a man." He paused and swiped a thumb over his eye. "I screwed everything up with my sons and my wife. For that, I'm truly sorry," he choked.

Tears welled, pricking Quinn's eyes. Stunned speechless, all he could think to do was draw his dad in for a fierce hug, pounding him on the back. "It's okay, Dad. It turned out the way it was supposed to." His dad returned the embrace, nodding against Quinn's shoulder.

After a few moments, it grew awkward, so they pulled apart. Tears streaming down his face, his dad squeezed Quinn's nape. "In spite of your old man, you made it—all on your own. I'm so proud of you, son."

The tears Quinn had been blinking back rimmed and spilled. "Not all on my own, Dad. You set the bar high, and that was the best thing you could've done for me. It gave me something to shoot for, something to prove." He paused and smiled. "And maybe it's better you *didn't* butt in."

His dad laughed, and the mood lightened, lifting an old, toothy wound out of the way. The air was clearer, sweeter, as father and son continued their chores, exchanging stories and bantering about this and that.

"What are you two yukking it up about out there?" Quinn's mom called. "And why wasn't I invited?"

"Nothing, Mom. We're just giving Ronan a ration of sh—crap behind his back."

His dad laughed low. "She's really got you buttoned up with the swearing."

"She's been training me for a while. I guess it's sticking, which is too fucking bad because swearing is so goddamn … liberating."

"Amen to that."

Quinn's mom appeared around a corner, surprising them both. "I heard that."

"Of course you did." His dad winked at her. "We said it for your benefit."

"So what were you saying about Ronan?"

"Nothing interesting because Ronan's not interesting," Quinn quipped.

"Did you know he whisked Jen away for a romantic, us-only staycation?" His mother's eyebrows bounced.

"Hadn't heard that. What motivated him?" Quinn imagined a showdown where Jen threatened to leave the douchebag.

His mom shrugged. "Beats me. He said something about how lucky he is, and how he needed to step it up. Apparently, he's got it in his head she might walk out on him some day, and he doesn't want that. Wonder who planted that bug in his ear?"

*He listened?* "Who knows? Maybe he finally wised up."

"Well, it was long overdue. Hopefully my youngest son will wise up too." His mom bobbed her head as if to emphasize her words.

He gaped at her. "What does *that* mean?"

Gleaming, wise blue eyes darted to the ceiling and back again. "Don't let Sarah get away."

"I don't want to," he spluttered. "But that girl has a mind of her own, and I'm not sure that mind is convinced I'm anything but a fling."

"Give her time. Then convince her otherwise. Show her you *are* the man for her, just like you showed your team you're their best winning goal-scorer."

# Chapter 38

## Boys in the Bubble

Sarah and Lily sat on the couch, eyes glued to the TV, where the Blizzard played Arizona in Game Five of the Western Conference Semifinals. The Blizzard were up three games to one, and a win tonight would move them to the Conference Finals. But the teams were locked in a heated two-two tie, and the clock was winding down on the third period.

In the background, Daisy danced with Blizzard pom-poms while Archer turned circles at her feet.

The buzzer sounded, and Sarah and Lily let out a collective groan. "Overtime," Lily groused. "Anything can happen."

"Let's clean up the kitchen while we wait," Sarah suggested.

"Okay. At least it'll keep my mind off whether I'm flying to Canada tomorrow or not."

Players had been living in COVID-19 "safety zones," or "the bubble," since arriving in Canada two months ago. No contact with people outside the bubble, including families, had been allowed, but that was all going to change for the teams headed to the Conference Finals, and Lily's excitement was palpable.

Sarah rinsed dishes while Lily scoured the counters. "I don't know how much longer I can wait, Sarah. Assuming I do go to Canada, I'll have to quarantine in the bubble for four days before I can be with him."

"Well, if they don't win tonight, they still have a good chance of winning game six. And if they lose the whole enchilada, he'll be coming home. Either way, you won't be separated much longer." *Unlike Quinn and me.* They hadn't seen each other since their breakup, though they'd texted a few times. Except for one message where Quinn had said he was having "Sunshine withdrawals," their comments had remained on safe subjects firmly planted in the friend zone. And it felt all wrong.

"I know. I just miss Gage so much." Lily inspected the counter, huffed, and immediately went back to scrubbing. "Quinn is sure looking good tonight," she threw out casually.

"Mm-hmm." Hell, he'd been looking good the entire playoffs, and not just in his play. Sarah had kept herself busy trying to forget just how good by helping Lily get the main house settled and continuing her job hunt, though her enthusiasm waned with each passing day. Not that she wasn't getting offers or a shot at some really interesting positions, because she was—all from out of state. Somewhere along the way, she'd fallen into a funk where she couldn't muster excitement. Consequently, she kept putting off potential employers. She'd have to shit or get off the pot pronto. Being stuck in limbo wasn't any way to live.

Lily bumped her hip. "That wasn't a very enthusiastic response. I expected more from you."

"What are you talking about?"

"Quinn. Looking good. You miss him, don't you?"

*God, yes!* "*That* full-of-himself pain in the ass?"

"I knew it!" Lily cried in triumph.

"Knew what?"

"Something *did* happen between you two, didn't it? Gage said Quinn's been grumpy ever since you moved out, and Quinn's never grumpy."

"Gage said that?"

Lily leaned against the counter and parked a fist on her hip. "Don't worry. Gage doesn't suspect a thing. So tell me what's going on."

"If I tell you, you'll tell Gage, and I'm not ready for that."

"I'll eventually tell him, but I'll give you a chance to tell him first. Fair enough?"

Sarah matched Lily's posture and narrowed her eyes. "How long is 'a chance'?"

"A couple of weeks? Wouldn't you rather he hear it from you than Quinn anyway?"

"I don't think Quinn's going to tell him. Team chemistry and all that. Plus, Quinn's fear of being spit-roasted slowly over an open fire."

Lily giggled. "Gage doesn't have it in him. If he weren't so forgiving, I wouldn't be standing here with you right now." Lily's eyebrows bounced. "So about Quinn?"

Sarah had been holding it in so long that when the story came out, the details spilled from her like water through a crumbling dam—with the exception of their incredible sexcapades, of course—and she felt a whoosh of relief. Somehow saying it out loud made it real and brought her closer to Quinn. How ironic, considering she'd been the one to cut away. In her own defense, she'd been convinced taking a break was the smart thing to do, that it would expose their relationship for the convenience it was before anyone got in too deep. As time lumbered on, though, she realized how far she'd fallen and how much she missed him, but she had no idea what to do about it. Run for the hills and protect her heart? Ask him to take her back? But what if he'd already moved on?

What was it about him she missed anyway? Besides his cocoa eyes, his mischievous smile, and his warm, easy laugh, it was the way he didn't let her take herself too seriously. She missed collaborating with him in their own private world. His engineering curiosity. His pout when she beat him at games. His swagger. Wrapping herself around his big frame and how safe—and cherished—he made her feel when he held her. His heated looks that conveyed just what he wanted to do to her. His annoying, overprotective side. Hearing him call her Sunshine—her nickname alone.

Her mind and heart had converged, and she'd been turning over the same question: Could she build a life with Quinn? Lately, she'd been answering that one with another question: How would she know if she didn't try?

"You know," Lily said, snapping her out of her musings, "I was hoping you and Quinn would get together."

Sarah's eyebrows hit her hairline. "You were? Why?"

"I don't know. He's cocky, and you're kick-ass." She mouthed the last word. "I haven't seen you two in action, but I suspect you may be the only woman on the planet who can put him in his place. You're different from his usual disposable dates."

"Yeah, I certainly don't fit in his typical big-boobed-blond category," Sarah chuffed.

Lily flicked Sarah's arm. "Hey! What's wrong with big-boobed blonds? Well, okay. Average-boobed blonds?"

"Nothing, if they're you." Sarah pecked her cheek.

Lily's big blues brightened. "I have an idea! If—no, *when*—they move on and I fly to Canada, come with me!"

"Are you nuts?"

"Probably, but hear me out. Daisy's going to stay with her grandparents for a few weeks. Come with me and keep me company."

Sarah scoffed. "I'm not sharing a room with you and Gage. Sharing a house was bad enough."

Lily reddened. "You weren't supposed to listen."

"I couldn't *help* but listen!" Sarah elbowed her playfully. "Believe me, I tried not to."

Lily's blush turned crimson. "Moving on. You and I will share a room until our quarantine's over, and then you can stay with Quinn." She shrugged as if this were the most feasible arrangement in the world.

"You forget. We're not speaking at the moment."

"And whose fault is that, exactly?"

"Mine, but he went along with the 'break.'" Sarah reminded herself of a bratty kid.

"Did you leave him any choice? No. Have you apologized?"

"For what? *He's* the one who walked out," the bratty kid replied.

Lily puffed out a breath that lifted her hair. "Let me ask a more basic question. Do you love him?"

Sarah's knee-jerk reaction was to deflect, and she opened her mouth to do just that but stopped. And sighed. "I … Yes. Does that make me a total sap?"

"No, but it makes the other stuff just a bunch of noise. Besides, why would loving him make you a sap?"

"Because I don't want to repeat the mistake I made with Wolf." The word "mistake," spoken in Quinn's deep timbre, rolled around in Sarah's head, and she cringed inside.

"I never met Wolf, thank God, but the two men don't sound anything alike to me. Besides, you have to break a few eggs to make a cake … or whatever the saying is. One mistake doesn't doom you to a repeat, nor does it mean you never dip your toe in the water again. If you want Quinn back, *you* need to make the first move. Take this from a girl who learned how to grovel and was glad she did."

"So I make my big move by busting into his hotel room? And what if …" Sarah's voice cracked, and she shook it off. "What if he's, you know, up to his old tricks and his bed's already occupied, if you catch my meaning?"

Lily's blond curls bobbed as she shook her head. "No. They're in the bubble and can't have anyone in their rooms—not even their own teammates."

"Lily, don't be naive. There are *women* in the bubble too. Servers, bartenders, NHL staff, you name it. Plenty of opportunity. And you think a horny hockey player isn't going to sneak a woman into his room if he gets the chance? He doesn't have a roommate to rat him out!"

"Then you'll keep our room, just in case. I mean, you might take one look at him and decide you don't want to share his room anyway, though I doubt that, just like I doubt he's messing around." Lily winked. "C'mon, Sar. What do you say? Come with me! We'll get to see some great hockey in a cushy suite with the other WAGs."

Sarah blew out a breath. "I'm not a wife or a girlfriend."

"You're the *S* for 'sister.'" Lily grinned.

Sarah bit back a laugh. "I'll think about it. In the meantime, overtime's about to start."

Lily topped off their wines, and they scurried back to the living room, where Crazy Daisy was starting up her pom-pom routine again.

An hour later, the teams were halfway through their second overtime. The boys should have been exhausted, but they still had jump in their skates, moving with speed and intensity up and down the ice. Sarah could scarcely breathe. Bouncing in place behind the couch with Archer at her heels, Daisy squealed with excitement. "That's Gage!"

Deep in his own zone, Gage was in a scrum with two Arizona players, trying to fish out the puck trapped against the boards while T.J. banged away at one of the Arizona guys. The puck squirted free, and another Arizona player corralled it. As he was teeing it up to fire on the Blizzard net, Quinn made a beautiful poke check and stole it. An Arizona defenseman stood him up at his own blue line, but Quinn executed a fleet sidestep and blew past him. As he raced through the neutral zone toward

Arizona's net, two opposing players hot on his heels, the remaining Arizona defenseman skated out to confront him. Sarah interlaced her fingers with Lily's and squeezed. In a thrilling move, Quinn deked, skating a half-circle around the D-man before lifting a perfect shot over the goalie's right shoulder that found the back of the net.

Lily, Sarah, and Daisy leapt into the air, screaming for joy, while on the ice Quinn's teammates mobbed him against the glass.

"Oh, what a win for the Blizzard!" the announcer enthused. "That's Quinn Hadley's fourth game winner of the playoffs, folks! Number eighteen has found an extra gear and has become the team's clutch player. What a post-season for the left-winger!"

Lily shook her hands in the air. "Oh my God! I haven't seen Gage in two months, and now I only have to wait a few more days! I have to book my flight! Our flights! You in?"

Caught up in the moment and breathless from watching Quinn, Sarah didn't hesitate. "I'm in."

Quinn nursed his fourth beer in the sports bar—the only bar in the hotel where they were allowed to hang out tonight—where he shared a table with a few straggling teammates after their big win. Most of them had already turned in, but with a few days off, he figured he could kick back and enjoy the glow of victory—and avoid facing the same four walls of his room alone.

Nelson had just left, leaving him with Grims, Wyatt, and Hunter.

"So what do you boys think of the crowd noise they're piping into the empty arena?" Wyatt asked.

"I think they're getting more creative as we go. I hear cheering when T.J. hands out a bone-crushing check or the rare time Wyatt flashes the glove," Hunter laughed.

"Better than the crickets the rare time you take a shot, asshole," Wyatt groused.

These two jokers were the odd couple. Just as Quinn was debating which was Oscar and which was Felix, they got up to flirt with a bartender, leaving Quinn alone with Grimson.

Quinn began to ramble. "On the IR at playoffs again, Grims. That's some bad luck. This year, a broken hand in the quarter finals. Last year … Oh shit." Now Quinn had stepped in it. What was he thinking? He wasn't. *What an idiot!*

Grims shot him a dagger-filled look. "What are you getting at, Hads?"

"Sorry," Quinn mumbled. "We weren't supposed to know about the doping last year—"

"But you found out. How?"

Quinn cleared his throat. "Nicole passed it on to the other SOs."

Grims's eyes narrowed. "What the fuck? First off, she's not an SO. Not anymore. Second, when did she supposedly do this?"

"Right before the season started last October. At least, that's when I heard about it." Guilt and a modicum of sadness pulsed inside Quinn. Despite Grims's epic mistake that could've tainted the entire team, he *liked* the guy. He was a fearless, no-nonsense D-man you wanted at your back when you went into battle. A fierce, quiet warrior—no flash, more show than tell—and damn effective. He might be out of the lineup with his broken hand, but his presence in the locker room brought a rock-solid steadiness the team fed off of.

Grims leaned back hard and blew out a breath. "She dumps me *because* she was 'so embarrassed'"—this he said in a falsetto—"I got caught. Like it tarnished her reputation somehow. But instead of keeping it to herself, she comes back and tells everyone? That's bullshit!"

"Sorry, man. I thought you knew."

"No, and had I known—"

"Hi!" A cute blond in pigtails, short shorts, a tight T-shirt, and knee socks—the establishment's uniform—bounced on the balls of her feet at their table. "Your waitress just clocked out, and I'm taking over her shift. Can I get you anything?" She looked from Grims to Quinn and stopped. "Quinn? Oh my God! I was hoping I'd run into you!"

Quinn glanced up, took in her big blue eyes and the rack filling her T-shirt, and recognition dawned. One of his Canadian hookups from last year. "Oh hey, Whitney. Haven't seen you in a while," he drawled. "How've you been?"

She did the hip jut thing with the parked fist, looked him up and down, and smiled wolfishly. His neck heated, and he felt like a bug on display. A piece of meat in a butcher's case being evaluated for consumption. He squirmed inside.

Back in the day, he'd have pulled out the big guns and flashed her a dimpled smile, and he'd have had at least one hand on her by now. One singular purpose, spurred by one body part. Everything had been one-dimensional. Now the thought made him recoil. His old life? No, thanks. The memory simply deepened the pang for Sarah.

They exchanged a few words, ending with her letting him know she'd be happy to stop by his room when her shift was over so they could "catch up." She was, she pointed out helpfully, in the bubble too. He deflected, introducing her to Grimson. Maybe she'd turn her attention on him. Dude looked like he could use a good time, especially after finding out his ex had dumped on him—twice. But Whitney wasn't going for it, so Quinn asked her to close out his tab. Hanging in his room alone was gaining appeal.

Grims watched her swaying ass as she strutted away from the table, the shorts not fully covering her cheeks. He grinned. "That has to be a first, Hads. Can't say as I've ever seen you turn away a choice opportunity."

"Not interested tonight." *Or ever.* "Feel free, though."

Grimson shook his head. "No, thanks. I'm done with the 'fairer' sex for now. Not worth the aggravation. I'm going to focus on upping my game. On getting this hand healed, on getting better, on getting stronger. There's a chance I could be back in the lineup if we go much deeper in the playoffs, and I want to be ready."

"That'd be sweet. We could use you." Quinn tipped his bottle back and finished his brew just as Nelson came rushing back into the restaurant, an idiotic look plastered on his face.

Grims gave him a barely there chin jerk. "What's with the jackass grin, Nelson?" The rapport between the two had landed in the shitter after Nelson busted Grimson doping. Though they put on a show of having kissed and made up in front of the team, their differences were palpable, and their relationship skidded across thin ice.

"Just heard from Lily, and she'll be here tomorrow before lunch."

"Who flies from Denver to Edmonton in the morning?" asked Quinn.

"The Gulfstream I just hired. Otherwise, it would have taken her four cities and over a day to get here."

"Jeez, dude. Desperate much? You still can't see her for four days," Quinn quipped. "That must have set you back a fair piece."

"Not that bad. And the sooner she gets here, the sooner she'll be out of quarantine. Besides, she thinks I'm a hero." Nelson's grin broadened—so did his chest. Quinn couldn't blame him. After months of celibacy, he was glad to see *someone* getting lucky soon.

Grims looked poised to make a snide comment, so Quinn jumped in. "Daisy coming too?"

"No, she's staying with family. But Sarah's tagging along."

Quinn's back went ramrod straight so fast that Grimson shot him a questioning look. Forgetting he'd already drained it, Quinn put the beer bottle to his lips to coat his suddenly dry throat. Now Grims arched a covert eyebrow.

"Where, ah, where's she staying?" Quinn managed.

"Not with Lily and me, that's for damn sure." Nelson's tone was emphatic. "She and Lily will quarantine together, and Sarah will stay in that room after Lily moves in with me."

Whitney reappeared with Quinn's bill and a pen. "You can charge it to your room." While Nelson and Grimson watched, she leaned in so close he could smell her perfume and feel her tits pressed against his shoulder. She pointed to a line on the tab. "Just write your room number right there, and I'll see you later." With a sly wink, she sashayed away.

Ignoring his teammates' guffaws, he waited until she was gone, pulled out his wallet, and left cash. No way was he letting Whitney know his room number. The only woman he wanted showing up at his door was arriving tomorrow. All he had to do was convince her they belonged together—an undertaking far more daunting than getting the winning score past a goalie who was playing out of his mind. He had four days to figure out how.

Hours later, Quinn lay in bed, staring up at a dark ceiling. Exhausted as he was, he should have been sawing logs, but he couldn't settle down while Sarah traipsed through his brain. What would he say when he saw her? Was she coming to see him? He could only hope. Wouldn't she have texted to let him know, though? Should he tell Nelson and risk upsetting the applecart when the team was playing so well? Was there anything to tell anymore? The thoughts tossed and turned and got wadded in his head.

He'd been relieved to get on the road after spending weeks in the behemoth mansion alone. Unlike here, where everywhere he looked it was all about hockey and his buddies and bubble living, the house had been filled with echoes of Sarah. He'd found himself in the solarium, looking at the 3-D puzzles with longing, picturing himself alongside her as they built them. Or stepping into her bedroom and surrounding himself with her fragrance that still lingered on the linens and pillows.

She'd left her engineering magazines behind, and he'd riffled through those without seeing a damn thing. He'd pulled his stuff out of the mirrored closet and put it elsewhere so he didn't have to set foot in there again and imagine their bodies reflected in bright silver. In the kitchen or family room, he pictured her there, and the space was suddenly imbued with a warmth he'd never known he wanted before meeting her. Not only did he want it, but he *craved* it.

And tomorrow she would be here.

# Chapter 39

## VOILA!

Four days in the hotel room had felt like fourteen, but finally, the wait was over. As Sarah and Lily emerged from the elevator on the main level, Gage greeted them. Correction: he greeted Lily with an embarrassing PDA and acknowledged Sarah's presence.

As she waited for her brother to end his liplock on his fiancée and come up for air, Sarah glanced around casually, her radar on high alert for a tall, dark, exquisitely cut man with eyes like hot fudge sauce and a dimpled smile that turned her knees to mush. But Quinn was nowhere in sight. Probably didn't even know she was there. *She* certainly hadn't told him. And why hadn't she? In case he didn't want to see her or she saw him with someone else, at least she could make a quick exit with some dignity intact.

The longer she stood there, the more her stomach knotted. She reassured herself it was a big place; she probably wouldn't even run into Quinn. During games, in the WAGs suite high above the ice—with a mask on—he'd never know she was there.

Yeah, right.

Gage had knocked himself out, hiring a private jet to fly them to Edmonton and a limo to drive them to the hotel when they'd touched down. But he'd booked the room in Lily's name, so he was now escorting them to the front desk to get the room transferred over to Sarah.

While Lily reconciled the charges on the hotel folio, Gage watched her with hawkeyed interest. A flush colored his cheeks, and the stupid grin he'd been sporting grew wider. While he studied Lily, Sarah studied him, really studied him, and suddenly saw him as the man he was, not the little brother he'd been her whole life. Four years divided them, but those edges had blurred. For as long as she could remember, it had been him and her winding their way through their family minefield, standing up to their overbearing mother, taking care of their loving grandmother. Together. He'd relied on her when he'd been younger, but somewhere along the way their roles had become interchangeable. And lately, she'd leaned on his strong shoulders, thinking of him more as a peer or a *big* brother. Four years.

Quinn was only five years younger—not such a stretch. Before her eyes, he'd transformed from a selfish pleasure-seeker into a loving son, a loyal and generous human being, and a blade-sharp sparring partner who could take and fire back barbs with elegant ease. Bonus: being a smoking hot, adventurous lover didn't hurt either. His devilry and a libido that matched her own were the spicy cherry on top. Most of all, he'd become her hero, replacing her brother in the number one spot.

God, for the chance to lay eyes on him and tell him, in person, how much she missed him, that she'd screwed up. But first she needed to walk the walk; she had a bomb to drop.

Gage stood by while Sarah signed paperwork and got a new room key. It was obvious how ready he was to ditch her and hustle Lily upstairs for some private time. "Gage, before you two take off and I don't see you for days, there's something I need to tell you." His eyebrows arched.

Lily patted his arm. "Why don't you give me your key, Professor, and I'll let myself in? I'm sure the bellboy got my bag transferred over by now. While you two talk, I'll settle in and freshen up." She gave him a smoldering look.

"Uh, sure." After he'd gotten a good eyeful of Lily walking away, he turned to Sarah. "Our choices are limited, Sar. There's a designated rooftop hangout for the team, or a ballroom where we take our meals, play ping-pong, poker, whatever."

"Where would be the most private?"

"Rooftop, I think."

As they made their way up, Sarah kept her head on a swivel. Yes, she wanted to see Quinn, but not before she finished with Gage. By the time they found an out-of-the-way table under an umbrella, Sarah's stomach was kinked so tight she wasn't sure she'd ever get the knots loosened.

Gage handed her a bottle of water she hadn't seen him snag. "So what's on your mind, Sar-Bear?"

She twisted off the cap and took a long drink. "I need to come clean with you, but I don't want you getting mad or taking it out on anyone. Promise?"

His eyebrows dipped in a frown. "Promise."

She drew in a lung-filling breath. "When I first got to Denver and told you about Wolf, you said something like we can't help who we fall for, remember?"

He gave her a cautious nod. "Vaguely. Don't tell me you're going back to that douche."

"No, never. But I have fallen for someone. A rather unexpected someone." She waited, but he merely blinked. "We didn't mean to, but Quinn and I—"

*"What?"* Gage's mouth swung open, and his eyes turned to hard, cold flint. "I thought you two *hated* each other!" he hissed.

She shrugged. "We did. But the more time we spent together, the more we found out about each other. Turns out we have a lot more in common than we ever knew."

"No way," he growled. "He's a womanizer who's going to destroy your heart. Just last night, a waitress invited herself to his room right in front of us."

Sarah steeled her spine. "And did she go to his room?"

"I don't know, but he didn't say no."

Sarah's stomach wobbled. So did her heart. "Well, don't worry. We're not really together. I sort of broke it off before you guys started training camp."

"So why are you telling me now?"

"I don't like keeping secrets from you, and I didn't want you getting blindsided in case you heard it elsewhere." Another cool sip to soothe her parched throat.

He drummed his fingers on the tabletop. "Why did you break it off?"

"I wanted to see if we felt the same when we weren't forced to shelter together."

Gage hmphed. "Sar, he's all wrong for you."

She wasn't sure she agreed, but curiosity drove her to ask, "How is he all wrong?"

"The waitress last night is how! That's who Quinn is."

*No, he's more than that.* A need to defend Quinn welled inside her, and she locked out the possibility he'd reverted to his romping ways. God, she *was* a sap! "Whatever else he is, Quinn's funny and kind and generous. Oh, and very smart. Even you said he was a good guy who'd do anything—"

She let out an audible gasp, and Gage turned in his seat. The subject of their conversation was making a beeline for them, decked in flip-flops, shorts, a T-shirt that hugged his chiseled torso, and a backward ball cap that seemed to be restraining his long-again locks. Dave Grimson, the team captain who resembled a deranged mountain man, trailed behind.

Though his expression was unreadable, Quinn's eyes were focused solely on her. In that moment, he could have made her believe no one or nothing else existed.

Gage broke that focus when he stood abruptly and squared himself in Quinn's path. "Did you take that waitress back to your room last night?"

Sarah dropped her forehead in her palm. *Can I just die now?* When she dared a peek, Quinn look confused, darting his eyes between her and Gage.

Dave stepped up and tapped Gage's arm. "Time out, man. What's eating you?"

"I want to know if he took that waitress up on her offer." Though he directed the answer at Dave, Gage's seething gaze didn't waver from Quinn.

Quinn opened his mouth to speak, but Dave took over with practiced calm. "You're jumping to conclusions *again*, Nelson. You didn't see the whole exchange. Yeah, she wanted to get friendly with our boy, but it was strictly a one-way street. If you remember, he paid in cash and got the hell out of there. I never saw him give her his room number. In fact, he told *me* to chase her."

"And did you?" Gage spurted.

Dave crossed his beefy arms. His beard was so long it practically brushed the tops of his forearms. "Exactly why is that any of your fucking business?" he snorted.

Sarah tugged on Gage's shirt. "Gage, I don't think—"

Dave glanced at her, then landed his gaze back on Gage. "No, I didn't. To my knowledge, she didn't sleep with anyone on the team—unless *you* hooked up with her."

"Hell no!"

Dave pointed a finger in his face. "So stop making up shit about your teammates." Then he gave Gage a chin lift, one side of his mouth curling into a smirk. "Chillax, Boy Scout."

Dave sent Sarah a wink. "Nice to see you, Sarah." And with that, he walked off, leaving the three of them in charged, awkward silence.

Quinn swiveled his head to Sarah and locked on her wide eyes. She took his breath away, and he gawked at her for a beat. Glossy dark hair brushed behind her perfect ears, tiny diamond twinkling on her pert nose, full mouth hinting at a smile. She was wearing a blue sundress that brought out the color of her eyes and showed off her curves and shapely legs. His mouth had gone dry, and he couldn't swallow.

Damn Nelson! Why'd he bring up Whitney? Until this moment, she'd been relegated to a nonexistent blip in Quinn's memory bank. When he'd seen Sarah, he'd let himself believe he had a chance, that she'd traveled all the way here to tell him she'd changed her mind. Nelson had just turned any chance into a climb up fucking Mount Everest. In Quinn's peripheral vision, his asshole best friend stood stony and rigid.

"Hey, Sparky," Sarah said with a lightness not reflected in her diamond-brilliant eyes.

"Hi, Sunshine." He congratulated himself on his own fake-casual air. Could she hear his heart slamming against his rib cage?

Didn't matter because Nelson snarled, "Wanna tell me what's going on, Hadley?" Deep vertical creases between his knitted brows broadcast his irritation.

"I told him," Sarah blurted. "About us."

A tap dance broke out in Quinn's gut, and he restrained a smile. "Yeah?"

"Yeah. As you can see, he's not happy about it." She gave Quinn a conspiratorial smirk.

He pulled himself a little taller and faced Nelson. "Doesn't matter whether you're happy or not, Nelson. I'm crazy about your sister, and I sure as hell hope she feels the same way." He darted her a look and was rewarded with a head bob that made his heart race faster.

"I thought you two *hated* each other," Nelson practically whined. "I expected to deal with a dead body after one of you murdered the other."

"It might have started that way, but we got to know each other, and … Voila!" Quinn flung out his hand.

Nelson narrowed his eyes. "Voila?"

"It's French for 'ta-dah,'" Quinn and Sarah said at the same time. She folded over with mirth. Her contagious laughter soon had Quinn chuckling. God, he'd missed hearing her laugh, laughing with her.

"See, Bro? I told you he and I had a lot in common." She tried to get herself under control, but she continued to bubble over.

Damn, she was adorable! The possibility she *had* come to Canada just for him about blew him off the rooftop. Was she ready to put the unbearable limbo of the last few months in the rearview mirror like he was? Fuck, he hoped so. He reminded himself it was up to her, and he reined in his optimism.

Nelson stood like one of the hotel pillars.

"I like you, Nelson. Always have," Quinn said. "But whatever happens between your sister and me is totally her call, and you're gonna need to get over it. Yell, take your best shot, let me have it. Let's get it out of the way now."

Nelson's shoulders eased, and a smirk formed. "I think I'd rather wait until we're on the ice and I have a bag of pucks at my disposal."

"Shit. You wouldn't."

"Better believe I would, *Sparky*. Nothing I'd like better than to rearrange your pretty face." Nelson jabbed a finger at Sarah. "That's my *sister*, and I've always thought she was smarter than me, but clearly I was wrong. I have no idea what you did to make her lose her mind."

*More like she made me lose mine. And I don't regret it one bit.* "So are you kicking me off your line?"

"Not up to me, but I hope Coach doesn't move you. I'll be able to take more shots at you on my wing."

"Um, Gage, don't you think Lily's done 'freshening up' by now?" Sarah wore a devilish smile that had Quinn's insides hip-hopping. "Her suitcase was crammed with new lingerie she was dying to show you, but I wouldn't wait *too* long. She might nod off—neither of us slept well last night."

Nelson blew a breath through his nose, clearly torn between leaving his sister behind and following his dick to Lily waiting in his room. Quinn nearly hissed a "Yes!" when Nelson gave into his baser, sex-deprived self.

He glared at Quinn. "Keep your hands off my sister, understood?"

*Only if* she *says so.* "Understood." *Now get the fuck out of here!*

Gage gave Sarah a warning look and finally left when she made a shooing motion. The guy practically raced toward the elevators, and Quinn corralled a laugh.

"So," she said. "Want to have a seat, or do you have someplace to be?"

"No place to be, although I'd prefer some privacy." He dropped into the seat beside hers.

"What do we need privacy for, Sparky?"

"So we can talk without being interrupted by your anal brother or my dumbass teammates?" On cue, Hunter and Wyatt strolled over. Quinn suppressed a groan.

"Hey, Gage's sister. You're looking mighty fine." Hunter stood beside Sarah with a lewd grin, and Quinn could have sworn he was looking straight down her neckline. Which made Quinn see red.

He stood to his full height, stepped between Sarah and Hunter, and wrapped his hand around her bare upper arm. "We were just leaving, boys," he growled. She rose even as he lifted her from her seat. Apparently, she was ready to leave too.

"So where do we go?" she asked as he steered her inside.

Her fragrance filled his nose, and he lost his bearings for a moment. "My room?"

"Sounds dangerous."

"Why? Afraid you can't keep your hands off me?" He was pushing his luck, but he couldn't contain his delight.

"More like my brother won't keep his hands off you," she tossed back. "Good to see you haven't lost your sense of humor."

They rode downstairs and wound up by the curtained testing booths, where he pulled her into an empty one. "This'll do for now, huh?"

"As long as they don't find us and try to swab our brains through our sinuses."

He drew in a deep breath. "First things first. You know I didn't sleep with that waitress, right?"

Sarah folded her arms across her chest. "Mmm. But you knew her."

"Yeah, I knew her from before, but I wasn't interested last night." He rushed to add, "Or any other night. In fact, you've kinda wrecked me for anyone else, Sunshine, so I sure as hell hope you're here to put me out of my misery." *Shit, that didn't come out right.*

Her delicate eyebrows inched up her forehead, but she remained quiet.

He shoved his hands in his shorts pockets to keep them from wandering to her arms, her back, her hair. After all, he still didn't know why she was here.

"I can't believe you told your brother." The thought had him suddenly verging on giddy, and he schooled his features.

She shrugged her creamy bare shoulders. "I should've told him a while ago. I just hope I didn't screw up your line chemistry. That was a gorgeous game winner you scored the other night, by the way."

He *knew* it was a gorgeous goal—he'd watched it on the highlights—but hearing her say it had heat rushing up his neck. "Thanks. Uh, so you were watching?"

"Of course I was! How do you think I got here?"

"How *did* you get here? Wait. Let me rephrase. What, specifically, made you come?"

"Great playoff hockey?" Her eyes glittered with amusement. She was toying with him, the little minx.

"Or was it to tell your brother about our 'attraction'?"

She laughed. "Never gonna let me live that down, are you?"

A sigh eased his shoulders a fraction. "I've missed hearing you laugh."

Her eyes suddenly misted, and her smile slid. "I've missed *you.* I wanted to tell you in person. That's why I came."

She about knocked the wind from him. "You came all the way to Canada to tell me you missed me? You could've done that on the phone or in a text."

"No, I couldn't have. It needed to be face-to-face." After an awkward little cough, she raced on. "So did you get yourself settled back in your condo before leaving Denver?"

The sudden switch confused him. Maybe she'd traveled here just to tie up loose ends. "I tried, but I couldn't do it. I extended the lease on the house and had Paige list the condo instead."

Her hazel eyes popped wide. "So you're living in that big-ass house by yourself?"

"Dad's buddy wanted his place back, so Mom and Dad moved into Mom's wing—your wing—after I came here."

"I thought you loved your condo?"

"Yeah, well, I realized when I went back that that love affair had run its course." *I want what I had at the huge house. You.* "So how's the job hunting going? Moving to Texas anytime soon?" He held his breath.

She brushed her hair behind her ears. It had grown longer, and a thick, touchable curl called to him from where it nestled on her shoulder. "No. I sort of took a break while I helped Lily get settled in their new house."

"You in the guesthouse?"

"Yeah," she sighed.

"You don't sound happy about that."

"It's just … It's not *my* place. It's theirs. I felt more at home in that ridiculous house of yours than I feel there."

*Killing me here.* His hands twitched, and he found himself looking around for something to juggle. "So what are your plans?"

"Now or future?"

He tucked his hands under his armpits. "Yes."

"Well, for now I plan to stay and cheer from the stands as long as you guys are in the hunt. After that, I guess it depends on you." She peeped at him from under her dark lashes.

His eyes darted to the ceiling while he tried to puzzle out what was she was telling him. He decided to help her along. "You flew up here to tell your brother about us and to tell me you missed me. What else am I missing?"

Unwavering eyes fixed on his and filled with tears. It took every ounce of willpower not to pull her into his arms.

"I, um, came to a few realizations I wanted to share." She paused a moment to dab and sniff. "First, my independence means a lot to me. I love my career, I like supporting myself."

His heart sank. “Thought we’d established that and that I’m good with it. It makes you who you are. I just had a hard time with the notion of you living so far away when I wanted you with *me*. Selfish, I know, but—”

She let out a teary laugh. “Would you let me finish? This is hard enough to say as it is.”

“Why? Since when have you been shy about saying what’s on your mind?” It was one of the things he loved best about her. “Just spit it out.” He would have gone for light with a smile, but he couldn’t marshal it. He braced himself against a table instead in case she was about to level him with something he didn’t want to hear.

“It’s harder when it comes from the heart.” She blinked back tears, and he swallowed hard. “What I’m trying to say is that the career and taking care of myself are important, but with you gone, I realized there’s something I care about more. I wanted to be with you more than I wanted those things. I guess that means I have to turn in my badass badge.”

He stood motionless, recycling her words to be sure he fully understood their meaning.

Unchecked tears were spilling down her cheeks in a free-for-all. “Don’t you get it?” she said. “I’m in love with you, Quinn.”

*That* he understood, loud and clear. He just couldn’t get his mouth to work.

“Aren’t you going to say anything? ‘Too bad, Sarah. You’re too late.’ Or—”

A single heartbeat, and he had her face cradled in his hands. “Or how about I fucking love you, Sarah, and I don’t want anybody else? Or I like me better when I’m with you, so let me be with you?” His eyes searched hers while his thumbs stroked her soft skin. “Let me love you, Sarah, and I’m not talking about sex. I want *all* of you.” There. He’d said it. It was out.

Her hands covered his, and she returned his gaze with such tenderness he nearly lost it. He forged ahead despite the tears clogging his throat and brimming his lower lashes. “I like that you know the real me, that you know my past, what I’ve done and what I’ve been, and you accept me. I can be me with you. You trust me. Do I have regrets? Lots. But the biggest regret I have is not meeting you sooner.”

One side of her beautiful mouth curled up. “You weren’t ready for me, Sparky.”

“I still might not be ready for you, but that sure as hell won’t stop me.”

"Sparky doesn't do things halfway."

"Not when it comes to you, babe." He kissed her with all the pent-up fervor that had been building inside of him during these long months, taking charge of her mouth in a way that left no doubt he was in all the fucking way. Her arms wound around his neck, pulling him close until the heat of their mouths and bodies practically fused them together.

Though he stood in a COVID-19 testing booth surrounded by flimsy metal frames holding flimsy blue curtains, he was home.

He broke the kiss and nuzzled her neck. She smelled so fucking good he wanted to inhale her. Bottle up her fragrance and take her with him everywhere he went.

A deep throat-clearing made them both jump. When Quinn looked toward the source, he realized a large, unamused health worker was watching them.

"Did you miss every single message on social distancing?" the man said dryly.

Quinn put up a hand in surrender and maneuvered himself beside Sarah to hide his raging boner. "Sorry, we just—"

"Get a room! Better yet, get a room and quarantine yourselves." The guy shot them a thoroughly disgusted look.

"Shit, I hope neither of us gets *him* for a tester," Sarah giggled as they scurried toward the elevators.

"He's just jealous." Quinn leaned down to her ear. "You heard the man. He said we need to get a room."

"I believe we have a choice between two."

Quinn punched the elevator up button with his elbow. "You didn't check out of Lily's and your room?"

"No, I kept it. I didn't want to *assume* you'd want me in yours."

"Babe, assume I'll *always* want you in mine. And speaking of mine, wanna come upstairs and have a look?" He flashed her both dimples.

On cue, the elevator doors opened, and they stepped into the empty car. He pressed the button for his floor.

She stood on tiptoe and purred against his ear, her warm breath shooting tingles through him. "Does it have mirrors?" His boner had eased into a semi, but her closeness and throaty voice turned it rock hard again.

"There's one in the bathroom. Bet we can figure something out, being the creative team we are."

Breathless, she pulled back and ran her fingers through his hair as she stared deep into his eyes. “Is this just sex?”

“Hell no. This is ‘I love you’ all the way. You good with that?”

“I’m more than good with that.”

Inside his room, he hung out the do-not-disturb sign and locked the door. Enfolding her in his arms, he relished her silky hair against his cheek, her pliant body beneath his hands. She pecked his lips, and he caught her mouth with his. Tightening his hold, he drew her closer. Her mouth parted when the tip of his tongue touched her lips, and soon they were tasting, rediscovering, then consuming each other with unbridled hunger. Unable to hold back another second, he picked her up and carried her to the bed, deposited her on its pillow top and followed her down, settling into her welcoming arms, where he wanted to stay forever.

# Chapter 40

## The Winning Score

Months later, on a cool fall day in a sunny Denver park, the season-ending team picnic was wrapping up. The boys were clustered together, some still lamenting their Stanley Cup loss in a seven-game run against Tampa. But Quinn had gotten over it—it helped to have distractions, like a smoking-hot, sassy girlfriend you were nuts about who'd agreed to move in with you—and house-hunting for that just-right place with her.

Wyatt, apparently, had no such distractions. "I still say that if that motherfucker hadn't run Hadley and boarded him, Hads would've been on the ice and gotten us the winning score instead of sitting in the training room waiting for repairs," he groused.

Sarah was cleaning up picnic tables with Lily and some of the other WAGs, and Quinn caught her eye and crooked his finger. She ambled over and wrapped her arms around his waist, tucking herself under his arm, where she fit so perfectly.

Quinn smiled down at her. "I *did* get the winning score."

His teammates obliged him with exaggerated eye-rolls, groans, and a few choice snide comments. Nelson went into a coughing fit brought on by fake hurling.

"I have no idea what you're talking about, but you're cute, so I'll kiss you anyway." Sarah raised on tiptoe and pecked Quinn's lips.

"Jeez, not in front of the kids, please!" Nelson protested. "Shit, I don't think I'll ever get used to this."

Ignoring him and the rest of his teammates, Quinn tapped Sarah's nose. "Ready to go meet Paige and look at houses?"

"Let's go!" She bounced in place. Sarah *loved* looking at houses, could spend hours studying them, but today, he'd whittled down the choices to three he'd already checked out. He was especially excited for Sarah to see the last one.

"Buying a new house, Hads?" one of the guys asked.

"Yep. Time to downsize to something less ostentatious," he quipped.

After touring the first two places, he and Sarah followed Paige to house number three, which was a stone-and-timber affair that sat on a golf course with spectacular mountain views.

Paige unlocked the front door and ushered them in. "Quinn, why don't you show Sarah around? I'll be in my car making calls if you need me." She sent him a wink.

They stepped into an open entryway, and Sarah gasped. *Yeah, she likes it.* In the center of the entry, an enormously thick chain was suspended from the vaulted second-floor ceiling to the walkout basement level. It twisted its way through railed openings in the stone floor on each level, and water skittered over its links, giving it an old-world, rusted look.

Sarah craned her head upward. "This water feature is amazing!"

His chest swelled with pride as she walked around it. He could practically see the calculations zipping through her brain as she took it in and disassembled its secrets.

"There's lots more to see." He took her hand and led her toward a series of NanaWalls—glass walls that opened completely, letting exterior living spaces blend with the interior.

"Oh my God! I *love* these movable walls." Again she paused, transfixed as her eyes scanned the wall systems, and he had to pull her away.

"So the house has six bedrooms, two family rooms, a wine cave, a billiards room, a gym, and this." He led her into a vaulted, two-storied master bedroom with a marble bathroom that was straight out of a luxury spa.

Her head on a swivel, eyes wide as pucks, she didn't see the room until he opened the door. She peered inside. "Is this another bedroom attached to the bathroom?"

"Nope. Guess again."

She shook her head.

"It's a big-ass closet. Now imagine every surface covered in mirrors, white fur rugs on the floor, and a leather lounge for two." He grinned and stood back to enjoy the transformation in her expression. She didn't disappoint.

Her hand flew to her mouth, but not in time to stifle a raucous laugh. "Oh. My. God! This would be perfect! Can you say mirror room?"

"Yes, I can, and I can also say 'scorching-hot sex.' It'd be a great room to shelter-in-place. Or shelter-in-lace." He waggled his eyebrows at her.

"And here I thought you liked this house because you can step right onto the golf course and play through," she chuckled. "Now I know the *real* attraction."

He let her linger and ogle the space a while longer before he showed her the rest of the house. He felt like a kid on Christmas morning, and every expression, every word, every reaction from her were his presents to open—and he couldn't wait.

They finally came to a stop in the airy great room and kitchen. He spread his arms wide. "So picture family dinners with you, me, Archer, Mom, Dad, Gage, Lily, and Daisy. Plenty of room for everyone. What do you think?"

Sarah folded her hands on the granite island counter and looked around with an expression he could only describe as awe. "I love it," she whispered reverently.

"More than the others we've looked at?"

She positively beamed. "Absolutely."

Quinn executed an inner fist pump. *Scored again! Yes!*

From his cargo shorts pocket, he extracted three objects. His heart rate kicked up a few notches, and he started to juggle. Sarah glanced at him and smirked. "Didn't get in enough juggling at the picnic?"

He kept his eyes fixed on the items looping through the air. "Nope."

She poked her head in cabinets and took another tour around the great room before stopping in front of him. Folding her arms across her chest, she tracked the circling objects. "Are you nervous today or just fidgety, Sparks?" she teased.

"Honestly? A little of both," he murmured.

He could feel her heat as she drew closer. "Why?" Her eyes continued following the motion. Without waiting for his answer, she pointed at one of the items spinning in midair. "What's that?"

Quinn snatched it, letting the others thud to the floor. "You mean this?" He opened his palm and presented her a small box.

Her eyes widened, and her mouth parted. "What is it?"

"Open it and find out."

She stretched her fingers toward it, then snatched them back as if they were about to be sacrificed to a set of pointy fangs.

"Open it," he urged. Excitement and nervousness twined inside him.

Curiosity lit her eyes as she plucked it out of his open palm. Oh so carefully, she opened the lid. He pulled in a breath that he nursed in his chest. She let out a gasp, and those wide, glittering hazel eyes drilled into him. "Is this … are you …?"

"Yes, that's an engagement ring, and yes, I'm proposing." No way did he want this girl to get away from him.

Stunned, she stared at the ring, then at him, and back again.

He pointed at the open box. "And *that* goes"—he twirled his finger in the air—"with the house." Then he opened his arms wide. "And me. A total package. If you don't like the house or the ring, we'll trade them for something else. But *I* have a no-trade clause."

Her diamond-bright eyes shimmered with tears. "It's so beautiful." Her fingertips played over the round brilliant stone sparkling in a platinum band set with smaller diamonds, but she didn't pick it up.

Plucking the ring from its velvet nest, he took her left hand in his and held it to the tip of her ring finger. Then he swallowed. "Please say yes."

In those glittering eyes danced mischief. "What's the question?"

*Killing me here, Sunshine.* He was sweating bullets and praying he didn't give himself away with some embarrassing blunder. This was more nerve-racking than going into overtime in game seven of the Stanley Cup Finals with a zero-zero tie—which he'd done only recently, so he knew.

He cleared his throat to keep his voice from sliding up an octave or three. "Sarah Sunshine Nelson, I love you." His hand shook as he slid the ring on.

It looked huge on her small finger, and a giggle escaped her. "Nothing halfway."

*So maybe I overdid it.* "Nothing halfway, ever, babe," he agreed. He tipped her chin up, and they locked gazes. He could barely catch his breath or coat his desert-dry throat for drowning in her hazel depths. "Please marry me? That's the question."

Her head bobbed vigorously, but nothing came out of her mouth. Tears coursed over her cheeks. Finally, in a voice so choked with emotion he barely heard her, she said, "I wouldn't trade you. Ever."

He caught her as she leapt into his arms and wrapped her legs around his waist. "I love you," she breathed against his neck. God, it felt so right having her pasted against him.

Laughing, he spun them. "Does this mean yes?"

"Yes, it means yes! Do you need me to spell it out on T-shirts?"

"Oh Jesus. I'm scared to ask, but what would the T-shirts say?"

"Yours would say, 'I Asked,' and mine would say, 'I Said Yes.'" She crinkled her nose. "Too cheesy?"

"Cute, but I think yours should say, 'I'm His So Back Off,' and mine should say, 'She's Mine. Best Score of my Life.'"

**THE END**

TAKE ONE GRUMPY HOCKEY PLAYER, add one frazzled landscaper, and mix together not-so-gently in one car crash. Here's an excerpt from *Defending the Reaper*, Book 5:

> Dave took the opportunity to steal another glance at the other driver. The paramedics were gone, and she stared at her phone as though it were a foreign object that had somehow landed in her hand.
>
> Slowed by crushing guilt, he took tentative steps toward her. "So you're okay?"
>
> She raised her head. Slate-blue eyes narrowed and pierced his. "No thanks to you."
>
> He heaved out a breath. "I am so, so sorry. If I—"
>
> Her hand flipped up in a stop-right-there-buster motion. "Mr. Grimson, I *know* you're sorry. It doesn't help right now."

"You know who I am?" A modicum of pride ballooned in his chest. He didn't normally play on his celebrity, preferring to fly under the radar, so the fact she recognized him—

"Yes. I copied it from the paperwork. You're Darryl—or is it Daniel?— Grimson."

The balloon deflated. "David. Dave." Why hadn't *he* thought to discover *her* name? "And your name is?" Fuck. Could he sound any stupider? He acted like he was meeting a dance partner at a hoedown. Next he'd be asking if she wanted a cup of punch.

When she didn't respond, he said, "Is there anything I can do?"

"Yeah," she bit. "You can replace the gardenia plants and the thousands of lights you destroyed, take them to my client's, and get them arranged in the next, oh," she tilted her forearm and glanced at a rugged watch that was too big for her slender wrist, "two hours, so I don't lose this project." Before he could ask what she did for a living, an old-fashioned ringtone chimed. Her voice softened when she answered. "Hey, Finn."

Dave turned away while she gave *Finn* her location. He pulled up his Uber app with a sigh and ordered a ride.

Behind him, the other driver was ending her call. "See you in ten."

"You've got a ride to … wherever it is you need to go?"

"I'm covered," she retorted.

"Okay. Good." He stuffed his hands in the front pockets of his track pants. "Um, so pick out whatever replacement vehicle you want, and I'll pay for it."

She snorted. "I doubt the vehicle I need will be covered by what insurance pays."

He shook his head. "Doesn't matter. This is on me. I'll cover whatever insurance doesn't. In fact, keep the insurance money, and I'll pay for the whole thing."

Her arms seemed to cross her chest on their own, and her eyebrows pinched together. "Are you for real?"

"'Fraid so."

Tilting her head, she scanned him and seemed to see him for the first time. "So what are you? A trust fund Wookiee?"

"A … what?" He didn't school the bewilderment that surely commandeered his features.

"A Wookiee. You know, *Star Wars.* Big, hairy animal that growls and scares the crap out of people."

Unable to hold back, he burst out with a humorless laugh. "Is that the impression I give off?" Okay, so maybe the beard needed a trim—and the hair. And oh, that's right: he hadn't put his front teeth in before he'd stormed out of the arena. Not that he usually did anyway. Why bother? He didn't go to the trouble unless he was making an appearance at a black-tie fundraiser. Or going out with a woman he wanted to impress. Which he hadn't done since before Nicky.

"Trust me, you don't want to know my impression of you," she snarked.

*You're probably right.*

Get your copy of *Defending the Reaper* at Amazon and find out if Dave and Ellie can skate out of this disaster with their hearts intact.

SEVEN PLAYMAKERS COUPLES unite for a winter wedding getaway, but there's trouble in Paradise. Claim your free copy of *Puck the Halls* at www.gkbrady.com and see if they can find the spirit of Christmas—and each other—before it's too late.

# *Author's Note*

Thank you so much for reading *The Winning Score*! I loved Sarah's spitfire personality from the moment she hit the page in *Gauging the Player*, and I couldn't resist pairing her with Quinn, the king of flirts.

If you enjoyed Quinn and Sarah's story, I would love it if you would leave a review on Amazon, BookBub, or Goodreads to help readers like you find the story. And if you do leave a review, I would love to read it! Email me the link at gkbrady@griffin-brady.com.

Stay up to date on upcoming releases, cover reveals, giveaways, and discount deals by joining my newsletter. Simply go to: www.gkbrady.com.

**Trouble is brewing. Disaster strikes. Can they conjure a mistletoe miracle?** Claim your free copy of *Puck the Halls* (Book 7.5), a Playmakers novella, when you join. Download it at www.gkbrady.com/bonus-content/pth/or scan this code:

Listen while you read! The playlist for *The Winning Score* can be found on Spotify.

# *Acknowledgments*

To my readers, who make this so much fun for me. Keep those emails and comments coming. I eat them up!

To Risa B., for patiently fielding my questions and generously sharing your experience as a structural engineer … and for taking such good care of my son.

To Stephanie H., for designing and babying my website and social media. Your creativity is amazing, as are your organizational skills. You make me look good!

To the Marbles and the non-Marbles (you know who you are), thank you for your invaluable critiques.

To Jodi B., thank you for your swift and honest feedback. And thanks especially for fearlessly slapping my characters around when they needed it most.

To my editor, Jenny Q, thank you always for your expertise, your intuition, and your generosity. It really does take a village to write a book, and I'm so glad you're in my village!

To Judith at Word Servings (aka Persnickety), for the sound-barrier-breaking speed at getting this story turned around, and for all those little bubbles that hold your suggestions and humor, which I always appreciate. Thank you for making me laugh out loud, especially when things aren't so funny.

And always, to my husband, Tim, my rock. You are as steadfast as your father was. What a way to carry on his legacy. I don't know how you put up with me, but please don't ever stop.

# *Also by this Author*

## The Playmakers Series®

## The Fall River Series

# *About the Author*

Since childhood, all sorts of stories and characters have lived in G.K. Brady's imagination, elbowing one another for attention, so she's thrilled (as are they) to be giving them their voice on the written page.

An award-winning writer of contemporary romance, she loves telling tales of the less-than-perfect hero or heroine who transforms with each turn of a page.

G.K. is a wife and the proud mom of three grown sons. She also writes historical fiction under the pen name Griffin Brady. She currently resides in Colorado with her very patient husband.

Connect with her on these platforms:

www.amazon.com/author/gkbrady

www.twitter.com/GKBrady_Writes

www.facebook.com/AuthorG.K.Brady/

www.bookbub.com/authors/g-k-brady

www.goodreads.com/author/show/19488321.G_K_Brady

www.instagram.com/authorg.k.brady

www.pinterest.com/gkbrady0993/

www.ingramcontent.com/pod-product-compliance
Lightning Source LLC
LaVergne TN
LVHW010559100826
845148LV00014B/2773
*9781735455846*